The Sword

Bhagwan S. Gidwani was born in 1923 in Karachi (Sindh), and remained there until Partition merged his province with Pakistan. Gidwani specialised in technical, economic, and legal fields of civil aviation. He was counsel for India at the International Court of Justice (*World Court*) at The Hague; and negotiated India's air transport agreements with foreign governments. He has variously served as India's additional director general of tourism; representative of India on ICAO Council, Montreal, (1979-81), and director of Legal Bureau of ICAO (United Nations), Montreal from 1981-85.

The Sword of Tipu Sultan has been reprinted in forty-four editions and has sold more than 2,50,000 copies. He also wrote the script, screenplay and dialogues for the television serial based on the book, which ran for many years and was also telecast in Europe, U.K., U.S.A. and West Asian countries.

Gidwani has authored *Omar & I* – a poetic rejoinder to *Omar Khayyam*, which discovers fresh and vibrant insights in Omar's poetry and mysticism; his other book, *Return of the Aryans* received much critical acclaim.

Based in Montreal, Canada, Prof Bhagwan S. Gidwani continues to participate in international projects to promote safety of air transport and tourism. Largely though, he concentrates on historical writing and research.

The Sword of Tipu Sultan

A historical novel about the life and legend of Tipu Sultan of India

Bhagwan S Gidwani

Rupa & Co

Copyright © Allied Publishers Ltd. 1976

Published 2009 by
Rupa . Co
7/16, Ansari Road, Daryaganj
New Delhi 110 002

Sales Centres:
Allahabad Bangalooru Chandigarh Chennai
Hyderabad Jaipur Kathmandu
Kolkata Mumbai

All rights reserved.
No part of this publication may be reproduced, stored in a retrieval system, or transmitted, in any form or by any means, electronic, mechanical, photocopying, recording or otherwise, without the prior permission of the publishers.

Printed in India by
Nutech Photolithographers
B-240, Okhla Industrial Area, Phase-I,
New Delhi 110 020, India

The artistic representation of history is amore scientific and serious pursuit than theexact writing of history. For the art of letters goes to the heart of things, whereas the factual report merely collocates details.

Aristotle

Dedicated

*To the Country which lacks a historian
To Men whom History owes rehabilitation
To Faith in the Destiny of Man
To Conviction that Sun rises in the East &
To my sons Manu and Sachal and all the youth of
India who must be told the Truth.*

CONTENTS

Part I
THE MESSENGERS

1.	The Night of the Double Retreat	3
2.	The Ruler is Dead	25
3.	A Traitor is Born	32
4.	Born in Battle	44
5.	They Also Mourned	46
6.	They Were Thirteen	50

Part II
MOTHER, MOTHER! FATHER, FATHER!

7.	My Lady of the Flowers	55
8.	The Pilgrimage	60
9.	The Promise	62
10.	Rejoice, a Son is Born	65
11.	Come, Take Over a Kingdom	67

Part III
THE PRINCE

12.	Forty Days	77
13.	Sixty Days	81

14.	Three Years	85
15.	The Fourth Year	86
16.	Brother Karim	90
17.	The Commandant of Dindigul	92
18.	Two Are Enough	94
19.	The Pandit and the Maulvi	98
20.	The Ladder of Fortune	102
21.	The Stars of Our Sons	108
22.	Tales and Stories	110
23.	Let the Birds Live	112
24.	Rescue	116
25.	God, You Rejected My Offering	120
26.	Parting of the Ways	125

Part IV
DREAMS AND MEMORIES

27.	We shall Endure	129
28.	The Traitors	139
29.	The Doubt	143
30.	Tiger, Tiger!	144
31.	Ruqayya, My Darling Wife!	159
32.	The Sultan Remembers	171
33.	A Soul in Torment	190
34.	Do Not Let Your Dreams Die	203

Part V
INHERITANCE

35.	The Crown	211
36.	Did they burn Jesus Christ?	213
37.	The Anantpur Massacre	215

CONTENTS

38.	Who is the Killer?	220
39.	The Three Suppliants	226
40.	The Doomed Peace	232
41.	The Surrender at Yorktown	240
42.	Rights of Man	246
43.	The Maulvi from Muscat	264
44.	Four Years of One Man	269
45.	Four Years of Another Man	273
46.	The Hour Strikes	300
47.	Our Faithful Ally	305
48.	The Shadow of an Axe	306
49.	The Governor-General from France	310
50.	Stand up and be Counted	313
51.	The Grand Army	316
52.	Two Years of War	324
53.	Thus Died a Horse	334
54.	Farewell, Ruqayya	336
55.	Where Are My People?	339
56.	Preparations for Peace	351
57.	Let My Sons Go	361
58.	Who is Your Enemy?	366
59.	A Sweetmeat After a Meal	368
60.	Torch for Tomorrow	370
61.	Ambition of His Masters	379
62.	Monarchy and the Masses	381
63.	Is My Strength My Weakness?	384
64.	The Price of Laughter	387
65.	Until Further Notice	390
66.	Letter from Napoleon	392
67.	None shall Forgive	398
68.	A Scream of Anguish	402
69.	Did Bansi Lal Desert?	410
70.	The Duke of Wellington	413

CONTENTS

71.	Enemy Within Our Gates	415
72.	How Did They Come This Far?	419
73.	We Are Assassinated	426
74.	The Destiny of Our Land	431
75.	Profile of a Traitor?	436
76.	The Last Day	444
77.	The Last Hour	466

AUTHOR'S NOTE

IT WAS SOME THIRTEEN YEARS AGO THAT I BEGAN COLLECTING material on Tipu Sultan. A chance conversation led to my interest in him. It so happened that whilst in London, a French student and I were leaving the British Museum at the same time. We nodded to each other as strangers would. I offered him the protection of my umbrella against the slight drizzle which had just begun. We were both headed for the nearby restaurant and there we shared a table. It was then that I learnt that he was not there merely for sight-seeing as I was but had interests of a more serious kind. He had come to the museum in search of material for a thesis which he was writing on kings and emperors who had died in battle. There were so few of them, according to him, and it seemed to be his complaint that in the face of defeat, kings often chose either to surrender or to flee in order to live to fight another day. I continued to listen somewhat uninterested until he caught my interest with his concluding remark: 'But your Tipu Sultan was the one who died on a battlefield—what a great man he was.'

With a courteous smile, I acknowledged his compliment to my countryman though silently I remembered that the history books imposed on me during my school and college days had not rated Tipu Sultan very high.

The observation of the French student remained in my mind.

Back in India, I bought and borrowed a few books on Tipu Sultan. They did not satisfy. Later, I read all the books on him that my friends and I could lay our hands on. The more I read, the more curious I became. It was barely two centuries ago that Tipu Sultan had lived and died. Yet, there was so much of ambiguity, so much of contradictory and conflicting testimony that it seemed that between us and Tipu Sultan there would always be a gulf of mystery. A conviction was also growing on me that ever since the English commentators of the eighteenth century had developed their portrait of Tipu Sultan as an arch-villain, no one had attempted a fair portrayal of the events in his life and the general shape of his character. Even some of the subsequent writers had been content to accept the many distortions passed on to them by those commentators. True, some did try to write with sympathy and understanding but what they left us was a narration of a few facts which neither recreate a life nor reveal a character; and so wide were the gaps left untouched by them, that what they had produced was more in the nature of a patchwork.

Someone, I thought, was needed to tear away this veil of mystery. Having no one else whom I could command, I appointed myself for the task.

Thus began my voyage of discovery. I read all there was to be read in the archives and libraries of India. The National Archives of India at Delhi and the Madras Government Records Office provided the largest number of unpublished records. Besides, I had the good fortune to obtain access to the many manuscripts of the Asiatic Society (formerly known as the Royal Asiatic Society of Bengal and established originally as the Asiatick in the eighteenth century). There were also a large number of documents and records which I could get from the libraries at Calcutta, Madras and Pondicherry.

Thereafter, I continued my search elsewhere. Frankly, I had little hope of being able to obtain a great deal of material from foreign countries. But I was wrong. The libraries and archives throughout the world yielded treasures far beyond my expectations. My next visit to the British Museum itself was rewarding. From then on I moved to the India Office Library in London and in my various contacts with them, personally and through friends, I came across what proved to be a vast storehouse of information on Tipu Sultan. There were manuscripts, published and unpublished, records of secret proceedings and top-secret consultations, memoranda and minutes on the affairs of the East India Company, Council deliberations of military and political affairs in all the three Presidencies (Bengal, Bombay and Madras), private collections and confidential correspondence of the British Governors and Governors-General. Taken together, they constitute the most extensive and unique record of how the English empire-builders thought, felt, acted and reacted about Tipu Sultan. Also remarkably informative were the collections available in the Public Record Office at London, the Bodeleian at Oxford, the National Library of Scotland and a host of other libraries, record offices and museums scattered throughout Britain.

Having obtained so much material in Britain, I knew that the trail obviously could not end there. There were so many clues in that material itself to indicate that much would be available on the other side of the channel. France, then, became my next hunting ground and off and on, over a long period I continued my research there. Of the long list of libraries and archives there which yielded the most relevant papers and documents, I must mention specially the Archives Nationales and Bibliotheque Nationale. Through a friend, I had also the opportunity of obtaining copies of some documents which are particularly relevant to the history of Tipu Sultan from the Archives du Ministere des Affaires Etrangeres.

In the meantime, partly through personal efforts though largely due to kindness of many friends, I was able to obtain copies of Dutch records, Ottoman archives and Iranian papers relating to Tipu Sultan and his contemporaries. The amazing fact was that wherever I held out my hand, and kept it there patiently and for long, the material poured in, in amazing quantities. The only difficulty I had was in obtaining first-hand source material from the Portugese archives and in their case I have had to content myself to rely on secondary material.

It was not without apprehension that I viewed the vast research material which I had collected over the years. To collate it, to analyse it and to arrange and organise it in a systematic fashion was not proving to be an easy task. Besides, the problems of getting so much of the material from the French, Dutch, Persian, Turkish and the Portuguese sources translated to enable me to understand it all, had tried my resources, both of ingenuity and finance. Somehow I had successfully met that challenge. Perhaps, I am digressing but I think it is worthwhile to record that the painstaking process of collecting my research material and having it translated, had at least resolved one question in my mind. Often, I had wondered why Indian authors had failed to come forward to correct the so many distortions and contradictions planted in our history books by hostile, motivated or misguided commentators. Now, I came to realise that the cost, effort and time that it would take is normally far beyond the resources of individual authors—howsoever dedicated—and until someone comes up with a proper, rational scheme, our history will hold neither truth nor inspiration for the coming generations. The task of correctly re-presenting our history, I appreciate, is colossal, but then all the more reason for beginning earlier rather than later or never.

This digression apart, the problem of how I should organise my work remained. To begin with, I started a historical work on Tipu Sultan but almost half-way through it I lost the mood for it with the realisation that history by itself would prove to be a poor medium to recapture in our imagination all that Tipu had lived and died for. In any case, history as I know it has served to retain not the fire but the ashes of the past, for it knows but little of the agony and ecstacy of the soul. Thus a novel it had to be to portray the life, love and sacrifice of Tipu Sultan and to establish what manner of man he was, the events and impulses that moved him, his hopes and aspirations, his sensations of pleasure and pain, and something of the times of which he was a part. Such a presentation has obviously to speak also of those that loved and betrayed him, of the charming ladies and brilliant men around him, of his greatness and the crafty stupidity of his contemporaries, of the wit and folly of his times, and of the struggle of men and ideas when faced with the march of history. Yes, clearly for this purpose, a mere historical work would have been inadequate. It is, of course, possible for a historian to conclude from this that I do not have the equipment, training or talent for writing a book of history. The historian would not be far wrong if he were to so conclude, though the fact also is that I cannot claim to possess the equipment, training or talent for writing a novel either—never having attempted one before. All I am convinced about is that Tipu's portrait must be drawn fairly and accurately and that must be viewed by a larger audience. A novel, in my view could achieve this purpose more effectively than a book of history.

Now that I am about to present this novel, I do appreciate that the accuracy of my portrait of Tipu Sultan ultimately depends on the validity of the imaginative judgements which I have formed but it is also my submission that these judgements have a firm foundation in historical truth from which I have tried my best not to stray away. I have not discarded the fruits of my patient research of Indian, English, French, Persian, Dutch,

Turkish and Portugese sources. On the contrary, my attempt has been to let the facts as they emerge from those sources, speak for themselves and if I have intervened, it is only to separate the lie from the truth. There are, of course, dialogues which had to be invented and at times the interpretations have also been mine. But I have no hesitation in taking full responsibility for them since it is my sincere belief that they have been drawn with care from facts and source material contemporary with Tipu's times. I shall continue to so believe until some historian conclusively shows me the error of my ways.

I would not like the reader of this Note to be misled into believing that my sole reason for writing this work is to rehabilitate Tipu Sultan in national memory. As my research developed, I began to acquire another, more important reason. I do believe that the past has a remarkable tendency to extend itself into the present, and at times when we forget the past, we run the risk of building without foundations and cutting off the roots of national growth. Tipu himself knew that in order to understand contemporary history, it was necessary to make a voyage of discovery into the past; and the one lesson which the past history of his unhappy land had taught him was that India was weakened not so much by an outside power but by the peril within us, the weakness within us and the sickness within us—disunity. He knew that the land he loved was in danger of dying an unnatural death—from assassination by the enemy *within* us. In that sorry plight, Tipu had seen not only a repetition of the historical process but also a lesson for the future. I am convinced that that lesson is as valid today as it was in Tipu's times.

All that remains for me is to thank those who have helped me. First and foremost, my gratitude is to the French student who initially inspired this research. I am sorry that I had not asked him his name, nor had he asked for mine. I hope his thesis has prospered and it is also my hope that some day he will come across this novel. I am immensely grateful to the directors, registrars, record-keepers, cataloguers, librarians and assistant librarians of all the archives and libraries, here and abroad, who have unhesitatingly assisted me so much to obtain material for the novel. Many also have over the years helped with translations of sources from foreign and regional languages. Their list is almost endless and if I do not individually mention them, I know they will understand. My special gratitude to Leila, my wife, for her assistance and encouragement, and to my brother Mangha, who because he shares the same faith helped me with enthusiasm in my research.

Bhagwan Gidwani
28 Lodi Estate
New Delhi-110 003
July 1976

Part I

THE MESSENGERS

1

THE NIGHT OF THE DOUBLE RETREAT

(i)

THEY CALLED IT THE NIGHT OF THE DOUBLE RETREAT.

At dead of night—at almost the same hour—the two opposing armies that had stood lacing each other for some days began their hasty retreat in opposite directions.

Fleeing to the north was the British army. Its Commander, Colonel Humberstone, was convinced that an attack from the enemy was imminent and that successful resistance was impossible. While the last of his units marched back, the Colonel ruefully scanned the heavy guns and cartloads of luggage that had to be abandoned to ensure a hurried and stealthy retreat. He was not so sorry for the guns, these were always replaceable and did not involve any personal loss. What saddened him was the necessity to leave behind so much of the treasure plundered by him and by his troops. Still there was some consolation in the diamonds resting in his hip pocket and the bag of gold coins hanging from the saddle of his horse. They would be worth, he mentally calculated, about one hundred years of his salary. Not bad, he thought. But he again looked at the mountains of brocades, skins, gold and silver utensils left for replunder by the enemy and cursed the need for camouflaging the movements of his troops not only from the opposing army but also from one of his own units stationed at a lower hill in the forward area.

The unit at the lower hill was composed solely of Indian troops with the exception of its commanding officer Lt Johnstone, and was in such close proximity to the enemy lines that its withdrawal would have been noticed by their scouts resulting in immediate pursuit. Lt Johnstone was therefore invited by the Colonel, ostensibly for drinks and dinner, so that he could leave with the main army while as usual the troops on the lower hill kept exchanging intermittent fire with the enemy unaware, at least for the next few hours, of the exit of the main army.

'They will discover their loneliness when the dawn breaks and will have the sense to disperse,' the Colonel soothingly tried to assure Lt Johnstone.

'Disperse where?' was Lt Johnstone's query.

The Colonel was about to shrug away such speculation, but the bewildered expression on the younger officer's face prompted him to say:

'Why worry? They will find their way, at least most of them will. They might surrender to the enemy and, in that case, will be treated well. Royally, in fact, when they hand in without a light all this treasure we are leaving behind. Tipu Saheb will gloat over these prizes and his first task will be to have an inventory made out for despatch to Hyder, his father. That will delay our being pursued all the more.'

Warming to the theme, and to while away the few moments that remained before the retreat was to begin, the Colonel added, 'Then, there will be some enterprising lads on yonder hill who will loot a part of the booty which we are leaving behind, while their colleagues go in for surrender. What do you think Tipu will do? I bet his instructions to his officers will be to give up everything else and hunt down those lads in order to recover the loot. Again, that gives us more time to be on our way. The lads who get away with some of this,' continued Col Humberstone, pointing to the tents containing the plundered treasures, 'might become richer than you and me, my boy. So don't waste your thoughts on them.'

'But they will not have the time to surrender or run away,' remonstrated Lt Johnstone. 'At sun rise, sir, they will know of their abandonment but Tipu's scouts will discover it even earlier. Without the protection of the heavy guns from this hilltop these wretched abandoned troops will be mowed down in one sweep.'

'Very well, very well,' replied the Colonel in a tone that brooked no further contradiction, 'then they will go down fighting, to the greater glory of our arms.'

Regretting immediately the harshness of his tone, the Colonel added:

'Do not grieve, my boy. If I abandoned a single white soldier, it would be on my conscience. These are natives I am leaving behind. If the natives choose to kill their native brethren, must we intervene at the risk of losing the entire army?'

The look of understanding that at last crossed the Lieutenant's face did not particularly please the Colonel. Sadly he mused on the quality of the present-day youth who insisted on knowing the reason for everything, and having been presented with a variety of explanations, chose the least logical as the most acceptable. The Lieutenant wants to run away as much as I do, thought the Colonel, but he wants a justification to ease his conscience for deserting his own troops. Gruffly he told the Lieutenant to take his appointed place with the columns, but before doing so he was invited to take whatever he fancied from the prize tent, without of course overburdening his own horse.

While the last of the columns was wheeling about, the Colonel remained on the hill. He wanted to be the last of the whites to leave. Men like Johnstone, he thought, would be impressed by such a gesture. In any case the Colonel knew that the gesture would cost nothing for his swift horse would soon overtake the vanguard of his retreating army. He had a more practical reason for staying behind and wanted to avoid the looting of the prize tents which would only have resulted in burdening the men and the beasts, slowing down thereby the retreat of his army. Looking back in the direction of the enemy camp, he said,

'See, Tipu Saheb, I guard the treasures for you.'

On an impulse, he tore out some note sheets from his diary and wrote on each one of them:

From Col Humberstone, Commander of the British Army to Tipu Sultan:

Greetings. Knowing you as a patron of arts and a connoisseur of beauty, I leave these treasures for your pleasure. Take what you will, distribute what you desire and if your generosity—universally acclaimed and honoured—impels you, send me a gift of whatever is unworthy of your notice from amongst these treasures, in acknowledgement not only of the esteem in which I hold you but also of my services in having given into your custody all these prizes, rejecting the advice of my counsellors who urged their destruction.

He pinned this message on each of the prize tents. An excellent example of making a virtue of necessity, thought the Colonel, and he wondered what Lt Johnstone and his other officers would have thought of this message had they had an opportunity of reading it. The last bit in the message was indeed factual. Lt Johnstone and all other officers had urged that the prizes be destroyed and prevented from falling into the hands of Tipu. The Colonel however had reminded them of a story, which he could recall only vaguely and in dim outline, of a Russian and his dogs being pursued by a pack of hungry wolves. On each occasion when the wolves were about to overtake the Russian, he would shoot one of his dogs and the wolves would stop to make a meal of him while the Russian pressed on. Seven dogs were sacrificed to halt the wolves sufficiently for the Russian to reach a place of safety.

'So, gentlemen,' the Colonel had said pointing to the moral of the story, 'we must also throw a few pieces of meat to the enemy in the hope that they will halt him sufficiently.' And then, he had added, 'senseless destruction of guns and the treasure will serve no purpose and will only lend fury to Tipu's pursuit of our retreating army. Your fear that this trash will strengthen the enemy militarily and financially may be correct, but the loss of so many valiant soldiers under my command will weaken our forces all the more. And this loss will be inevitable, if Tipu gives his undivided attention to pursuing us. Hence, we must offer him temptations and distractions. Possibly, he will annihilate or imprison the forces we leave on the lower hill. He will then move on to this high hill which we will have evacuated. Having shed blood, having gained guns, prizes and prisoners, he will proclaim himself a victor, receive the homage of the countryside, hold court, confer titles and bask in glory. When he does decide to pursue us, we shall be far ahead.'

'My mission, gentlemen, as I see it,' concluded the Colonel, 'is that since I cannot lead you to glory, I must at least lead you to safety. Let therefore the arrangements for the retreat, as I have already outlined, be undertaken forthwith.'

With that pronouncement, the meeting of the officers was over and they hurriedly dispersed to look after the tasks that must be completed by the hour set for evacuation. Now that the moment when he also must finally depart was arriving, the Colonel noted with wry satisfaction that all arrangements for the retreat had progressed according to the plan he had explained to his officers. He had worked out each detail—the water, salt and food rations, the equipment to be moved, the load to be carried by each horse and man, the moment of departure of each column, the route and a host of other major and minor matters, and, above all, measures for secrecy so that neither his own forces on the lower hill which were to be abandoned, nor the enemy scouts swarming the area should guess his intentions. Yes, everything had been planned. The only unplanned act was his own—to leave a pinned message for Tipu on the prize tents, making a gift of what he could not in any case take away.

'Why did I do it?' wondered the Colonel.

When he had torn out the pages from his diary he had thought of writing merely in jest or impudence, to divest Tipu of the role of a conqueror and to disabuse any possible feeling that the guns and prizes were coming into Tipu's hands as the result of a well-earned victory. Then he had changed into a different mood—half-servile and half-humorous—and had even ended with a request for gifts in appreciation of his services for leaving the guns and the prizes intact. Now he knew what was at the back of his mind in writing the message finally in that manner.

'Well, you bastard, you do want something for nothing,' he thought to himself.

Somewhere at the back of his mind lurked the hope that Tipu might respond gracefully to the message and the Colonel might reap a rich harvest of gifts—and if perchance his retreat was a failure, he might be dealt with leniently if he fell into enemy hands. He had never met Tipu but had heard countless stories of his unpredictable generosity. There was an instance last year when Tipu, having captured a fort after a bloody battle lasting for some days, had instantly released all the prisoners with their personal belongings and horses in honour of his patron saint whose birthday fell on the day of the capture. A young British subaltern who had come into possession of an emerald felt so relieved at being treated with such leniency that he gave it to his captors who were releasing him saying, 'Give this as my gift to your master to mark my gratitude for his generosity.'

The emerald was taken to Tipu who had the subaltern called into his presence. Tipu thanked him for the emerald and saying that one gift deserved another, handed the subaltern a bag containing many more precious stones and a hundred gold coins. Tipu then asked the subaltern if he would like to join his army. The subaltern stammered his reply which was translated to Tipu in the following terms: 'This foolish youth says that unfortunately he has taken a vow not to change masters and is therefore prevented from taking service under you.'

'Tell him,' replied Tipu, 'that in this court we honour such foolishness,' and having said this he took off from his finger a ring with a glittering stone as rare and precious as a king's ransom. This he presented to the young subaltern. There was another instance when the wife of an English Lieutenant on being informed that her husband was missing after a battle with Tipu's army in which many were slain and several were taken as prisoners, wrote to Tipu beseeching him with tears to let her know if she was a widow or a wife and if the latter, to convey to her husband her assurances of undying devotion as also affectionate regards from his son who was to be four years old in the coming month. Tipu released the Lieutenant with a gift of a necklace with thirty pearls for his wife, saying that he wished he could send a pearl for each tear she had shed. For the son, there was an abundant gift of toys—horses, elephants, tigers, soldiers and guns, all made of ivory and studded with precious stones. The wife learning from her husband of his release and of the magnificent gifts he was bringing for her from India, wrote a gushing letter to Tipu thanking him and hoping that one day she would have the honour of kissing his hand. In the meantime, she begged for his portrait so that 'it could adorn our humble home, always to remind me and my son of the debt we owe you'. Tipu responded by sending his portrait in a heavy gold frame to the Lieutenant. The heavy gold frame, the Colonel remembered, did not reach its destination, though the portrait did. But that was another story and the fault was not Tipu's. When the portrait addressed to the Lieutenant was brought to the English camp, the Lieutenant had already sailed for England. Tipu's messenger then had it delivered to a Director of the East India Company for onward transmission. The Director frowned on such clandestine correspondence and exchanges between an Oriental Prince and an English woman. However, he did not wish to be too harsh. He sent the portrait to England for the Lieutenant but had the gold frame confiscated and later purchased it himself at a nominal price at the auction, through which such confiscated goods were sold. Now, it adorned the portrait of the Director's third wife.

There were many instances indeed, recalled the Colonel, in which Tipu, sworn enemy though he was of the British army, had filled British pockets and warmed British hearts with magnificent gifts.

'Tipu, my friend,' thought the Colonel, 'may Allah guide your hand to dip deeply into your coffers and reward yours truly for the treasure I leave behind intact for you.' Then he looked at the sky and admonished, 'listen, Allah, don't go about telling Tipu I had no choice in the matter. Let this be a secret between you and me.'

With an inward chuckle, the Colonel tried to detach himself from his thoughts. He mustn't allow his thoughts and fancies to run wild, he told himself. In his earlier days in India, his erstwhile commander, Capt Jacobs had, in his confidential report, said of him, 'Humberstone is a man of mature action but of frivolous thoughts. He must check and discipline the latter lest they come to influence his decisions and he comes to grief.'

Well, I haven't come to grief yet, mused the Colonel, though Capt Jacobs has, having been felled, it was said, by a sword thrust on his head from Hyder Ali himself. They said that his thick skull had dented Hyder's sword and in consequence Hyder cursed the fallen soldier, abused the British army, ranted against the cowardice of his own troops and even blasphemed against the Almighty. Certainly, he ignored the time-honoured custom of immediately distributing alms, presents and titles to celebrate a victory and it was only at Tipu's intervention, four days later, that the ceremony was held, with Tipu presiding at Hyder's command. The munificence of the gifts, then, more than made up for all the tardiness. Capt Jacobs, recalled the Colonel, was extremely good at writing stern reports but not so good at lining his pockets. He robbed, extorted and plundered, as most English officers did and therefore was not a good example to men of bigoted honesty. But then he robbed, extorted, and plundered so little and so clumsily that he was not a good example to the rest either. The little that he had shipped to England to Mrs Jacobs from time to time enabled the widow, now, no more than the luxury of buying a modest cottage and a husband somewhat younger than herself. The Colonel loved his wife too much to consign her to widowhood and he loved himself too much to live in penury. Yes, he had ambitions, the Colonel had.

While he was about to picture to himself his expectations and aspirations in the foreseeable and distant future, the Colonel saw his orderly, Munawar Khan, approaching. Munawar Khan reported what the Colonel had already expected: that the first column had reached the appointed place without interception and that there was no indication of any activity from enemy scouts; that the rest of the columns were also moving smoothly including the last column which had begun its movement; that the Colonel's horse was ready and that the unit, composed of an officer with thirty soldiers which was to form the rearguard, awaited the Colonel's signal to move.

The rearguard was given the word to depart.

Now that the Colonel walked over to his horse, he was glad to be getting rid of the accursed hill. He had been lured here by the prospect of booty en route and an easy victory at the end of the journey. The objective of his masters in sending Col Humberstone to Malabar was to cut off all source of supplies to Hyder Ali. In his declining years Hyder Ali was loath to part with his son Tipu; and Col Humberstone, so calculated his masters, would have an easy walkover for he would have to contend neither with Hyder nor with Tipu but with the notoriously incompetent soldier Jung Bahadur Arshad Beg Khan who had been nominated by Hyder Ali to control the civil and military administration of Malabar. There were many who sneered that Jung Bahadur whose name signified 'Brave in Battle', was good at pacifying quarrels in a harem but had no fondness for battle and bloodshed. But his worst detractors had to admit that he was an excellent Quarter Master, an able administrator and could keep supplies moving to provision Hyder's armies locked in various battles. His chief asset lay in building a reserve of buffer stocks to meet the unexpected and emergent demands which Hyder Ali frequently made. While others, equally loyal, sent despatches to Hyder promising provisions, the caravan of supplies of Jung Bahadur would have already arrived, and in most cases, well before the statement of promises from others had reached Hyder.

'He is worth to me more than three generals,' Hyder Ali had said of him, and Tipu had asked, 'Thirteen generals you said, did you not, father?'

Col Humberstone's masters had been right. There was booty en route, plenty of it. The Colonel had seized Calicut and stripped the prosperous town of all that it possessed. Then he had moved on to Palghatcherri, capturing some forts and looting many a treasure. Now at the end of the march also, facing him were the forces under the supine leadership of Jung Bahadur who even allowed the Colonel to take over without harassment an extremely advantageous position on the crest of a high hill from which he despatched a small force to take over a lower hill as well. Entrenched in this position, the Colonel waited for the arrival of a large body of his army which had formed his rearguard—not because a military movement was feared in the rear but because a systematic, methodical and comprehensive plunder of booty could only be achieved by devoting time and effort to it. This was the task allotted to the rearguard. The benefit, however, of all the success which the rearguard achieved in its mission reached the Colonel only partly. Many ingrates in the rearguard, having had more than their share of the booty, decided to call it a day and deserted. Many others moving in small detachments, intent on exploring the hinterland and securing larger plunder, did not keep to the schedule of the march. The excesses of some of them, crazed by the feeling of power, drunk with wine or lured by sex, were such as to lead to reprisals when caught alone or in small numbers. The Colonel cursed the malarial fever that had overtaken the Captain left in charge of the rearguard and as if that was not enough misfortune, the only capable Lieutenant with the rearguard had also been wounded with his own musket whilst cleaning it. Stragglers from the rearguard came trickling in but not in the shape of large formations which the Colonel had left behind.

Meanwhile, contrary to expectations, Hyder Ali commanded Tipu to proceed forthwith to protect Jung Bahadur and face Col Humberstone's forces. Tipu left Hyder Ali's camp with 705 soldiers and when his intelligence system reported to him the atrocities of Col Humberstone's rearguard, he despatched Gopal Rao with his seven hundred men to harass the English rearguard and hinder its joining the Colonel.

Tipu arrived at Jung Bahadur's camp after forced marches with only five men, the rest having accompanied Gopal Rao to the rear of Col Humberstone. Jung Bahadur, always modest about his military genius, was overjoyed to welcome Tipu.

'I have arrived only with five men,' said Tipu.

'You have come, Sultan. That is enough. With you arrive not only your five men, but my own army arrives as well,' replied Jung Bahadur.

Jung Bahadur was right. Tipu's arrival had such an impact on the army that Jung Bahadur was quite correct in saying that his own army had 'arrived' with Tipu. His army was now as certain of Humberstone's defeat as it was only a moment ago certain of his victory.

That Col Humberstone did not share Jung Bahadur's joy on the arrival of Tipu was to be expected. What was not expected was that Gopal Rao, with his small force in the rear, would carry out a thorough job of annihilating or dispersing Humberstone's rearguard. The English Captain in charge of the rearguard, still suffering from the effects of malaria, was allowed to pass in his litter, to rejoin the Colonel, on the plea that he was dying and could obtain medical attention from the doctors in the Colonel's camp. Gopal Rao let him go on parole and with a curse:

'May you communicate this and every other disease to your white compatriots on the hill.'

When parleying with the Captain, Gopal Rao had kept almost his entire force with him, pretending that it was merely his bodyguard, while the rest of his forces were devoted to hunting down English units in the rear. The hope with which Gopal Rao allowed the Captain to pass was that the Colonel would get, from his own trusted subordinate, an account of the disorganisation and disintegration in his rear and of the superiority of Gopal Rao's forces for mopping-up operations.

The Captain did not rise to Gopal Rao's expectations in communicating the malarial disease to the Colonel, who remained hale and hearty but the Captain did deal a severe blow to the Colonel's hopes. The rest was done by foraging parties that Tipu sent in the rear to supplement Gopal Rao's efforts in stopping supplies to the Colonel's forces. Now even Gopal Rao's slender force had joined Tipu's army which almost in its entirety had been turned into a labour force working on fortifications to face any threat of attacks. Of the four surprise night attacks which Humberstone's forces had made, the last three had been dismal failures. Tipu's attacks on the other hand, though not decisive, had a crumbling effect on the morale of Humberstone's troops. His soldiers felt let down; they were promised much and could at best look forward only to a miserable retreat.

'Well, I cannot advance,' the Colonel had told himself, reviewing the gloomy prospect, 'and if I remain on this miserable hill any longer, I shall grow into a vegetable. So all that remains is to retreat.'

The thought of parleying with Tipu to get favourable terms for the retreat, did cross his mind. But he had in his army eleven white officers who had once been prisoners of Hyder Ali and were released on parole having given a promise never to engage in war with his forces. This promise had been broken. Some of them had even engaged in plunder and violated women at the border village before crossing over. Tipu would demand their surrender. Then there was a Captain with him, who, in a drunken orgy, in the forward march, had molested one of the temples maintained by Tipu, trampled on the idols and killed the priest. His name had been ascertained by Tipu's men and Hyder's court had proclaimed him as an offender. His surrender would also be demanded. Of the Indian troops, a contingent of four thousand under Abu Wafa had deserted from Hyder Ali a few months back. Abu Wafa was under a sentence of death in Hyder's court and so were the troops under him. In any terms for withdrawal, however liberal otherwise, Tipu could not be a party to an arrangement which permitted parole violators, criminals and deserters under a sentence of death from his father's court, to go free. Col Humberstone though often quite generous in sacrificing others, could not possibly persuade himself to contemplate seriously an arrangement involving a death sentence on so many of his men. The ignominy that would attach to him by such a deed would certainly finish his career as a soldier and might even entail far more serious consequences. If it was a question of surrender of Abu Wafa and his troops, he could have explained it away, as one of the grim necessities of war. Privately, the powers-that-be would have doubted his explanation but, officially, they would have accepted it. In any case, they were Indians and could be treated as cattle. The question of surrender of the English officers would, however, have been viewed differently.

'In any case,' the Colonel said to himself, 'dash it all, whatever be the twists and turns of my conscience, I am regarded as a model officer. I should not shatter that image at this late stage of the game. So let it be. I cannot parley. Let me, instead, retreat in the cover of the night. And if luck favours me on my return, and some prizes come my way, I shall proclaim my victory, almost simultaneously with Tipu.'

He knew of the new atmosphere which had now begun to prevail. Many a bunch of fresh recruits with a journalistic flair had been brought over from England. No longer were victories won only on the battlefield but often with paper and ink, which conveyed fanciful accounts of the most routine engagements. With a chuckle, the Colonel recalled a sortie some time back in which his men had been engaged and all there was to capture was a dead camel, with the added mortification that the camel had died not by bullets or bayonets but through natural causes. Sheepishly, his men had returned in safety, and besides tiring their leg muscles from running and walking, bore no other marks of battle. But the story as it appeared in the Bulletin recorded the heroic exploit with zest and was entitled 'The natives left their dead behind'. When the Colonel was accosted by his compatriots off and on and congratulated for organising this or that brilliant sortie, he soon learned that it was bad form to deny or discount what had appeared in the Bulletin with official blessings. So, with becoming modesty, he accepted the laurels that came his way, time and again, for equally brilliant skirmishes that had their source in journalistic fancies.

'Truth,' he told himself, attempting a definition, 'is what is believed to be true'. And he added, 'if I don't believe in the glory of our army, how will the enemy believe in it, or be frightened by it?' He was a good soldier, an efficient officer and had many successful engagements to his credit. That was also true of many of his colleagues. Still these journalistic props were good for morale and they often built for the British army an aura of invincibility which sometimes added to the demoralisation of hostile forces.

In any case, the Colonel enjoyed this journalistic jingoism not so much because it attributed heroic deeds to him and to his colleagues, nor for its possibly lasting effects in consolidating the British supremacy in India, but because it amused him, brought some fun and frolic into a conversation and took away the tedium of a humdrum existence involved in a patient siege or the pursuit or a retreat covering hundreds of miles, without firing a single shot. He did not particularly relish the other journalistic and psychological activities that were beginning to be pursued, all the more vigorously—of sowing seeds of discord between various communities, races and religions in India, of instigating molestations of mosques and temples, inciting each religious community to blame the other for the sacrilege and of encouraging missionaries to convert the natives to Christianity. Not only the journalists, but several others, song writers, storytellers, minstrels, religious fanatics were being hired for this purpose. Humberstone did not mind when it came to spreading stories amongst the Hindus that Hyder and Tipu were bigoted fanatics of a different faith, or amongst the Muslims that father and son were violating all tenets of Islam. It was all right, the Colonel thought, to tarnish the image of the princes and war lords who were hostile to the British and to make the people hate them. But he wondered if it was worthwhile to carry war into the homes of the people, invade the privacy of their ideology and religion and to impose on them new hatreds, new enemies and new distrusts. And how, in heaven's name, asked the Colonel himself, will Christianity thrive or even survive in this land if people are encouraged into new realms of religious bigotry and racial fanaticism. If a Maratha is to be goaded into regarding a Mysorean as a foreigner and, therefore, hold him in contempt and anger, how

THE NIGHT OF THE DOUBLE RETREAT

would it help the imperial design of English supremacy over the country? Will the Maratha not, trained to hatred of what is foreign, reject the British equally, or even more strongly? The Colonel concluded this mental debate within himself and said: 'Well, I don't know all the answers. Let them that frame the policies worry about it. Maybe, when I reach the Biblical age of three score and ten years, I will have time to ponder over the problem more deeply. Meanwhile, if I am to reach that ripe age, my first task should be to put in many, many miles between Tipu and myself.'

The Colonel knew that his decision to retreat on that very night had been made none too soon. Barely a few minutes back, his scouts had reported to him feverish activity in the enemy camp, indicative obviously of intention to attack at dawn. With his field glasses, he could see hundreds of torches moving to and fro in the enemy camp and he could sense their excitement.

'Sorry, boys,' he said, as if speaking to the unseen enemy in the distance, 'can't oblige you now. Maybe next time I will sit back and fight.'

His sense of professional propriety was, however, revolted. 'These baboons,' he thought, 'do they not know the first rudiments of battle? Must they expose so brazenly their intention to attack?'

He remembered the stories—fanciful undoubtedly—of ancient chivalry amongst the Indian kings. They would inform the adversary of the date, time and venue of the attack and the strength of the army that they proposed to bring into the field. Gracefully, the other side would keep the strength of its army at the same level. If it could not muster an equal number of men, elephants, horses and camels, the advancing army would reduce its own size, correspondingly. 'Crazy beggars,' the Colonel had said on hearing the story but he recognised the charm of it. Fighting, he had been told, was in those days restricted to the royal classes—royal by birth or by nomination; agriculture, art, industry and all economic activity remained unaffected; the kings ruled by the consent of the governed except within the first half year of the conquest and must thereafter periodically receive a 'confirmation' from each of the four classes of which society was formed—Brahmins, Kshatriyas, Vaishyas and Sudras; a contrary vote from a single class led to renunciation by the king of not only the territory held by him but all his worldly goods. The Colonel had thought that the story was too good to be true but he did suspect that it was not wholly a yarn and possibly much of it was based on facts. How else, he wondered, did this land, barren almost from coast to coast, come to accumulate vast and almost unending hordes of treasures and magnificent masterpieces of art and craftsmanship. Uninterrupted peace and freedom from persecution undoubtedly enriched the land, thought the Colonel. 'But they won't be here for long—these treasures and masterpieces. For we are here, the French are here, and the others are here—to shake the golden tree and to pluck its ripe fruit.' 'Your rape,' continued the Colonel, speaking to an imaginary audience of virgins representing the vast multitudes of the country, 'has begun'.

The Colonel's scouts apart from reporting intense activity in the enemy camp had also told him of recitations of the Quran and of the Gita by two groups from Tipu's motley army, composed of both Muslims and Hindus. It amused him. 'The Indian prince is learning fast,' he thought.

This was the first occasion, as far as the Colonel knew, when Tipu was resorting to the aid of religion to whip up some fervour and frenzy amongst his troops.

'You are undoubtedly planning a messacre, my friend,' said the Colonel, speaking to the absent Tipu, 'but, I won't be here to be massacred. In any case, it is quite, quite unfair of you to try and face me, with both the Quran and the Gita at the same time, when I am not guilty of even having seen, much less read, a Bible for the past so many years. May the holy Quran dull the wits of your troops and may the Gita cramp the muscles of their legs—and may Allah guide you tomorrow morning in directions different from mine.'

He almost heard himself say 'Amen' as he mounted his horse and beckoning to Munawar Khan, his orderly, who was following at a respectful distance, said:

'Munawar, you have your instructions. Remain at this hill forty-five minutes. Should any of our men be tempted to return for loot of the booty, ask no questions. Just shoot—and shoot to kill. Not that anyone will come since the officers have strict instructions to watch out for possible desertions. Still, be vigilant. After forty-five minutes, follow in the direction of our rearguard. You have a swift horse. But don't join the rearguard. Maintain a distance of fifteen minutes. If anything suspicious takes place, give an alarm and join them. In any case, join them just before sunrise, and ride out to meet me later in the day. Now, repeat to me what you have been told to do.'

Munawar Khan politely repeated his instructions.

'Any questions?' asked the Colonel at the end of the recital.

'None, Master.'

'Goodbye, then, for the time being.'

'Khuda Hafiz, Master.'

'Khuda Hafiz, Munawar.'

With that salutation, the Colonel departed.

Munawar Khan went back to the hill. When his forty-five minutes' vigil was over, he felt relieved. He had not been afraid at having been left alone but his was a soul that rejoiced in company. He was at his happiest when the crowd around him was the largest. In his younger days, the visit to the annual village fair always thrilled him, not because of the amusements it had to offer but on account of the considerably large number of people that it attracted. He would sit quietly in a group, hardly saying anything to his companions; much of their chatter was also lost on him for he rarely listened—so wrapped up was he in his own thoughts. But it delighted him to be in the midst of the group. He loved the camp life and was even reconciled to its savagery. Because, he said so little, his opinion was respected and because he rarely listened, in the first instance, every one had an opportunity of restating his viewpoint. Now that Diler Khan had died and he had taken over as orderly to the Colonel, his stock amongst the Indian troops had risen all the more, though he met his friends less often than before. Sometimes his companions mocked him, 'Oh! thou, that rubbest shoulders with the high and mighty.'

But they said it with a smile and he listened to it with a smile. He knew they loved him and he loved them in return. He had been a lonely man, his three wives having died without presenting him with a son.

Munawar Khan fully remembered the Colonel's instructions. He was to follow the direction of the rearguard, now that his lonely vigil of forty-five minutes was over. But what of so many of my friends who were to be abandoned on the lower hill? he wondered. Should he warn them? He would be violating a direct order from the Colonel himself. This he had never done before. But, then, he had never deserted his friends either. Amongst them was Daulat Khan with whom he had discussed an aspect of death and after-death. Munawar Khan had told Daulat Khan, 'I do not mind dying in a battlefield, but, I do want to be decently buried, preferably not in an isolated place. I would like to rest where many come and go and where there is a patter of children's feet, with possibly even a garden, nearby.'

'Well, leave it to me, my friend. I will have your carcass carried to the right place,' Daulat Khan had replied with a laugh.

'Will you, will you really, my friend?' earnestly Munawar Khan had asked.

Daulat Khan had been joking, of course. But something in that wistful longing in Munawar's heart had reached him and arrested his laughter. Solemnly, he had replied, 'Yes, Uncle, I promise you, I will, if at all it lies in my power.'

Then there was young Ashraf also on the lower hill. Ashraf's widowed mother for whom Munawar Khan cherished a tender regard, ever since the death of his third wife, had promised to marry him on his return from the campaign. He is not of my blood, thought Munawar but he is to be my son. 'Do I desert him, too?' he asked himself.

And what happens to all those, Salabat, Mehfuz, Satyanarain, Pande, Barkat and Tajadod—with whom he shared a pipe? Or, the youngsters, Srikant, Kamran, Mahmoud, Abdul and Tantia, who all ragged him once in a while but invariably addressed him as 'Uncle'?

Munawar Khan knew that in the Paradise that had been promised to him for the Hereafter, the nectar that the maidens would offer him would taste bitter indeed, if he were to carry out the soulless order of his Commander. Defiantly, with slow, measured steps, he walked in the direction of the lower hill. 'Go, wake up, Wafa, Daulat and Maqboo,' Munawar barked to the sentry at the entrance of the lower hill.

To these three elders, Munawar told the story of Humberstone's departure along with Lt Johnstone. Of the prize tents left behind, Munawar said nothing. He knew that such a disclosure would lead these men into a temptation which would ultimately destroy them. Every man and beast on the lower hill was roused. By common consent, Abu Wafa took over command and thus began the retreat of the last of the troops of the British army.

(ii)

Facing the hills was the army of Tipu Sultan. That night a message had reached him that his father Hyder Ali Khan, the ruler of Mysore, was dead. Prayers began and then the evacuation.

2

THE RULER IS DEAD

(i)

OUTSIDE HYDER'S TENT THE MORNING RITUAL HAD BEGUN. THE handsome drummer stood at the entrance and as the last notes of the far-off bugle faded away, he began his roll of drums. This was Hyder's way of greeting his followers at the camp every morning. The soft beat of the drums, followed by swift and lusty notes, proclaimed that Hyder was well and thanked the Almighty for this morning's sunrise; that he invoked His blessings for every one in the camp and wished them success and life with honour. The men around the camp paused and with a smile lifted their right fingers to their lips; the women solemnly raised both their palms to heaven while the older children—the few of them that were there—looked up to the sky. This was how each one in the camp responded to Hyder's greetings every morning.

This morning it was no different. No one in the camp knew that Hyder was dying. None, except his five Ministers and the physician who watched him day and night by his bedside, knew of Hyder's mortal sickness. The five now ceremoniously entered the tent, as indeed they did every morning. Each one saluted at the entrance of the tent, as if in reply to Hyder's salute, for it was customary for Hyder to salute first when someone entered his tent. Those who, from a distance, idly watched the procession of the five Ministers into the tent, thought that they saw Hyder on the other side of the entrance, greeting each Minister. For that was how it was, every morning. This morning, however, Hyder was not there to greet anyone. He was lying in bed in the rear section of that large tent. He knew, this was his last battle on earth—a battle of a different kind, in which he was alone and defenceless. He had led a full life and had found it beautiful. He had tasted of every pleasure that the world offered. Always there was merriment in his eyes, a smile on his lips and laughter in his heart. Even when he lost a battle or had to retreat, the zest for life did not forsake him for long. He had seen many a comrade die in battle, others in famine and pestilence and several in the natural course of events. He knew that each life had to end and that God had willed it so; surely, therefore, the Angel of Death was to be regarded as a benign messenger of God. Much as he loved life, Hyder knew that when the call came to him to end it all, he would willingly heed it and would go along without a regret, if not with a smile.

But benign or malignant, surely the Angel of Death was now playing games with Hyder. Hyder could plainly see his Presence, just behind the physician who had been keeping a constant vigil by his bedside. Hyder's lips moved as if to utter a welcome and also to wave aside the physician impolitely standing in the way of the illustrious Visitor. Hyder could now feel himself bathed in a ray of light. The agonising pain in his body melted away, leaving a sense of wellbeing. But as the ray of light entered into his dim consciousness, Hyder perhaps saw something of what lay ahead, in the future, for those that were to be left behind. He shuddered and the pain that had left his body, re-entered his entire being. 'I must warn Tipu, I must; please wait awhile. He must know what is to happen, dear friend, wait a little,' he implored; but he was being mocked. 'Tipu will follow you soon,' he was told. Again, he begged and pleaded, even offered a bribe or two and volunteered to plunge himself in the fires of hell so that he might be given the time to warn his son. But the Angel of Death was unmoved and therefore was no longer an Angel but an enemy who must be subdued. Gone was Hyder's resignation. 'I shall fight,' he said, waving his fist. It was then that the physician stood up in alarm. Although he understood nothing of Hyder's incoherence, he could sense his agitation. The five Ministers also now entered the bedroom as witnesses to the unequal struggle in which Hyder was locked.

(ii)

For once, the wise and venerable Hakim Al Batar, Chief Physician to Hyder Ali, was proved wrong. The night before, Purnaiya, the trusted confidante and Minister of Hyder, had visited him.

'How long?' Purnaiya had asked. It was not an idle question, the Hakim knew. Six messengers had been kept on the alert, day and night, to carry at a moment's notice the fateful message to Tipu, the son and heir of Hyder Ali.

'How long?' Purnaiya repeated the question.

The Hakim looked at the sky as if to indicate that answers to such questions should come from the heavens above. He turned to Purnaiya, gazed again at the moon and softly whispered: 'Tonight's moon shall be his last.'

'And tomorrow?' Purnaiya asked, as if to be certain.

'Tomorrow? It shall look for him in vain,' was the reply.

By Purnaiya's orders, the six messengers left, unknown to each other through different routes, each one bearing a message in code which only Purnaiya and Tipu shared. Prematurely, Purnaiya informed Tipu of his father's death and begged him to return.

(iii)

For four days and four nights, Hyder lived, through nightmare and agony, through delirium and pain.

(iv)

Purnaiya gently rubbed his head, as he watched the messengers galloping away with his message to Tipu. He knew that if Hyder lived, he would be answerable for his hasty summons to Tipu.

Twice before, Tipu had been summoned, in the midst of his campaigns against the British, to Hyder's bedside when his nervous ministers had thought that the end was near, while the Hakim was hopeful. On both the occasions, Hyder had recovered but how he had stormed and raged at the innocent Hakim, at the ministers and above all at Tipu! Tipu, he knew, had deprived himself, twice, of decisive victories in order to be near his father. Hyder knew very well that it was not the fear of losing his inheritance that brought his son to his bedside. On that score Hyder was supremely confident. The consolidation that he had carried out, the legend around the prowess of Tipu, the loyalty of his commanders and the affection in which Tipu was held, would ensure a smooth succession. It was not therefore to seek the throne of his father that Tipu had come. Hyder knew that and knew also that on both occasions, Tipu had rushed back to comfort him in his sickness, out of the love that the son bore to his father. Purnaiya knew of Hyder's joy and Hyder's rage over Tipu's love for his father. The rage triumphed, for Hyder the father was overruled by Hyder the Monarch who could not tolerate the weakness of a general abandoning a campaign and the prospects of a victory, merely for the sake of attending to a sick father. Tipu was ordered, never again to interrupt his campaign, whatever be his father's health.

Purnaiya had agreed with Hyder. The astute minister knew that sentiments which interfered with political ambition were luxuries which kings could ill-afford. Purnaiya knew also of the lengths to which Tipu could go to sacrifice himself. He vividly remembered the incident of not long ago when Tipu was ready to sacrifice his all. The Maratha cavalry under Trimbuk Rao had encircled Hyder's forces during his retreat to Seringapatam. Drunk though Hyder was, after an orgy, he managed to gallop away on a horse on which a groom put him. Trimbuk Rao's search for Hyder's person ended when Yaseen Khan, one of Hyder's commanders, surrendered to the Maratha army under the pretence of being Hyder himself. Yaseen Khan was the only man in Mysore who had the audacity of imitating Hyder by having his beard and whiskers shaved and this now helped the pretence. But while Trimbuk Rao had been fooled, Tipu and the rest of the Mysore army also believed that their missing Chief had been captured. Hyder, in the meanwhile, was lying by the roadside, having fallen from his horse in his drunken stupor. Under a flag of truce, Tipu himself went to Trimbuk Rao, intending to beg for Hyder's liberty and ready to promise, in return, the Kingdom of Mysore. He had already written out the terms of the surrender of Mysore and sought no more than a small principality for Hyder, 'the details and dimensions of which may be determined by your honour at your discretion and command and meanwhile, I, Tipu, the son of Hyder shall be your hostage.' The message never came to be delivered for Tipu had first insisted on seeing that Hyder was alive before he could parley with Trimbuk Rao. On seeing Yaseen Khan instead of Hyder, he understood the game and keeping up the pretence, bowed low before Yaseen Khan, as he would have before Hyder. But instead of delivering the forthright message, he merely entered into some desultory conversation with Trimbuk Rao, respectfully enquiring the terms on which Hyder could be released and peace could be restored. Tipu returned safe, for Trimbuk Rao was a man of honour who would never violate the Maratha tradition of chivalry by restraining an envoy.

When sobered, Hyder had returned to his fort in Seringapatam, tended in the meantime by a peasant who had carried him from the ditch by the roadside to his nearby hut, unaware of his identity. On hearing how Tipu was prepared to sacrifice his kingdom and liberty to save him, he had, at first, said nothing but later had much to say. At Hyder's bidding, Purnaiya also launched into several harangues and homilies, the purport of which was that kingdom and kingship were more important than the king himself and that ties of neither blood nor love could be allowed to stand in the way.

Purnaiya knew that Hyder had remembered that incident too, when he had ordered Tipu, never never again to leave the field of battle to be near his father. To the ministers he had said, 'If any of you should send for Tipu while I am alive, you shall answer with your head, I swear.'

Watching the messengers leave, Purnaiya rubbed his head again, wondering if it would have to answer for the hasty summons to Tipu. A small price to pay, if Hyder lives, he said to himself.

(v)

The six messengers left Hyder's camp with Purnaiya's message for Tipu. Each one carried an identical message. Different routes were assigned to them to safeguard against accident, ambush or treachery. It was enough if even one of them reached Tipu.

Of them, five followed the routes assigned to them by Purnaiya. The sixth had an assignment of his own. He deviated from the route and went towards the camp of Sheikh Ayaz—the trusted and favoured lieutenant of Hyder, but ready now to don the mantle of treachery.

3

A TRAITOR IS BORN

(i)

SHEIKH AYAZ, THE GOVERNOR OF THE PROVINCE OF BEDNUR, SAT in his tent. From the flap of the tent, perched on the crest of the hill, he could see, for miles, the path which would bring the messenger with the message that Purnaiya never intended for him. Patiently he waited.

Ayaz knew that the next few days would decide his destiny. Would he be the supreme lord of the empire or would he have to go limping back to Bednur—was the question. He came out of the tent, surveyed his camp which he had set up a fortnight earlier at Hyder's orders, mentally counted his forces and returned to his tent, satisfied. He kept thinking of the sonorous phrases of the proclamation which he would issue when the fateful moment arrived to give the marching orders to the troops under his command.

Ayaz had come a long way. He was the son of Ashila Banu, the famous courtesan of Calicut. So famed was she, and so sought after, that they said that it cost a handful of gold to hear her sing and three handfuls to see her dance. But of her love, she gave free—whenever she was inclined to. Only the Zamorin (ruler) of Calicut could take her as of right. For the rest, she dispensed her favours, never for a purse of gold but out of sheer love and fancy. Many claimed that it was Maqbool, the stable boy across the street—a handsome lad of seventeen—who was the father of Ayaz. Others singled out Hayat, the stepbrother of Ashila for the deed. Ashila, on her part, whispered to every one that the father was none other than the Zamorin.

The Zamorin, himself, did not believe it but was nonetheless pleased. He was an incompetent lover, who was always flattered by rumours which did such credit to his virility and vigour. He was not only the father of his people but was also supposed to have sired the largest number of bastards in the land.

For reasons best known to herself, Ayaz was brought up by Ashila Banu as an orthodox Hindu Nair. When he was eight years old, he moved into the Zamorin's court as a page boy and later, when he came to manhood, succeeded as the Chief of the Palace Guard.

Ayaz had by then matured into a handsome young man, well versed in the arts of war, swordsmanship and horse riding. His duties as the Chief of the Palace Guard were light, for the Zamorin was a popular ruler who was in no danger. Ayaz passed his time reciting poetry and composing songs. Often, he organised theatrical performances for the amusement of the Zamorin. He was at peace until Hyder threatened it.

The Nairs of Calicut under the Zamorin had fought Hyder gallantly. After heavy losses and tremendous carnage, Hyder had stormed the headquarters of the Zamorin. Ayaz was one of the thirty chiefs who followed the Zamorin when he made his submission to Hyder. Along with the Zamorin and other Chiefs, he swore life-long fealty and loyalty to Hyder.

They had come in fear of their lives. Hyder, however, impressed by their gallant defence, had received them kindly

After settling the military reparation at four hundred thousand sequins and receiving the oath of allegiance, Hyder sent them back, with some gracious words, free to resume their lives.

(ii)

That night the Zamorin lay drunk in his palace. Though generally abstemious, the tension of the past few days, the disgrace of the defeat and finally his relief at his life being spared, were enough to make him seek the companionship of wine. He had silenced his musicians and waved his courtiers away. Only Ayaz had remained to fill the cup. Shortly before midnight, Ayaz left the palace while the Zamorin slumbered through his drunken, fitful sleep. Ayaz woke the Chief Minister up and conveyed to him the sharp, crisp orders of the Zamorin—the treasure chests are to be moved away, the zenana (harem) is to be shifted and the army is to march to the Paldha fortress. After assuring himself of immediate compliance, he rushed to Hyder's camp and laid before him the tale of the Zamorin's supposed treachery. Hyder could hardly believe it, for he had been generous with the Zamorin. Still, he despatched his scouts in the direction indicated by Ayaz and they all reported troop movement. Livid with anger, Hyder ordered his army to swoop on the Zamorin's troops and to give no quarter. To Ayaz, his newly recruited lieutenant, who pleaded that he felt bound by the oath of allegiance to his new master, Hyder entrusted the task of attacking the Zamorin himself and of bringing him alive if possible 'so that I may keep him in a cage like that traitor Khande Rao, as a warning to mankind'. The body of troops led by Ayaz first arrested the Chief Minister of the Zamorin and at the orders of their leader, immediately the torture began. In a few moments the hiding place of the treasure chests was revealed while the Chief Minister was torn from limb to limb, his blood trailing on the road to the Zamorin's palace. Ayaz sent Hyder's soldiers to take custody of the treasure and removing now the turban with which he had hidden his face, went into the Zamorin's palace. He was challenged, recognised and allowed to pass with deference, for no one there yet knew of his change of sides. He called the palace guards to arms and all were kept near the gates in readiness to meet the attack from Hyder's forces of which he warned them. Alone he repaired to the Zamorin's bed chamber. The twelve soldiers who kept vigil at the Zamorin's bed chamber were ordered by him to the wall to join others in the defence of the palace. There unguarded now lay the Zamorin, lost to the world in his drunken sleep. Ayaz knew that he must not permit the Zamorin to be captured alive for then Hyder would come to know the truth. From the guardroom outside the bed chamber he picked up the burning torch from its stand and moved to the Zamorin's bed. For a moment he paused while the light flickered over the Zamorin's face. Gently he turned the Zamorin to the other side. Something of his forgotten decency stirred within him. He did not want to face the Zamorin. Averting his eyes, he applied the torch to the sides of the bed and watched fascinated as the flames began to move towards the Zamorin. In the intense heat of the fire, the Zamorin woke up, startled and sober now, but as he started to leave the bed, Ayaz, after a brief moment of panic, struck him with the burning torch again and again. The Zamorin lay writhing as the flames enveloped him. Ayaz now fled, applying the torch to everything in sight. As he reached the gate of the palace, he signalled the guards to be in readiness and galloped away to Hyder's soldiers who had by now assumed control of the Zamorin's treasure. The fire in the palace had spread and could be seen from a distance. He rushed to Hyder's camp. Hyder, who was delighted with the abundant treasure and his new lieutenant, had hardly a moment to grieve over his fallen foe who was assumed to have set fire to his own palace to perish in the flames rather than face the wrath of Hyder.

Hyder offered Ayaz the realm of the Zamorin. Ayaz, fearing that the Nairs, his erstwhile compatriots, would suspect treachery and would somehow seek their revenge, pleaded that he saw greater glory in being by the side of his master. Hyder was delighted.

(iii)

Many rewards had come to Ayaz since then. He was, after all, a forceful commander, a superb organiser and a gay companion. He held Hyder's trust and affection. While Hyder was for ever plagued by his followers for honours and rewards, Ayaz was the only one who had twice declined to accept governorship of a province on the ground that such an office would come in the way of his accompanying Hyder on his campaigns frequently—a pleasure which he regarded far above the honour, prestige and riches, of a governorship. Finally, when Hyder pressed him to accept governorship of Chitaldrug, he came out, with even a better objection, designed to please his master.

'Let me remain a soldier. I cannot even read and write,' said Ayaz.

'Read and write!' exclaimed Hyder. 'How have I risen to the Empire without the knowledge of either?'

'There is only one Hyder and we all know it, sire,' was the response of Ayaz.

But Hyder also needed governors whom he could trust fully and without reservations. Apart from his other duties, a trusted governor had also charge of a part of Hyder's treasury, which had to be kept distributed in three or four places for safe custody and to guard against a surprise attack.

(iv)

It was during his governorship of Chitaldrug that Ayaz had himself converted to Islam and gave himself the title of Sheikh. When Hyder heard the announcement, he shrugged his shoulders for he set little store by religion. Tipu, however, had a comment.

'He changed his master once, now his religion and his name. What next?' asked Tipu.

Ayaz was now the Governor of Bednur, custodian also of a third of an entire treasury of Hyder. Hyder knew that his own health was failing and he wanted his loyal commanders nearby, so that in case of his death, Tipu's inheritance suffered no challenge. Not that Hyder had any serious doubts about the succession. It was only a question of taking abundant precautions. Ayaz was commanded to set up his camp at a distance of fifty miles from Hyder's and to wail for summons 'from me or, if God so wills it, from Tipu whose succession you have sworn to safeguard and uphold'.

So, Ayaz knew that Hyder was dying. He also knew that Tipu was far away. Here was his chance to seize the kingdom before Tipu arrived to claim it. He had been in correspondence with the English. They would support and uphold him. He had his friends at Hyder's court who would strike but only when Hyder was dead. It was important therefore for him to have the news of Hyder's death, well before Tipu could arrive to claim the succession. Purnaiya would undoubtedly use Gulam Mohamed, the fastest courier in Hyder's court, to carry the message to Tipu. Gulam Mohamed was in the pay of Ayaz and it was for him that the Governor of Bednur had been watching for days the paths that led to his camp.

Sheikh Ayaz came out of the tent and looked again in the general direction of Hyder's camp. The midday heat and the bright sunlight reminded him somehow of the night in the Zamorin's chamber. He walked back into the tent and waited.

(v)

Late in the afternoon, Gulam Mohamed arrived in the camp of Sheikh Ayaz and delivered to him the message intended for Tipu.

Courteously, Ayaz motioned the messenger to the chair and passed on to him the flagon of wine.

The poisoned wine took effect even before Sheikh Ayaz could break the seal to open the letter.

Gulam Mohamed would betray no one, any more.

(vi)

Of late, ambition had spurred Sheikh Ayaz to learn reading and writing. He had come to acquire passable knowledge but the paper he was trying to read meant nothing to him.

Ayaz knew enough to understand that it was written in Sanskrit—a language of the highly educated Brahmins, which naturally Purnaiya, but surprisingly Tipu also, knew very well.

Ayaz, after his voluntary conversion to Islam, had banished Brahmins and other Hindus from all offices in his court. Hyder, on receiving the complaint had dismissed it by saying, 'Let him have whosoever shall serve him well.' Tipu who sat next to Hyder when the complaint was heard, had the temerity to ask, 'If the religion of your subjects means nothing to you, Father, should it mean more to your governors?'

Hyder viewed the question differently and said, 'Son, the question before us is not of the religion of our subjects but of the right of my governors to choose their servants.'

In his camp, therefore, Ayaz had no one who could read the letter for him. From a distance, a scholarly Brahmin was brought. The letter was read out to Ayaz but still it meant nothing to him. It began and ended with a quotation from the Gita—an ancient religious classic and a philosophic treatise revered by the Hindus. The text of the letter was simplicity itself. It consisted of salutations from Purnaiya to Tipu, with the regret that the former, so busy with the life at the Camp, had not been able to write a detailed report on the matter which they had earlier discussed but promised to do so in the coming weeks. That was all. The two quotations from the Gita signified even less. The first quotation was translated to read:

I am the goal, the upholder, the
lord, the witness, the abode,
the refuge and the friend. I am
the origin and the dissolution,
the ground, the resting place
and the imperishable seed.

And the second:

Better is one's own law though
imperfectly carried out than the law
of another carried out perfectly.
One does not incur sin when one
does the duly ordained by one's
own nature.

The scholarly explanations of the venerable Brahmin could shed no light. He was quickly dismissed by Ayaz to be seized outside the tent by the orderly and silenced for ever.

Ayaz realised that it was a message in code. If it was merely an innocent letter, how was it that Purnaiya did not even mention Hyder's illness which had caused so much anxiety and speculation all over, amongst friends and foes?—and why did Purnaiya send the fastest courier in Hyder's court with a message, so routine on the face of it? Yes, Hyder is dead, concluded Ayaz, and this coded message is surely intended to recall Tipu to claim his inheritance. The only doubt that troubled him was that not even one of his many spies littered in Hyder's camp had come to inform him of this momentous event. He dismissed the doubt. The wily Purnaiya must have conspired to keep Hyder's death a secret, he surmised. This would not cause any serious change in the plan though. The original plan had seen that on the night following the announcement of Hyder's death, followers of Ayaz would seize Purnaiya and other trusted commanders of Hyder. They would spread the rumour that Hyder was murdered by Purnaiya in league with other commanders. Thereafter they would hastily summon the nearest commander, Sheikh Ayaz, who would come with his army, investigate and having judged them guilty of Hyder's murder at Tipu's orders would have all the inconvenient ones beheaded, The stage would then be set for installing Abdul Karim, Tipu's feeble-witted brother, on the throne as a puppet. The English, with whom Ayaz was in daily correspondence, would wait for the summons to block Tipu from marching anywhere, proclaim him guilty of conniving at the murder of his father, release the propaganda material already in readiness suggesting that the tyrant was planning to convert all Hindus to Islam and consign to slavery all Christians. Abdul Karim was not intended to live long but long enough for all power to slip into the hands of Ayaz.

This then was the plan—and if Purnaiya and others had conspired to keep Hyder's death a secret, this was all to the good from the point of view of Ayaz, for the accusation of murder would then have all the greater credibility. He sent a courier to Hyder's court, with a message to his agents Muhammad Aramin and Shums-ud-din informing them of Hyder's death, charging them to whip up the rumour of his murder and thence proceed as planned.

Muhammad Aramin was the cousin of Hyder, a cavalry general who commanded four thousand horses while Shums-ud-din Bakshi was the paymaster of Hyder's army.

Ayaz now waited with his divisions on the alert for the night arrests, uprising and the summons to him.

(vii)

The supple Purnaiya heard impassively the rumour of Hyder's death as it spread throughout the camp. His orderly told him of it, with tears in his eyes. Later he saw groups, apparently discussing it in whispers. Shums-ud-din's three wives, beating their breasts, were going from place to place and so were many more, to exchange the sad 'news'.

Purnaiya knew that the sorrow was genuine but, naturally, he suspected its inspiration. He made his preparations. Well before sunset, he had the drums beaten and the entire camp thronged in the square to hear him.

'They have lied to you,' he said. 'Hyder Ali Khan is alive, though in fever. His physician tells me that God will spare him for us.'

'Prove it,' retorted Muhammad Aramin, who was a relative of Hyder but unknown to Purnaiya was also the secret agent of Sheikh Ayaz.

'Or, is it that you have murdered him?' needled Muhammad Aramin.

'I forgive you,' Purnaiya replied, 'for your grief no doubt blinds you. But I repeat, Hyder Ali Khan is alive.'

'Prove it, prove it,' was the chant on all sides, though here and there Purnaiya could also hear a heckler or two, hurling abuse and calling him a 'murderer', 'a vile Brahmin' and such other epithets.

Purnaiya spoke the truth. Notwithstanding the coded message he had sent to Tipu, Hyder still lived, though raving, gesticulating, through nightmare and agony of pain. Purnaiya did not like the mood and the temper of the troops fed on the rumour of Hyder's death, and possibly of his murder. He consulted Hakim Al Batar, and Hyder's physician agreed. All those who doubted Purnaiya's word were invited into Hyder's tent and the procession began. Hyder's fever was clear for everyone to see. Some thought that his eyes were open and others thought that they were closed but all of them could plainly hear his strident though incoherent shouts that came through his delirium. When outside they wanted to know what exactly Hyder had been saying, Purnaiya admonished them.

'He is in fever and in pain,' said Purnaiya, more in sorrow than in anger. 'You insist on violating his privacy. Should you wonder, if he shouts.'

Ashamed, the crowds dispersed, convinced now that Hyder lived and satisfied with Purnaiya's assurance that the fever and pain would not last long.

Purnaiya, however, was not fully reassured. His preparations were made. He had feared a conspiracy and it erupted at the dead of the night. The contingency plan of Ayaz had provided that if Hyder's death had not occurred, let it be contrived, with Purnaiya and his associates to be held responsible.

Sixty French mercenaries of Hyder had also been enrolled by Muhammad Aramin for the infamous task and they now proceeded to arrest Mir Sadik, Hyder's Minister of Finance. Of the four thousand vavalry troops, Muhammad Aramin could rely on only a few to engage in this treacherous task but he expected all of them to rally to him after initial success. The other agent of Ayaz, Shums-ud-din, with eighty men in the pay of Ayaz, went to Purnaiya's quarters, They walked into a trap.

Meanwhile the troops sent by Purnaiya disarmed Muhammad Aramin and the French mercenaries. The French officer of the Guard, Bouthenot, disclosed the plot on being given assurances of personal safety. The two principals—Muhammad Aramin and Shums-ud-din—were put into chains and sent away to Seringapatam as though on the orders of Hyder.

Sheikh Ayaz was warned by a courier who slipped away. Ayaz marched back to his fort in Bednur to await better times. Couriers sped from his fort carrying his messages of treachery and treason to the English and to others.

4

BORN IN BATTLE

ABDUL KARIM, SON OF HYDER ALI KHAN AND BROTHER OF TIPU Sultan, appeared in his father's camp, the next day.

He had been summoned by Sheikh Ayaz to the camp, with utmost speed and the messenger had whispered to him, 'Tomorrow you shall be our King.'

A man of weak intellect but amiable disposition, he came with an air of mild enquiry.

No one had told him of the plot that was afoot or that it had failed. He could be relied on to permit anyone to rule in his name and ask no questions. But now he had a question to put to Purnaiya. 'Am I to be the King?' Karim asked.

'Your father is a King and your brother shall be a King. Should that not suffice?'

'Yes, of course,' came the cheerful answer of Karim.

'Do you want to be a King?' playfully Purnaiya asked.

'Will I have to go into battle?' parried Karim.

'Sometimes,' replied Purnaiya.

'I want no more of battle. I was born in the midst of a battle. Should that not suffice?'

'Yes, of course,' Purnaiya replied with a smile.

Abdul Karim went to Hyder's tent to sit by the bedside of his father, while Purnaiya mused on how Fakhr-un-Nissa, wife of Hyder, had given birth to Karim in a palanquin while a battle had been raging. On being informed, Hyder had rushed to the palanquin. The cry of the newborn babe had spurred Hyder to greater effort—and soon he was awarded with victory.

In Karim, Hyder had placed many hopes. What greater omen of his coming glory than being born in the midst of battle in which Hyder had chalked up a great feat of arms!

Tipu was promised to God—to go into the priestly order, to pass his life in prayer and meditation. This was the solemn pledge that Hyder and Fakhr-un-Nissa had taken. That Karim would carry the proud banner of his father had been their hope—a hope that soon turned into ashes.

5

THEY ALSO MOURNED

(i)

SADHU RAM, ONE OF THE SIX COURIERS SENT BY PURNAIYA, was the first to reach Tipu's camp. He had covered the long distance through uneven terrain in four days and four nights. Even though he was unaware of what the message was about, he knew that it was important. A reward awaited him, if he delivered it safely and quickly, Purnaiya had said. Sadhu Ram had promised to himself that he would give a portion of the reward to the temple at which he regularly prayed. He was now escorted to Tipu's tent.

'How is my father?' asked Tipu, before breaking the seal of Purnaiya's message.

'He was ailing at the time I left but Hakim Al Batar was certain of speedy recovery. God willing, he must be fully recovered by now.'

Tipu broke the seal and silently read. A chill went through his heart. The message was clear to him. He did not need to read it the second time. Still, the minutes passed by and his eyes remained bent on the letter before him. The camp gong struck the midnight hour. Through the storm raging in his heart, Tipu dimly heard it and looked up from the letter.

'My father is dead,' quietly he said.

Both Tipu and Sadhu Ram prayed, each in his own way.

Arshad Beg and the Brahmin Shivji, who had escorted Sadhu Ram to Tipu's tent, left. They would pray later, for the departed soul—Arshad in the mosque and Shivji in the temple, or possibly even in the privacy of their tents. Now they had something more important to do—to alert the camp commanders to be ready for the retreat rather than for the battle and to make arrangements for Tipu's departure.

(ii)

Brahmin Shivji was Tipu's Secretary. He loved Tipu who had rescued him from the English prison. Brahmin Shivji's wife had perished during the famine that swept Bengal in the wake of the English ascendancy, while Shivji himself had gone to the nearby town to raise a loan from a friend. His friend had also been wiped out and in his house, instead, resided an English Lieutenant. Shivji had fallen sick and it took him some time before he returned, only to find that his wife and his three sons were missing. The story of his wife's death was simply told by the neighbours. The comely but foolish woman had gone to the English camp to sell her last belongings in order to feed her children. She was dead when the last soldier raped her. The tormented children were then released. Abdul Gafoor, the next-door neighbour, took them in for the night. Next morning, Gafoor lodged a complaint. An Englishman called and he promised action against the criminals and undertook to look after the children until their father returned.

After three years of vigilant search, Shivji located the Englishman, Father Wilson, a missionary. The two older children had died, he was told, and the youngest was converted to Christianity. He demanded his child. He was shown a document, bearing a signature which was falsely witnessed as his own, whereby not only the custody and the legal guardianship of the three children was transferred to the society of the Missionaries, but a fervant plea was made to bring them up as Christians. Shivji, who persisted in claiming his child, was shown the door and finally when he lost his temper, was beaten by the servants of Father Wilson. They handed him over to the English police. There he was lodged, in a dungeon, reserved for dangerous political offenders. When the English in Madras needed help against Hyder Ali, prisoners were sent from Bengal to help in preparing road blocks and such tasks. Shivji was one of them. He was also one of those freed by Tipu when the Sultan routed the English division. Shivji sought service with Tipu and served him until the end.

As Tipu's Secretary, it was Shivji's task to take down what Tipu dictated and to transmit his orders to all concerned. Sometimes, however, he wrote on his own—letters to his sons—letters that were never despatched, letters that somehow filled the emptiness within him. In the early hours of the morning, he was writing one of them.

'At the stroke of midnight, the Sultan after reading Purnaiya's message said that his father was dead. His voice was gentle and the tone quiet. In the stillness of the night, I left the tent with Arshad Beg; he, to arrange the movement of the troops and I, to supervise the arrangements for the departure of the Sultan. I returned to the tent shortly to find that Sadhu Ram had gone to sleep, worn with the fatigue of travel. The Sultan sat in his chair with his faraway look. I called the guard to remove Sadhu Ram to the nearby tent, but the Sultan intervened and said, 'Let him be, he is tired. He doesn't disturb me. Let him sleep.' As the guards were about to leave, the Sultan added,

'But if you can gently take off his shoes, loosen his tunic and put a pillow under his head, he will sleep more peacefully.' The Sultan watched this being done and then relapsed into his reverie. What was he thinking of, my dear sons? Was it grief at parting with his father whom he loved as much as I love you? But I saw no sorrow on his countenance. Was it the fear of responsibility that awaited him, the wars he would have to wage, the plots, conspiracies and intrigues that he would have to contend with? Yet, I saw no lines of anxiety on his brow. But I will tell you what I think I saw on his face and in his heart. Compassion. Yes, compassion for the weak, for the innocent and for the helpless—countless thousands upon thousands on whom the aliens would now unleash their remorseless war machine in an effort to gain supremacy, to take territory and to plunder treasures. With Hyder Ali gone, this would be their heaven-sent opportunity to trample the soil under their iron heel, to shed rivers of blood, to separate lovers from their beloveds and fathers from their sons. Yes, my sons, the Sultan has seen this in his mind's eye and grieves not for his loss but for the unfortunates like me who pine for their sons. Yes, he grieves for you. May he....'

The letter remained unfinished like all other letters of Brahmin Shivji to his sons. Invariably, in the middle of his letters, tears welled up in his eyes and in the anguish, he could write no more.

6

THEY WERE THIRTEEN

AT PRECISELY THE SAME MOMENT, WHEN TIPU SULTAN ANNOUNCED the death of his father, 280 miles away from his camp, Hakim Al Batar pronounced Hyder as dead. Legend, which has thus invested Purnaiya with the feat of conveying an instantaneous communication of Hyder's demise, failed to take note of the fact that prematurely, though for good and valid reasons, Purnaiya had sent the message four days earlier. Destiny had willed that Tipu Sultan and Hakim Al Batar should know of the death at the same moment.

When Hakim Al Batar pronounced his fateful verdict, Purnaiya, Krishna Rao, Shamaiya, Abu Muhammad, Gopal Nath and Mir Sadik were around Hyder's deathbed. Purnaiya called in the other seven chief officers and swore all of them to secrecy.

Hakim Al Batar was to remain in vigil in Hyder's tent. His assistant physicians and surgeons were to keep visiting at regular hours. Hyder's commanders and chief officers were to keep calling as if to be in audience with Hyder. Couriers, messengers and others were to follow the same routine as if Hyder was alive and in full control. The army was already on the alert but everyone related it, not to the possibility of the death of Hyder but to the recently suppressed mutiny by the agents of Sheikh Ayaz. Who knows it might erupt again! The treacherous rebels had even spread the rumour of Hyder's death and Purnaiya had proved it to be false. The camp was cautioned to watch out for anyone spreading such false rumours again.

Early next morning, a large chest containing costly and rare jewels was shown around the camp, with the joyous announcement that the Ottoman Caliph had sent these from Constantinople as gifts for Hyder Ali Khan Bahadur as a token of his friendship. The chest was then used to deposit Hyder Ali's body and sent under a heavy escort as if it still contained the Caliph's presents which were being sent to Seringapatam. It found its temporary resting place, sixty miles along the route, at Kolar where it was placed near the tomb of Fatah Muhammad, Hyder Ali's father, until it was finally removed to be buried in the grand mausoleum which Tipu built for it in Seringapatam.

Before depositing Hyder's body in the treasure chest, a solemn ceremony took place at which in the presence of the dead, the commanders and chief officers of Hyder reaffirmed their oath to serve Tipu. Purnaiya took the oath and administered it to the Hindu chiefs—Krishna Rao, Shamaiya, Gopal Nath, Ram Murari, Maha Dev and Vishwanath. Abu Muhammad followed suit and administered the oath to the Muslim chiefs—Mir Sadik, Badr-uz-zaman Khan, Maha Mirza Khan, Muhammad Ali and Ghazi Khan.

Purnaiya looked around and idly counted the officers again. Including himself, they were thirteen. Christians, he knew, regarded this number with superstition. One by one, his glance rested on them. By the light of the lantern he could see these tried and trusted men who had borne the scars of countless battles of Hyder. Only Mir Sadik he could not see, for he was silently praying with his palms shielding his face.

'No, these men would never betray their trust,' Purnaiya thought. 'None,' he was convinced, 'would turn Judas.'

Still, Purnaiya dismissed the supper that was to follow the ceremony.

'If you agree, tonight we shall fast and pray, to honour the illustrious dead.'

Others echoed his sentiment.

Part II

MOTHER, MOTHER!
FATHER, FATHER!

7

MY LADY OF THE FLOWERS

(i)

FAKHR-UN-NISSA, WIFE OF HYDER ALI KHAN AND MOTHER OF TIPU Sultan, was in her bed chamber, alone. She had sent away her maids and companions. She did that often, whenever she wanted to sketch. In the high-walled private garden outside her bed chamber there was a profusion of flowers. She loved to watch them grow and brush them against her cheeks to feel the coolness of the morning dew on her soft skin. Their living fragrance held for her a fascination far greater than all the perfumes with which her dressing table was littered. When a flower stood out alone, growing away from its companions, she loved to take out her sketch book, to recapture it in pencil or paint. Was it her mood that determined the mood of the solitary flower? She frequently wondered. At times, she would draw a flower as it stood proud and alone in the universe desiring no companionship. Her next flower would be restless, whispering messages to the breeze for friends far away. Then there would be a solitary soul, with a bowed head and knowledge of the guilt that condemned it to its loneliness.

Whatever be the mood that she caught them in her sketch book, flowers were her passion.

Whenever Hyder departed on his campaigns, his parting gift to his wife would be flowers—white flowers. A day or two before he was to return, a courier would speed to the palace to lay at her feet a bouquet of multi-coloured flowers sent by her husband to signal his immediate return. White flowers signified to Hyder the sadness of parting, his tenderness for his wife and the purity of their love, but the joy of homecoming and reunion was best expressed, he thought, in flowers of different hues and colours.

At midnight, the courier had come with a large bouquet wrapped in white silk. With a happy heart, she unwrapped it. They were white flowers—the flowers of farewell.

It was now the hour of dawn. She had not slept all night. Savagely, she fought against all the doubts that assailed her mind. Clearly, there was a mistake. Never did her husband send white flowers. He always gave them to her personally when about to depart. Now all that could have happened was that on this occasion her husband did not obtain the flowers himself but entrusted the task to some dolt who chose wrongly. How was she to know that Hyder in a lucid moment some time before he closed his eyes for ever had asked Purnaiya, 'You must send flowers to Fatima [Fakhr-un-Nissa].'

'That will be done,' Purnaiya had replied.

'White, white flowers, only white,' Hyder had said.

She had arranged the flowers—most of them in the large porcelain vase at the centre table. She began to sketch but the lines did not come out right. The lovely flowers on the table had a withered, vanquished look in the sketch book. She gave up and sent for news from the Palace Commandant who personally came with a courier, just arrived from Hyder's camp. All was well and nothing—absolutely nothing—to worry about. And from Tipu's camp? The messenger had arrived only last night. All was well. All.

She did not know, then, that at the stroke of midnight when she had unwrapped the bouquet of flowers, her husband was dead.

(ii)

Fakhr-un-Nissa sat thinking of her husband and her son. Most of her life passed by, waiting for them. When they came back with their trophies and treasures, with news of battles won and armies routed, she heard the lusty cheers of the multitude but she also counted the many who had not returned with them. Silently she would render thanks for their homecoming but would pray also for those lost on the battlefield and for the widows and orphans left behind. Then, the night would arrive and Hyder would steal into her bed chamber. She would lie in his arms and he would gently caress away her fears and torments.

She had married Hyder, at the behest of Shahbaz Begum, Hyder's first wife. Hyder had been married at an early age to Shahbaz Begum, the daughter of Shah Mian Saheb, a holy man of Sira. Shahbaz Begum was frail and often sick. Amongst the visitors who frequently called on her was Fakhr-un-Nissa, daughter of Mir Muin-ud-din who was for some years the Governor of the Fort of Cuddappah. Others carried rich gifts to Shahbaz Begum. Fakhr-un-Nissa carried only flowers. As time passed by, Shahbaz Begum began to love the young visitor and would insist on her company every day. The ailing Shahbaz Begum gave birth to a daughter but while in child-birth, she was stricken with dropsy which made her paralytic for the rest of her life. Fakhr-un-Nissa would comfort her with flowers, wipe her brow with perfumed towels and draw comic sketches of the little daughter, over which Shahbaz Begum giggled; but when Fakhr-un-Nissa left, the pain would return to her.

Physician after physician pronounced Shahbaz Begum incurable. Hyder did not even once countenance the thought of re-marriage. He loved his wife and the little daughter she had given him. He would sit by the side of his bed-ridden wife for hours, hold her hands and kiss her brow and lips whenever she was in pain. Shahbaz Begum was tormented all the time—except for the brief moments when her husband or her friend Fakhr-un-Nissa were there to comfort her. More than her physical pain was the agonising thought that she could not give a son and an heir to her husband.

Shahbaz Begum had reached a decision and was comforted by it. When Hyder went into her bed chamber one afternoon, he was delighted to see her looking well rested, and comfortable.

'I have reached a decision,' responded Shahbaz Begum when Hyder complimented her on her cheerful look.

'And what is the decision?' Hyder enquired with a pleasantry. 'A new ring, a new dress, a new necklace?'

'No,' replied Shahbaz Begum. 'A new wife. You need another wife.'

'One wife is enough for me, madam,' Hyder Ali had answered quietly.

'But a daughter alone is not enough,' countered Shahbaz Begum.

Shahbaz Begum was not deterred. She had called in all the companions and colleagues of Hyder, one by one, and also their wives. She had taken a promise from them to look for a suitable wife for Hyder. It was then that Hyder began to be accosted by proposals of marriage. Portraits of lovely girls of suitable families were shown to him. Their wealth and accomplishments were narrated. One by one Hyder rejected them all.

When fever returned to Shahbaz Begum, she pleaded with Hyder to marry, if not for his sake, at least for the sake of his daughter who would be left uncared for. Sullenly, Hyder agreed. He told her of the proposals he had received and why each one was unsuitable on account of this or that reason.

'You select a wife for me, madam,' concluded Hyder.

'You will marry my Lady of the Flowers,' said Shahbaz Begum.

(iii)

Two years after the second marriage of Hyder, Shahbaz Begum, his first wife, died in the arms of Fakhr-un-Nissa, his second wife. During these two years, Hyder who had resentfully married Fakhr-un-Nissa came to love her. He had seen her tenderness towards Shahbaz Begum, her affection for his daughter and her devotion for him. She had also been mortally afraid of this strange, swashbuckling and rough soldier who spoke in such strident voice and impatient tones. But alone with her, he was a gentle lover. He calmed her troubled spirits, gave her flowers and kisses and each night became a night of joy. Still, their pleasures were barren. Hyder Ali was still without a son and an heir.

On her deathbed, Shahbaz Begum took a promise from them both that they would go on a pilgrimage to the shrine of the saint Tipu Mastan Oulia in Arcot to seek the blessings of this holy man.

8

THE PILGRIMAGE

SAINT TIPU MASTAN OULIA WHO WAS ALSO CALLED MAST KALANDAR and Sachal Fakir was a vagabond. He had no house of his own. He would sleep wherever he felt like—on the street, in the forest, on the mountain, on rough ground or on grass—always uncovered and without a pillow. No one saw him praying, never once did he enter a temple or a mosque and none knew of his religion. He would come to Arcot as suddenly as he would leave it. If anyone came after him, he ran to avoid being followed. If he was still followed, he threw stones to shake off the pursuit. Often, he would be dancing away in drugged frenzy for hours until he fainted. At times he would talk to himself, his eyes closed. He would address the trees and speak to them for hours. Strangely, the birds remained in the trees and flew away only if some one else approached. Stray dogs would crowd round him, but that was not surprising for he gave them the food that was presented to him by so many. Some had sworn that they had seen him in the forest talking to tigers and other wild animals. Many a time he would refuse sumptuous food offered to him but would be seen eating the leaves of a tree. The sick would be brought to him for healing but he would turn them away, though sometimes he got up, blessed the sick and it was said that they recovered. When Nawab Sadutullah Khan came to beg him personally to cure his daughter who was in high fever and said to be dying, he sent him back, saying she had already recovered—and indeed she had. Then there was the story of the night guard, permanently blind in one eye, who had stumbled against the holy man, sleeping on the pavement. In anger the holy man snatched his lantern, broke it against the wall and cursed the guard as a 'blind fool'. Instinctively, the guard struck back and as Mast Kalandar reeled, the guard immediately lost the sight of his good eye as well. In the morning, blind in both eyes, he was taken by his sons to Mast Kalandar. He braved his abuses and curses and in the end was admonished to look where he was going. He left Mast Kalandar with sight in both his eyes restored.

Mast Kalandar tolerated no human company, except one youngster who sometimes quietly sat by his side. It was said that he was his son.

To Nawab Sadutullah Khan's entreaties that he should reside in a house which the Nawab would build for him, Mast Kalandar had pointed to a spot, saying that he would live everywhere but would die there. 'Then you can build a house for me, when I die.' Several months later, Mast Kalandar was found dead at the spot that he had indicated. The Nawab had a tomb constructed in his honour.

Men and women from far and near, some in faith and others with wounds to be healed, came to the tomb. Sometimes they would catch the glimpse of the son of Mast Kalandar who was now said to be as mad as his father, but possibly without his healing touch.

It is to this tomb that Hyder Ali and Fakhr-un-Nissa repaired to seek the blessings of Saint Tipu Mastan Oulia.

9

THE PROMISE

(i)

HYDER ALI BOWED PERFUNCTORILY AT THE TOMB OF SAINT TIPU Mastan Oulia and left soon after depositing a large offering. Fakhr-un-Nissa remained behind to pray. Every morning she came for seven days and remained until late afternoon in prayer and meditation. The atmosphere at the shrine gave her a feeling of peace and contentment. The architectural design of the shrine also pleased her but the environs were rocky and barren. 'Why hadn't some one thought of planting some trees and flowers?' she wondered. She spoke to her servants who waited outside and soon they collected a small labourforce. She had asked the trustees and the caretakers of the shrine and they welcomed the idea of a garden being planted. As the digging started, a wild-looking man rushed out of the shrine and asked why the peace of the shrine was being disturbed. He was the one who was said to be the son of Mast Kalandar and though he was intensely disliked by the trustees and caretakers of the shrine, none of them dared to interfere with him. As the labourers pointed to Fakhr-un-Nissa, she herself approached him, saying that her idea was to have flowering trees planted.

'Why?' the young man demanded gruffly.

'Why?' repeated Fakhr-un-Nissa, 'I think Tipu Mastan Oulia would be pleased.'

The young man raced back to the shrine only to return after a few moments.

'No,' he said. 'Tipu Mastan Oulia would not be pleased. He wants nothing done by a woman for himself. Send your son if you want flowers to be planted.'

'But I have no son,' Fakhr-un-Nissa stammered, 'Perhaps my husband....'

'I know, but you will. You will have more than one son. That is why you came here. Your prayers have been heard. Go now.' As Fakhr-un-Nissa silently stared at the youth, he continued, 'But what is the use of having sons, only to have them mown down in battle!'

It sounded like a curse.

'No, no,' cried Fakhr-un-Nissa, 'grant that they shall live.'

'Will you promise to deliver your first born to God's service?' quietly the youth asked.

'Yes, I will,' was the fervent reply.

'Go then in peace. Your first one will be a prince, a Sultan, a king amongst men. Let him know the ways of the Lord, so that he may carry his banner. Let him serve God and none else. Go.' All the wildness had now left the youth. He stood transformed. His tone was soft but commanding and Fakhr-un-Nissa felt the presence of some one else.

'Thank you,' she said with a trembling heart, kissing the hem of his robe.

She returned to her palanquin and as she was entering it, the youth regained his wildness and shouted, 'Your son is a Sultan, do you hear? Tipu says so.'

(ii)

Hyder Ali could not make head or tail of the account which Fakhr-un-Nissa gave him.

'Well, this much is clear,' he summed up, 'that even though we don't have a son yet, we have got a name for him. Tipu Sultan is what we will call him.'

'And he is to be brought up in the service of God,' added Fakhr-un-Nissa.

'Amen,' said the irreverent Hyder, 'but you better quickly deliver the son to me, so that I may keep your promise of delivering him to God's service.'

As the palanquin kept moving, every five minutes or so Hyder kept enquiring with mock seriousness if the pains (of childbirth) had started or if he should ask the palanquin-bearers to go slow if the birth was imminent. At times, he asked if God wanted a son of his to be delivered to His service, why did He have to take the trouble of having Fakhr-un-Nissa deliver him first. Could He not do so without human intervention or assistance? Then he wondered what people would say if he named his son a Sultan (or a king) when he himself was only a junior commander still. 'Perhaps, I shall have to try to become a king, too,' he added. Fakhr-un-Nissa was in too good a humour herself to prevent him from joking but she did repeat: 'A Sultan, not in the temporal or earthly sense but in matters of spirit and in service of the Lord—that, dear husband, is the destiny of my son.'

'Our son, you mean.'

'Yes, our son,' graciously Fakhr-un-Nissa conceded.

The rest of the journey passed away with both sharing perhaps the same thoughts.

10

REJOICE, A SON IS BORN

(i)

AT DEVANHALLI, ON FRIDAY, 20 NOVEMBER 1750 FIVE YEARS AFTER her marriage and nine months after her first visit to the shrine of Saint Tipu Mastan Oulia, a son was born to Fakhr-un-Nissa.

He was named Tipu Sultan.

(ii)

Fakhr-un-Nissa had visited the shrine again during her pregnancy and asked the guardian of the shrine about the son of Saint Tipu Mastan Oulia.

'He was no son, madam,' reproachfully the guardian said. 'He was a pretender. Always deep in drink and drugs. Mercifully, he died and we are now spared his violence.'

'Where is he buried?' Fakhr-un-Nissa enquired.

'Buried?' snorted the guardian. 'He was no Muslim. He had asked that he be cremated.'

'And his ashes,' Fakhr-un-Nissa persisted, 'where are they kept?'

'Nowhere, madam, nowhere,' the guardian was almost cheerful. 'He had asked that his ashes be scattered so that the wind would take them anywhere and everywhere, to alight on rivers and oceans, to scale the mountains and the stars and to visit every home and every garden. He was mad, madam, absolutely mad,' concluded the guardian on an angry note.

'Did they not say the same of Saint Tipu Mastan Oulia?' Fakhr-un-Nissa enquired.

'Madam!' The guardian was so aghast at the blasphemous comparison that Fakhr-un-Nissa felt sorry, but still she continued her questions.

'Tell me,' she asked, 'there were many who were devoted to him and they called him the son of the Saint. Do they pray for him? Where?'

'There were some such misguided souls indeed, madam,' admitted the guardian, 'but they are as scattered as his own ashes, for he had willed that no shrine be built for him, no temple, structure or samadhi be erected in his honour and that no congregations or meetings of devotees should be arranged to pray for him. Only...', and here the guardian stopped in mid-sentence.

'Only?' prompted Fakhr-un-Nissa.

'Only, only, he had said,' with reluctance, the guardian replied, he had said: let him or her who loves me sometimes light a candle for me so that when my ashes pass by, it will light up their path.'

Every night in Fakhr-un-Nissa's bed chamber a candle was lit. It was burning when Tipu Sultan was born. For fifteen years thereafter it was lit every night. Then it burnt no more. The promise made by Fakhr-un-Nissa to Saint Tipu Mastan Oulia and his son was broken, finally and irrevocably, on the fifteenth birthday of Tipu Sultan. He became a warrior now, no longer to be delivered to God's service.

11

COME, TAKE OVER A KINGDOM

(i)

PROUDLY, HYDER LOOKED AT FAKHR-UN-NISSA'S FIRST-BORN. 'TOO small to be called a Sultan, much too small,' was his first comment. When he saw him hungrily glued to Fakhr-un-Nissa's breast, he added, 'and too greedy to serve God'.

To Fakhr-un-Nissa, he said, 'There are two of us now, I notice, madam, who admire those lovely breasts.' Fakhr-un-Nissa blushed. The child whimpered. Hyder Ali apologised.

'I take it back, my son,' he said, 'such jests surely have no place in the presence of the servant of God.' He bent down to kiss the child, who, tickled by his hair, cried lustily.

'All right, I know when I am not wanted,' he said and after kissing Fakhr-un-Nissa, left to distribute wine and sweets in celebration of the birth of his son.

Hyder was then a junior though promising officer. He had not yet reached the pinnacle of glory that was to be his, a few years hence. Still, he was most lavish in the celebration he had organised for his friends and companions. When he announced the name given to his son, he also good-naturedly joined in their jests.

'How come, Hyder, you beget a son with a royal designation [Sultan]?' asked one, 'and yet provide such poor ancestry for him.'

'But don't forget, my friends,' said another, 'not one amongst our friends has taken as long as Hyder has to produce a son. He has been at it for more than a decade. Surely you don't expect the result to be anything less than royalty.'

'True, very true,' said yet another, 'it takes seven months to bring forth a musician, eight months to make a cobbler, nine months to produce a trader, ten for either a thief or an uncouth soldier like Hyder. But, royalty, yes, it must take time.'

'But Hyder won't be a common soldier for long,' added one more. 'He will petition the Sultan, his son, for a principality.'

'No,' added one sententiously, 'it is the duty of the father to give, not to receive.'

'True, true,' was the chorus, and the mock silence that followed was broken by another.

'To be worthy of his son and not to dishonour his son's name, Hyder must be made a king.'

'Accept, accept,' they chorused, and to crown him, placed on his head wine jars, bowls and nut plates.

'I accept, I accept,' said Hyder again and again, shielding himself from the crowns that his drunken companions were showering on him.

Festivities over, Purnaiya, completely sober—for he never drank—accompanied Hyder to his house. Hyder himself had drunk little. He hadn't got over the miracle of the son in his house. He wanted to be sober enough to enjoy his company.

'There was a point in the jest,' said Purnaiya.

'It was fun,' said Hyder, missing the import of Purnaiya's observation.

'Still there was some truth,' repeated Purnaiya.

'What point, what truth?' Hyder asked. He liked Purnaiya but did not always relish his habit of analysing everything.

'The truth, simply, is this,' responded Purnaiya, 'that kingship is going abegging. Anyone can take it over. Corruption is rampant, the farmer has been liquidated, trade has been paralysed, the army is seething with discontent and the whole population is resentful. The king is powerless, his ministers Devraj and Nanjaraj—brothers though they are—are engaged in a savage power struggle of their own.'

'So?' asked the mystified Hyder.

'So, so as I said, the kingship goes abegging,' replied Purnaiya. 'Anyone can take the crown. Let him, who will come forward, take it.'

In astonishment, Hyder looked at Purnaiya. No, he was not drunk, Hyder knew.

'Do you,' Hyder had some difficulty in formulating the question, 'do you mean to tell me that I can take over the kingdom?'

'No, Hyder, no,' replied Purnaiya, I was just drawing your attention to the truth there was in the jest. Still, since you ask, let me say this that for you and for whosoever shall boldly look into the future, there is a golden opportunity ahead. If you cannot be a king—and perhaps that is too great an ambition—there are other avenues, great avenues, open to you; to be the Chief Commandant, Governor, Minister; who knows what heights you can reach in the holocast that surely is near at hand.'

Hyder laughed. It was an open-hearted and uproarious laughter. Playfully, he slapped Purnaiya's back and then became serious for a while.

'I am not so young, Purnaiya,' he said, 'I started late. I had my first taste of battle when I was as old as twenty-four. They gave me an independent command when I was twenty-nine. I have, at my age of thirty, a son who is not even one day old.'

'There is need for mature men in the troubled times ahead,' Purnaiya rejoined.

Thereafter, for days, weeks and months ahead, there were many such conversations between the two men. In them, it is said, lay the seeds of ambition with which the affable Hyder, later, armed himself.

(ii)

Gone were his easy ways. No longer was Hyder content to drift. Like a hawk, he watched the political scene, invested in powerful friends, took his military duties seriously, volunteered for battle and was always in the forefront to invite notice and attention.

The titular ruler of Mysore was a puppet. The real power rested with the two brothers, Nanjaraj and Devraj, who were his ministers. It was as their protege that Hyder rose to power. In 1749, he had distinguished himself in the siege of Devanahalli and was, as the result, given an independent command of fifty horse and two hundred foot. This was his position—the position of a minor Commander—in 1750—when Tipu was born.

Within a short while he was swept to power and came into the full limelight of history. In the war for the Nizamat of Hyderabad, a few months after Tipu was born, Nanjaraj conferred on Hyder the command of three thousand foot and five hundred horse. The war was inconclusive but a portion of Nazir Jung's treasure was seized by Hyder. Of the three camels, laden with gold, one he sent to Nanjaraj who was delighted and the remaining two went to Devanahalli, which was now Hyder's home town. With this loot, Hyder was able to recruit retainers and began to train them with the help of French deserters.

In another campaign—in Trichinopoly—again Hyder distinguished himself. Nanjaraj, remembering the gold-laden camel and Hyder's exploits, appointed him Faujdar (Commandant) of Dindigul, where a strong man was needed to discipline the rebellious elements. Now, Hyder had immense opportunities to amass wealth, recruit and train men, organise his artillery and establish arsenals.

Meanwhile serious quarrels arose between the two brothers—Devraj and Nanjaraj. In a huff, Devraj parted from his brother, taking a part of treasury with him. Nanjaraj, impoverished already by the costly campaign to Trichinopoly was now attacked by the Marathas and was forced to buy peace at the cost of a heavy tribute. The Nizam also threatened him. Nanjaraj plundered even the temples and crown jewels to satisfy the Nizam's extortions.

Another crushing blow which Nanjaraj received was the revolt by his own troops whose pay, naturally, had fallen in arrears. The proud Nanjaraj summoned Hyder to save the situation.

This was Hyder's great moment—a moment of destiny. Purnaiya had prepared him for it.

He marched into Seringapatam and even contrived to bring Devraj with him. A touching reconciliation took place between the two brothers. He seized the ring leaders of the revolt and plundered them. To the rest, he paid not only the arrears but a bonus as well, backed as he was by Devraj's treasury and his own accumulated wealth. The grateful Nanjaraj embraced him, the army saluted him and the population saved from the depravations of the mutinous soldiery hailed him as their saviour.

So much was his influence and prestige that when the Maratha invasion threatened again, Hyder was appointed

Commander-in-Chief. Engaging the Maratha forces for several months, he finally obtained from them favourable terms of peace and returned to Seringapatam in triumph. The once-obscure soldier of fortune, known until then as Hyder Nayak, was now given the title of Fatah Hyder Bahadur. Purnaiya was present at the investiture. After the investiture was over Hyder sought him out. 'Tell me,' asked Hyder, 'can you still say that I have failed you?'

'This is the beginning of a beginning,' replied Purnaiya.

(iii)

Nanjaraj was getting old.

Devraj had died shortly after the reconciliation between the two brothers. He had cancer and knew that he did not have long to live. His disease, he had regarded as punishment from God for deserting his brother in time of need. Hence, readily, he had listened to Hyder's advice to come back to Nanjaraj's side. Now he died, at peace with his brother.

In Nanjaraj's heart lay the sorrow of separation from a brother whom he had loved. In his mind was the intense fury and contempt at the unjust rumour that he was responsible for poisoning his brother in order to avoid future desertion and also to misappropriate his brother's wealth. Constantly he was being reminded of his repeated military defeats. In contrast, the prestige which his own protege Hyder had gained began to anger him. The upstart kept making demands on the treasury which Nanjaraj could not meet. Instead of disbanding part of the army, now that the kingdom was at peace, Hyder kept recruiting fresh troops. The conditions were becoming chaotic and again the pay of the troops fell into arrears. None could blame Hyder, for not only had he stopped drawing his own salary but he had started selling off his belongings to meet the needs of his hard-pressed troops. No longer did he, like a noble lord, eat the delicacies prepared in his kitchen. He joined the common mess in their frugal meals. Nanjaraj saw the seething discontent that surrounded him. He felt lonely and lost, unable to cope with the problems that faced him. Hyder was the only one who showed respect for him. Others ridiculed him and mocked at him. He decided to retire to the country, with a hope lurking in a corner of his heart, that they would recall him when Hyder failed to organise State finances.

Nanjaraj left and Hyder quietly slipped into his shoes. But then a palace conspiracy followed against Hyder, organised by an erstwhile friend and a favourite. Taken by surprise, Hyder had to flee. He went to Nanjaraj for help. Nanjaraj and Hyder had parted company ostensibly as the best of friends, with expressions of regrets on both sides. Nanjaraj knew that in Hyder, and Hyder alone, lay the hope of his recall. He now made available to Hyder his vast resources of wealth which he had appropriated for himself from the Mysore treasury. With these, Hyder was able to recruit an army and returned to batter his enemies into submission.

To Nanjaraj, he returned the gold that he had borrowed. An equal amount he sent to him in token of his gratitude. For himself, he took the supreme command of the Kingdom of Mysore—no less.

Part III

THE PRINCE

12

FORTY DAYS

TIPU SULTAN, THE SON OF HYDER NAYAK AND FAKHR-UN-NISSA, was four weeks old.

'When will you be ready, madam?' Hyder asked.

Fakhr-un-Nissa blushed. This was the question Hyder had asked every day since Tipu was a week old. Despite its repetition, it had not lost its effect on Fakhr-un-Nissa. The first time Hyder had asked the question, she had been puzzled, somewhat.

'Ready for what?' she had asked.

'Ready for what!' Hyder's eyebrows went up in mock surprise. 'Ready, madam, to share the bed with your husband again and to restore to him the love and consideration that he has been denied for long. Incidentally,' he added with tenderness, 'you are looking more beautiful and desirable than ever.'

Fakhr-un-Nissa had blushed crimson. Gently she rested her hand in his to arrest its wanderings. When Hyder pressed the question, she reminded him of the moratorium of forty days that the custom in her family prescribed after childbirth.

'I did not know,' she added playfully, 'that I was married to a lecherous, old man.'

'Old, yes; lecherous, no,' was Hyder's rejoinder. 'Duty, madam,' he lectured to her, 'the stern call of duty is the compelling factor. Purnaiya, if you would listen to him, would tell you that one must not deviate from duty, however distasteful it might be. By the same token, should I deviate from my duty just because it happens to be pleasant and tasteful? Yes, madam, old I am, so I have to be in a hurry. Your first-born, you say, shall be devoted to God's service. Who shall look after me in my old age, then? Hence, have I time to lose? No. Therefore, I say this to you, madam, we cannot deny the urgent call of duty. In short, our immediate, inevitable and unalterable mission in life is,' here he paused, groping for words to bring the sentence to a grand conclusion but then added lamely, 'love-making and baby-making—yes, that indeed is our mission. So let us make haste.'

The dignity of his words was marred now by the restlessness of his hand and Fakhr-un-Nissa, always sensitive to tickling, was in paroxysm of laughter.

'No wonder,' she said, when her laughter subsided, 'that soldiers follow you to the jaws of death and come back victorious. Who can resist such charming speeches!'

'No one, madam, no one,' said Hyder, and then asked tenderly, 'tonight, then, is the night of love?'

'Let forty days be over, dear husband,' she replied softly. 'I too wish to engage in, what was it you said? Yes, love-making and baby-making—strictly in the line of duty, as you said, if that will please you more.'

'Forty days!' exclaimed Hyder sadly. 'You know how long that is in an old man's life?'

'Hyder Nayak,' she said, calling him by his official title, 'if I called you old, I withdraw it. I have seen younger men. None is as handsome and as strong as my dear husband.'

'And where, if I may enquire,' asked Hyder with pretended jealousy, 'have you seen younger men?'

'Oh, keep quiet, here and there, everywhere. On the parades which I watch from the window, on horseback and when they bring you back after a tavern brawl.'

'Let me say this, my dear lady, I too have seen younger girls. None I swear is as pretty or desirable as the mother of my son.'

'I have no doubt that you have seen younger girls,' rejoined Fakhr-un-Nissa. 'In fact, ever since our son was born, you return late every night and I am told that you are at Purnaiya's. Surely, you do not go to share his milk. He does not drink wine, I am told.'

'You have been correctly told. He does not drink wine but he stocks it and offers it to his friends. I will request him next time to offer me milk. Do you think it will make me younger and stronger?'

Fakhr-un-Nissa disdained to answer the question and instead asked, 'How is it that Purnaiya's wine is better than the wine in our house? Or, is it that there is something more there—some music and some company?'

'There is company there and some music too. Purnaiya's wife, ailing and with a squint in her eye, is there. His small son sometimes practises on the sitar. You think,' asked Hyder with seriousness, 'that I am in mortal danger of being corrupted?'

'What takes you to Purnaiya's house, every day for hours?' was the practical question of Fakhr-un-Nissa.

'Not matters of flesh, madam.'

'What then?'

'Politics,' was Hyder's reply.

'Politics?' Fakhr-un-Nissa asked. 'What does that mean?'

'Ah, there you have me,' expansively Hyder replied. 'For a perfect explanation, you will have to ask Purnaiya. But generally speaking politics means self-advancement; it involves taking the road of golden opportunity; to get ahead of your fellow men; to manoeuvre yourself into a commanding position so that your equals or even betters should recognise you as their leader, if not out of free will, at least out of fear; to make your virtues known and to conceal your vices so that you are acclaimed as good, just and strong; to watch your enemies so that they never prosper; to keep an eye on your friends so that their loyalties do not waver; to know the weakness and the strength and even the innermost secrets of those that work for or against you; to keep your opponents divided and your adherents even more so; to create conditions of drought in times of plenty and manipulate bankruptcy and economic ruin when the treasury is bursting with hoarded wealth: to learn logistics, warfare, communication, geography, history....'

'Not love-making though?' interrupted Fakhr-un-Nissa.

'No,' replied Hyder. 'For that Purnaiya's quarters are not appropriate. For that I must come to your bedroom.'

'Welcome, most welcome, my lord, when forty days are over,' said Fakhr-un-Nissa, with a smile.

13

SIXTY DAYS

'I SEE NO SPARK OF DIVINITY IN HIM,' SAID HYDER, WATCHING Tipu, when the child was two months old. 'But he does smile beautifully. You agree?'

Fakhr-un-Nissa looked on happily, with the smile of a proud mother, while Hyder made facial contortions to win more smiles from his son. Now he had the son in his lap.

'Well, madam,' asked Hyder, 'have you started his religious training?'

'Wait awhile,' replied Fakhr-un-Nissa, with a laugh. 'At the moment, I am more concerned with his toilet training.'

'Do not tell me, madam,' asked the irrepressible Hyder, 'that servants of God also have the same human weakness?'

Fakhr-un-Nissa did not answer but Tipu did, for immediately Hyder cried out, 'They do, they do!'

Fakhr-un-Nissa looked up in surprise. 'I have just discovered to my sorrow, madam,' said Hyder, 'that servants of God indeed do have the same weaknesses. My best dress is spoilt'

To all appearances, Tipu was being brought up like any other first-born. If there was a difference, it was subtle and subconscious—and hardly discernible. It lay, perhaps, in the reserve with which Fakhr-un-Nissa invariably and Hyder often treated the child. When Tipu was asleep, Fakhr-un-Nissa would kiss him from head to foot fervently and ardently. She would wait for him to go to sleep before hugging him passionately to her breast or kissing him on the lips but when he was awake, her kisses would be light and gentle—a mere caress of the cheek or the forehead—so timid and tender as if she was seeking his permission for the familiarity. Fixed in her mind was the thought that her little one was destined to serve the Lord. She had learned to honour seers and saints, and in her mind's eye her son was already the chosen one of the Lord. She did not, therefore, consider it strange that he should inspire in her feelings of respect and humility. But when he slept, she surrendered to her hunger to smother him with burning kisses and wrap him in her arms.

Hyder also stood in awe of the child, though he concealed it behind his banter. Hyder and Fakhr-un-Nissa shared a large bed and Fakhr-un-Nissa would often pick up the sleeping Tipu from the baby cot and put him on their bed. Hyder would gently separate the son from his mother's arms and shower kisses alternately upon the mother and the son. If Tipu showed signs of waking up, Hyder would scamper to his side of the bed, right to the edge, as if to reassure Tipu that he was peacefully sleeping and had not been taking any liberties—either with the son or with the mother. Tipu would wake up, nestle against his mother and go to sleep though at times he would also roll over towards his father, his tiny hand reaching for Hyder's bushy eyebrows or the long hair on his head which always fascinated him. Hyder would then whisper aloud in mock dismay, 'Oh, spirits of my forefathers, save me for I am caught in the act and my holy son has me by the hair.'

Even through the midsummer heat, when other children would be naked or half-naked, Fakhr-un-Nissa would keep Tipu fully clothed.

'People would suspect, madam,' Hyder often complained, 'that this little one of ours has something very little about him if he has to be so meticulously covered from neck to foot all the while.'

But when neighbours and relatives sometimes commented on Tipu being always overdressed, Hyder casually mentioned that his skin was unfortunately sensitive to mosquito bites—a reason which was understood and appreciated.

Hyder could dimly guess what was in Fakhr-un-Nissa's mind though he had never discussed the subject with her. She had seen many fakirs and holy men walking around the countryside wrapped up in nothing more than a loin cloth. Perhaps, she did not wish her son to get used to that kind of lifestyle when he attained holiness. Or, was it that she wanted him to make up for all the deprivations of the future? Hyder was not sure.

Before Tipu was a year old, he had discovered a strange phenomenon that his parents were somewhat undemonstrative towards him when he was awake but kissed him and petted him repeatedly when his eyes were closed.

A child whose hunger for love matches perhaps all the yearnings of the universe knows by instinct how to react to such a situation. He would pretend to be asleep and in his innocent ecstacy would enjoy the rapturous love of his fond parents.

If in later years Tipu was aloof and remote, it was not as if there was a barrier in his heart. Always he hungered and craved for companionship and affection, but at times he could not shake off an attitude of conduct he had developed in his formative years. In the years to come he also continued the same delicacy of feeling and modesty which his parents had for his dress. Even his closest acquaintances rarely saw any part of his person except his face, feet and hands, so fully clothed he always was.

14

THREE YEARS

THREE YEARS PASSED. FAKHR-UN-NISSA AND HYDER ALI CONTINUED to yearn for a second son.

'Madam, if you break your word to me,' admonished Hyder, 'you will not be able to keep your word with God. Our little Sultan does not then get enrolled to God's service. Remember that?'

'Patience, my lord. There will be another son,' replied Fakhr-un-Nissa.

'Was there a specific promise at the shrine [of the Saint Tipu Mastan Oulia]?' asked Hyder.

'You know, there was.'

'What were the exact words he used?' Hyder persisted.

'Do not trouble yourself so much. Have faith.'

'And suppose he misled you?'

'Do not blaspheme, my lord. Believe, as I do,' pleaded Fakhr-un-Nissa.

15

THE FOURTH YEAR

(i)

'HOW PRECISELY, MADAM,' ASKED HYDER ONCE WHEN TIPU WAS four years old, 'are we to deliver him to God's service?'

'Surely, He will know,' replied Fakhr-un-Nissa.

'Yes, but I also want to know,' protested Hyder. 'Do I have to send a courier to Him and, if so, some one must tell me where He can be found. Or, is it that a chariot will descend from the Heavens above with minstrels and maidens from paradise to claim my son?'

'I hope not,' said Fakhr-un-Nissa with a smile, 'for I fear that if such a chariot came, you will be the one to desert us.'

'Ah! so you really think,' asked Hyder in self-admiration, 'that once the lovely maidens from paradise have seen this virile and handsome husband of yours, they will insist on taking him?'

'I have not the slightest doubt about it, my dear husband,' replied Fakhr-un-Nissa.

'Maybe, you are right,' Hyder conceded graciously. 'But I will tell you this. I shall not go. Of course, I might be tempted a bit, if they are as charming and as sweet as my dear wife, but frankly I doubt it. Truth to tell, I have a shrewd suspicion that they do not make them that good in Heaven. I think, this Heaven or paradise has its own inadequacies and shortages.'

'Shortages in Heaven?' asked Fakhr-un-Nissa, losing the drift of the conversation.

'Of course,' replied Hyder, 'if it was a region of plenty why would God claim our little son for His service? He could just requisition the supplies from His own territory.'

'I know, dear husband,' Fakhr-un-Nissa said with a troubled expression, 'that you like to joke, but even so, you should not reach the edge of blasphemy. Can we set a limit to God's territory?'

'You are right, madam,' Hyder was quick to admit, 'we waste our time with empty jests. But the question still remains: how do we prepare our son for his appointed destiny?'

'I, I do not really know,' replied Fakhr-un-Nissa, as if groping for words, 'but first he has to learn to read and write. He has already made a beginning.'

'Very true,' said Hyder, 'though already the illiterate Hyder Nayak is feeling the pangs of jealousy that his son is to embark on such an illustrious course. His tutor says that he has acquired considerable skill in calligraphy. What else?'

'Well, we will have to get him a religious teacher,' said Fakhr-un-Nissa, 'someone well known, someone like Maulvi Obedullah or Al Hussaini or Mirza Shams or Abdul Gafoor.'

'Muslims only?' queried Hyder. 'Is it of Islam alone that you wish him to learn?'

'What else?' questioned Fakhr-un-Nissa.

'There always will be more Hindus in this land than Muslims,' responded Hyder. 'To be in the Lord's service, I thought, would mean serving both of them—and perhaps people of all religions.'

'But could there not be a conflict, if he was to be given training in many religions?' Fakhr-un-Nissa asked.

'There never is a conflict between religions, madam,' said Hyder. 'Religious men sometimes quarrel, religions never.'

'Then, surely, let him serve the Lord by serving all His religions and all His people. You select the teachers for him.'

'Maulvi Obedullah, whom you named, will be good,' said Hyder. 'The other person I have in view is Goverdhan Pandit. Purnaiya speaks highly of him.'

'Oh, so you have been thinking about it?' cried the delighted Fakhr-un-Nissa.

'Of course, madam, I am essentially a thinking being though most people regard me as nothing but a man of action,' proudly Hyder replied.

(ii)

'Now that we have discussed the problem of his religious training,' asked Hyder, 'what about other matters?'

'What, for instance?' asked Fakhr-un-Nissa.

'Horse riding, for instance,' replied Hyder.

'Horse riding?' queried Fakhr-un-Nissa, 'why does he need to learn horse riding?'

'Have you, madam,' asked Hyder with asperity 'considered which of the two courses is better: to carry the message of the Lord on bare, blistered feet and reach as few as possible or to travel on a fleet-footed animal and reach as many as possible.'

'But I have not seen holy men on horseback,' protested Fakhr-un-Nissa.

'Let us hope,' said Hyder, 'that what the past has denied to you shall be unfolded by the future.'

'Very well,' Fakhr-un-Nissa said, ignoring his pleasantry, 'let him learn horse riding, if you think it is necessary.'

'And what of other things,' asked Hyder, 'like archery, musketry, combat, marksmanship, military arts?'

'Hyder Nayak!' cried Fakhr-un-Nissa, 'are you making a fool of me? Surely, a holy man does not need to learn military arts!'

'That is why,' said Hyder, 'there are such few holy men left in this world, madam. They could not defend themselves.'

'But what need is there,' asked the perplexed Fakhr-un-Nissa, 'for him to learn warfare? He is to be a soldier of God and of none else, or have you forgotten it?'

'No,' replied Hyder, 'I have not forgotten it. But let me present before you two propositions; first, let us assume that even though we have not forgotten it, God might, and our son might be rejected for His service; second, the failure might not be God's, but you, yourself, might fail.'

'I fail?' she asked, 'how so?'

'Well, you may not give us,' replied Hyder with a smile, 'our second son and in that case we do not surrender our son to anyone—not even to the Almighty.'

'Hyder Nayak, I notice with regret,' her soft tone however was in contrast with the harshness of her words, 'that more and more you begin to engage in blasphemous thoughts. But let me say this to you that God has promised me and I have promised you that we shall have another son, come what may.'

'A very pretty speech,' said Hyder, clapping his hands, 'and believe me, it was to hear this that I started this conversation.'

The pillow missed him, as he was leaving the room. Hyder laughed and said, 'Poor marksmanship never pays, madam, be it by a soldier, a holy man or a lovely woman.'

16

BROTHER KARIM

(i)

HYDER WAS ESCORTING FAKHR-UN-NISSA AND TIPU TO DINDIGUL where he was to take over his appointment as Faujdar (Commandant). This high promotion had come to him in recognition of the distinguished services he had rendered in the struggle for the Nizamat, the Trichinopoly campaign and several other severely contested battles. Accompanied by a small force, he was now on his way to that remote southeasterly region where a strong man was needed to discipline refractory elements.

Fakhr-un-Nissa was pregnant. She was in her sixth month.

Hyder's cup of happiness was full. His son Tipu Sultan was nearly five years old. Honours, riches, position and prominence had overtaken Hyder during the five years since Tipu's birth. Now he was expecting another son.

(ii)

An ambush awaited Hyder and his forces at the outskirts of Dindigul. In the vanguard was Hyder with thirty companions, much ahead of the columns that followed. In the rear were the palanquins conveying Fakhr-un-Nissa, her maids and Tipu. A well-trained pony had accompanied Tipu's palanquin so that he could get on to it any time he felt bored in the palanquin, but now that they were in the hilly region, Hyder had forbidden the use of a pony by Tipu. A horseman sped to Hyder saying that Tipu was insisting on mounting a horse and wanted his father's permission. Hyder denied permission. A few moments later, Fakhr-un-Nissa's message came to Hyder requesting him to come and discipline his son before he reached Dindigul in order to discipline others.

'Well, I will put that brat on my own horse,' said Hyder and raced back to the rear, towards the palanquins. Hardly a minute passed, when in the narrow valley through which the vanguard was passing, huge rocks suspended on chains and levers were unleashed by the enemy hidden in the hills. Simultaneously from the adjacent hills musket shots rang out and a savage battle ensued. Of the thirty in the vanguard, twenty-eight had died before they could engage in battle. Hyder himself would have had to share their fate but for the miracle of his turning back in view of his son's sudden insistence on riding a horse. There were also several other instantaneous casualties amongst Hyder's forces but he was unhurt and rallied his troops all along the line. The battle raged for some hours when at last the enemy retreated, leaving their dead and wounded behind.

Abdul Karim, the second and the last son of Hyder Ali and Fakhr-un-Nissa, was born in the palanquin during this battle.

17

THE COMMANDANT OF DINDIGUL

HYDER ALI, THE FAUJDAR OF DINDIGUL, DID NOT PUT TO DEATH the rebels who had treacherously attacked him. He began his rule by granting amnesty to all political offenders. He removed the economic curbs and constraints on the local population and allowed them, within limits, freedom of action that they had not known for generations. Generously, he gave remissions of taxes and extended time limits for their payments in deserving cases.

No, it was not to practise a new political philosophy or to carry out an experiment that the Faujdar of Dindigul became a benevolent ruler. He was superstitious. He wanted to be blessed by all and cursed by none, while his prematurely-born son, Abdul Karim, hovered between life and death. Hyder grew thin and lost his sleep in his anxiety, rising several times every night to listen to the infant's breathing; every cry and cough of the infant tore at his heart.

Fakhr-un-Nissa prayed, Hyder prayed, but more steadfastly than both of them, the five-year-old Tipu prayed, that God may spare the life of the newborn.

The first few anxious weeks passed. Abdul Karim would live. He was gathering weight and strength. Fakhr-un-Nissa and Hyder still prayed though not as often as Tipu. He was at the bedside of his brother during all his waking hours.

Hyder was jubilant when the physicians finally pronounced Abdul Karim as completely out of danger and were confident that he would lead a strong and healthy life.

Meanwhile, his policy of leniency and gentleness was having its effect. The rebels laid down their arms; the refractory incidents were few and far between; the enormous expenditure of punitive or pre-emptive raids was avoided; the trader, the traveller and the farmer felt safe; economic activity and even normal life returned to the region, so much so that Hyder's tax collections went up by leaps and bounds. He collected three times as much he was expected to. To his masters in Mysore, he surrendered far more than the target set for him. A little portion he gave for the construction and upkeep of temples and mosques in thanksgiving for Karim's life. The remainder he kept for himself, to recruit more troops and to build factories and arsenals under the supervision of the French engineers whom he had appointed.

The grateful response of the people of Dindigul to his kindness taught Hyder a great political lesson that it was not necessary always to rule by the sword. He reminded himself to tell Purnaiya of the great thought and deliberation with which he had embarked on his wise and sagacious policies, forgetting for the moment that it had its roots in the hope of cajoling Providence to be merciful with Karim's life and forgetting also the silent vow he had made to himself to reduce the entire region to ashes if Abdul Karim did not live.

Nevertheless, it was a great political lesson and one from which he was to profit in the succeeding years.

18

TWO ARE ENOUGH

FAKHR-UN-NISSA HAD ALSO BY NOW RECOVERED FROM THE ORDEAL of premature birth. Her listlessness was gone. The colour on her face returned. Hyder was delighted to see her well and cheerful.

He had had a pleasant morning, having counted large amounts of gold, silver and grain that had come in the way of taxes. He had been able to extract confessions from eight hated tax-collectors and he confiscated not only their concealed gold but also satisfied every one with their public flogging. To top it all, a letter had arrived that morning from Mysore congratulating him on his extraordinary zeal but more so, on the tribute sent by him with an expression of hope that he would continue to send the same amount every quarter. He had, in fact, despatched a larger amount for the subsequent quarter, only a day earlier. He knew how delighted Nanjaraj would be when his courier reached Mysore. Greedy and grasping though Nanjaraj was, he knew how to reward those that served him well—and Hyder counted on this.

He lifted Tipu to his lips and knelt to kiss Karim lying on the bed. Tipu rewarded him with a shy kiss and Karim gave him a winning smile before exploring his bushy eyebrows.

When Hyder was alone with Fakhr-un-Nissa, he gave her a gift of flowers before claiming a kiss.

'It is good to see you looking so well, dearest,' he said. He told her of the letter from Nanjaraj and all the developments that had taken place, the wealth he had amassed and the factories he was planning to build.

'All our problems are behind us now,' he added. 'Tipu is shaping very well and Karim is doing beautifully. Well, Tipu can be yours for God's service; make a priest of him, if you will. Karim will be mine and, God willing, he shall be the greatest warrior on earth, a conqueror, an emperor, who knows!'

Then playfully, he asked, 'But what, madam, of the third child that we have to plan? What future shall we set in store for him?'

Fakhr-un-Nissa looked at her husband. There was tenderness and love in her glance—and tears in her eyes.

'There will be no third son from me, my lord,' gently she said.

'Don't say such things, my dear. You have been ill. You will get over it, soon. Already you are looking fresher than the flowers I have just given you.'

'But it is true,' said Fakhr-un-Nissa.

'Of course, it is true. You are lovelier than the loveliest of these flowers.'

'What is true, dear husband, is that you can have no more children from me.'

Hyder understood now that it was the medical verdict by the physicians that she was telling him about. He was silent for a while. 'Is this final?' he asked. 'Can such things not be cured?'

'I fear not, my lord,' was the sad reply.

He asked for details about the physicians who had been consulted and what they had said.

Then he mastered the gloom that had crept into him. 'So be it,' he said. 'We can still make love, it seems without paying the penalty for it. Who wants more children, anyway? The two gems we have are enough for the two of us.'

Fakhr-un-Nissa also brightened up. Cheerfully, as if it did not wrench her heart, she said, 'My lord, it is I who cannot have a son, but you can.'

'What riddle is this, Begum?' asked Hyder.

'Simply this,' Fakhr-un-Nissa went on with a cheerful smile, 'that you have to marry again. Do please allow me the privilege of choosing a wife for you. I promise you, that you will be pleased with my choice. Or, better still, let me give you an idea of a few that I have in view and we can then go over the list and select one. There is, for instance, the daughter of Mian Mumtaz Sahib—Oh, I have a whole list here.' She picked out a large sheet of paper from the jewellery box on her dressing table and was about to read, when Hyder interrupted her.

'Is that the list of females you have in view for me?' he asked.

'Yes.'

'Give it to me, please,' Hyder demanded.

'What for?' Fakhr-un-Nissa asked. She knew he could not read.

'Give it to me,' he commanded. She handed over the list to him. He looked at the list and said, 'You see, I cannot read.' He tore the paper into bits and threw the pieces on the carpet. He kicked those that fell near his right foot.

'Hear this, madam,' he spoke slowly, in firm, clear tones, 'and mark my words well. Let me not hear from you again—never again—any suggestion for my remarriage. The subject displeases me and the subject is closed.'

'But. . . . ,' Fakhr-un-Nissa was about to protest.

'Enough,' Hyder cut in, 'I forbid it.' Now he had raised his voice, for the first time in his life with Fakhr-un-Nissa. 'Fatima, I repeat, I forbid it, now and for ever. Do you understand?'

He strode from the room in anger. In his absence, Fakhr-un-Nissa said, 'Thank you, my lord.' Was she addressing God or Hyder?—she did not know.

Hyder soon returned. They passed the night in love. Hyder was always a gentle lover. That night he made love with tenderness and a fervour which Fakhr-un-Nissa had not met with before.

19

THE PANDIT AND THE MAULVI

(i)

MAULVI OBEDULLAH AND GOVERDHAN PANDIT TOOK OVER AS Tipu's religious mentors. They were to give effect to Fakhr-un-Nissa's silent hopes that her son would not be a wandering fakir but a learned teacher, renowned and respected who would spread the word of God and his Gospel far and wide. She could picture in her mind's eye princes and pandits bowing before her son, in reverence and awe, and he dispensing enlightenment wherever he went. Hearts laden with grief would turn to him for solace and her son would be the healer, the teacher and the pathfinder. To both Maulvi Obedullah and Goverdhan Pandit she had respectfully said, 'Make him worthy of your knowledge.'

In her heart of hearts she believed that he would be more than worthy. More, far more.

(ii)

'God is not confined to any form of religion, nor is he excluded from any,' was the message which Goverdhan Pandit sought to implant in young Tipu's mind.

Tipu's religious training began in right earnest in Dindigul where Hyder had taken over as Faujdar (Commandant) and Fakhr-un-Nissa gave birth to Karim, her second son, on the eve of their arrival.

Maulvi Obedullah was less outspoken than Goverdhan Pandit. He did not come out with ringing declarations and final judgements. Notwithstanding his lifelong piety, prayers and meditation, he had many questions that were open and unanswered in his mind. This did not trouble him too much. He knew he would soon meet his Maker and perchance would have the answers. The answers he knew were, he thought, enough for a lifetime. He also thought that there were many highways and pathways to reaching God—and religion was one of them.

Fundamental, however, to his belief were the tenets of Islam—of universal brotherhood, charity, compassion, love and the indissoluble association in which all are linked. He knew that the seemingly different streams of tradition which prevailed were actually united currents of philosophical and religious thought over all of which was the living grace of God. Islam never taught him and he never believed that there could be hostility with various religions or different tendencies of thought. Passionately, he rejected the clamour of doctrines and dogmas which denied to the individual, his special place in the world or divested him of equality before God and man. He was certain that God treated every aspirant with favour and granted him his heart's desire.

Goverdhan Pandit and Maulvi Obedullah complemented each other's teaching. Tolerance, prayer and devotion were what the venerable Maulvi sought to instil in the young pupil.

Goverdhan Pandit was more demanding. It was not enough for him that the devotee should surrender himself to the Divine in prayer, piety and meditation. The doctrine of Grace and Salvation meant much more to him. He held that anyone who gave up his duty to pass his time merely in prayer or to proclaim the name of the Lord but devoted not his energies to protecting righteousness, was a sinner. No one, according to him, had the right to lose himself in inner piety alone when heart's heavy laden cried out for help or when the poor died at our doors or when there was even a single person in this world who was naked, hungry, maltreated or humiliated. Thus prepared though he was to exalt the life of contemplation, he was convinced that Man could not make himself a perfect instrument for His use or attain the highest spiritual wisdom unless he sought out action and adventure to fit God's transcendent pattern, purpose and will.

These were the early mentors for Tipu's young and receptive mind. This training they imparted, not like an avalanche but gently, very gently, through stories, tales and anecdotes and often through song and verse. Slowly but persistently, they sought to implant their ideas but more so they wished to invest him with a thirst for knowledge, a philosophical outlook, a heart with compassion and a mind that enquires and questions.

To these teachers was due the breadth of intellectual vision and curiosity which Tipu displayed in later life and on which even his worst enemies have grudgingly complimented him; to them also he owed in some measure his sense of justice and fairplay, his belief in the one Supreme, his desire for truth and virtue, his mandate for action, and above all his willingness to sacrifice for his principles and national honour, everything he possessed, including his own life—and indeed, he did make that supreme sacrifice and courted certain death when the enemy, with treachery and superior numbers, had surrounded him and most of his adherents had deserted him.

20

THE LADDER OF FORTUNE

THE POLITICAL MUSCLE OF HYDER ALI WAS BUILDING UP.

Not only had he amassed wealth, enlisted recruits and set up factories in Dindigul but he had also earned for himself a reputation as an able administrator. It was he who had brought peace to the region and with it economic stability which in turn enriched him, his masters and the entire province as well.

With the entry of Maulvi Obedullah and Goverdhan Pandit into his household, as tutors for his son, Hyder's political image was at its peak. Hyder was known as the Commandant of Dindigul, a military leader and a man of the sword—and he was respected and feared as such. But how was anyone to know that in the deep recesses of his soul lay so much veneration for the Lord that he should have recruited two renowned teachers of theology for the teaching of his son! It was as if people had suddenly begun to see the other side of Hyder—of a man who believed more and more in the spiritual side of life, whilst continuing to perform the duties that the world demanded of him. They did not know that he had promises to keep and had a superstitious terror of breaking them. Instead, they invested him with piety, hitherto unrevealed.

Purnaiya himself had been surprised when Hyder had initially approached him with the problem of finding suitable teachers to inpart religious training to Tipu Sultan. Their conversation had taken place well before Hyder's departure for Dindigul.

'Why?' Purnaiya had asked.

Hyder had been reticent but soon Purnaiya thought that he saw it all.

'I salute you, Hyder,' he had cried exhuberantly. 'Yes, you, who I thought were my pupil, are indeed my master.'

'What are you talking about?' Hyder had demanded.

Purnaiya had merely nodded as if to indicate not only his complete understanding but also complete approval. The infuriated Hyder had shaken him by the shoulders and repeated the question.

'Enough, enough,' Purnaiya had laughed. 'You fooled me for a moment—no more. I see very well that the great commander now wishes to be known as a man of God so that people who merely bow to him out of fear should bend lower out of respect as well, and that his name be on everyone's lips with reverence. Not a bad idea, really, Hyder.' Then he added, 'Rather clever of me, to have seen through your game so quickly, what do you think?'

'I think,' ponderously Hyder had replied, 'the goat whose milk you drink must have drunk a lot of wine.'

'I drink only cow's milk,' Purnaiya corrected him.

'A curse on your cow, goat, camel, cobra or whatever the animal or fish that gives you milk,' Hyder had said testily.

With some hesitation, however, Hyder had told Purnaiya of the promise which Fakhr-un-Nissa had made at the shrine of Saint Tipu Mastan Oulia—a promise which he himself had vowed to keep, for he firmly believed that it was divine intervention that had graced his home with a son after so many years of longing and he feared the consequences if he failed to keep his vow.

Purnaiya who had soberly heard the recital, laughed in the end and Hyder had chided him, saying, 'For a Brahmin, who should listen to such matters with a bowed head, you display a great deal of frivolity and a total lack of reverence.'

'Forgive me, Father of the God-chosen,' Purnaiya had replied with the humility he did not feel. 'I laugh at my own foolishness in thinking that wisdom prompted you and not... er... piety.' After a moment, however, he seriously added, 'Be that as it may; you see this as a necessity; perhaps it is so, though for different reasons I regard it as a great experiment; whatever the reasons, the results will be all to the good.'

They had then discussed the names and merits of the various teachers who might be willing and available.

Before Hyder left, Purnaiya had warned him. 'Let this be a secret,' he had said, referring to the vow that Hyder had taken, 'between you and your wife. Let no one else hear it either.'

'You are the only one I have told,' said Hyder.

'I have the poorest memory for things I wish to forget,' Purnaiya assured him.

Purnaiya had remained in Seringapatam and when word reached him of Hyder's achievements in Dindigul, he was happy and saw to it that every one heard about them. Later when soldiers on furlough, couriers and countless civilians moving between Seringapatam and Dindigul had brought the news that Hyder, the great commander, had enlisted the services of two great religious teachers, Purnaiya was delighted with the impressive effect it had on every one. He passed the news along, often embellishing it, with many a tale of Hyder's virtue. Some of Hyder's erstwhile comrades and Purnaiya's friends had made a joke of it.

'See, the moment he got away from this corrupt Brahmin,' they said, referring to Purnaiya, 'he saw the light.'

Purnaiya laughed good-naturedly. He was quite happy that Hyder's image was taking shape and he did not mind a jibe or two at his own expense. Sometimes, when they asked him if he had ever suspected that Hyder, the vagabond, merrymaker and reveller, would ever go near religion, he had a long reply to make. He always had, he said, detected in Hyder not only the qualities of an able administrator and a brilliant soldier but also of utmost honesty, integrity and trustworthiness as also loyalty to his friends. Did he ever cheat his officers and men on the share of the booty, as most commanders did? he had asked. Did he leave the sick, the wounded or disabled unattended on his campaigns? he further questioned. 'Did he not see to it that the widows and the children of those that died in his battles were provided for and how many times he personally went to the Treasury officials to see that their claims were settled?' He continued with such questions, ending with the statement that while he himself had not detected any direct evidence of Hyder's leanings towards religion, it was clear that he was a man of honour, a man to be trusted and a man to lead—and in any case, concluded Purnaiya, the dividing line between a man of honour and a man of religion was mighty thin indeed.

Thus, Purnaiya kept Hyder's name and image alive. At Purnaiya's suggestion, a trickle of gifts flowed from Dindigul to Seringapatam intended for various commanders. 'Of what use is so-and-so to me?' at times the exasperated Hyder had asked.

'Learn to invest in goodwill,' Purnaiya had replied. When some one with whom Hyder was acquainted died, his wife or children would receive a well-composed letter of sympathy in Hyder's name accompanied often with a gift in cash. Purnaiya saw to it that such gifts were well advertised. Hyder noted with annoyance and Purnaiya with delight that each mail brought to Hyder ever-increasing number of letters seeking financial assistance. To some Hyder responded favourably at Purnaiya's suggestion. At times, sparingly though, Hyder would even write to the supplicant through Purnaiya pleading his own difficulties at the moment but suggesting that his letter be taken to such and such banker with the request to advance the specified amount and treat it as a loan to Hyder at the current rates of interest. Purnaiya had seen to it that the banker would honour the request.

'What a man,' it was said. 'To help his friends, he would even borrow.' 'And that too at exorbitant rates of interest,' Purnaiya would add.

Purnaiya was in his element when the near-mutiny broke out as the result of arrears of pay due to the troops. While Nanjaraj temporised, Purnaiya and his friends went from camp to camp and from tavern to tavern, saying that if only Hyder was here, he would have found a solution. Somehow, they said, he would have extracted the money from those grasping and corrupt officials who had concealed it from the deserving soldiery to whom it was due. When Nanjaraj met the military commanders to negotiate with them, he had pleaded that since Devraj, his brother, had deserted him, he would send for some one trustworthy to look after the finances of the realm and until then they should wait.

'I will send for Mir Shahab, my senior-most Governor.'

The commanders grumbled. No one trusted the Mir Shahab, they said. The soldiers were in an ugly mood and so were the officers, they added. The appointment of Mir Shahab would only add fuel to the fire.

'Well, who do you suggest?' Nanjaraj asked, 'Alam Khan? Ismail Beg? Nandlal? Surajmal? These are our Governors.'

'Are there none others?' the commanders enquired in dismay.

'The junior ones, yes. Prithiraj and Hyder Ali,' replied Nanjaraj.

The commanders thought it over and then one of them said with an air of uncertainty, 'Well, Hyder Ali might be a good choice.'

Others readily nodded their assent. Nanjaraj was delighted. Hyder was his own man, without a doubt. He, and he alone, was responsible for his elevation. In the case of others, Devraj his brother had also played some part but Hyder owed his position only to Nanjaraj and could be counted upon to the hilt Also, he was sufficiently junior to be amenable to advice and discipline. With a sigh of relief, Nanjaraj agreed with the commanders' choice and a courier left with an urgent summons for Hyder.

Purnaiya arranged Hyder's rendezvous with Devraj, the estranged brother of Nanjaraj, and pleaded for reconciliation between the brothers. The rest is history—that Hyder officiated over the touching reunion of the two brothers, subsequently became Mysore's Commander-in-Chief as a stepping-stone to becoming eventually its supreme overlord.

21

THE STARS OF OUR SONS

TO THE HISTORIAN, TO THE POLITICAL OBSERVER AND EVEN TO THE courts and kings far and near, Hyder Ali's rise to power was a mystery they could not explain. How did an obscure and insignificant soldier, who in 1750 commanded no more than fifty horse and two hundred foot come to acquire in 1761, the supreme and undisputed command of the kingdom of Mysore? There were no riots, no massacres and no holocaust over this transition of power. The grim battles and gruesome warfare, which invariably characterise every succession of such authority were missing. Here, not a shot was fired. True, Hyder had distinguished himself in several battles but this was no more than what several other commanders had done. Also, he had proved himself an able administrator of a remote province but there were others, far more senior with greater prestige and proximity to the centre of power. Why, he did not even know how to read and write! Yet, Hyder rose, easily and effortlessly, each rung of the ladder carrying him to heights that were well beyond even his own dreams.

Idle gossip did not share the helplessness of the historian in explaining this mystery. It saw what the historian does not see—that the stars of the son affect the destiny of the father—for was it not from the moment of his son's birth that Hyder began his rise to power?

22

TALES AND STORIES

HYDER WOULD OFTEN STEAL INTO THE NURSERY, TO WATCH TIPU at play or work. The moment Tipu espied him, he would come running to his father who would gather him in his arms. The huge ceiling was enough for the child to be thrown higher and higher, through squeals of laughter and playful fear.

Initially, Hyder had felt sorry for the imposition of religious training on his son. What a frightfully boring and cheerless experience that would be—he had thought. He was all in favour of educating his son, for this unlettered man, though he would be the last to admit it, had profound respect for education and the educated. But to subject his child, to what he thought would be a chanting of hymns, psalms and prayers, was hardly fair, he thought. Soon, however, his misgivings were no more. Often, unseen by Tipu and his teachers he had eavesdropped on them and what he heard enchanted him—stories upon stories, interwoven with poetry and imagery. If this was religious training, he was all for it.

These were the legends of the mountains and rivers—of the mystic wonder of the Himalayas and the Vindhya mountains; of the eternal life-giving waters of the Ganges and the Cauvery;

there were stories from the lives of Ashoka and Akbar—how one renounced war and how the other sought to establish a new order embracing all sects; there were poems from the ancient Sanskrit poet Kalidasa and the medieval teacher Kabir who taught the brotherhood of Hindus and Muslims alike in the fatherhood of one God; there were tales of the heroes of the *Ramayana* and *Mahabharata*; then there was much that was said of Jesus, who was the son of God; of Mohammed who was the Prophet; of Gautama who was enlightened; of the Holy Quran which preached the gospel of universal brotherhood; of the Bhagavad Gita which inspired men to action; of the Upanishads which developed human thought; of Manu the law-giver and of Patanjali the teacher of Yoga.

Above all, there were stories of India's ancient culture which did not perish or wither before the onslaughts but assimilated every external influence, welding it into a single harmonised and gracious unity. Cultures that came with the conquerors -cultures that lived by the sword alone—inevitably died, absorbed as they were by the gentler, the more intelligent and spiritual civilisation that they came to conquer.

23

LET THE BIRDS LIVE

THE RIGOURS OF HIGHER AND MORE INTENSIVE RELIGIOUS training for Tipu Sultan were to come—Maulvi Obedullah and Goverdhan Pandit knew that. At the moment, however, they were more concerned with planting the seed and of developing in the young mind a thirst for knowledge and a curiosity that does not cease to question until the ultimate reality has unfolded itself. He was not ready yet for asceticism, self-denial, mortification of the flesh or deeper meditation. Enough, if his soul was awakened and his heart full of pure joy. His mind was like a tender plant, his teachers knew that. Slowly and patiently, through successive stages, it had to be nursed until it was ready to stand on its own to be in company with the wind and clouds, to bear fruit and offer shade to the weary traveller.

Nor did they allow the neglect of his physical training. Goverdhan Pandit had already initiated him into the rudiments of yogic exercises. The early morning hour was reserved for horse riding, when Tipu was accompanied by Ghazi Khan, an officer in Hyder's service. Often, Hyder would join them and both, father and son, would race each other across the countryside. Sometimes, Hyder would allow Tipu's pony to outdistance his fleet horse. The child, with the sure knowledge that his father had so contrived it, would still be delighted. Soon enough, Hyder's horse, Dilkush, got into the mood of the game and would race along Tipu's pony, head to head, maintaining the same speed throughout.

It was Ghazi Khan's duty to teach Tipu Sultan what was beyond the jurisdiction of his more learned teachers.

'They addle his brains,' complained Ghazi Khan to Hyder, pointing to Maulvi Obedullah and Goverdhan Pandit. 'They keep him so occupied with their holy trash that one would think that you wanted your son to be a fakir. What time do I have to teach him to be a man and prince?'

'Ghazi Khan, your reputation,' retorted Maulvi Obedullah, 'as an unjust man is not unjustly earned. I am told that you have taught Tipu archery so well that he excels your own son whom you have taught longer. But surely, you know why. It is the power of concentration that comes to him from his yogic exercises that Goverdhan Pandit teaches him.'

'Well, Tipu Sultan excels my son in swimming and water diving also,' rejoined Ghazi Khan. 'I suppose you will say that it is because you have taught him to search so frantically for truth, that he plunges into water and rushes ahead of everybody, chasing the unseen God.'

'That could well be,' said the Maulvi, unperturbed by the irony, 'though I think here again the art whereby breath is controlled and held through Yoga may have much to do with Tipu's proficiency in water.'

'Ho! Ho! tell me reverend Maulvi,' asked Ghazi Khan, 'you would say the same of Sultan's proficiency in wrestling, fencing and other sports.'

'I have not,' replied the Maulvi with weightiness, accompanied by a smile matching Ghazi Khan's, 'considered the matter in depth. I shall certainly study it further and let you know.'

'Hyder Sahib,' said Ghazi Khan, now with some exasperation, 'I think the conventional training of our soldiers should be given up and they should all be consigned to the care of Maulvi and his tribe, since so much can be gained from their teachings, here and Hereafter.'

'Thank you, my son,' said the Maulvi, and while Hyder laughed, the Maulvi placed his hand on Ghazi Khan's head as if to bless him. 'God, who hears all, will no doubt reward you for such pious advice to Hyder Saheb.'

When the Maulvi had withdrawn, Ghazi Khan returned to the charge. 'It is a mistake, Hyder Saheb.'

'But you tell me,' countered Hyder, 'that Tipu is faring well.'

'True,' replied Ghazi Khan. 'He has talent. He excels in sports—be it horse riding or swimming. But how much better would he do, if he did not have to waste time with all that! Why does he have to have so much scholastic education?' he finally asked.

'Much has been denied to me, Ghazi Khan,' replied Hyder. 'I am unlettered and untrained in the ways of God. Perhaps, I must do more for my son than was done for me. Maybe, he will atone for my past sins and many more that I will commit in the future.'

'Maybe,' said Ghazi Khan, 'but also, he may not acquire the nobility of his ancestry.'

'My life shall be more than satisfied if he achieves nobility of the soul,' was Hyder's reply. 'But tell me, how has the Maulvi's or the Pandit's training interfered with yours?'

'Not very much, but still there are indications which bother me,' said Ghazi Khan.

'For instance?'

'Well, it is his attitude,' replied Ghazi Khan, 'that sometimes puzzles me. When he wins a race, politely he waits for the opponent to reach the goal. Does not get rowdy, does not taunt him and does not even show any jubilation. When he loses, he smiles and congratulates the adversary. It is unnatural in a boy of his age. He will not join others in pilfering bananas from a fruitseller's cart, nor in pelting stones at the milk vendor's jar, nor in ragging a youngster. Winning or losing a game seems to mean nothing to him. Yesterday,' continued Ghazi Khan, warming to the theme, 'the Sultan declined to shoot at birds saying that he would not shoot at a living target.'

'Well, let the birds live. Man was not created to destroy all other creations of God. In any case,' asked Hyder, 'why does he have to learn shooting? I thought I had told you that he is not to engage in any bloodthirsty games.'

'He is the son of a nobleman. Would you have him feeling inferior to boys of his age and class?'

'Please, Ghazi Khan, leave such decisions to me,' Hyder said. 'There are reasons that my heart alone knows.'

24

RESCUE

THERE WAS A CRITICAL PERIOD IN HYDER ALI'S CAREER JUST BEFORE he assumed supreme command of the Kingdom of Mysore in 1761. Suddenly a palace conspiracy had erupted, taking him unawares. The conspirators had mustered sufficient force. Hyder's life was in danger. He had to flee by night. A handful of horsemen who accompanied him with his treasure-laden chests crossed over by swimming the calm waters of the river Cauvery. He did not pause until he had reached the safety of Bangalore, some eighty miles away.

Left behind in Seringapatam was his ten-year-old son Tipu Sultan along with his five-year-old brother Abdul Karim. Fakhr-un-Nissa had been away visiting her father and was safe. The conspirators removed the two children to the top floor of the tower house near the mosque inside the Seringapatam fort. They were treated kindly and allowed to carry whatever they wanted, but they were to remain, under heavy guard, as hostages with an uncertain fate depending upon the success or failure of moves and countermoves that their father would undoubtedly make. They were permitted the company of one of their servants, who was locked up with them. Goverdhan Pandit, Maulvi Obedullah and Ghazi Khan who had accompanied them on their return from Dindigul as also the large number of male retainers and maid servants were left unmolested. None of them knew where the two children were imprisoned. They watched the windows of the countless rooms in the Seringapatam fort.

The room in which the two children were kept along with their servant was large, dark and cheerless. It had one iron door, always barred and guarded from outside all the time by a platoon of soldiers. There were no windows. Its only source of light and air was a ventilator at a level just below the ceiling. The servant stood on the iron bedstead and perched on his shoulder, Tipu gripped the bar of the ventilator. It was of no avail; even if the rotting bar could have been wrenched, what awaited him was a sheer drop of over one hundred feet to the huge boulders below. Just beyond the boulders was the mosque and Tipu knew that Maulvi Obedullah would pass that way, but he was tired, hanging on to the bars. A few minutes later he went up again, tied firmly the ends of a bedsheet to the bars of the ventilator and after several efforts was able to place himself in the uncomfortable loop that the sheet provided. Ready with him was his bow and arrow which he had been permitted to bring along with so many other things. Soon enough, he saw Maulvi Obedullah passing by. Along with him were two others he could not recognise. Tucked in the arrow was a message he had written saying where they were imprisoned, requesting that his mother and father be informed that they were alive, well and happy. The arrow landed barely a yard away from Maulvi Obedullah and his companions, one of whom picked it up. The Maulvi snatched the message, read it and put it in his pocket. If he went into the mosque by one door and came out by the other, ignoring his prayers, he knew that the good God would understand and forgive. The dignified Maulvi almost ran to the house and announced to the despairing members of the household that the children were alive. To Ghazi Khan he requested that he should leave immediately to inform Begum Fakhr-un-Nissa about the safety of her sons; Fakhr-un-Nissa had already been warned not to come near Seringapatam and to remain hidden. Ghazi Khan agreed but did not go himself and sent a servant with the message to Begum Fakhr-un-Nissa. He had other arrangements to look after.

At dead of night, a tall ladder was placed against the wall. A man went up with a rope tied around him. Reaching the top of the ladder, the man continued his ascent, balancing himself precariously on the thick, long and pointed iron nails which he kept pushing into the wall with the aid of a strong hammer. Tipu's servant woke him up as he heard the soft taps against the ventilator. Tipu went up, again tying up the loop of the sheet. He caught the rope that was being thrown up. The man below could not come up to the ventilator for about ten feet below the ventilator, stuck into the wall were broken and sharp pieces of glass, designed to make it impossible for anyone to scale that part of the wall. As Tipu pulled the rope in, he found attached to it a small pointed saw, obviously for cutting away the iron bar of the ventilator. The servant tied the rope to the bed. He also kept coughing to muffle the noise of the saw grinding against the iron bar. It was not necessary. The huge iron door between them and their guards as also the furious rain which kept up all night accompanied by the roar of thunder, were enough to drown any noise that Tipu made. Nor did the rotting bar resist much. Tied to the bedstead and gripped firmly by the servant at one end, the rope was held on the ground by Ghazi Khan and his companion, stretched at an angle, away from the wall and safe from the sharp edges of the broken glass below the ventilator. With some difficulty, Karim was persuaded to hang on to Tipu's back and the servant cut up more sheets to strap them together. Cautiously, Tipu, with Karim tied to his back, began his slow descent on the rope. After what seemed an eternity, he reached the ground into the arms of Ghazi Khan. His hands were bloody and blistered from sliding on the rough rope. If his eyes were wet, so was his face, hair and his entire body from the rain—and if there were tears in them, they were the tears of triumph and thanksgiving. He kissed his brother Karim.

The servant was left behind. He was too large to have passed through the ventilator. He had thrown away the rope and Ghazi Khan had taken it away. He had so arranged the beds as if the children were asleep but the escape was discovered in the morning. The servant was strangled to death. The guards at the iron door also met the same fate.

Soon, Hyder returned victorious and the family was reunited. Hyder avenged the death of the faithful servant.

25

GOD, YOU REJECTED MY OFFERING

THE MOST CAPTIVATING THING ABOUT ABDUL KARIM, IN HIS infancy, was his smile. His features were hazy and his colouring indistinct but the smile that lit up his face reached every one's heart. It was Tipu Sultan who had first seen the smile, while Abdul Karim was still regarded as hovering between life and death, immediately after his premature birth. So excited were Tipu's shouts for his father and mother that Fakhr-un-Nissa woke up startled and the rest of the household rushed into the room while a servant ran to call Hyder. If Tipu, usually so quiet and reserved, shouted, there must be an immediate cause for alarm—they thought. Not so. Tipu just wanted to share with them the delight of his brother's smile. They laughed in relief and waited for Karim to smile again. They did not have to wait for long. The smile came, spreading to his eyes and lighting his whole face, while they all basked in its warmth. It was from that moment that the physicians felt the glimmer of hope and the parents became certain that their son would live.

The surge of pride and happiness that filled Hyder's heart over his second son was incomparable. He lifted his eyes to the sky and prayed. He gave thanks that his son had been spared. He prayed for his son's health and lustre. He prayed for his fame and glory. He was sure that his prayers had been heard.

Frequently, Hyder was away from Dindigul. When he came back, he could not be parted from his favourite son. He heard official reports, received visitors and dictated despatches, with Karim in his lap. If Karim cried, he was not taken away but the work in hand was interrupted. If he continued to cry, Hyder would take him in his arms and carry him to Fakhr-un-Nissa. Once Fakhr-un-Nissa, with equal loyalty to her first-born, chided Hyder for such open favouritism.

'He belongs to us, only us,' Hyder would reply.

Meanwhile, Abdul Karim continued to smile—a smile that continued to captivate, fascinate and charm. With icy dread, Fakhr-un-Nissa saw the smile turn into a grimace and finally into a twich. Abdul Karim was three years old when she permitted the first hint of suspicion enter her mind that there was something wrong with her loved one. He was slow and lethargic, but, at times he grew so excited as if under a spell; his eyes would then take on a wild look, his hands would be trembling, his teeth clenched and his forehead wet with sweat. 'Oh God, dear God, protect my son, I beg of you,' was Fakhr-un-Nissa's constant prayer. In the beginning she had waved away her misgivings. If he could not focus his mind on various things, she realised that each child must have his own individual developmental process. She also knew that some children are slow in the beginning but later catch on. What really frightened her were the brief periods of frenzied excitement that overtook Karim. She prayed constantly. These periods grew, both in length and in frequency. She confided in Hyder. He watched, shaken. He had the physicians called. They came, first from Dindigul, then from Seringapatam and thereafter from every corner of the country. Every kind of medical treatment was tried. Special prayers were offered in mosques and temples. Holy men were invited and their blessings invoked. Astrologers were called in. To no avail.

Fakhr-un-Nissa went on a pilgrimage to the shrine of Saint Tipu Mastan Oulia. For days on end she prayed that her son may recover. She begged for an answer. The wind howled. The rest was silence. She prayed before the candle—the candle that burnt in her bed chamber every night ever since she heard of the death of the son of Saint Tipu Mastan Oulia. The candle flickered as if to mock her.

Karim's condition worsened as months went by. Any noise upset him and brought on the excitement. Anything shining, colourful or even slightly unfamiliar put him into shivers. If a toy broke or if a glass or a cup dropped, his trembling would begin. Fakhr-un-Nissa would then hold him closely to her breast until slowly he recovered. If Hyder picked him up at such times, he would resist, hitting out with his feeble hands. Hyder felt dejected. Still, in Hyder's heart was the conviction that it was a passing phase. It was not. Karim was never a whole personality.

Strangely enough, when he was imprisoned along with Tipu in the tower house in Seringapatam fort, he was quite happy and normal in those unfamiliar surroundings. When Tipu had brought him down to safety, sliding on the rope strapped to himself, he had behaved as if he enjoyed the adventure. He had kissed Tipu's bleeding hands and had embraced Ghazi Khan at the deliverance. Also, when the brothers were in hiding with Ghazi Khan, he was the model of good behaviour. Even the reunion with the parents did not result in the dreaded excitement. He was happy, ecstatic, yes, as any normal child would be, in circumstances such as these. He watched the parades in honour of his father, as he took over the supreme command of the Kingdom of Mysore, clapped his hands in joy and joined the celebrations and merrymaking that followed. He saw himself and his family installed in the palace and was in awed delight at the splendour in which he was to live.

'God has given me a kingdom,' said Hyder to Fakhr-un-Nissa, 'and has returned my son to us.' Silently, Fakhr-un-Nissa prayed.

Six months later, Karim picked up a sword and cut out the eyes from every portrait hanging in the palace. 'They were watching, me, those strange, unfamiliar eyes,' he explained.

Later, he would pick up a chalk and draw eyes all over the walls of the palace. He would then hammer at them with his fists until his hands were ready to bleed. They watched him, day and night. Still, he dodged them once in the garden and jumped into the swimming pool where the water was deep. He could not swim. In his lucid periods, he knew of his capacity to shock and terrify when such spells came over him. Often he was penitent, but slyly sometimes, he even pretended to be under a spell to get, perhaps, a feeling of greater importance. Once he scissored off Tipu's collection of books and amongst them precious manuscripts which Maulvi Obedullah had presented to Tipu on each of his birthdays. Tipu was sad but said nothing and just put his arms around Karim in tenderness as if he understood it all. It was Karim who shed tears. By and large, however, Karim was amiable and even charming except when those dreadful spells came and then without notice, without warning.

Later, his trembling fits became more serious. The procession of physicians commenced. They came from near and far. The Caliph from Constantinople sent his own physician. Others came from Muscat, Persia and even France. Every one gave hope but none the cure.

The rage that seethed within Hyder was boundless. How could he passively submit to such monstrous injustice! How could he tolerate that a common soldier or a humble peasant should be able to sire a dozen children, each healthier than the other but that he—he who ruled over the realm with powers of life and death—should be so mercilessly dealt with! When Maulvi Obedullah told him, 'God's ways are wonderous,' he had an almost insane desire which he restrained with difficulty to strangle the frail, aged Maulvi with his bare hands if only to see if the Maulvi would continue to be enchanted with God's wonderous ways when the breath of life was being snuffed out of him. Hyder had regarded kings—and he was no less—as God's representatives on earth for carrying out the business of the world. Was he supposed to protect righteousness, when he himself was being so humiliated! What crime had he committed, in what had he failed God that such vengeance should be wreaked on him—on him who had glorified the Lord, praised Him, prayed to Him, made gifts to His temples and mosques and had even surrendered his eldest son to God's keeping! Was this His reward! Was there any justice in His scheme of things or is it that for those that serve Him, He reserves only retribution and chastisement!

Behind every smile, however innocent, he saw mockery and ridicule. In Karim's malady, he saw nothing but cruelty from Heaven—both wanton and purposeless. Hyder continued to fear God but loved Him no more.

'I offered my eldest child to you, God,' said Hyder in anguish, 'but you have rejected me and my offering. So be it. I shall still go Your way and not offend You, but I take back my Tipu in my service.'

26

PARTING OF THE WAYS

(i)

'I TAKE BACK MY TIPU IN MY SERVICE,' HYDER HAD SAID.

Thus ended Tipu Sultan's religious training, from that day. He was now to be brought up as a man of war—an heir to Hyder's throne.

Tearfully, Maulvi Obedullah and Goverdhan Pandit parted from Tipu Sultan on his twelfth birthday. They had been with him for seven years. The two of them now left with handsome gifts and pensions from Hyder. Maulvi Obedullah would now be able to satisfy his ambition of building a monastery while Goverdhan Pandit had no fixed plans, though to begin with, he wanted to go to Rishikesh. The two theologians embraced each other.

'He will always be a man of God,' said Maulvi Obedullah. Goverdhan Pandit knew that the Maulvi spoke of Tipu Sultan.

'Always,' agreed Goverdhan Pandit.

Each went his own way. Both had been Tipu's teachers but both had learned much from each other. The one abiding truth that they had come to recognise was that in the kingdom of God, there is no difference between a Hindu and a Muslim. Also, they had come to recognise that the currents of philosophical and religious thought, diffused along many varied and devious courses, did not represent hostile or even conflicting beliefs but were a part of a single harmonised unity of Indian culture and tradition. Both departed in peace. They did not realise that in the years to come the alien enemy from distant lands, already within the shores of India, would begin to preach a doctrine of hate that would divide the Hindu from the Muslim and set brother against brother.

(ii)

When the two ecclesiastics left, Ghazi Khan emerged as the sole tutor of Tipu Sultan.

'I am short of sons,' Hyder had told him ruefully. 'See that he lacks neither valour nor will. Make a mighty man of him and I shall make him a mighty king.'

Ghazi Khan placed his hand on his heart and said, 'God willing.'

Hyder glared at him without speaking.

Part IV

DREAMS AND MEMORIES

27

WE SHALL ENDURE

TIPU SULTAN RODE ALONE. HIS COMPANIONS FOLLOWED AT SOME distance. The rain had come suddenly in the middle of the night rampaging through the heavy velvet skies. Thunder and lightning had rent the air with awesome and primeval fury. It was getting lighter, now that the dawn was approaching, giving way to a gentle drizzle and cool breeze. Still, the tempests in Tipu's heart continued to rage.

Only a few hours ago, the messenger had arrived from Purnaiya announcing his father's death. An overwhelming loneliness and silent despair had come over him. He loved his father, who was more than his father. He was also his companion, his mentor, his king and his commander-in-chief; side by side, they had fought and marched; together they had shared glory and victory—and sometimes frustration; each was the delight and pride of the other—and each protected the other, through various campaigns and varying fortunes of war. Silently, Tipu had waited in the tent, wrapped in the memories of the past, while preparations were being made for his departure.

Tears had come to him as he approached his horse Dilkush the Second. Proudly, the horse had borne him to many battles.

He was now to bear him on his mournful journey. Dilkush the Second was sired by Hyder's favourite horse, Dilkush. Both horse and man understood each other's sorrow—such was the bond between them. Through blinding tears, Tipu could not see the way ahead but Dilkush the Second went dashing forward unmindful of the rain and thunderstorm.

Far beyond the grief that gripped Tipu, far beyond the anguish that tore him and far beyond the loneliness that surrounded him, was his bewilderment, at the question to which he must find an answer. Someone, unknown, from somewhere unseen, had shouted the question, voiceless. Barely he could formulate the question in words though he understood its import and sensed its purpose.

'Where am I going and for what?' he asked himself.

His father had fought for glory—his own and his son's. Out of nothing, he had carved out a kingdom for himself, enlarged it, rendered it comparatively safe from depredations, encroachments and brigandage. Constantly, he had fought, in the end with one overriding ambition, that he should leave for his son a glorious inheritance.

'But what shall I fight for?' was the question that incessantly troubled Tipu.

'To protect my father's kingdom?' 'For my glory?' 'For the glory of my sons?' 'To establish a royal dynasty?'

No, this was not the answer. It was not even a question. He knew that something which he could only dimly realise, something which he could not put into words, something beyond the realm of his immediate consciousness, was dragging him to a destiny unknown.

As a child, he had been offered to God. He had spent his childhood in serenity with his books and with his loving teachers. Above all, they had taught him to be just in all ways, ardent in piety and eager for justice. It was not in him to be a secret server of the wrong, to seek imperial power or lustful ambition. In those childhood days, he had met no torments, no turmoil, no anguish of body or spirit. His tears and laughter were innocent, never self-seeking. If he wept intensely, it was over a sparrow that had fallen in his garden, wounded; and boundless was his joy when he nursed it to survival. The storm through which his father lived had not touched him and he lived in peace—in love with his father, mother, his baby brother Karim and his teachers but he always felt around himself the Presence of Another whom he loved all the more.

His lamp was shattered when he was twelve. His loving teachers parted from him. Hyder was now convinced that, with Karim's illness, the Lord God had released him from his vow to bring up Tipu Sultan as a seer and a sage. Tipu, at fifteen, was trained for war and was constantly by the side of his father.

Tipu Sultan was now thirty-two. For seventeen years he had fought for his father and had become his most trusted general. With his courage that defied death, he had helped his father to defend his kingdom, to extend its boundaries and to strike terror in his enemies. He fought as a duty, as something without pleasure or interest but he fought furiously, nevertheless. At the end of a victorious battle when jubilation surged around his camp and wine would be brought out copiously, he would politely accept congratulations but not the cup of wine and his immediate attention would be directed to the dead and the wounded on both sides. In the beginning, the horror of the battle and the merciless murder and senseless slaughter that went with it had revolted him. How could he, with his own hands, take a life and extinguish the spark with which God had sanctified every human being? He had been shaken to the very core of his being. He had pleaded with his father to release him from his service. His eyes were lowered but he was unafraid when his father had threatened him. He had not even flinched under his father's lash. He would renounce war, he had said and neither threats nor the lash would break his resolve. But he had submitted, finally, to his father's tears. His father told him of the dangers that he faced, within and outside the boundaries of Mysore and how defenceless he would ultimately be without the supporting arm of his elder son when the younger one was so helpless. Ghazi Khan, whom Tipu loved, told him of the duty of a son to his father. Fakhr-un-Nissa, whom Tipu adored above all others, had wept when he had gone to her for understanding and sympathy. She had gathered him in his arms and with his cheek moist from her tears, he had heard her whisper, 'Do as your father bids you; you are the only one he has; do not fail him as I did.' No, she would say no more, nor explain herself and Tipu sensed that even what she had said had been torn out of her, in grief, against her will. Wily Hyder had even enlisted the support of Karim who once asked his brother:

'I hear, dear brother, that you will not go to wars. Who will protect me when father is gone?'

'Quiet, little one,' Tipu said, pinching Karim's cheek. 'Father will not be gone.'

'And if he does,' Karim persisted.

'I,' replied Tipu, pinching his other cheek and kissing him on the forehead, 'shall be there.'

Karim had put his tiny hand into his brother's. He needed no further reassurance.

Could Tipu have resisted further? His mother whom he regarded as a poem in self-effacement, who never asked for anything and imposed nothing, had begged him to follow his father. His brother, helpless and loving, had asked for no less.

No, these seventeen years of war had not steeled his heart to its horror. He knew that anguish and death were its bitter fruits and that the victims were not only those that fell on the field of battle but also the widows and orphans who wept in countless homes.

Each campaign had brought him victory and his fame became so illustrious that people told stories of him as they tell stories of legendary gods or heroes. Still, joy and laughter had eluded him. He felt alone.

His father had been proud of him. He doted on him. Often, Hyder would magnify Tipu's victories and slur over his own. His pride in his son's prowess was far greater than in his own achievements. His son could do no wrong. Once a senior commander said to Hyder, 'Sultan fights but his heart is not in it.'

With his powerful grip, Hyder had picked up the Commander from the back of his neck. 'You, son of a whore,' he shouted at the hapless commander, 'do you know where your own heart is located?' To make his point clear, he hit him with his knee in his backside.

Every one had laughed, though somewhat uneasily. It became clear that in Hyder's company, merry though it always was, with many jests and ribaldry, no one could get away with a crack at Tipu. Praise Tipu, if you want Hyder's favour or be silent, but criticise him, never.

Tipu continued on the path of war. With each victory, his father's pride grew.

Now the father was dead. Tipu had promised to serve him all his life. The life had ended and with it perhaps, the promise to serve. He was now the master of his destiny—or was he?

'Where am I going and for what?' Again, Tipu had asked himself. He was rich. What he had was enough for himself, for his brother, his mother, his wife and children. He was weary of war. He longed for peace and quiet. He knew that if he chose to quit, there would be many aspirants for his father's throne which would always remain the centre of bitter warfare. He could install the worthiest amongst his father's commanders and leave for lands far away—removed from the pain and strife of war. For himself, he needed nothing but an opportunity to study and meditate. To others near and dear to him he could provide all the luxuries that life could offer. Why was he then being drawn by some strange, irresistible force? And what was it telling him! Why? Why? Why do I have to fight? Why do I have to go to wars? he kept on asking himself. Why am I a prisoner of destiny unknown?

All his life he had yearned for truth and piety. They had eluded him and he was sad. He had sought neither fame nor glory, neither lustre nor wealth. They had come his way, but his heart had not rejoiced. Now that death had separated his father from him, why had the iron entered into his own heart, bidding him—nay, commanding him—to fight. Fight for whom and for what? For his glory, riches and family fortune as his father had fought? No. But what else? What else?

Dilkush the Second galloped on. The rain had stopped. The sun was trying to assert itself though the clouds still disputed its passage. Tipu Sultan did not know when he became conscious of the light and warmth. Softly, and tenderly, he felt his feverish mind caressed. He was no longer distraught. His questions ceased.

He knew now where his destiny goaded him. He could not find the words for it but he felt it, sensed it, deeply, vividly, in the inner most consciousness of his being. No, he would not fight for his glory nor for wealth but fight he would, he knew. For himself, he expected nothing, desired nothing, coveted nothing. A vision rose before him—a vision culled from stories of the days gone by when he sat at the feet of the learned Pandit and the venerable Maulvi—vision of a country with an ancient culture and colourful history. He felt within him the stirring of an emotion which thrilled him. No longer did he feel himself rootless, without moorings. He had the support. He belonged.

Several scenes from the moving drama of the Indian people came before him. He saw their age-old culture, the continuity of their traditions and the richness of their philosophical thought, spreading the civilising message of truth and love. He saw their love of beauty, their vigour, dynamism and deep humanity which had inspired the art, literature and aesthetics of many countries. He saw their spiritual strength and their underlying unity through all this apparent diversity of language, sect and race. He became conscious of the conception of a common national culture—from the Himalayas to Cape Comorin—and its immemorial sway over the people of this land. He saw the culture, proud but without arrogance, a culture that withstood hostile influences from outside and did not decay, a culture that assimilated within its loving fold new impulses and ideas. He saw the conquerors who had come from lands far away, establishing dynasties that came to merge themselves indissolubly and spontaneously with Indian culture enriching it with freshness, and creating a synthesis of thought and the ways of living.

Tipu Sultan saw this and he also saw another scene. He saw a band of impoverished adventurers, belonging to a trading corporation in collusion with effete upstarts and servile, self-seeking feudatory princes, getting a stranglehold on this proud land. He saw the corrupt, perfidious and rapacious government of the British spreading its claws over India, not only to disorganise her trade and industry and impoverish her people, but also to demoralise and sap the spirit of her cultural traditions. Theirs was an army of dacoits bent on pillaging and plundering the people under the pretence of trade and commerce. Wherever they went, they brought destruction, destitution, death and famine. These were the foreigners—and they would always remain foreigners imbued with purposes hostile to Indian thought and bent on its desturction. He knew of the gold lust of these men of monstrous immorality. He knew of the corruption, venality, nepotism, violence and greed of this early generation of British rule. He knew also of the missionaries who were being imported from England and were moving around in bazaars, schools, hospitals and even prisons. They ridiculed in public the tenets of Hinduism and Islam. They were out, he knew, to uproot the most ancient aristocracy in the world.

But another wave of thought and feeling came flooding into his mind. It is not the English who are to blame. It is not they who are out to degrade us to the condition of pariahs. No, we ourselves have done this to ourselves. A civilisation, he knew, deteriorates and decays much more from inner failure than from external attack. India had become dormant and exhausted, torn by dissensions and disunity. The age-old dream of Indian unity—vivid, vibrant and full of life—had degenerated itself into empty murmurings of troubled sleep. Princes driven by their insane ambitions, petty rivalries and mutual hatreds were ready to seek the help of an alien authority. The British had after all come to India as traders and their troops and their military establishments were intended merely to protect their commerce. The Indian powers, with scores to settle against each other, regarded them as mercenaries to be hired. Surely, these foreigners were not to be considered as contestants for the sovereignty of the country; they would earn their profits, amass their fortunes and go back to their cold, distant land. But it was not to be. The British had their own hopes, their own aspirations and their own designs—the conquest of India. They were not there to play anybody else's game. They were there to stay, to consolidate and expand their power. The disintegration of the Moghul empire had brought into the field several adventurers, aspirants and claimants, each supplicating the British for support from their well-trained, disciplined troops. The British obliged, helping one rival against another. But they extracted a heavy price for their support. Thus, more and more territory came under their sway, their power grew and also their military establishments. The painful realisation that the British had designs for total military and political domination of India did dawn on the Indian powers but by then it was too late and the British had already established themselves firmly in the country. Even so, did the Indian princes halt their own quarrels to present a united front against a common enemy? No, they buried their national sentiment and continued to scheme and plot against each other, engaging in bitter rivalries, civil wars and defections, frequently turning to the British for help to further their narrow and petty interests. Thus, they ultimately paved the way for their own shameful subservience and timid submission to the English.

Will India find herself again? Tipu asked himself. Will she survive the danger and horror of today and recapture the dream of her past to rebuild herself on secure foundations of freedom, justice and national unity? Tipu's mind went to the mountains and rivers of India, to the forests and the broad fields, to the valleys and the plains, to the panorama of India's cultural heritage of thousands of years, to the faces and figures of the men, women and children of this proud sensitive land. He tried to fathom what lay behind those millions of eyes of theirs. He could see in them their capacity for immense self-sacrifice. No, they would not lose their hope, nor their dignity nor their faith.

'We shall endure,' said Tipu Sultan, fervently.

Tipu knew that India was in this predicament through her disunity. She was not conquered from without. Whenever the

British won a battle, it was always a battle in which a section of the Indian army went over to the side of the British and fought against their own countrymen. It was an incontrovertible though shameful fact, that the British were not conquering India with their sword, but that Indians themselves were conquering their country with their own swords and handing it over to the British. He knew that cold-blooded treachery was the established policy of the English. Princes were betrayed into war with each other; and one of them having been helped to overcome his antagonist, was then himself dethroned for some alleged misdemeanour. Always some muddied stream was at hand as a pretext for official wolves.

Yes, India was caught like a bird in a net. But was this just an unhappy interlude in India's long and colourful history or was destiny writing the last page of the chapter? Tipu wondered. But again his mind went to the millions of his countrymen and he saw in their eyes a light of deep understanding which went far beyond any spoken words.

'We shall endure,' repeated Tipu, identifying himself with the emerging hopes and aspirations of the vast multitudes of the Indian subcontinent. It was the surge of a new emotion that he did not recognise, a sensation that he could not name, a thrill of which he was previously unaware.

It was the breath of nationalism that had entered into Tipu's soul. In the decades that followed, there were others who appeared on the Indian national scene with magnificent feats of heroism and valour. But Tipu was the first—the first nationalist—the first to identify himself with the soul of India.

28

THE TRAITORS

THE ROAD DIPPED, LEVELLED, TWISTED, TURNED AND OFTEN disappeared altogether, interrupted by streams, forests and rocks. It was five days since Hyder Ali had died. In those five days, Tipu Sultan and his horsemen had travelled nearly two hundred miles, though they were still two days short of their destination. Purnaiya had come to greet Tipu Sultan. He lowered himself to his knees, bowed low and waited for Tipu to command him to rise. Tipu was confused by the courtesy. For a moment he thought that Purnaiya was making fun of him, then he saw he was not. It was his submission to his new sovereign.

Tipu put his hand on Purnaiya's chin, raised him from the ground and the two embraced each other. Silently, they sat, each respecting the grief of the other. Tipu loved his father; Purnaiya, he knew, loved him no less.

They went into the tent pitched for the night's rest. It was some time before they spoke. Tipu asked and Purnaiya told him of the last days of Hyder Ali. He did not tell him of the pain and anguish he suffered but of the gentleness of his death. He told him of the fondness with which he remembered Fakhr-un-Nissa, Karim and above all Tipu Sultan, right till the end, his whispered words of love, his orders that flowers be sent to Fakhr-un-Nissa and his insistence on being covered with the embroidered blanket which Tipu had given him as a gift on his last birthday.

The conversation moved on. Purnaiya wanted to retire. 'Be with me,' said Tipu, 'I have been alone for long.' Purnaiya remained. He told him of the means by which Hyder's death was kept a secret. He also told him of the treachery of Sheikh Ayaz through his secret agents Muhammad Aramin and Shams-ud-din Bakshi. The agents were in chains but Ayaz himself was in Bednur with the vast State treasury in his clutches and was frantically sending agents here and there to foment plots against his sovereign. Only three days back, they had obtained a confession from Rasool Khan that he had been in touch with several senior officers of Hyder Ali on behalf of the traitor Sheikh Ayaz.

'Rasool Khan?' asked Tipu in surprise. 'You mean Ghazi Khan's son?'

'Yes.'

'And he confessed to treachery!' Tipu was aghast. Rasool Khan had been his boyhood friend. Ghazi Khan, his father, had been Tipu's teacher.

'Yes, he confessed,' replied Purnaiya, 'but not willingly. Only after a severe beating.'

Tipu looked at Purnaiya sorrowfully. 'How could you torture Rasool Khan, Purnaiya? Don't you realise how much we owe his father. My life, to say the least.' Tipu remembered vividly the incident when Ghazi Khan had rescued him and Karim from the tower house in the Seringapatam fort when he was ten years old.

'It was Ghazi Khan, his father, who questioned him. It was his whip and his lash which obtained the confession,' Purnaiya replied, and then he added, 'Rasool will survive but Ghazi Khan may not. Immediately after obtaining his son's confession, he had a massive heart attack.'

'Poor Ghazi Khan, poor Rasool,' said Tipu at last.

'Poor Rasool!' Purnaiya objected.

'Yes, poor Rasool,' said Tipu with compassion.

Purnaiya gave him the list compiled by Mir Sadik, Qamar-ud-din and Burhan-ud-din of the various commanders and senior officers suspected to have been corrupted by Sheikh Ayaz and other traitors. The list was long. Tipu read the names on the first page and cried out as if stung. These were the names of men with reputation for faithfulness and loyalty to his father. With some, he had ties of blood and family connections. Others had risen from obscurity, helped by Hyder's trust and generosity.

'What are you up to, Purnaiya?' Tipu asked. 'Is it to break my heart that you give me such a terrible list?'

'Not to break your heart,' replied Purnaiya, 'but to steel your heart. To forewarn you against surprise and to put you on guard against treachery.'

'I suppose your advice would be that I should have all of them shot, straightway,' Tipu asked.

'That was the advice of Mir Sadik, Qamar-ud-din and others.'

'And yours?' asked Tipu.

'No, not mine,' replied Purnaiya.

'And what is your advice?'

'To be on guard, to investigate and maybe to bring some of them to trial.'

'And if they are found guilty?' insisted Tipu.

'Then the law must prevail,' said Purnaiya.

'Do you realise, Purnaiya, what you are saying? These are men I have grown up with. Some of them are my kinsmen. Do ties of blood mean nothing?'

'If they meant less to them, why should they mean more to you? Incidentally, forgive me, Sultan, I think it is relevant that I remind you of one of your father's observations. He had said that a murderer might be forgiven but never a would-be murderer.' Thus, Purnaiya tried to divert Tipu's mind back to the memory of his father. Tipu sat as if in a trance. Purnaiya begged leave to retire so that they could leave in the morning refreshed. The morning was only three hours away. Purnaiya left.

29

THE DOUBT

TIPU DID NOT SLEEP THAT NIGHT. THE MORNING FOUND HIM, DEEP in thought, sitting in the same posture in which Purnaiya had left him.

Purnaiya's revelations had shaken him to the core. They had almost shattered his dream—the dream of nationalism and the dream to fight for a cause bigger and nobler than his own personal glory. He realised now that he would have to struggle for his own safety and self-preservation, to battle against conspiracies and plots, and to hunt his kinsmen and friends who had turned disloyal. He who had been secure in the belief that he and his father were loved and that the kingdom waited for him to follow his lead felt now lonely, lost and rejected.

His dejection lasted for a while to be replaced by a sense of release, as if the irons that shackled him were taken off. No longer was he required to fight. He would turn his back to the kingdom, go where he chose, lead a simple life amidst his books, study, pray and meditate. The memory of his early years came to him. The peace and sunshine of those days returned to him.

He allowed his thoughts to wander in the past.

30

TIGER, TIGER!

(i)

TIPU'S MIND WENT OVER THE IMAGES AND PICTURES OF THE PAST. He thought of his wife Ruqayya Banu. He remembered how he met her the first time. She was seven and he was ten. It was the day after Ghazi Khan had rescued him and his brother Abdul Karim from the tower house in Seringapatam fort. They were hidden in the half-covered boat moored five miles down the river. The long boat had in the past been used for the purpose of river-burial. It was a common practice to immerse the coffins of dead children in the river instead of burying or cremating them and it was from such boats that the coffins were lowered into the water. This boat was now in disuse. Also, it was in a dilapidated condition. Few approached it, due to its association with death. It was in this boat that Ghazi Khan had placed the two children. Somehow his arrangements had misfired. The horsemen who were to meet him there to take the boys to safety had not reached. Ghazi Khan passed the entire night with them and left them the next morning to bring provisions and food. He left strict instructions to them not to leave the boat. Meanwhile, their escape from the fort had been discovered and house-to-house searches had begun. Ghazi Khan reached his house only to find the police closing in on him. He feared that he might be arrested since, as an associate of Hyder Ali, he could be under suspicion. The policemen knocked at the door. Hurriedly, he wrote a short note. He opened his window. Opposite that window was the window of another house, belonging to Lala Mian. The two houses were divided by a distance of three feet. Ghazi Khan knocked at the window of the other house with his stick, while the police was outside banging away at his door. Lala Mian's seven-year-old daughter Ruqayya Banu opened the window. Ghazi Khan asked for her father. He was away, she told him, and would be back shortly. Ghazi Khan gave her the note he had written and asked her to promise—promise faithfully—that she would give it to her father. She promised. The windows were then closed.

Before Ghazi Khan could go to open the door, the police had forced it open. They arrested him. Ruqayya Banu had also rushed out of her house, hearing the commotion of the door being broken. She watched Ghazi Khan being escorted by the police. They did not speak a word to each other. A look of understanding passed between them.

Soon, Ruqayya's parents returned and she gave to her father the note which Ghazi Khan had given her. Excitedly, she told them of his arrest, exaggerating the number of policemen, the crowds that had collected and the strength with which the door had been broken. Quietly, Lala Mian read the note. His face fell.

'What is it?' his wife asked.

'It is a letter from Ghazi Khan,' he quietly replied.

'I know that. What does it say?'

'It says,' Lala Mian was angry now, 'that Ghazi Khan has hidden Hyder Ali's children in the boat at Sirni, which is used as a launching pier for river-burials and that I am to take food to them and look after them.'

'So?' enquired his wife.

'So, nothing,' Lala Mian replied. 'I do not wish to die hanging from the gallows.'

'But what will happen to the children?' his wife asked.

'I don't know madam and I don't care. I have children of my own to worry about.'

'Ghazi Khan is a friend of yours. You have served Hyder Ali. What will they say?'

'Listen, woman. Ghazi Khan is an adventurer and so is his master. As you say, I served him, but only so long as he was in lawful command here. He is no longer in lawful command.'

'Suppose, he comes back,' persisted his wife.

'If he does, which he won't, we can always say that Ruqayya forgot to give me the letter. She is after all a child, you see.' Here, he smiled at his cleverness.

Lala Mian's wife was not amused. 'Can you not think of asking someone else to look after the two children?' she asked.

'Can you not think of a better scheme to tighten the noose around my neck?' was the exasperated reply.

It also occurred to Lala Mian that he would be in poor shape if Ghazi Khan, possibly under police questioning, blurted out that he had left a message with Ruqayya. The police would then hold Lala Mian as an accomplice for not reporting the matter to them.

'Listen, little one,' he said, handing over Ghazi Khan's letter back to Ruqayya who had been a listener to all this conversation, 'go and keep this in your desk and if anyone, anyone, should ever ask you about it, say that you got it from Ghazi Khan but forgot to give it to your parents. Understand?'

Ruqayya understood. She kept the note in her desk. The whole day she was worried about the two boys kept in the boat, without food, unattended. Her mother snapped at her for her questions about them.

'For the hundredth time, I have told you Ruqayya, forget about the whole matter. Just forget about it. Your father is right. If you talk about it, we all will suffer.'

'I won't talk about it, Mother,' she had promised. But Ruqayya Banu was worried. She could not shake off from her mind the picture of the two boys, hungry, lonely and forlorn waiting for someone to bring them food.

It was evening. Ruqayya's father and mother slept early. She was tucked into bed. She soon got up and went into the kitchen. There was plenty of homemade bread, several biscuits, pickles, jam and a small jar of honey. She filled up a basket. She stuffed sweets into her pockets and put one or two into her mouth. Silently, stealthily she crept out of the house.

Five miles is a long walk. When one is barefooted, it can be an agony. At night it can also be frightening. The shadows on the calm, serene river can appear like spirits and demons. Somehow she braved it all with tears in her eyes, a prayer in her heart, half-running, half-walking. She reached the boat unaccosted. Tipu and Karim were frightened to see someone enter the boat. It was only a little girl with a basket.

'From Ghazi Khan?' Tipu asked, looking at the basket. Ruqayya nodded. She hadn't caught her breath yet, her feet were sore and tears were in her eyes. Tipu could not see her face clearly in the moonlight but he could hear her sob. He brushed the dust from the bench with his handkerchief and gently asked her to sit. She noticed now the basket which she was still gripping tightly and gave it to Tipu.

'Eat,' she said, mumbling through her sobs. He waited for her to sit down, leaned from the boat to wash his handkerchief in the river water. He gave her the wet handkerchief. She wiped her face.

'Please eat,' she was now in control of herself. 'I brought it for you.'

She had dropped the basket on the way half a dozen times. The bread, biscuits, jam, pickles and honey had mixed and intermixed.

It was still the most delicious meal that they had eaten throughout their lives. They had been hungry since morning.

Ruqayya Banu enjoyed seeing them eat. Her fear had left her. She was smiling. The boys finished their meal. The wet handkerchief was in use again. They dipped it into the water and washed their hands and faces. As Ruqayya wanted to take out her own dry handkerchief, the sweets which she had stuffed into her pocket dropped out. The three began to eat them contented. Soon, her fear returned. How would she go back in the dark! Tipu offered to take her home. No, his danger was greater. She decided to pass the night in the boat.

It was there that Lala Mian found her in the morning. His wife had got up well before dawn as usual and had missed her daughter. She woke up her husband. They searched the house and found the mess in the kitchen. The basket was missing. They knew now.

She was sleeping in Tipu's arms. The towering rage and desperate fear with which Lala Mian had come disappeared. Instead, there was relief and gratitude that his daughter was unhurt and safe. For a moment he watched her tenderly and then woke her up. Her arms went round her father. Tipu and Karim woke up.

'Come,' said Lala Mian to his daughter.

'Come,' she said to the two brothers. They left the boat together. Lala Mian did not object. His heart had softened though he wondered how he should take them to his house. The crowded streets through which he would have to pass might lead to instant recognition of the young fugitives. He led them a mile or so in the opposite direction towards a place from which litters, palanquins and horse-carts could be hired. None were available. The place was closed, for it was the day of the Holi—the festival of joy—the day on which children and adults revel in throwing coloured water and powder on each other. Although in its origin a Hindu festival, every one in those days—Hindus and Muslims—came out to celebrate it. Already though it was early in the morning, he could see people stirring out, getting ready to play Holi. Lala Mian who always considered himself resourceful had reason to congratulate himself. He walked to the nearby shop selling coloured water, coloured powder, water pistols, shining caps, face masks and other paraphernalia for the celebration of Holi. He played Holi with the children. Their hair became multicoloured, along with their clothes. None, he was sure, could recognise them, particularly with the colourful masks they wore. None did. They reached Lala Mian's house, half-jumping, half-running, sprinkling coloured powder on each other almost like a dust cloud and inviting jets of water from passers-by. Of the three, Ruqayya Banu and Karim had enjoyed the colourful escapade and so had Tipu though he alone was aware of the danger. As Lala Mian closed the door behind them, he said, 'Thank you, Uncle.'

Lala Mian, proud of his feat at having escorted them safe through huge crowds of merrimakers, smiled and said, 'Ghazi Khan is a silly ass.' This was his comment—chest out—on the sloppy way in which Ghazi Khan had bungled and by contrast the adroitness with which he had completed the dangerous and delicate mission.

Ruqayya was already in her mother's arms who was both kissing and beating her at the same time. With trembling heart she had waited for her daughter. She then looked up and through her tears laughed outright at her husband's multicoloured beard and dishevelled appearance. With all the dignity he could muster, he told her, 'Madam, you have guests to look after. Attend to it.'

'Oh dear ones, dear ones,' she cried, hugging both Tipu Sultan and Karim against her ample bosom.

'I am glad you brought them, Ruqayya,' and then added with absurd logic, 'but you shouldn't have gone.'

She led Ruqayya and Karim to the bathroom to help them clean up. She was about to assist Tipu likewise but something held her back. She did not know why she felt shy with him; perhaps his reserve made him seem older and more mature; quietly she handed the soap and towel to him. Soon, however, she was worried. Where would she get the clothes for him? Karim was alright. Ruqayya's clothes would fit him. But what about Tipu? His own clothes, dipped in every possible colour, would not be clean even with a hundred washes. On the festival day, all shops would be closed except those that sold colours, sweets or such other things as were needed for the celebration itself. Soon, she thought of a lady a few blocks away who did tailoring work in her own house and always had ready-made clothes, some of them rejected by disappointed clients from time to time. There she repaired carrying a box, and braving coloured powder and water from neighbours—for who would be out on Holi day except to participate in its merrymaking! To ensure that she was not overcharged, she explained that she needed the suit of clothes for her servant's son who had spoilt his only set of clothes playing Holi. Perhaps, it influenced the price or perhaps it did not but she did get the right size. She put the suit in the box and was soon back home. Tipu who had in the meanwhile wrapped himself in large towels and was waiting for his multicoloured clothes to dry received the new suit. He came out wearing it and Ruqayya clapped her hands.

'Pretty, pretty, very pretty,' she said.

'Thank you,' Tipu said, politely smiling at her raillery.

'Ah, but you also looked very handsome and very gallant in your Tiger mask,' said Ruqayya.

'Tiger mask?' Tipu asked in surprise.

'Tiger mask, of course. That is what Papa got you this morning and that is what you wore. Everybody on the street must have said "Oh! here comes the handsome tiger," and they must have got afraid that you would eat them up so no one came too near us. That is what protected us.'

Tipu went to look for the mask which he had hurriedly discarded, found it and looked closely at it. It did resemble a tiger, though the artist had undoubtedly taken some liberties.

'It is a tiger mask,' said Tipu.

'Of course, it is,' Ruqayya said, surprised that anyone should have doubted her word. 'How funny, he wears a mask that protects him and he doesn't know what it is!'

Ruqayya's mother intervened. 'Keep quiet,' she said.

'Can I keep the mask, Uncle,' Tipu asked Lala Mian.

'Certainly, my son,' Lala Mian replied. 'But I can get you a better one. This one is spoilt with Holi colours.'

'No, this one, if you permit,' Tipu urged.

'But, of course, son.'

'Thank you,' said Tipu, and then irrelevantly added, 'I never had a mask before.'

'You will have this one,' said Ruqayya's mother, 'and many more.'

'No, this is the best.'

'Ho, ho,' Ruqayya chimed in. 'He never had a mask before and he says that this is the best.' Then with a wrinkle on her forehead as if she had deeply pondered over the problem, she added, 'Perhaps he is right. He did look very brave, very ferocious with his tiger mask. Isn't that so, Papa?'

Lala Mian pinched her cheek lightly and said, 'You are always right, my love'

'See, see, Tiger, I am always right,' happily Ruqayya crowed.

With a grave smile, Tipu replied, 'I am sure you are.'

'Oh, the brave handsome tiger also says so,' she announced, waving her hand.

'Idiot,' said Ruqayya's mother.

Throughout the day that they were together, Ruqayya made Tipu wear the tiger mask often. Both Karim and she would pretend to be frightened, running here and there. The first one Tipu caught had to sit down while he tried to catch the other; if the other one repeated 'Tiger, brave handsome' ten times before being caught, the first one could get up and re-enter into the game until both were caught which Tipu saw that it took a long time, much to the delight of Ruqayya and Karim.

Well before sunset, Karim had gone to sleep. Lala Mian and his wife sat in another corner of the house, discussing in whispers the next step to ensure that none comes to know of their harbouring Hyder Ali's children. They were worried about the gossipping maid servant who would return the next day in the evening after the leave granted to her the previous day for celebrating Holi with her relatives in the nearby village. How to silence her—with what threats and bribes?

Meanwhile, Ruqayya and Tipu silently watched the evening sky from the window. They held hands, their innocent hearts not knowing why. Or, perhaps, they knew that there would never be another period like this in all their lives—that they would never be so happy, never so young and never so free.

Ghazi Khan came that night. He had been released from custody. He had cajoled, begged and sworn that he had nothing to do with Hyder Ali's escape or that of his children. Why would he have been sleeping away peacefully in his house for anyone to nab him if he was guilty? Actually, he was not under any special suspicion but was one of the many who had been taken in for routine questioning, just in case he could reveal something about the escape. It takes time to question so many and his turn would have come next morning but the festivities of Holi intervened. He was questioned late in the evening and released after being warned to report if anything came to his notice. The police officer questioning him was an acquaintance and said, 'See, Ghazi Khan, we kept you in on Holi day and saved you a suit.' Ghazi Khan laughed so uproariously as if this was the best joke he had heard in all his life. The delighted police officer told him a few more jokes and sent him home in his horse-drawn carriage. The sentry outside his door gave him another fright. 'Just to guard your door, I have got it repaired and put a lock on it too. Here is the key,' explained the sentry. Ghazi Khan took out some money to tip.

'That is not necessary. I am Roop Singh's brother, the one whom you saved at Dindigul,' said the sentry.

'How is he now?' asked Ghazi Khan, without remembering the incident.

'He is well. He has a larger farm now. He has married.'

'Well, well, then you must drink to his health and mine,' said Ghazi Khan, pressing the money on him. As soon as the sentry's footfalls died, Ghazi Khan closed the door and tapped at Lala Mian's window.

'I had left a message before I left,' he said when Lala Mian opened the window.

'I received it. All is well.'

'Thank you. I was worried. I will rush to the boat.'

'Don't bother to do that. They are here.'

'What!' Ghazi Khan was astonished enough to ask loudly.

'Speak softly,' Lala Mian admonished and then added, 'come to my house as soon as you can. Don't knock. The door will be unlocked. Close it when you enter, softly.' Lala Mian enjoyed giving these instructions as if he was speaking to someone quite capable of overlooking the most obvious precautions.

'God of my Gods, I thank you,' said Ghazi Khan to himself, and went outside his house. There was no one in the street. He went into the next house. Lala Mian and his wife awaited him.

'Where are they?' he asked.

Lala Mian motioned to the next room. There on a large bed slept the two boys. The low burning lantern far away did not shed enough light on them. Ghazi Khan lifted the lantern near the bed.

'There is no mistake,' said Lala Mian, as the light fell on them.

'How did you manage to bring them to the house?' asked Ghazi Khan, thinking of the streets congested with people and police.

'That is not important,' said Lala Mian relishing the question. 'Certain risks were inevitable, the matter had to be organised and all necessary precautions had to be undertaken but what is important now is to consider the next step.'

Ghazi Khan had many ideas. Patiently, Lala Mian explained the flaws in each of them. The soldier Ghazi Khan finally surrendered to the strategist Lala Mian who unfolded his plan, prefacing it with the profound observation that in great gatherings and crowds lay the greatest anonymity and the least prospect of detection. Tipu was to wear the veil as girls of orthodox Muslim families do. Karim was also to be dressed as a girl but without the veil. Both would get into the litter, which should join the hundreds of litters and palanquins in the marriage procession of Seth Devi Dayal's son which was scheduled to leave the next day afternoon. An extra litter won't be noticed. The procession would be proceeding to a quiet suburban place nine miles out of the city gates and horses, pre-arranged, could take on from there. Such a procession would not be subjected to any checks at the gates considering Seth Devi Dayal's eminence and influence. In any case, the authorities must be convinced by now that Hyder Ali's children had already been spirited away.

The plan worked. Ghazi Khan had left ahead of the marriage procession to reach the appointed place. He did not want to invite suspicion on the procession by accompanying it in case anybody recognised him. He had arranged the horses. Lala Mian had joined the two boys in the litter.

Ruqayya remained behind with her mother.

'Goodbye,' Tipu had said to her. 'You have been very good to us, Ruqayya.'

'Oh, Tiger, Tiger, the things you say!' she laughed, but there were tears in her eyes.

'Goodbye,' Tipu repeated.

'Have you taken your tiger mask?'

'Oh, yes, I have.' It was in the thick paper bag in his hand which Ruqayya's mother had given him, stuffing it with biscuits and cakes.

Ruqayya's mother came leading Karim, dressed as a girl. They laughed. She now slipped the long veil on to Tipu. She had herself stitched it, altering one of her own.

'I can't see you, I can't see you,' cried Ruqayya.

'Keep quiet,' Ruqayya's mother said.

'Please let me see you,' Ruqayya begged.

Tipu lifted the veil awkwardly.

'I don't like your veil,' she said. 'I like you as a Tiger. I want my Tiger.'

'I shall always be a Tiger,' he said, holding her hand for a moment and then letting the veil down.

Lala Mian fussed over Karim, inspected Tipu and was finally satisfied. Quite a few houses along the street had litters and litter-bearers waiting outside. They were to join the wedding reception. Lala Mian, the generous soul that he was, had asked the litter-bearers to go and have refreshments at his expense at a stall some distance away. Tipu Sultan and Abdul Karim entered into the litter, unnoticed. Lala Mian called out his litter-bearers and entered into the litter. Four hours later and nine miles away Ghazi Khan took over.

The rythmic movement of the litter and the music of the bands accompanying the procession had put Karim to sleep. Lala Mian retained his pose of the alert and watchful general on the battlefield, waiting for the enemy hordes to arrive. Tipu Sultan thought of the little girl whose hands he had held and who called him Tiger.

(ii)

While Tipu sat in the tent in which Purnaiya had left him, his wandering thoughts continued to caress every event in his past. His mind went back to the incident of fifteen years ago. It was 1767, seven years after he had met Ruqayya Banu. He was seventeen. He had won a resounding victory against the English army of Joseph Smith at Vaniyambadi and had followed this up by routing the combined English forces under Gavin and Watson who had raided Mangalore. The panicky English battalions retreated leaving their dead and wounded behind along with their artillery and stores. The well-entrenched English battalions hardly put up a fight. Tipu did not have enough forces and had recruited a mock army of 15,000 peasants, each one armed with dummy wooden muskets with banners flying over every five hundred men. Thus, he had marched to Mangalore. The enemy panicked against this 'overwhelming mass of soldiery'. Tipu occupied Mangalore and expelled the English from the rest of his father's Malabar possessions. His father had also then joined him and for two years Tipu continued his relentless fight, side by side with his father, until March 1769, when they reached such a commanding position that Hyder could dictate peace terms to the English before the very gates of Madras.

Hyder had rejoiced over the victories, more so because his son had distinguished himself so brilliantly in achieving them. He decreed that his son would be entitled to a special battle flag and banner. Tipu Sultan had demurred with becoming modesty and stated that his father's battle flag and banner gave him all the strength and assurance that he needed.

'Enough,' Hyder had replied. 'I too wish to draw strength and assurance from your battle flag. Carry mine by all means but carry yours as well.'

'Very well,' Tipu had agreed.

'What should be the emblem on the flag?' Hyder had asked Tipu and others present.

'Emblem?' Tipu had asked.

'Yes, emblem,' Hyder explained. 'What would you like, a sword, a musket, a crescent, a crown?'

'I would like a tiger, Father, if I may, as the emblem,' said Tipu, remembering Ruqayya and her teasing.

'Tiger! why tiger?' Hyder had asked.

'Why not, Father?' politely Tipu had countered.

'Yes, indeed, why not?' said the delighted Hyder. 'It would be an excellent symbol. Can you think of a better one?' he asked others present.

None could. From that day the Tiger became the symbol and emblem of Tipu Sultan. It embellished his flags, banners, guns and other paraphernalia. The uniform of his soldiers was decorated with a tiger stripe. Although simple in his dress otherwise, on ceremonial journeys he himself wore a coat of golden cloth with a red tiger streak embroidered on it.

Thus the light-hearted words of Ruqayya Banu, the girl whose hand he had held some nine years back, became the inspiration for the symbol adopted by the grave, contemplative Tipu Sultan. The work of the unknown artist who had drawn the tiger mask which Lala Mian had bought for him on that Holi day was copied in bronze, silver and gold, carved in wood and stone and painted on silk and cotton.

31

RUQAYYA, MY DARLING WIFE!

IN THE SILENCE OF THE STILL NIGHT, TIPU SULTAN'S MIND KEPT roving over the past. It now dwelt on his wife and children. He had married Ruqayya Banu in 1774 at the age of twenty-four.

Fourteen years earlier, he had passed the night with her in the dilapidated boat and a night in her house. Soon, Hyder had returned victorious, to take over the undisputed command of the Kingdom of Mysore. Tipu Sultan and Abdul Karim were reunited with their father and mother. Hyder went with Tipu to the boat, out of curiosity, to see how his sons had fared. The food basket which Ruqayya Banu had brought was in the boat still. Ruqayya had forgotten to take it back when Lala Mian had come to them on the morning of the Holi. Tipu wanted to keep the basket. Hyder had the replica of it made in solid gold and went with Fakhr-un-Nissa, Tipu, Karim and Ghazi Khan to call on Lala Mian and his wife in gratitude for their help to his children. Profusely he thanked Lala Mian and his wife. He lifted the little girl Ruqayya and kissed her on her cheeks and lips. She was hanging on to her mother's robe, shy now, before the magnificent Hyder, with his ample robe of white satin with gold flowers and his turban of brilliant scarlet. Lavishly, Hyder gave them presents including the gold basket, explaining, however, that the basket was not a present but merely in exchange for what Tipu wanted. Apart from Hyder's presents, the other gifts were symbolic. Fakhr-un-Nissa gave Ruqayya's mother an embroidered shawl and to Ruqayya a scarf woven in gold thread. Karim gave Ruqayya a mirror with a frame studded with semiprecious stones. Tipu Sultan gave her a miniature painting on ivory. He had made the selection from the hundreds shown to him. It depicted a tiger roaming in the forest. Prettily but shyly, Ruqayya thanked them all. With her lips she framed a word, without voicing it. Perhaps Tipu understood.

Lala Mian until then a junior commander in the Mysore army, rose by leaps and bounds under Hyder's patronage. His growing military duties took him to other districts. Tipu Sultan did not meet Ruqayya for the next fourteen years—until they were married—although each year when the Holi festival was celebrated, a gift from Hyder's household would invariably arrive for her and her parents, until her father died.

Lala Mian had become a general. He died bravely fighting in 1771 in Hyder's house at Melukote. Tragically, he fell on the day of the Holi. Hyder settled large estates on Lala Mian's family. His command went to Burhan-ud-din, his son and Ruqayya's brother. He had been away visiting his uncle when Tipu had passed the night in their house.

Tipu Sultan had called on Ruqayya's mother to condole her loss. The house was full of others who also had called. Ruqayya did not appear, as was only fitting; she was in mourning and in any case grown-up unmarried girls did not appear before company.

During these years, Tipu's legend had taken root. He went marching from battle to battle keeping his enemies at bay. Imperceptibly, his father was slowing down. Illness came to him often. More and more he left the conduct of war to his trusted son. Still, he was a force to reckon with and could vie with the younger man in bravery, lightning marches and stratagem. Hyder with only two sons, one of whom was retarded, could recognise the need for an early marriage to raise a large family. The first time that the thought of Tipu's marriage firmly entered his mind was when his son was about seventeen. It was the time when the first Anglo-Mysore war began. The English had the support of the Nizam of Hyderabad. Hyder was keen to detach the Nizam from that alliance, although he did suspect that the Nizam would be a fickle and perfidious ally, who would change sides with each gust of wind. Still he hoped for the best. Of equal import to him was the praise that he had heard of the beautiful daughter of the Nizam's brother Mahfooz Khan who, he was assured by his astrologers, would be a suitable wife for Tipu, provided 'Mahfooz Khan can succeed in his claim to become the Nawab of the Carnatic.' Thus Hyder sent a delegation to Hyderabad under the leadership of Tipu though along with him he also sent trusted and experienced counsellors. Many were the sleepless nights that Hyder passed after he had impulsively sent Tipu on this diplomatic mission. To his confidants, he said, 'I am afraid of the perfidious and cruel Nizam; he has assassinated his own brother; will he spare my son? Or at least have I no reason to fear that he will detain him, and compel me by the apprehension of my son's danger either to pay him a large sum or make great concessions to him? For, in short, I trust my son in the hands of a wretch to whom nothing is sacred.' However, everything went well and the treaty was ratified. The slender though martial figure and the commanding dignity of the young prince impressed the Nizam as he led his six thousand horsemen with the train of presents—elephants, horses and treasures. Tipu was well received. The Nizam conferred on him the title of Nasib-ud-

Daula (the fortune of the State) and invested him with the right of the overlord—to pass on the Nawabship of the Carnatic to anyone. Mahfooz Khan's daughter was promised to Tipu. More practically, the Nizam bound himself to turn against the English. Thus, Hyder's design and Tipu's diplomacy proved effective. Not only did the Anglo-Hyderabad alliance break up but the Nizam also became Hyder's ally—at least for the moment.

Tipu returned in triumph after his diplomatic success in Hyderabad. But the Nizam changed sides often—so often that some said that he had to refer to his diary to remind himself who his allies were on that particular day. To Hyder Ali's suggestions that the marriage with Mahfooz Khan's daughter might be solemnised, Tipu never offered any opposition but asked with humility if his father considered it safe for him to be in the midst of such a treacherous family. Hyder began to have second thoughts. He looked elsewhere to exercise his matchmaking talents. But whenever he came out with any definite suggestions, Tipu was always there ready with his objections and reservations. When his own ingenuity failed him, he enlisted his mother's help. His mother was as keen as her husband, if not more, that Tipu should get married but she wanted a daughter-in-law worthy of her son and if any defect was pointed out to her, howsoever slight, she would plead rejection of the match. At first Hyder was looking for alliance with powerful princes, which would, he hoped, bring tremendous influence and rich dowry. Later, as he himself amassed wealth, renown and territory, his ambition to ally himself to powerful houses waned. All he wanted now was to find a virtuous and beautiful wfe for his son someone who would fulfil his need for grandsons—and he wanted many of them.

Time and again, his matchmaking proposals were vetoed by Fakhr-un-Nissa at Tipu's prompting and, finally, he stormed at his wife and son, announcing that on the next occasion he would, without consultations with them, choose the bride for his son and impose his will as indeed was his privilege and prerogative both as a father and as a sovereign.

Hyer Ali chose a worthy bride—Raushan Begum, daughter of Imam Saheb Bakshi of Arcot—a girl whose mother had borne eight sons and whose grandmother had given birth to eleven sons. Proudly announcing his selection, Hyder had said of the girl '... of an ancient family, a girl of beauty, chastity, purity and—don't forget—fertility.'

That very morning, however, there had been another matchmaker at work. Tipu had met the six-year-old Salim, son of Burhan-ud-din and nephew of Ruqayya Banu. Always— either out of politeness or because of an emotion that stirred unknown—Tipu would enquire about Ruqayya Banu, whenever he chanced to meet anyone known to her. After a pat and a hug, he put Salim on his horse and led him to the palace shop where he could obtain sweets for the child. Thereafter they chatted—their conversation ranging from one topic to another—sweets, games, horses, birthdays and festivals. Casually then Tipu had enquired about Ruqayya but Salim was engrossed in the topic of the circus he had recently seen. Tipu interrupted to remind him about the question.

'Oh, Aunt Ruqayya? She is fine,' Salim had replied, and then went on to describe the elephant in the circus.

'I hear that she is to get married soon. Is that so?' Tipu had enquired.

It took Salim some time and help from Tipu to discover whether the question was about the marriage of the circus elephants or of his aunt Ruqayya. Still, as soon as the mystery was cleared, he was quite informative.

'Aunt Ruqayya! No, she is never going to marry a man,' Salim had said, 'she is waiting for a tiger to marry her.'

'A tiger to marry her!' Tipu had laughed in disbelief. 'Are you sure?'

'Yes,' Salim had responded. 'It is a secret between her and me. No one else knows it.'

'Do tell me,' coaxed Tipu.

The know-all Salim knew the sanctity of keeping a secret but surely one could not hide it from so lovable an uncle like Tipu Sultan. He looked around and flinging a pebble at a nearby sparrow and squirrel so that they might not be around to overhear, he unfolded his tale in a whisper.

'You know, Uncle, she herself told me, after grandma and my father had scolded her sternly for not agreeing to get married, that once—many years ago—a prince met her in a boat. He came to her house to marry her. So charming was the prince, so handsome, so brave and so strong that a magician became jealous and cast a spell on him. Thereupon, the prince turned into a tiger and went to the forests to roam. She is now waiting for him to come back. Every now and then, the wicked magician comes in different disguises and sends her a proposal of marriage. Grandmother and father try to persuade her in vain and then leave her in anger. But she is only waiting for her tiger. She will marry none else.'

Little Salim had much more to say and on many other things. Tipu kissed him gently. It was a kiss intended for another—the girl he had met in the boat fourteen years earlier and in whose house he had passed one enchanted night. The vision of that brave, beautiful girl rose before him, giving shape and substance to his dreams and emotions that had stirred within him ever since that night. Silently, Tipu sat while Salim kept chattering away until Salim's father Burhan-ud-din came to collect his son. Tipu had always been specially friendly to Ruqayya's brother Burhan-ud-din. Now he embraced him. Burhan-ud-din was pleasantly surprised.

'I hope Salim has not been misbehaving,' he said.

'Misbehaving!' Tipu smiled, 'You have no idea of how much he has helped me—and of how grateful I am.'

Burhan-ud-din was puzzled but asked no questions. Tipu put his hand on Burhan-ud-din's shoulder.

'My father and I,' said Tipu, 'have been indebted to your late father. For you, we both have a special friendship. Would you object, Burhan-ud-din Mian, if our friendship became even closer—and came into a near-relationship?'

'It would be an honour, Sultan—an honour beyond our dreams,' Burhan-ud-din respectfully replied, but without fully understanding the drift of Tipu's observations.

'Begum Fakhr-un-Nissa will speak to your mother further,' Tipu said.

Burhan-ud-din thanked him and left happy but mystified.

Tipu went to his mother's chamber. Hyder Ali was also there, extolling the virtues of Raushan Begum, the girl he had chosen as the bride for his son. Fakhr-un-Nissa who had already enthusiastically agreed with the choice of her husband, put her arm around Tipu as soon as he entered and asked him to listen carefully to his father.

'I have decided, Sultan,' said Hyder Ali sternly, as if to silence a protest or quell an uprising for he knew how his son objected to getting married, 'that you shall marry, now.'

'Such is my wish also, Father,' replied Tipu calmly.

Hyder's eyebrows went up in delighted surprise. Fakhr-un-Nissa's arm around Tipu tugged more firmly. This was the first time that Tipu had given such a positive response to the idea of marriage.

'Very well, my son.' Hyder's tone was no longer sharp and strident but gentle and contented. 'You are to marry Raushan Begum, daughter of Imam Saheb Bakshi and sister of Ghulam Husain Khan, the Pondicherry Nawab. I have promised.'

'Forgive me, Father,' softly Tipu replied, 'but, if you permit, I have something to say.'

The dark clouds reappeared on Hyder's eyebrows while Tipu told of his wish to marry Ruqayya Banu, daughter of Lala Mian and sister of Burhan-ud-din. Fakhr-un-Nissa had already begun to nod approvingly.

Hyder who knew that he could rely on Fakhr-un-Nissa's full and undivided loyalty in all matters except where they concerned Tipu's wishes, was reduced to pleading. Plaintively, he repeated: 'But Raushan Begum's father has my word for it. I have promised.'

'But Tipu is promised to another,' Fakhr-un-Nissa remarked.

Hyder Ali glared at his wife and said, 'Madam, Hyder Ali does not break his word—neither as a man nor as a sovereign.' Turning to Tipu, he asked, 'Would you like that your father breaks his solemn promise?'

'No, Father,' was the brave though agonised answer.

Tipu knew that thereafter there had been many conversations and several meetings between Hyder Ali and Fakhr-un-Nissa on the subject. Hyder's decision was unalterable. He thought highly of Tipu's choice of Ruqayya Banu and would have given his blessings readily and happily but he was not prepared to break his word to Imam Saheb whose household had in fact already begun to rejoice and celebrate. Still, Hyder had seen the appeal in Fakhr-un-Nissa's eyes and though it sometimes infuriated him, it also had its softening effect. Tipu wore an expression of calmness and resignation as if he was ready to set stones in his heart and seal it in order to accept his father's command. Hyder capitulated but only partly. He suggested—nay, dictated—a compromise. Tipu was a Muslim and entitled to marry four wives. Let him marry two—Raushan Begum for his father's sake and Ruqayya Banu for his own. Let the marriage to Raushan Begum be in name only, while Ruqayya could be his true and real wife, if he so wished although Raushan Begum would be equally entitled to all the respect, dignity, position and wealth due to the wife of a crown prince.

So, it came to pass that on the same evening in the spring of 1774, Tipu was married to two girls—one of them was Ruqayya, the girl who had brought the basket to the boat and the girl who had been in his dreams for the last fourteen years. Ruqayya was slender and beautiful when she had first met him. She was slender and beautiful when she married. In the depth of her eyes was the same glint of smiles as in the waters of a deep well.

There was little that Ruqayya and Tipu said to each other on the marriage night. Quietly they lay in their nuptial bed, their thoughts wandering to re-enact the dreams of their past and thence to return to the warmth of the soft-lit bed chamber while the distant music could still be heard. They moved gently and unhurriedly, and together they stitched the night into an unbroken tapestry of love and fulfilment. He knew that the memory of that night would last him beyond eternity. Clearly, he remembered how time had stood still and how their hearts had stopped beating each time their lips met. No, he would never forget her first cry of pain, joy and ecstacy!

Sitting in the tent and waiting for the morning to break when Purnaiya would rejoin him, Tipu Sultan remembered that night. He thought of his lovely wife—so full of laughter and surprises, and so abundant, spontaneous in her passion. When he had parted from her to join the campaign against Colonel Humberstone, she was expecting her third child. Not even her third confinement had dimmed her loveliness. She seemed younger and more radiant than before, a shining thing of innocence and gentleness.

'You will come back soon?' Ruqayya Banu had asked at the moment of parting.

Tipu kissed her silently, without answering. He knew it was more a prayer than a question, for who knows, how long a campaign would last—and how it would end!

'You will forget me, as soon as you are gone,' Ruqayya repeated.

'Never.'

'You say so now, when I am in your arms.'

'Believe me,' teased Tipu, 'I find you as attractive in my dreams as I find you in the flesh.'

Ruqayya laughed, through her tears of farewell. She then left his embrace and looked into his eyes intently with mock seriousness.

'Really!' she asked. 'You do remember me in your dreams? Me, an old girl!'

'Your eyes, when you look at me, are far from old and I am glad of it,' said Tipu, scrutinising her as if he was inspecting a piece of merchandise, 'but no hasty judgements, let me feel the rest of you.'

He pulled her back into his arms and with an air of solemnity began his probings, kissing and feeling her on the forehead, lips, neck and breasts.

'Do not despair, dear one, but I fear that much waiting is ahead of you before your youth departs,' was his verdict.

He did not know what her silent thought was. Sadness had come into her smiling eyes. Much waiting is ahead of me—she was thinking—before my husband returns. When the moment of parting had come, they faced each other like shy lovers, in silence. 'God be with you,' Tipu had uttered the traditional words of farewell while mounting his horse,

Dilkush the Second. 'God and you; I need both. Both,' softly Ruqayya had whispered. Tipu heard her.

Thus they had parted. Ever since they were married, life had been almost an endless series of farewells—with one campaign after another, claiming Tipu's presence. Both father and son had been constantly in action, protecting and strengthening the boundaries of the kingdom. Now that his father was dead and the greedy English eyes would be fixed on Mysore all the more intently, he wondered how much time he would have for Ruqayya and his children! He knew that his concern for the kingdom would not allow him to come close to his family. He must almost forsake them, if he was to be king in his father's place. He would have to struggle long and hard to keep the ambitions of the enemy at bay and this would absorb every moment of his life. He knew also what was required of kings in those cruel and rapacious times. He must prove his fitness for supreme power. Not only must he remain denied of family affection and forsake alliances of blood and marriage but he must be invested with supreme and unrestrained power. Tipu knew of the absolute power wielded by monarchs, sometimes used in a good cause but more often employed corruptly. He knew how morally ravaged many kings and chieftains had become as a result of unrestricted authority invested in them. If the ruler could punish, he could punish unjustly and thereby degrade himself.

'Could a king,' he wondered, 'exercise unlimited power and yet be neither cruel nor callous but just and merciful?' Yes, he could think of many such shining examples from the history of India but he feared that this could not be in the evil war-torn times that lay ahead. Kings must learn to stifle their remorse, restrain their sympathy and grow more and more lonely.

'Why, why must I live in such awful isolation, imprisoned by an ambition which is not of my seeking, unable to pronounce the words that are in my heart and afraid to show my heart to those that I love?' Tipu asked himself.

As if in reply, the memory of Ruqayya's smile came to him, bringing instant calm to his turbulent mind.

32

THE SULTAN REMEMBERS

TIPU SULTAN REMAINED IN THE REALM OF HIS DAYDREAMS, with pictures of the past flashing before his mind's eye. He remembered his sense of wretchedness when he had to part with his religious teachers—Goverdhan Pandit and Maulvi Obedullah—and he had been persuaded by Hyder Ali to go to wars with him. He who had initially been trained for a life of peace, piety and asceticism, was at the age of fifteen sent out to have his first taste of the blood and bustle of battle.

Balam, a hilly town lying to the south of Bednur on the borders of Coorg, had provided the setting for Tipu Sultan's first experience of warfare. Its ruler had offended Hyder Ali by raiding Seringapatam territory. Tipu was ordered to accompany his father on the campaign but he was also cautioned to remain well in the rear under the protection of Ghazi Khan, his military perceptor. Hyder had this advice for him: 'Remain at the back of the headquarters. Just watch the battle grow, from the distance. Grumble away at my caution, by all means, but do not come near where the bullets are flying or the bayonets are flashing. Later expound to me what you would have done in my place but while the battle is on, keep your distance.'

Ghazi Khan with two thousand troops was told to remain around Tipu Sultan so that no harm came to him. Hyder Ali had promised to send a courier to Tipu Sultan every hour to inform him of the progress of the battle. Three hours had passed. Not a single courier had arrived. Hyder had forgotten. Fighting in the meantime had developed in the thickly wooded forest. Hyder's banner, visible for some time, had disappeared amongst the tall trees. Ghazi Khan became anxious, Tipu, more so. Leaving five hundred troops behind with Tipu, Ghazi Khan left with fifteen hundred to reinforce Hyder Ali. Another hour passed. In the thick of the battle and heavy resistance from the ruler of Balam, neither Hyder Ali nor Ghazi Khan sent any messages. Tipu ordered his five hundred to follow him. Avoiding the direct route, he led his men into a semi-circle and making a flanking move entered the middle of the forest. Then he backtracked to where he thought the battle was raging. Suddenly, he came to a sharp halt He was face-to-face with the hideout where the ladies of the household of the ruler of Balam were concealed along with their escort. The nonchalance and abandon with which Tipu's little army had burst upon the hide-out was such that the zenana guards had no doubt that they had to deal with Hyder Ali's main army. Those who could not run away and hide themselves in the forest surrendered. The wife of the ruler of Balam with her infant son, three daughters and other ladies came forward and sought Tipu's protection. Tipu dismounted, bowed to the ladies and assured them of their safety and honour. It took only a little time for the news to reach six miles away, where the ruler of Balam was furiously defending himself against Hyder Ali's onslaughts. In the midst of this gallant defence, Hyder was surprised, suddenly, to see the white flag of surrender going up in the Balam camp. Was it some sort of a ruse, he wondered. No, the ruler of Balam was riding alone towards him to surrender personally. Soon, he laid down his turban on the ground at the feet of Hyder's horse in token of submission and pleaded for the release of the members of his household, which surprised Hyder all the more. The battle had ceased all along the line. Maqbool Khan, one of Hyder Ali's commanders, darted with his body of troops towards the thick of the forest to unravel the mystery. There, he came upon Tipu Sultan and his five hundred men in command, standing at some distance from the zenana tent. He waved his congratulations to Tipu and went right into the tent, dragging the frightened wife of the ruler of Balam out, while his soldiers stood by, ready to seize other helpless victims so that all of them could be taken in a victory parade before Hyder Ali who would no doubt reward those who had brought such prizes. Tipu called upon Maqbool Khan to desist. Maqbool smiled with the contemptuous familiarity of an old soldier but did not release the captive. By then, the three princesses and other ladies were also being dragged out. Tipu repeated the command. Maqbool ignored him altogether. Tipu Sultan lifted his gun and shot Maqbool Khan through the head. The soldiers released the sobbing women who rushed back into the tent. Silence reigned.

This was the first time that Tipu Sultan had killed a man. He walked to the dead body of Maqbool Khan. Respectfully, Maqbool's soldiers retreated, as Sultan came forward. Tipu watched the dead figure lying in the dust. The grin still remained on the lifeless face. One eye was smeared with blood but the other was open. It stared at him as if in astonishment. Tipu Sultan placed Maqbool's inert hand in his own. Was it to check the pulse or to say farewell, no one knew. He bent his ear on the dead man's chest, then stood up and looking far beyond the men around him, said, 'Forgive me.' Was he addressing Maqbool? None knew.

Tipu asked for a blanket. It came from the zenana tent. He covered the dead body.

In the years that had followed, many were slain in the wars that Tipu Sultan had to wage. The inexorable march of history was to lead to a bloodstained thread of countless graves. Yet, the memory of the first man he had killed lived with Tipu Sultan for ever, eating at his heart like fire.

Ghazi Khan, his military teacher, had soon arrived on the scene. He had Maqbool Khan's body removed. Shortly thereafter, Hyder Ali also reached. Along with him was the main body of the army as also the prisoners including the ruler of Balam.

Hyder embraced his son and congratulated him for his capture of the household of the ruler which led immediately to the surrender, saving Hyder any further anxious moments as to the outcome of the battle.

'Name your price,' Hyder had said.

'Price!' Tipu had wondered.

'Ransom, my son, ransom,' Hyder explained. 'I have agreed to release the ruler and his men and also restore to him his territory in exchange for fifty camel-loads of treasure. This is the reparation he must make. But these,' continued Hyder pointing to the zenana tent, 'are your prisoners. You alone must name the price for releasing them.'

'They are women and children, Father,' said Tipu, almost in an accusing tone.

'So?' asked Hyder with a smile. 'Are they to be released free?'

'Yes, Father, and with honour, if you permit,' pleaded Tipu.

'So be it,' Hyder replied, pleased with his son's answer and added sententiously, 'Hyder Ali never waged war against women and children, nor shall his son. Here, Balam,' continued Hyder waving, to his erstwhile foe, 'take these prisoners away, free and with honour, by the grace of my son and heir, Tipu Sultan.'

The ruler of Balam came forward, and bowed before Tipu, 'I bowed to your father in fear,' he said, I bow to you in respect.'

'Go in peace,' Tipu replied, absent-mindedly with the memory of dead Maqbool's face.

That night, Hyder Ali learnt of the circumstances of Maqbool Khan's death.

'I shall mourn Maqbool,' he said, 'for I do not have a bigger rascal nor a merrier fellow in my entire outfit. But what my son did was right. Is it not so, Purnaiya?'

'He was honour-bound to protect his prisoners. You would have done no less. Maqbool deserved to die.'

'Yes,' Hyder had agreed with sadness.

(ii)

Tipu remembered vividly also the battles and wars that came thereafter. One action followed another in swift succession and both father and son had to fight ceaselessly to face the imperial designs of the English. Tipu emerged as a dashing, daring and successful leader of light horse. Still Hyder Ali, timorous where his son was concerned, had charged Ghazi Khan, his military tutor, to keep a strict eye on Tipu and to ensure his personal safety 'whatever the outcome of the battle.' Despite the success at Balam and rejoicing over Tipu's exploit there, Ghazi Khan had received from Hyder Ali a terrible tongue-lashing for leaving Sultan to join the main army.

Tipu's real test as an independent military commander came when he was seventeen. The year was 1767 and the occasion was the Anglo-Mysore war forced on Hyder Ali by the English after their emissaries had given every assurance of peaceful intentions. Quickly and treacherously, however, the English were at work and formed an alliance with the Nizam of Hyderabad and the Marathas. Suddenly, almost without a warning, war clouds gathered and the guns boomed. Hyder Ali hardly had a chance against the formidable triple alliance. Also, he had set too much store by the assurances given to him by the English while they were feverishly preparing for war. He did not lose heart but prepared to face the challenge. First, he succeeded in breaking the alliance. The Marathas agreed with him that their treacherous friend of today would be their treacherous enemy of tomorrow and made a separate peace with Hyder Ali. To the Nizam, he had sent Tipu as his ambassador. This was Tipu's diplomatic debut and he had accomplished it with poise and finesse. He had succeeded in impressing the Nizam and in detaching him from the coalition with the English. The English were thus isolated from their allies but their preparations had been well made. They had collected a huge army and their arsenals were bursting. No longer could Hyder Ali and his son fight side by side. Each had to supplement the efforts of the other in different theatres of war.

Hyder Ali faced the main English armies while Tipu Sultan with a small force of cavalry with light armour and irregular infantry was ordered to remain in contact merely to 'harass the English troops and to create a diversion'. Accompanied by Ghazi Khan, Mir Ali Raza Khan and Makhdum Saheb, Tipu marched southwards. Volunteers joined him on the way—men whose homes had been plundered by the English, whose wells had been poisoned, whose crops had been burnt and who had been uprooted from their native soil. Tipu's small force—though swollen now somewhat with the enlistment of volunteers—reached the very gates of Madras. The English troops fled in consternation. The English Governor himself narrowly escaped. When Tipu's horsemen arrived, the Governor was in the East India Company's magnificent garden villa near the beach. In a special room called the 'Love Chamber' which was exclusively reserved for the Governor and his guests, he was merrily drinking away while the dancing girls performed. He and his companions had barely managed to get away to a small vessel lying offshore.

Meanwhile, peremptory summons had come to Tipu Sultan to come immediately to the rescue of Hyder Ali who had suffered a defeat at Tiruvannamalai in South Arcot. Madras was now ready to fall into Tipu Sultan's grip but the message from Hyder for aid was far too urgent. He retraced his steps. Opposing his swift passage towards Hyder's main army was another English army under Col Todd and Major Fitzgerald. Tipu quickly outmanoeuvred them and succeeded in joining Hyder Ali, ten miles from Vaniyambadi. With Tipu's arrival, it was as if a new surge of life had entered into Hyder Ali. Here he had lain tired, wounded in spirit and humiliated by his defeat at Tiruvannamalai. Tipu was welcomed as a hero.

'In your safety lies my happiness and in your victories, my only consolation,' said Hyder to Tipu after the father and son had joyously embraced each other.

Hyder Ali had also embraced Ghazi Khan and thanked him for looking after his son.

'Thanks are due from me, Hyder Ali Khan, your son saved my life twice, not I his,' was the veteran's reply.

The delighted Hyder heard the account of Ghazi Khan's discomfiture on two occasions when he had been personally rescued by Tipu Sultan. Then he insisted that Ghazi Khan should tell him, from beginning till end, the account of Tipu's campaigns. 'Go slowly,' Hyder urged. 'Pleasure such as this must be sipped like fine wine, not swallowed at a single draught.'

'It is beginning to dawn on me,' said Hyder finally, after Ghazi Khan had concluded the tale, 'that the valour of youth outshines the experience of age.'

(iii)

Thereafter, the father and son had fought side by side. Tipu assisted his father in capturing the two forts at Tiruppatur and Vaniyambadi. Later, Hyder Ali was about to be trapped at Vaniyambadi when the English main army attacked it under Col Smith. Tipu rushed to the scene just in time, swept round and attacked the English flank, as Kirmani puts it, 'like a lion springing on a herd of deer, and sank the boats of their existence in the whirlpool of eternity'.

The year had ended with the defection of Nizam of Hyderabad who changed sides again. Treachery was becoming a compelling habit with him. Tipu Sultan's earlier visit to him had kept him aloof from the English for a year. Thereafter, he switched over to the English and in February 1768, he signed a treaty of defensive and offensive alliance with them against Hyder Ali. The threat to Mysore was real. Hyder Ali was getting worried. He longed for peace but knew that he could bargain with the English only from a position of strength. His only solace lay in the resounding victories that his son was achieving. Hyder Ali decided to wait before suing for peace so that in the interval a major victory or two by Tipu might improve his prospects for securing better terms. Tipu Sultan, however, exceeded all his expectations. He bad kept the Nizam's forces at bay. His lightning marches and manoeuvres had kept the English guessing and harassed. Later, he defeated the English army under Col Smith, thereafter another army under Gavin and Watson. He occupied Mangalore and expelled the English from Malabar. The stage was now set for a decisive thrust by father and son towards Madras. Soon, the outskirts of the city were in the hands of Hyder's forces and from there Hyder sent a message to the English Governor of Madras calling upon him to discuss a truce to pave the way for peace. He even dictated to the English who their negotiator should be. He nominated the English Council Member, Josias du Pre, for the peace talks. Later, when Hyder Ali was asked the reason for picking up an English negotiator, unknown to him, he had said, 'Well, the man carries a French-sounding name. Maybe, with the name, he has imbibed some traditions of French honour and gallantry. In any case, he would be better than an Englishman with an English name.' In March 1769 the peace treaty was signed. Hyder Ali was in a strong position. The city of Madras lay before him; facing him was the irresolute English Governor and the English forces thrice defeated by Tipu Sultan. Still, he did not demand his pound of flesh and dictated a treaty equally favourable to both sides. An English cartoonist, with a sense of humour, who was on a short visit to Madras, had drawn a caricature well before the peace talks had begun. It was a derisive drawing in which the Governor and his Council were represented as on their knees before Tipu Sultan and Hyder Ali who held the Governor's nose, drawn in the shape of an elephant's trunk which poured forth gold and diamonds, while the English Commander-in-Chief was shown holding the treaty in hand, and breaking his sword in two. Thus did the English cartoonist foresee the outcome of the peace negotiations. But Hyder Ali was not keen to drive a hard bargain. He did not wish to sow the seeds of further discord with the English and hankered after a lasting peace, though in his heart of hearts, a suspicion lingered that the English would break their word—as indeed they did, ever so often.

(iv)

It was, Tipu remembered, at the conclusion of the Anglo-Mysore war that he was elevated and became entitled to his own battle flag and banner that carried the emblem of the tiger.

During the four years of his military career, Tipu Sultan had already chalked up several brilliant victories to his credit. The army he had led swore by him to the man. They were astounded by his success.

'He is lucky,' they had said, for how else would one so young succeed against experienced commanders. To begin with, Tipu had permitted himself to be persuaded by the views of his senior advisers. Later, he had come into his own and did not hesitate to discuss and even overrule, though always with gentleness and without rancour. Through marches and counter-marches, through advances and retreats, through manoeuvres, onslaughts, attacks and defence, they had learned something of the commander that led this motley task force composed of veterans and volunteers.

They knew, their commander—Tipu Sultan—was courageous in adversity, resolute in war, prudent in decision, full of fortitude, fearless, temperate and honourable. They were proud of him. The veterans did sometimes grumble at the honour and attention their commander bestowed on mere volunteers who had recently joined his cause. They did not understand what exactly their commander meant when he said that they must instil a sense of patriotisim—a sense of nationalism—particularly in those who had been uprooted by the English. He had many foibles, enough to make another commander unpopular. He would not permit the pillage or plunder of the towns that fell to his army. He would not permit the execution of a single man when hostilities were over, except anyone caught molesting women or children. The prisoners were to be treated with humanity and gentleness, he had insisted. They tolerated him, he knew, and tolerated what they considered his strange and meaningless orders on such matters. It was a small price to pay to gain peace with the commander who led them from one victory to another where the lawful prizes themselves were compensation enough.

Formally, the war with the English was over. But not really. The English began mustering their forces for a further onslaught on Mysore. Meanwhile, they encouraged the Marathas and later the Nizam to declare war on Hyder Ali. This war which began in 1769 subsided in 1772 but erupted again thereafter. The English also kept arming and activating the chieftains and rulers of nearby territories to raid and harass Mysore. It was Tipu Sultan who had to bear the brunt of these attacks. Day in and day out, he was fighting, here, there and everywhere. Sometimes it was a major battle, often a skirmish, more often a sortie to cause disruption in the enemy ranks. He besieged Sira and after a prolonged siege captured it. He attacked Maddagiri, Gurramkonda, Chennarayadurga and Huskote and captured them. He rushed to his father's assistance in conquering Bellary and Chitaldrug and also occupied Hubli.

Thus by 1778, Tipu Sultan had succeeded in re-conquering for the Kingdom of Mysore all territories up to the Tungabhadra and also the part that lay between the Tungabhadra and the Krishna. The English forces had not remained on the sidelines. They had succeeded in routing and plundering several Mysore detachments. Surprise attacks by the English were the order of the day. The Mysoreans must be harassed and harried at all costs was their aim. They had supplied arms and men to those fighting the Mysoreans. They had done all they could, short of declaring a formal war, to frustrate Hyder Ali and Tipu Sultan and to assist their enemies.

(v)

The moment had come when father and son could look forward to an era of tranquillity and rest. Tipu remembered with nostalgia the year 1778. They were at peace with the Marathas. The Marathas would not break their word and would always, Hyder hoped, abide by the terms of the treaty, for treachery had never been a part of the Maratha State policy. The Nizam had been taught a lesson. In any case, he was a coward and lacked the daring to act on his own. True, he could be swayed by whosoever blew hardest upon him and the voice he followed was the one he heard last. Still, there was nothing to fear from him, not immediately at least. Others who had been encouraged and assisted by the English to raid and harass the Kingdom of Mysore had been repulsed beyond the borders.

But father and son were both wrong. There was to be no peace. The English were determined—more than ever before—to bring about the downfall of the house of Hyder. On this the English knew depended the expansion if not survival of their empire in India which could not coexist with the independent Kingdom of Mysore. Their preparations were complete, intensified by the memory of bitter defeats which Tipu Sultan had inflicted on them in the first Anglo-Mysore war. They redoubled their provocations and thus began the second Anglo-Mysore war in 1880.

A huge English army had been assembled under Sir Hector Munroe at Conjeevaram. The troops at Guntur under Colonel William Baillie were to join him there.

Baillie had reached the north bank of the river Kortalaiyar on the evening of 25 August. It would take Tipu Sultan some time to muster his forces to meet the enemy. Meanwhile, his three scouts watched the scene from a distance. They had his instructions, clear and precise. Baillie could see clearly from the north bank of the river several small fires burning beyond the south bank and it did seem as if there had been an effort to conceal them from view. In the fading light of the late evening, he could also discern some movement on the south bank—a man running here and there, sometimes two, and at times even three. Once or twice, he saw them running with a fire torch as if carrying messages from one tent to another. The river bed was almost dry. Baillie could have easily crossed it. But the stealthy movement on the southern bank worried him. Would he be walking into a trap? he wondered. He decided to wait till the morning when he would have a clear view of the situation. Until then, he would camp on the north bank.

The next morning ushered in a beautiful sunrise and a cloudless sky. There was stillness on the south bank and beyond, with no sign of activity. Tipu's three scouts had disappeared and the fires they had lit the night before had died out. But Baillie had many days to admire the view, for the river, as Tipu had expected, became flooded at night and it was not until 3 September that Baillie's troops could cross it. By then Tipu Sultan had arrived at the scene and began harassing Baillie. Sir Hector Munroe sent additional reinforcements to Baillie. Colonel Fletcher also joined him with an additional one thousand men. Baillie's original force of six thousand men had swollen considerably and Tipu with his slender force of 1,500 men could at best engage only in harassing tactics. On 9 September, Hyder's reinforcement of three thousand men arrived. More were promised but Tipu could not wait if he had to stop Baillie's rendezvous with Munroe.

Tipu attacked on the following day—10 September. He had, through his scouts, kept a sharp eye on the ammunition which the English had placed behind a ravine before the battle began. Tipu ordered his artillery to aim at it and soon one after another the English tumbrils were blown up, causing consternation amongst the English forces and jubilation amongst the Mysoreans. In the confusion that followed, Tipu Sultan, personally, led the charge of the Mysore cavalry. Men, metal and horses clashed with one another. The cries of the wounded and the dying rent the sky as their bodies were crushed into the mud. Disfigured corpses, trampled by horses lay all along the battlefield. For a while, none of the combatants knew how the battle was progressing and in whose favour. After a while, the chaos of the battle took a more ordered shape. The English ranks were broken and some of their troops were fleeing. Still the resistance was strong. Baillie and Fletcher were rallying the demoralised English. Baillie would not surrender. It was clear to him that the Mysoreans had attacked with a smaller force. Tipu led a fresh cavalry charge. The slaughter began. By then, Hyder Ali through forced-marches had also reached the scene of the battle with 1,500 cavalry troops. As his troops came into view, a cheer went up from the English who thought that Munroe's reinforcement had arrived to rescue them. Hyder wanted to wait until next day when more of his troops could arrive to match with his estimate of the English forces but Tipu begged for instant action, pointing to the disorganisation of the English troops and the possibility of Munroe's troops arriving shortly. Hyder charged with his cavalry. In the meanwhile, Tipu had collected his troops together and renewed his cannonade. The English ammunition was now getting short due to Tipu having blown up their tumbrils earlier. The sudden appearance of Hyder Ali had also added to their panic for they did not know that he had arrived only with a small force. Col Baillie put up the flag of truce.

Altogether two thousand English were taken prisoners along with Baillie, five thousand were killed and the remainder had scattered. The Mysorean losses were also heavy. Of their total force of six thousand, they had lost 2,500. There were many others who had lost a limb or an eye.

While Hyder Ali had been jubilant, Tipu had surveyed the scene with sadness. It was a harrowing spectacle. Anguish and death were the fruits of war, he said to himself.

(vi)

The battle of Pollilur in which Tipu Sultan had routed Col Baillie's forces on 10 September 1780, was regarded by the British as the 'severest blow that the English ever sustained in India'. Sir Hector Munroe was sharply criticised for not rushing to Baillie's rescue for he was barely six miles away at Conjeevaram with the main English army. His scouts had, however, given him a correct estimate of the Mysorean detachments and how was he, he exclaimed repeatedly in self-defence, to suspect that Bailie with his superior forces would succumb to the Mysorean force of six thousand! How indeed, was he to know that Baillie was in mortal danger! His scouts had given him the figures of Tipu's army but who was to tell him in advance of the boldness and enterprise with which Tipu Sultan would charge at the enemy!

Baillie had been wounded. Tipu had accepted his surrender on the battlefield and complimented him on the gallant defence, assuring him that his defeat was but the fortune of war. A palanquin was ordered and Tipu assisted Baillie towards it. In the effort, Baillie's wound, bandaged though it was, began to bleed and some of his blood was smeared on Sultan's sleeve. Baillie courteously apologised.

'Do not apologise,' the Sultan said. 'It is gallant blood,' and then after a long pause, looking at his sleeve, added 'it has the same colour as my blood.'

Baillie had looked surprised, as if wondering why such a highly educated man like Tipu Sultan should make a statement which was so self-evident.

At Tipu's command, stretchers were prepared for the more seriously wounded prisoners. Five palanquins were earmarked for officers amongst them. The English had lost their doctor—Doctor Hopkins—in the battle. Tipu's doctors took over the care of the wounded on both sides. Tipu and Hyder Ali had fought many battles but never before had they seen so much bloodshed in such a restricted area of action. Even Hyder Ali, normally indifferent to the sufferings of the enemy in battle, was visibly moved. Biscuits and water were distributed on the field itself. Later, in the improvised sheds the attendants came with a supply of wine and bread. Urgent summons were sent for clothing and the other needs of prisoners. Surgeons were sent for.

Later, Tipu Sultan had heard of the calumny heaped on him and his father regarding indifference to the care of the prisoners. The English had gone even to the extent of circulating rumours and publishing pamphlets to show that he had been cruel to them. Tipu had merely shrugged his shoulders at such fabrications. He knew of the blow which English prestige had suffered through his victory over Baillie. Naturally, they would like the battle to be remembered not so much as the one that led to a brilliant victory of Mysorean arms but as one in which a cruel and fanatical prince mercilessly slaughtered English soldiers even after the flag of truce had been hoisted. Thus had the English sought to divert attention from their defeat and disgrace to their fanciful image of a cold-blooded and horrifying tyranny. Did the English know, Tipu wondered, that he had suffered in spirit as much as the wounded prisoners had in flesh? After a moment's reflection, however, he dismissed the question from his mind by asking himself, 'What arrogance is this that I should seek to judge the suffering of another!'

Be that as it may, Baillie's guns and stores did not reach the expectant Munroe who had waited at Conjeevaram. Meanwhile, Hyder Ali's army was being reinforced. Munroe feared immediate pursuit and he marched back to Madras in haste abandoning the stores and throwing his heavy guns which he could not carry, into the Conjeevaram tank. Hyder Ali sent Tipu in hot pursuit with light cavalry. Tipu wiped out the English rearguard and captured the whole of Munroe's luggage. Munroe himself reached safely with most of his troops at Marmalong, four miles south of Madras. Hyder Ali recalled Tipu Sultan to capture Arcot. The Arcot garrison surrendered to him after a siege and fierce fighting which lasted for six weeks. The next to surrender to Tipu's arms was the strong fort of Satghur, almost without a fight. At Ambur the English garrison under Captain Keating fought for four weeks before capitulating. Thereafter, Tipu captured Tiagar whose English garrison had fought under Captain Roberts for over a month. Week after week, other forts had also fallen to Tipu's arms. During this campaign thousands had surrendered to him. They were received with utmost gentleness and the wounded amongst them were given the most humane treatment along with immediate medical aid.

After consolidating his gains, Tipu joined his father at Arcot to be received like a hero. He was given a brief period of leave to be with Ruqayya but ordered soon—in February 1782—to proceed to Tanjore, where he inflicted a crushing defeat on the English commander, Col Braithwaite—comparable in brilliance to his defeat of Baillie's forces. After a furious struggle lasting for two days, Braithwaite surrendered. This was also one of those numerous occasions when tribute was paid to Tipu's humane treatment of prisoners. He not only personally supervised their medical attention, food and clothes but also gave strict instructions to his officers to treat the prisoners with courtesy and gentleness.

Tipu Sultan saw the wounded enemy soldiers lying in pools of blood. A shudder passed through him. Often, as his men would pick them up to lift them on to the stretchers, Tipu would plead: 'Gently, gently, please move him gently.' It was as if Tipu Sultan suffered more than the wounded soldiers.

In that moment, he had forgotten that they were the soldiers of the enemy. No, it was the cry of one human being sharing the agony of another.

Tipu Sultan's troops had often cheered him. On this occasion he was cheered by the prisoners with a spontaneity which touched his heart. He released the ailing and the wounded with presents. He released also those who gave parole never to fight against the Kingdom of Mysore. Many of them broke their word later, Tipu came to know. He also came to know that some of them had falsely spread rumours about his cruelty to prisoners. Tipu Sultan disdained to deny the rumour. It amused him though that no one had said that he saw him acting cruelly. Each had pleaded that he was quoting another.

(vii)

A host of memories surged up and intermingled in Tipu Sultan's mind while he waited in the tent where Purnaiya had left him. He thought of that brief holiday with Ruqayya Banu. She had met him, her eyes brimming with happy tears, gazing at him with joyous love. Tipu saw her shining eyes which were beautiful. He heard the sound of voices behind them. He drew her to himself with gentleness. For three nights they slept in each other's arms. Then he received his marching orders. Ruqayya had promised herself that she would not cry when the moment of parting came. 'Thank you, Lord, for granting me this indulgence to be by his side for three days. I dare not ask for more,' her heart had said. Still, the tears came and the ache in her heart returned.

Tipu was ordered to proceed to Malabar where the Mysorean army had suffered reverses and his task was to aid and assist Arshad Beg Khan Jung Bahadur who was being harassed by Colonel Humberstone's forces. There he was on 7 December 1782—the night of the double retreat—when Sadhu Ram had brought him the letter from Purnaiya that his father Hyder Ali was dead.

Now he would be alone, to carry singly the burden which father and son had shared. To what end? he wondered. He knew that the battles that lay ahead would be far more terrible. Plainly, vividly and with horror, the images of the battlefield rose before him—crazed horses rampaging back and forth; the agonising cry of the wounded soldiers; stabbing, hacking, burning, pillaging; then death and silence—a silence far more shrill than the most piercing scream. He felt in his own person the sufferings he had witnessed on the field of battle. Then in his imagination, he saw himself with a naked sword seeking feverishly to draw blood from the heart of the enemy. He shuddered. The image disappeared and he now pictured himself dressed in coarse rags, walking down the dusty road from one saint's shrine to another, seeking salvation and bliss.

'Which path do I take?' he asked himself. 'Surely, not the road that lies littered with corpses under the shadow of the vultures!'

But he feared that some inner sentinel stood guard, prohibiting him to go where he wished. He prayed: 'God, I commit myself to you. Tell me what is Your Will, show me the path I must tread and teach me what to do.' He prayed, his heart yearning for an answer to his prayers.

33

A SOUL IN TORMENT

THE LONG NIGHT ENDED BUT THE VISIONS THAT ROSE ONE AFTER another before Tipu's mind did not end. The gallery of pictures before him was unending.

It was six in the morning when Purnaiya entered Tipu's tent.

Tipu Sultan sat on the rug-covered chair where Purnaiya had seen him the night before. Purnaiya could see that he had not slept. He looked at him intently, seeking in his face some explanation of what he was thinking but did not find it. Tipu Sultan's face wore a calm, peaceful expression. The eyes were tranquil and rested. For a moment, Purnaiya and Tipu Sultan did not speak to each other. Neither of them felt like breaking the silence.

'If you permit,' said Purnaiya at last, 'your breakfast can be served to you in the tent. Thereafter we could depart.'

'Let us eat together,' Tipu replied.

Purnaiya left the tent to order the food and to allow Tipu time to get dressed. After some time he re-entered and both sat down to eat. Halfway through breakfast, like a man who has secretly borne a heavy burden in his soul and suddenly decides to speak out, Tipu began to talk.

Purnaiya heard him in astonishment. The calm and peaceful expression on Tipu's face had disappeared. His face was now drawn and its every muscle quivered with impatient energy. His eyes were no longer tranquil. They had become intense, with brilliant, radiant light. The voice was forceful, commanding. But the words—oh, what was he saying? Purnaiya wondered. In themselves, they were clear, coherent and comprehensible. But could he be serious? Oh, dear God, no. Purnaiya almost wailed and kept asking himself. How can he desert his own cause? Can an emperor renounce his empire? Can a king surrender the keys of his kingdom to a timorous and frightened enemy? Why, but why? Purnaiya asked himself as Tipu recounted to him the strands of the thoughts and visions of the night before. Purnaiya raised his hand as if to stop the torrent of Tipu's narration. Each word was like a blow. Tipu understood. He gently took Purnaiya's hand into his own and said no more.

They sat facing each other, without speaking. In those silent moments, Purnaiya understood more of the solitary anguish of Tipu's heart than at any time before. Purnaiya had always known of Tipu's deep desire for commitment to God. He knew that Maulvi Obedullah and Goverdhan Pandit had inculcated in their pupil a longing for peace and truth. They had inspired in him a dream and hope for eternal joy and bliss and a state of mind in which there is neither sorrow nor sighing. Purnaiya had watched Tipu grow, rejoiced that his mother and father had steadfastly kept to the promise of offering Tipu to God's service and had grieved when Hyder felt compelled to send his son into military service. He knew that Tipu had rebelled for a while but then had been persuaded into submission. The father and son had then fought together until almost the entire burden of fighting had fallen to Tipu's lot. So brilliant had been Tipu's victories, so engrossed had he been in military activities that never for a moment had Purnaiya suspected that his heart had hungered for something else. For a fleeting moment, Purnaiya felt a thrill of joy. He himself was a Brahmin—a man of compassion, well versed in theology, sacred lore and scriptures. He had respect for kings but reverence for piety. Here was a king ready to renounce his all for the sake of piety! Purnaiya's love for Tipu, always abundant, overflowed. But no, Purnaiya said to himself, the sword had been drawn. It cannot be put back into its sheath.

Purnaiya remembered his own father, an ascetic Brahmin who loved God, man and his books. The English had stormed into his house, torn his books, broken his idols, pulled his beard and kicked him in the chest. Then they had killed a cow on his door step, smeared her blood on his person and pushed a piece of her flesh in his mouth. Three days later his father had died and his dying request to his son was to love all men. Yes, Purnaiya had said, he would love all men. But the English, he knew, were not men. They were beasts, devoid of mercy who killed and tortured in cold blood and for amusement; without hesitation they would rape women, murder children, insult Gods, burn crops and houses, leave innocents destitute and dying. No, they were not men, Purnaiya knew, but a scourge, which must be wiped out. As soon as the flames had consumed his father's dead body, the orphan Purnaiya was escorted by an English missionary to a large house where there were many children who were being brought up as Christians. He was clothed and fed. At night he had run away. He had gone to his house as if hoping that somehow his father would reappear. Then clutching at a half-burnt-out book of scriptures, he had left his house. After days and nights of wanderings he had crossed into Mysore where the English had not yet penetrated. In the pocket of his shirt which the English Missionary had given him, he had found an abridged version of the Bible. He wanted to spit on it, tear it to bits and grind it under his heel to return the insult which the English had heaped on his father's books. He restrained himself and decided to read it so that he might understand the bigoted religion of the depraved English which undoubtedly permitted such barbarism, cruelty, rape, murder and plunder. Later, he had read it and was moved to tears. His hatred of the English remained but not of their religion. He knew now that these godless men had forsaken their religion which taught universal love, respect for justice and holiness. These were the men he knew who 'would be punished with everlasting destruction from the presence of the Lord and from the glory of His power'. The message of love that the Bible taught fascinated him and he was moved by its conception of God who so loved the world, that He gave his only begotten son, that whosoever believes in Him should not perish but have everlasting life. Later, his studies matured and he came to acquire a deep knowledge of Hindu scriptures. Still, his love and respect for the Bible remained untarnished. Purnaiya broke himself away from these thoughts. Over the years Purnaiya had carved for himself a position of prominence in Mysore. He was the most trusted friend and Prime Minister of Hyder Ali. He was loved by Tipu Sultan. Hyder had placed on him the task of helping Tipu to govern the kingdom in accordance with the laws of God and morality. No, he must not fail the father or the son. He contemplated Tipu gravely. He knew he ought to come to his aid, to demolish his fears and discredit his arguments but he was afraid to begin, for somewhere in a deep corner of his heart he too believed in and cherished what Tipu Sultan held sacred—truth, goodness and renunciation. He too believed—firmly and fervently—in the divinity of God and the brotherhood of man, united in the aim of assisting each other in the path of religion and virtue. But he had a duty to perform—a duty imposed on him by Hyder Ali. He pulled himself together.

The argument between Purnaiya and Tipu Sultan began.

Purnaiya knew of Tipu's love for the country. He talked to him of the land and its people, reminding him also of its glorious heritage and of the men and women who had laid down their lives to preserve it.

'It seems to me that you are ready to forsake it,' Purnaiya said.

'Forsake it! No.' Tipu replied emphatically, and then added with gentleness, I am born of this soil. This is my native dust, the cradle of my being. Here I shall die.'

Purnaiya looked at Tipu as if dissatisfied with the answer.

'Do tell me, Purnaiya,' Tipu continued, 'is it not worthwhile to spend a serene life with my books and my thoughts than with the sword? Must I be on horseback chasing a battle when all I long for is to spend a quiet time with my wife and children? Is the call to arms mightier than the call to prayer? Is the battlefield more important than the shrine of saint? You know, Purnaiya, I love to paint but tell me if I wish to paint these native hills on my canvas, do you think I should do so with the blood of those that have been slain by me in battle?'

'You wish to paint, Sultan?' Purnaiya asked with a smile intending to divert Tipu from the serious trend of conversation.

'Yes, I wish to paint,' Tipu replied wistfully, T wish to paint the sunshine, the fresh air, the flowering trees and the blue seas but not with the colour of blood.'

Purnaiya was silent and Tipu continued, as if pleading: 'See, Purnaiya, I wish to paint the cry of faith, not the wail of the wounded; I want to bring on my canvas the dreams and yearnings of man and not his death and degradation. I wish to heal, not to kill.'

'Nevertheless,' said Purnaiya, 'a commander does not desert in the midst of a battle. A king does not forsake his duty in pursuit of his dreams.'

'You think the voice of conscience must for ever be stifled?' Tipu asked.

'The law imposes a duty on a common soldier and a subject,' Purnaiya replied. 'Are they allowed to listen to the call of their conscience and desert? Is the sovereign not subject to the same law and subordinate to the same duty? Or, is it that the common soldier alone faces the firing squad for desertion but kings and princes are free to flout the law? No, you have your obligations to fulfil and your duty to perform as much as the lowliest of your subjects.'

'And you claim to know what my duty is?' softly Tipu questioned.

'Yes, you have made a covenant with your father and your country,' was Purnaiya's answer.

'My father imposed his paternal will on me. But when did I make a covenant with the country?' Tipu asked.

'Tipu Sultan, I do not wish to tear away the veil from your heart nor invade the privacy of your soul, but tell me, did you not shed tears at the revolting cruelties and cold-blooded treachery which the English inflicted on the Indian people? Did your heart not cry out when they killed their prisoners mercilessly and barbarously—sewing Muslims in pig skins, smearing them with pork fat before execution and forcing the Hindus to defile themselves? Tell me, did not the cry of agony go out from your heart when you heard of their massacres, slaughters and plunders, when they destroyed the villages, poisoned the wells, burnt the crops and forced a degrading servitude on a peace-loving people? Yes, Sultan, you did shed tears and tell me, with those tears, did you not make a covenant with your people?'

'And what about my covenant to God, to my wife, to my children?' Tipu enquired.

'They can co-exist.' Purnaiya replied. 'Or, is it that you think that God has any use for a king who breaks his vows to his people and shirks his duty?' After a pause, Purnaiya added, 'Believe me, a king's first duty is to his people. Neither family ties nor alliances of blood relationship must intervene. Your commitment to your people precedes in point of both time and importance, your attachment to your family. Ask Ruqayya Banu, she will tell you the same. Ask her to tell you the story she told me of Dara Shukoh's wife who said she would rather die than leave her native soil.'

'Dara Shukoh's wife?' Tipu asked. 'What did Ruqayya tell you of her?'

Purnaiya was delighted that the conversation was being diverted to safer channels. He told Tipu of the story of Dara Shukoh's wife as Ruqayya Banu had narrated it. He told him first of Shah Jahan, the Moghul Emperor of India who had built magnificent buildings with fairy-like beauty representing the height of Moghul splendour and amongst them the Taj Mahal, the Pearl Mosque, the Diwan-i-Am, the Diwani-i-Khas and the Jama Masjid. Tipu, who had read history as vividly as Purnaiya, knew of the reign of Shah Jahan but allowed Purnaiya to tell the story in his own way. Purnaiya then told him how Shah Jahan's younger son, the bigoted and tyrannical Aurangzeb, seized the throne when his father's health began to fail. Shah Janan was imprisoned, denied even the commonest of conveniences and his only solace was that he could from the place of his confinement gain a distant view of his fairest creation, the Taj Mahal, where he was finally laid to rest beside his beloved consort Mumtaz Mahal. Meanwhile, the treacherous Aurangzeb had moved also against Dara Shukoh the eldest son of Shah Jahan and the lawful successor to the throne. Dara shared the liberal religious views and tolerance of his great-grandfather Akbar and was on the best of terms with Rajput princes, Jesuit Fathers and Jewish Rabbis. He was deeply interested in Hinduism and studied the doctrines of Vedanta. He had the *Atharva Veda* and the Upanishads translated into Persian with the aid of Brahmin scholars. He had studied also the Talmud and the New Testament and was indeed a scholar, a man of grace, charm and compassion but by no means a match for the cold, crafty, unscrupulous intriguer that Aurangzeb was. Dara Shukoh was on the run, pursued by Aurangzeb's army and with his was his wife, Nadira Begum, his nearest and dearest friend, his devoted and worthy helpmate. Hunted as Dara was, she accompanied him in all his wanderings from place to place—Rajputana, Cutch and Sind—but when Dara planned to cross over to Persia, she begged that she be allowed to remain in India.

'This is my land. Here my bones shall rest. What shall they do in an alien land?' she had pleaded.

Dara Shukoh wept but he also understood. Leaving his physician and an escort of soldiers behind with his wife, he pressed forward. In an hour, Nadira Begum dismissed the physician and the soldiers with instructions to join her husband whose need, she felt, was greater. Purnaiya completed the story.

'A few weeks later, she died but not amongst alien people nor on an alien soil. She did not desert.'

'1 had heard the story differently,' Tipu said. 'Nadira Begum was sick and did not want to hamper her husband's flight. She knew that her husband would not march an inch if he suspected her sickness. Her refusal to leave her native soil was only an excuse—a cloak for her sickness which she wanted to conceal from her husband lest he would delay his flight from the pursuing army.'

'I have no doubt,' replied Purnaiya with courtesy, 'that your version is more authentic than the one that Ruqayya Banu and I believe. Still, the point remains. Nadira Begum did not desert.'

Tipu's mind was on Ruqayya Banu.

'I see that Ruqayya has been entertaining you with stories,' he said.

'Oh, yes, she knows many. She told me of Jaswant Singh Rathor who fled to Jodhpur and whose proud wife shut the gates of the castle against him for retreating from the field of battle.'

Tipu did not comment on the moral of the story but said petulantly:

'See, Purnaiya, so many years I have been married to Ruqayya and so little is the time that I get with her, that I have to hear of her stories from others. Yet, you lecture me on duty. Do you think that Ruqayya Banu believes that a husband on horseback is more dutiful than a husband at home?'

'You know it as well as I do, Sultan,' said Purnaiya, 'that Ruqayya Banu is proud of her husband and proud of the cause he serves.'

A pause ensued, during which Purnaiya noticed that the food on the table had remained untouched.

'Shall I give the orders for the move?' he asked. 'It is long past the hour scheduled for departure. The army awaits you.'

'Give me time, a few days, no more,' Tipu urged.

'A few days!' Purnaiya was aghast. 'What for?'

'To silence a storm in my heart,' Tipu replied. 'To find answers to some questions that keep tossing in my mind.'

There was no time, Purnaiya pointed out to him. Hyder Ali was dead. Every possible stratagem had been employed to keep the news of his death from leaking out. But soon the

English would know. Like locusts they would try to sweep across Mysore. Traitors like Sheikh Ayaz had already hatched their conspiracies in which they had snared through bribery and blackmail some of the trusted lieutenants of Hyder Ali. Disquieting reports were coming day by day of defections and treachery. Sheikh Ayaz must be brought to book for he holds not only a strong fort but a sizable portion of the Mysore treasury.

'God is my witness,' concluded Purnaiya. 'You have not a moment to lose. You must move quickly before such rats multiply.'

Tipu smiled. 'Do you know,' he said, 'you have given me the best reason for following the inclinations of my heart. A little while ago, you imagined that I had made a covenant to the people. Now you tell me that they will go against me unless I move in to stem the tide. What about their covenant to me!'

Before Purnaiya could reply, Tipu raised his hand to silence him and said: 'Sheikh Ayaz, my father's favourite, has betrayed me, Rasool the playmate of my boyhood days has defected, our kinsman Mohammad Aramin has become a traitor, Shams-uddin Bakshi whom I once saved from a death sentence has joined my enemies. They even sought to corrupt my poor brother against me. You have shown me a long—almost endless—list of those suspected of treachery.'

Purnaiya was about to interrupt, but Tipu silenced him and continued:

'No, I bear them no grudge. I should be grateful to them. The realisation of their guilt leaves me free, without responsibility, to go my own way. I was hurt about it I know, and confused. But now I see it as a release, a breaking of the bonds of responsibility, an opportunity to advance beyond the restraint which their assumed affection had placed upon me.

So, Purnaiya, if there was a covenant, it is not I who have broken it.'

Purnaiya who had heard him calmly at first was growing angry. He controlled himself and said more in sorrow than in anger:

'Tipu Sultan, I have loved you as I would my own son. Forgive me, if for a moment I forget that you are my sovereign. You are not hypocritical nor will you deliberately utter a falsehood but I say this to you that you deceive yourself pitifully and insult the very soul of our people when you identify them with a few grasping, avaracious traitors who have betrayed you and your father. By what right do you close your eyes to the traditions of honour of your people and judge them by the standards of a few ingrates? By what right do you dishonour the God-given manhood of our people just because a few have fallen prey to lustful ambition? Would you condemn an entire nation because of one Mir Jaffar or even hundreds of them? Answer me, lest I should think that it is not merely an error that misleads you but a desire to find an excuse for your escape.'

'Escape!' Tipu asked. 'If I should seek the avenue of religion, you would call it an escape.'

'Permit me to remind you of one of your own observations,' Purnaiya shot back, 'that elements of duty, love and sacrifice are the foundation of religion. How can you then deviate from your duty?' 'And what is my duty?' Tipu asked.

'We talk in circles, Sultan, but let me repeat, your first task is to hunt out the traitors and let them have a taste of retribution. . . .'

Tipu interrupted him. 'Purnaiya, can you not see that vengeance sows vengeance, hate engenders hate and blood breeds blood! What satisfaction can revenge bring? I know that my revenge will eat at my heart like fire if I apply it to some of those with whom I have grown up.'

Meeting Purnaiya's sorrowful glance, Tipu continued, 'I know I disappoint you. You can see that I am not fitted for supreme power. Kings must be ruthless, you had once said. But, I, on the other hand, begin to see the viewpoint of those who have betrayed us. I was born to such greatness that I never needed to intrigue and to such wealth that I was never tempted to steal. But what about Sheikh Ayaz and his kind? He was raised from the gutter and I pity him for the dirt that still clings to him, but do I hate him? I wonder.'

Tipu Sultan rose from his chair and went near Purnaiya who had also risen. He put his arm around Purnaiya's shoulder.

'I know I disappoint you,' he repeated, 'but you must forgive me. My mind is in a turmoil. I need time to look at the river to seek counsel in its boundless expanse; I need time to look at the clouds floating in the heavens to discover if there is a meaning in their message.'

'Meanwhile, the enemy arms himself,' Purnaiya commented with grimness.

'What will be, will be,' Tipu said and then added, 'I need time. Above all I must go to Kolar where my father's body lies. Give me a week or ten days. I must silence the doubts that assail my heart. Then I shall know the path I have to tread.'

'Your path has already been determined, Tipu Sultan.'

'Surely, the final decision is mine, Purnaiya.'

'To speak, yes. To determine, no. You are committed to the cause of a nation in agony. God cannot will that you should abandon it.'

'Give me time,' Tipu repeated simply.

Purnaiya knew that he had much more to say. But he also knew the futility of further argument. Clearly, Tipu wanted time to set his doubts at rest. Sadly he began to discuss Tipu's immediate plans. To begin with, Tipu would visit the spot where his father's body lay. Purnaiya told him that he would possibly find Goverdhan Pandit also there. Goverdhan Pandit had met Purnaiya only the day before. They had not seen each other for several years during which Goverdhan Pandit had been wandering from place to place. He was the only one outside his immediate circle to whom Purnaiya confided the secret of Hyder's death. Goverdhan Pandit had decided to visit the place where Hyder's body lay. The prospect of meeting Goverdhan Pandit pleased Tipu immensely.

Tipu Sultan promised to meet Purnaiya on 28 December. 'By then, I shall know the path I have to take.'

They embraced each other. Tipu Sultan was moved by the tears in Purnaiya's eyes.

'If you have affection for me. . . .' Tipu began.

'Doubt anything but that,' Purnaiya interrupted.

'I know,' Tipu said, 'Therefore for the sake of that affection, I beg you to bear with me. What you said today was not in vain. The words that you uttered, I shall remember. Perhaps they alone shall show me the way. What I have said has no substance, for in my heart, I hear many voices and words. The sound of these voices and words re-echoes within me and each one seeks to pull me in a different direction.'

Purnaiya hugged him to his heart. Later, he watched him depart for Kolar where Hyder's body was temporarily rested. Purnaiya himself took a different direction to rejoin the army commanders who were waiting to greet Tipu in vain. Sombrely, Purnaiya thought of the efforts that would be necessary to continue the myth of Hyder being alive and of the measures to ward off further treachery and defection. Meanwhile, he would not tell a soul—not even the most trusted colleagues—of the seeds of conflict in Tipu's soul.

34

DO NOT LET YOUR DREAMS DIE

TIPU SULTAN HAD NOT MET GOVERDHAN PANDIT SINCE HIS twelfth birthday. That was the day on which Hyder Ali had terminated Tipu's religious training and both his teachers—Maulvi Obedullah and Goverdhan Pandit—had to part from him.

Tipu saw Goverdhan Pandit kneeling by the side of his father's grave. His eyes were closed in prayer. Tipu touched the grave with his forehead, kissed it and then sat next to Goverdhan Pandit.

It was later, much later, that Goverdhan Pandit, his eyes still closed, moved his hand to touch Tipu's. In that brief moment, Tipu Sultan felt as if he had unburdened his heart. The prolonged and measureless torment, through which his soul was passing, ceased. The noise of the tempests disappeared. The thunder of battering rams against the fort walls, the clash of steel and armour, the pitiful cries of outraged women, the wail of the wounded and the dying no longer assailed his ears.

In the evening, the two of them spoke to each other. They met as if they had not parted at all. There was no hesitation, no effort, no groping to pick up the old threads or to renew the companionship. If Goverdhan Pandit knew each step in Tipu Sultan's colourful career, there was nothing to be surprised at.

Much of it was public knowledge anyway. What was strange was that Goverdhan Pandit seemed to know even his innermost thoughts and the torments that surged within him.

They began their conversation, warmed at first by the fire that burnt in the hollow of the wall. Later, the fire went out, unnoticed. The morning arrived. They continued their conversation.

Tipu Sultan told Goverdhan Pandit of his intolerable sadness. It was the tale of a man oppressed by doubt, dread of waste, loneliness and insecurity. He who had aspired for the vision of reality and the riches of heaven, was being compelled to wage war, shed blood, slay people and meet evil with evil. His was heart-broken lament of a man who sought to live by divine principle and gain spiritual bliss; yet some inner compulsion drove him to violence and warfare. He had sought peace but was thrown into the midst of a threatening chaos. He had longed for the comfort of human affection but had to face the world as a stranger, invested with the isolation of kingly power. He had believed in piety, virtue and compassion; yet thousands died at his bidding and his heart had felt their suffering. Who would benefit by this bloody sacrifice? What goal would he reach over those dead bodies? He did not know. All he knew was that his mind was clouded, his convictions unsettled and his whole consciousness confused.

It was depression that could find no relief, restlessness that could not flow.

Tipu Sultan's tone was calm. His words were measured. Yet clearly, Goverdhan Pandit knew of his gnawing distress.

'Tell me, Tipu Sultan,' Goverdhan Pandit questioned softly though with a subtle hint of challenge. 'Have you asked yourself what it is you are after? Is it through renunciation that you seek to pursue a spiritual destiny—untrammelled by sorrows, tears and blood that surround this world?'

'Yes, that is what the voice in my heart seems to say but there is another part of my heart which tells me that I hear that voice in vain, that I must shut it out, expel it and hear it no more.'

'And this rebellious part of your heart—what role would it assign to you?' Goverdhan Pandit knew the answer but still asked.

'To stand up and fight the rapacious alien enemy who is out to disrobe and dishonour the nation.' Tipu told Goverdhan Pandit of the slaughter, butchery, vengeance and plunder by the English, of their deceit, greed and annexations, of their war against religion, honour and decency. It was the story of death and destitution, wanton and deliberate cruelty, human migrations, withering crops and starving livestock.

The tale was familiar to Goverdhan Pandit but he allowed Tipu Sultan to relate it. He knew that Tipu Sultan himself must find the answers to his own questions. No one else could resolve his doubts and conflicts. Goverdhan Pandit could help—but only up to a point—for he believed that in the final analysis each man must be regarded as the sole arbiter of his destiny, working his way to salvation and Godhood through his own efforts.

They resumed the conversation after evening prayers. They spoke of many things and many men. They spoke of the hesitation, despondency and despair through which man must pass. Clearly, the decisive issue lies in the hearts of men where battles between right and wrong are fought hourly and daily. The fight takes place every moment in the soul of man, until he is fully aware of his purpose in life. What then is the purpose of life? To achieve spiritual destiny? And is this destiny to be achieved by ceremonial worship, a chanting of prayers, a code of personal ethics, an inner piety or by total devotion to the Lord? Does devotion to the Divine involve a surrender of man's duty on earth? Are they not sinners who merely proclaim the name of the Lord and in their assumed devotion, surrender their duty on this earth, when the Lord himself has taken birth for protecting righteousness? Can man seeking a surrender to the Divine choose a path different from the one taken by the Lord? Can man obtain a release from the problems of the world or be indifferent to them, when God himself cares? Surely, then, man's purpose was to live in the world and save it. Life was, therefore, a mandate for action and none can be anchored in Eternal Spirit by mere renunciation.

For two days more, Goverdhan Pandit and Tipu Sultan passed much of their time in each other's company. They continued their discussion. Mostly, it was Tipu who spoke. Goverdhan Pandit listened, asking an occasional question here and there to clarify a doubt or pose a problem. It was not his intention to dominate the thoughts of the other nor even to influence. Each man must come to his own decision himself.

Tipu had unburdened his heart. Perhaps, that alone served to cast away his doubts. No longer was his spirit overwhelmed by sorrow. Peace was returning to an anguished soul. His mind began to resolve itself.

'No, man cannot give up,' he said. 'For the sake of an ideal, for justice and truth, for the freedom and happiness of his people, he must stand up to tyranny and face pain and death.'

The dreadful question: 'Why must I fight?' which had appeared to threaten all his spiritual longings and yearnings no longer existed for him. To that question, a simple answer was ready in his soul: 'I must fight because this is my country, my native soil and this I am honour-bound, duty-bound to defend and protect.'

They talked of men who had turned their backs on the world, happy in the hope of salvation of their souls. In their fervour for the Lord, such men had forgotten the purpose of the Lord. If instead, with all their vigour and might, they had gone out into the world, they might have done something to save it.

The conversation now took a different turn with entirely a new series of questions. Should one engage in battle when victory was uncertain? Was victory possible in the face of the formidable army that the English could command? Should not one abandon the struggle, when defeat and death was the inevitable result?

'Do you believe,' Goverdhan Pandit asked, 'that anyone who dies with honour, in the performance of his duty, dies in vain?'

If Tipu took time to answer, it was not because he had to formulate his thoughts. No, his mind went into the future—beyond the limits of the time and space of his own being and outside the level of horizon of his own life.

'No,' he replied. 'Such death cannot be in vain. Someone, somewhere, some time will pick up the fallen torch, for, once lit, it can never be extinguished.'

He was at peace now. His mind was made up. He would fight. The nation must be defended. Its honour must be preserved.

Tipu Sultan and Goverdhan Pandit said farewell to each other. Somehow both seemed to know that they would not meet again. They embraced.

'Do not let your dreams die, Tipu,' Goverdhan Pandit said in a low voice at the moment of parting.

Part V

INHERITANCE

35

THE CROWN

TIPU SULTAN REACHED CHITTOOR ON 2 JANUARY 1783 WHERE HIS army awaited him.

Sadhu Ram had reached him with the message of his father's death in four days on 7 December 1782. It had mystified many—and some still wonder about it—that Tipu should have taken twenty-six days to cover the same distance. Few knew that he had paused at Kolar by the side of his father's body to perform the religious rites and while that did not take all the time, his marathon discussions with Goverdhan Pandit did.

Purnaiya met him ten miles from the camp. The camp itself had been set up for Tipu Sultan about two miles from the main army. He entered the camp after sunset. He refused to be received with pomp and show. Seated on a plain carpet, he gave his first audience to the principal officers, receiving their condolences and compliments. Later in the night, in the presence of his senior officers and army chiefs while the Hindu priests and the Muslim Maulvis chanted their prayers, he sat on his father's throne. Pandit Durga Prasad and Maulvi Hafiz Rahman dipped their hands in the bowl which contained the holy water of the Ganges and both, together, picked up the crown resting on a jade table nearby. Step by step they went to the throne and placed the crown on Tipu Sultan's head.

Tipu's lips were seen to move. The moment was solemn and no doubt, everyone thought, he was praying. Purnaiya who stood by the side of the throne heard him.

'Today, I wear the crown and nail myself to the cross,' Tipu had said.

36

DID THEY BURN JESUS CHRIST?

MEANWHILE, THE NEWS OF HYDER ALI'S DEATH HAD LEAKED out. The English received it with joy and jubilation. Their arch enemy was dead. They would now, they thought, deal a crushing blow to the son, who had so humiliated them in scores of battles. Already in anticipation of the death of the ailing Hyder, they had sown the seeds of sedition. Sheikh Ayaz was in their pay and so were many of Hyder's lieutenants. With Tipu Sultan annihilated, the last bastion of resistance in the country would have crumbled. So great and enormous would then be the English power that the rest of the Indian kingdoms would fall like nine pins.

The Christmas of 1782, the day on which the news leaked out to the English, became for them a day of special festivity. Each church bell sounded as if it tolled the death and strangulation of the Kingdom of Mysore and its Sultan. All over the country—wherever the English were in control, the mosques and the temples were desecrated. Pigs, donkeys and cows were forced into mosques, tied to each other. Idols in temples were broken and spattered with filth and urine. In a display of sporting skill, infants torn from their mother's breasts, were tossed from one to the other, like a game of handball. A few heads were broken and some were treated with gun butts if they were foolish enough to protest but otherwise no mass killing took place—merely the mirth and frolic of punching noses, pinching breasts, pulling beards, tearing the veil of the orthodox ladies, forcing women to strip their dress and march naked.

Thus did the English occupation forces in India celebrate the Christmas of 1782 and remember its message of peace and goodwill on earth. At night, they had a large bonfire of the religious books of the Hindus and the Muslims. An effigy was also burnt. It was said to be of Tipu Sultan. Some said it was the God of the Hindus that the effigy represented. No, it was of the prophet of Islam, others urged. Some with cheerful abandon were dancing round the fire and of others there was hardly anyone who did not have a mug of drink in his hand. A yell of delight went up as the effigy was enveloped in flames.

An Englishman, on a short visit to India with his son, watched the bonfire with sadness. When his son wanted to know whose effigy it was that they were burning, the Englishman said: 'I fear, my son,' he said, 'that they are trying to burn Jesus Christ.'

37

THE ANANTPUR MASSACRE

TIPU SULTAN'S SUCCESSION TO THE THRONE WAS SMOOTH. THE internal situation was far from menacing. His ascendancy over the mind of Mysorean soldier, peasant and artisan was complete.

He tore the list of traitors and defectors which Mir Sadik and Burhan-ud-din had compiled and issued an order of amnesty pardoning them all.

'I am at war with the English—not with my own people,' he had said.

Mir Sadik and several other Ministers had protested. Such leniency and soft-heartedness would only encourage treason in the future, they urged. Tipu was adamant.

To Sheikh Ayaz, he wrote:

> Do not bring shame on the decorations you wear and the honour my father bestowed on you .... I have forgotten the sorry chapter of the recent past and I long to hold you in my embrace as my father did.

The messenger did not return.

The English were making feverish preparations for war. Tipu Sultan must not, they felt, be given time to consolidate. His liquidation, as the English Commander-in-Chief put it, would open to them the 'fairest prospect of securing to the mother country, the permanent and undisturbed possession' not only of the whole of India but of the entire eastern dominions.

General James Stewart, the English Commander-in-Chief of Madras, moved towards Wandiwash to attack Tipu Sultan.

'Let us be courteous and meet him halfway,' said Tipu and he set out to meet General Stewart. The battle of Wandiwash ended on 13 February 1783, with the English retreating in disorder closely pursued by the Mysoreans.

Gen Mathews, the English Commander-in-Chief of Bombay, marched towards Bednur which was commanded by Sheikh Ayaz who was already in correspondence with the English and had reached a secret understanding with them. Ayaz had sent off one of his English prisoners—Captain Donald Campbell, to the English to make overtures to them. Ayaz was to bring not only the town and the fort of Bednur under the overlordship of the English but the whole province as well, provided he could retain the governorship and the treasury. The English occupied the town and under orders of Sheikh Ayaz, who spoke in the name of Tipu Sultan, practically every other place in the province also surrendered.

The one exception was Anantpur. Its Commander—Narain Rao—received the letter from Sheikh Ayaz to surrender to the English but suspected either forgery or treachery. He sent a messenger to Sheikh Ayaz to confirm the order and another to Tipu Sultan, asking if the order really had his blessings. Tipu Sultan had already on hearing of the threat to Bednur despatched Lutf Ali Beg to proceed to its defence. Narain Rao's messenger met Lutf Ali's forces and promptly rushed back to Anantpur to report treachery. At the same time, the messenger sent to Ayaz returned, confirming the order and peremptorily

THE ANANTPUR MASSACRE

calling upon Narain Rao to surrender to the English. The English forces neared Anantpur fortress. Under a flag of truce, the English Commander sent a messenger asking for surrender. Narain Rao refused. He knew he was courting certain death. His garrison consisted of five hundred men. The English besieged the fortress. They, who had been enabled to occupy the whole of Bednur without firing a shot, were enraged at the stout and strong defence put up by a small fortress with such few defenders. General Mathews rushed reinforcements and on 14 February 1783, the English succeeded in capturing the fortress. Of the 500 defenders, 440 were dead. Narain Rao lay helplessly with a chest wound, unable to move. The English dragged him to the wall to hang him from the ramparts. What saved him from the hanging was that he mustered sufficient strength to spit at the English Commander. Promptly, he was bayonetted to death. Orders were given to shed the blood of every man who was alive. From the fortress, the English moved out to massacre the civil inhabitants. Wantonly and inhumanly they were put to death, their bodies strewn here and there or thrown into the tank. As the published English records were later to reveal, the victims included:

> four hundred beautiful women, all bleeding with wounds from the bayonet and either dead or expiring in each other's arms, while the common soldiers, casting off all obedience to their officers, were stripping them of their jewels and committing every outrage on their bodies. Many of the women, rather than be torn from their relatives, threw themselves into a large tank and were drowned.

What was Anantpur's crime? Alone, its fortress had resisted when the entire province of Bednur had surrendered under the order of the treacherous Sheikh Ayaz.

Tipu Sultan did not allow Gen Mathews to remain long in occupation of the Bednur province. But in the interval what havoc, devastation and brutality the inhabitants of Bednur had to face from the English! Early in April, Tipu Sultan came on the scene. Capturing Hydergarh and Kavaledurga, he sent his forces to the Ghats to thwart the English communications with the sea coast. He then proceeded to Bednur to challenge the main English army under General Mathews. He personally led the assault on the town and after its capture besieged the fort into which Gen Mathews was compelled to retreat with great loss. The onslaughts against the fort began with the thunder of thirteen batteries. For eighteen days, Gen Mathews held out. His sorties had been repulsed with tremendous loss. Tipu's guns had destroyed all places of shelter in the fort. The English were exposed and in great danger. Mathews surrendered.

Sheikh Ayaz had already slipped away to Bombay, as soon as Tipu had arrived on the outskirts of Bednur. Gone were his dreams of continued governorship of Bednur. He left almost destitute since Gen Mathews had confiscated the treasury and also what Ayaz claimed was his personal wealth. Gen Mathews had Ayaz searched before he left the fort and confiscated whatever he had hidden on his person, leaving him only with a hundred pagodas. 'Enough,' Gen Mathews said. 'Normally we shoot traitors. You are a traitor to your Sultan, are you not? However, somehow, I feel merciful this morning. Take these hundred pagodas and be gone.'

When Tipu Sultan entered the fort on 28 April 1783, he found the treasury empty. Mathews had already sent away vast sums of money. The remainder was secreted by the English officers and men. They were searched. Every knapsack was found to be lined with gold. It was hidden in the loaves of bread and while the search was going on, the English had crammed it down the throats of dogs and fowls. What was thus recovered came to about fifty thousand pagodas—a mere fraction of the tremendous treasure, traditionally deposited at the Bednur fort.

Tipu Sultan saw what the English had done to his people during their brief period of occupation. There were men whose eyes had been put out and they went their way groping. Others had had their limbs cut off. There were those whose tongues had been torn out. All this, only for sport or to terrorise though at times to extract information about possible hidden wealth.

'Do not ask us for the fate of our daughters and wives for their fate was more terrible than death,' they wailed.

Tipu Sultan wept. 'Is there no God in heaven to forbid such revolting cruelties?' he cried.

38

WHO IS THE KILLER?

IKRAMULLAH WAS A CAPTAIN IN THE ARMY OF TIPU SULTAN. Eighteen months back he had married a girl from Bednur. While he was called away to military duties, Yasmin, his wife, remained with her parents. They had an infant son. Ikramullah had parted from her when the infant was four days old. When Tipu Sultan's army captured Bednur, Ikramullah was one of the first to enter the town. Tipu noticed the young dashing Captain, fearlessly advancing into the town, beckoning the troops to follow him. He made a mental note of the Captain's gallantry, to remember him in the future and to consult his Commanding Officer for a decoration or a promotion for him.

Ikramullah's enthusiasm to rush into Bednur, ahead of his soldiers, was not so much for the glory of the Sultan. Still less was he thinking of decorations and promotions. He was thinking of the reunion with his wife and his infant son left behind in Bednur.

He found his wife. She was more dead than alive. Her account was incoherent and hysterical.

After the English occupation, soldiers had entered her house to loot. Some of them wanted to lay hands on her. Her old father, her brother and the servants who had watched silently the removal of valuables, intervened now to protect her. A commotion arose. They kicked her father. He died on the spot. They continued beating the lifeless body. Meanwhile, a servant ran out crying out to the neighbours who came out of their houses. Gen Mathews with his guard was returning from an inspection tour. He had the servant brought to him. On hearing the story, he rushed to Yasmin's house and immediately placed the English soldiers under arrest. He had the servants released and ordered restoration of whatever was looted from the house. He glanced at Yasmin's dead father, looked at Yasmin and the child in compassion, said nothing to her and left.

The neighbours came in to condole with Yasmin over her father's death while she sobbed clutching her infant. In the evening, a palanquin arrived. With it came seven soldiers. She was ordered to get into the palanquin to proceed to Gen Mathew's quarters. She did not want to go. The soldiers insisted. They were ready to use force, if necessary. The neighbours comforted her. Surely, this summons was related to the enquiry into the morning's dastardly attack on her house and the murder of her father. A neighbour offered to accompany her. The soldiers refused. She picked up her child. The soldiers looked at their corporal. He shrugged his shoulders. She entered in the palanquin with her infant. They left her in the ante-room of the General's quarters and left. The palanquin remained. The General escorted her into a study. He was in his uniform replete with ribbons, medals and decorations. She felt reassured. The General pointed to the sofa where she deposited the child. She took another chair. The General left and reappeared in a few moments. He had changed into pyjamas. He beckoned her into the next room. She refused. He pulled her. She resisted. The General caught her in his arms and pressed his lips on her. She did not know what object she picked up from the table. She stabbed the General's head with it. He released her. She saw his face contorted with rage and passion with blood flowing from his eyes. She ran to the door. It was locked. He moved to follow her and then paused, picked up the boy by his leg, dashed him forcefully across the distance against the glass window which broke into pieces. The iron grill beyond the window held the infant's smashed head. Yasmin shrieked and fainted. General Mathews undressed her and calmed his passion on the unconscious woman. Two hours later he called the guard and gave the naked Yasmin to their charge. He had ripped her dress off but could not put it on her again.

'Would you be needing her again, Sir?' the soldier had asked.

'No, never,' the General had replied, 'she is a cold woman. Go, warm her up, if you can.'

An hour later she had gained consciousness. The soldiers made sport of her. She was unaware of what was being done to her. Piteously she kept asking for the child. Yes, the General was right, they said, she was cold and unresponsive. They lost interest in her. The palanquin was still waiting for her. They put her into it. The palanquin-bearers stopped at Yasmin's house and helped her out. The servants opened the door and were shocked. They dressed her, called the physician and neighbours. In the morning, the body of an infant was found in the garbage heap outside the General's quarters. It was brought to Yasmin.

Since then Yasmin had died a thousand deaths. Somehow, life flickered in her by a slender thread, waiting perhaps for her husband to release her. She was now in her husband's arms. His tears touched her face and she felt as if they had washed away all her agony. Her mind went to their wedding night. The melody of that night came to her anew. She saw herself decked in flowers and pearls—her heart aflame with pride and the thrill of expectation. She could hear the sighs and murmurs of admiration from the crowd as she walked down dressed in gold to take the marriage vows and hold the hand of the man who was to be her husband. She saw herself—shy, her heart throbbing—on her nuptial bed, decorated with garlands and felt her heart lose its limits in joy—and then she heard her own cry of ecstasy.

Thus, Yasmin died in her husband's arms, regaining for a brief moment, the happiness that was gone for ever.

Ikramullah did not shed tears again. He had stood for hours by the grave of his son, without prayer, without words and if any thoughts whirled in his heart, he could not decipher them. He lowered his wife into a grave. Many wept. Not Ikramullah. War hardens a soldiers's heart, they said to themselves and went their way. Ikramullah returned to his duties.

Days later, Bednur fort itself was captured by Tipu Sultan. General Mathews and the English army surrendered to him. Ikramullah was one of those who was decorated by Tipu Sultan at a colourful ceremony, for gallantry in the field. Four days later, Ikramullah saw General Mathews, resplendent in his shining uniform, sitting in a half-open palanquin at the head of the English prisoners of war. They were being taken to the camp in Seringapatam, until the conclusion of peace. General Mathews and other senior officers were given the use of a palanquin while other prisoners were to march on foot.

Ikramullah ran to the palanquin. What was his conscious thought?

'I must tell him,' Ikramullah had said to himself, 'I am the husband of her whom you dishonoured, I am the father of him whom you killed.' There was no anger in him, no hatred. Perhaps just a nameless, senseless urge to share his sorrow with the killer.

The Mysorean soldiers at the head of the column halted. The palanquin-bearers stopped and rested the palanquin on the ground. Perhaps, the Captain had a message from Tipu Sultan to give to General Mathews. The General was about to stand up as he saw the Captain approaching. To steady his rise, he lifted his hand to catch the top beam of the palanquin. Ikramullah saw the hand. All else disappeared from his view. Was this the hand which dashed the life out of his infant? Was this the hand that disrobed his wife? His own hand clutched at his dagger and went pounding again and again at the General. The General was dead before the Mysoreans overpowered Ikramullah.

Later in the day, Ikramullah was brought before Tipu Sultan.

'How dared you, how could you, what impelled you to kill a prisoner?' asked Tipu Sultan in fury.

Ikramullah did not reply. Tipu Sultan asked again.

'I decorated you for bravery,' Tipu continued, 'but you shamed me with your cowardice. To kill a helpless, unarmed prisoner. . . .'

Something of Tipu Sultan's agony crossed over to Ikramullah. He must tell him, he thought, but the words would not come. 'He robbed me of all, he dishonoured me,' he mumbled incoherently. Tipu understood nothing though perhaps he caught the word 'dishonoured' and said, 'Yes, yes, you dishonoured me. You killed a prisoner whom I had promised life and safety.'

Ikramullah helplessly looked on without saying a word. 'Take him away.' Tipu ordered the guard, 'let the Military Court try his offence,' and then looking at Ikramullah in cold contempt, he added, 'Never, never let him come into my presence again.'

That night Ikramullah was lodged in a solitary cell. A comrade had sent him the daily necessities, for he was still an undertrial. He wrote a note which simply said, 'Forgive me, my Sultan.' To someone, unknown and unseen he said, 'Wait for me, I am coming,' and with his crude shaving razor he cut his vein. They found him dead, amidst blood, when they opened the door of his cell in the morning.

Thus ended the anguish of Ikramullah, but not of Tipu. He was given Ikramullah's note, informed of his suicide and told also of how Ikramullah's infant and wife had died. Tipu felt a terrible loneliness. Later, he dictated to his Secretary Shivji a letter to Ikramullah's aged parents saying that 'Ikramullah died after gallantly fighting for the honour and glory of the kingdom. He had avenged the death of his wife and child who were killed at the time of the English occupation.' To the letter was attached a note indicating the generous pension and land grants in perpetuity to Ikramullah's parents.

To Purnaiya, Tipu ordered, 'Announce that it was under my orders that General Mathews was killed. Let the blame not fall on Ikramullah.'

Purnaiya remained quiet. None, he knew, would believe that his sovereign would kill a war prisoner to whom he had promised safe conduct. Such was his code of honour; even his worst enemies knew of it and relied on it.

Little did Purnaiya know of those mindless little men of the future who called themselves historians.

39

THE THREE SUPPLIANTS

(i)

FROM BEDNUR, TIPU MARCHED TO FACE THE ENEMY ON MANY fronts. He was here, there and everywhere, sometime on one front and at another on the other. A strange coincidence that came to pass was that on one single day—18 May 1783—the three English commanders separated by hundreds of miles, originated a message to army high command in Madras urging reinforcements since Tipu Sultan had personally appeared with his army in their theatre of operations. The English Commander-in-Chief rushed reinforcements to all the three fronts; but had also the sense of humour to send to each one of them, copies of despatches sent by the other two and scrawled on each of them was a question: 'Shall we believe him?' The fact of the matter was that Tipu moved from one front to another, making lightning switches from east to west.

From that grew a legend that Tipu tore across the country like a pillar of cloud during the night and like a pillar of fire during the day. Every morning he was reported in some battle or the other. Often, at night, his horse, Dilkush the Second, would bear him to another front while his army at the first front rested or formed itself for a siege. Tipu would rejoin it well in time for the attack and until then the myth of his presence was kept alive.

At Mangalore, Tipu inflicted a crushing defeat on the large English army under Campbell. The English withdrew and shut themselves up into the fort. While the Mysorean army laid siege to the fort, Tipu left for Cuddapah to join his commander Qamar-ud-din. There, he defeated the troops under traitor Sayyad Mohammad and then routed the English army sent under Montgomery to assist Sayyad Mohammad.

At the end of the battle, Tipu looked down on Sayyad Mohammad who grovelled before him and begged for mercy. His cold calm figure glowed in splendid armour. He listened attentively but without change of expression. Every onlooker thought that he could forecast what the answer would be, for Sayyad Mohammad had added to his treachery by killing in cold blood hundreds of Tipu's loyalists. Tipu replied: 'I grant you your life, not in forgetfulness of what you did but in remembrance of who your father was.' Sayyad Mohammad's father was a man of religion, attached to the tomb of Gisu Daraz at Gulbarga.

The reply almost led to a quarrel between Tipu Sultan and his trusted commander, Qamar-ud-din. The quarrel ended only when Tipu Sultan cried: 'You call me a king but question each act. It seems I am your king only when I command to kill. But I cannot, it seems, command to spare a life, if I choose.'

This was not a kingly act, Qamar-ud-din thought to himself. We are only increasing the legion of wolves against us, he wanted to say. But after this outburst, he knew, it was no use arguing further.

(ii)

Despite severe reverses which the English suffered at Bednur, Cuddapah and Mangalore, the English kept their hopes alive. Hyder Ali's death, they knew, had given them a miraculous opportunity and they must not let it slip. Surely, the son must be strangled, before he could consolidate. On several fronts therefore the English amassed their armies to harass the Mysoreans. Messages went to all princes, jagirdars and chiefs to raise the standard of revolt against Tipu Sultan. Promises of extensive land, magnificent rewards and even kingdoms went with these messages. A legion of missionaries was enrolled to carry such messages. In Tipu's kingdom, they knew, a man of religion was safe from molestation.

General Stewart whom Tipu Sultan had defeated in the battle of Wandiwash, struck now in Cuddalore but he retreated after losing one thousand men. The only notable feat achieved by Stewart's retreating forces was that they captured a French Sergeant in Tipu's service. He was carrying a message for Tipu Sultan from Bussy who commanded the French serving in the Mysore army. Tipu remembered this Sergeant with affection. Once, when everyone was exhausted after a gruelling battle, news had come that Tipu Sultan had been blessed with a son. A cheer had gone up but it was this Sergeant who had gone out, collected a large bunch of flowers and presented it to Tipu Sultan on behalf of all the forces. On hearing of his arrest now, Tipu sent a courier under a flag of truce and for forty pagodas obtained the Sergeant's release. The Sergeant was Jean Baptiste Jules Barnadotte, who subsequently became a General in the French Army, married Napoleon Bonaparte's childhood sweetheart Desiree, later became a Marshal of France in Napoleon's army, thereafter was elevated as the Duke of Ponte Carvo, still later was elected as the heir to Charles XIII and finally achieved the Crown of Sweden as King Charles XIV.

The French contingent assisting Tipu Sultan withdrew its help altogether from him in June 1783, as soon as the news reached them that Preliminaries of Peace had been signed at Versailles on February 1783, between England and France. The English who had suffered so many reverses at the hands of Tipu Sultan were now jubilant and hoped that with the French neutrality, they would be able to make some headway. In actual fact, the French withdrawal made Tipu stronger. The French were often at cross purposes with the Mysore Army. Their demands for assistance were at times excessive. In any case, divided counsels now gave way to single-mindedness. When Qamar-ud-din and other Mysorean Commanders expressed indignation at the French desertion in the midst of a war, Tipu chided them, saying: 'This is our war, not theirs. Or, do you expect foreigners to fight your wars for you?' Then he added, 'In self-interest they fought with us; in self-interest they now withdraw from the fight. If need be, in self-interest they will fight against us!'

If the French withdrawal had an effect on him, it was only to steel his determination to redouble his own efforts.

The battles raged on several fronts. Tenaciously, the English armies fought. From Madras, Bombay and Bengal, reinforcements were rushed to bolster their striking power and morale. It was essential in their view to keep the pressure on and to win one or two decisive victories. Thereafter, they hoped that the process of degeneration of the hitherto victorious Mysorean army would begin. Other powers would also by then be encouraged to join the battle against Tipu Sultan. But all their hopes and calculations came to nought. The Mysore cavalry outrode and outmanoeuvred the enemy and everywhere the English suffered humiliation and defeat.

The English were now growing desperate. All their campaigns had brought nothing to them but death and disaster. They knew now that they must get out of this ruinous war and live to fight another day. They sent peace feelers to which Tipu replied, 'Peace! But I have always wanted peace. Leave my territory and we have peace.'

The English sent three Commissioners: Anthony Sadlier, George Staunton and John Huddleston to appear before Tipu Sultan to parley for peace. Macartney, the English Governor of Madras, his nerves frayed by continuous defeats, urged on his Commissioners that 'peace is not only so desirable but so necessary an object to us in our desperate situation that it is our duty to endeavour to accomplish it by every means'.

Meanwhile, when the peace feelers had come, Tipu Sultan had agreed to an armistice to the English garrison in the fort of Mangalore, which was heavily besieged by the Mysorean army. The English Commander Campbell, capitulated on after holding out valiantly for over eight months. The garrison, although Tipu Sultan had readily allowed food to pass to them as part of the armistice arrangement, was broken down with disease and exhaustion. Campbell himself was a dying man in the last stage of consumption.

As Campbell came out of the fort, Tipu Sultan saluted him.

'You and your garrison performed your duty valiantly,' Tipu said.

Campbell was touched. The memory of the curses of his comrades whom he had kept cooped up in the fort faded away from his troubled mind and he said, 'Your praise, Sultan, is my highest reward.'

The garrison was permitted to march with honours of war. Tipu Sultan provided boats for their journey along with provisions, medicines and other supplies. Campbell had much to say in his official memoranda of the generosity of Tipu Sultan and of his strict and honourable adherence to the articles under which the English capitulated. To his senior officers, Campbell, a defeated man on the sick list, was of no use. He met with harsh indifference. He died a month later. On his deathbed, to his friend Captain Lindsey, he said, 'I die despised by all who surround me, but do not remember me by my present misery. Remember, instead, the moment of my glory when a man of honour, a great commander and a great king, saluted my valour.'

The English Commissioners set out to meet Tipu Sultan in November 1783. The Commissioners desperately wanted peace, for the English army had suffered severe blows. Still, they had several quarrels amongst themselves. Also, whilst they were on their way to Tipu Sultan, they received conflicting instructions from the Governor General Warren Hastings and the Governor of Madras, Macartney. They had to waste considerable time in getting clarifications and confirmations. Thus, they lost nearly three months and by then the English position had deteriorated. It was in February 1784 that they finally appeared before Tipu Sultan in the position of suppliants.

On 11 March 1784, the Treaty of Mangalore was signed whereby the English and the Mysoreans agreed on restoration of each other's territory. It was a diplomatic victory for the English who had suffered some crushing defeats in the war. They were, however, dealing with a war-weary sovereign who had always longed for peace.

40

THE DOOMED PEACE

WARREN HASTINGS, THE ENGLISH GOVERNOR-GENERAL, HAD concurred in the Treaty of Mangalore with a heavy heart. He had called it a 'humiliating peace'. Yet, he knew there was no way out. The English had been lulled into the belief that Tipu Sultan without Hyder Ali to guide him, would fall an easy prey to their strength. It was not to be. The bitter truth had now dawned on them after several crushing defeats. They wanted time and this was precisely what the Treaty of Mangalore was intended to provide them with. Warren Hastings was quite clear in his mind that all traces of this humiliating peace must be wiped out as soon as possible and he regarded the intervening period only as a temporary phase. Tipu Sultan had to be humbled, if the English designs of expansion in India were to progress. Innes Munroe expressed the hope of Warren Hastings, the East India Company and the British government when he said: 'It is to be hoped that the treaty of peace which the Company has lately concluded with Tipu Sultan is only meant to be temporary.'

The vigour and success of Tipu's onslaughts had reduced the English to, what their historians describe, a condition of 'debility, dejection and despair'. Abjectly, therefore, they had to sue for peace and furnish profuse assurances of keeping faith in the future. They undertook to abstain from any interference in matters relating to Mysore and to maintain friendly relations with Tipu Sultan and his heirs. They even gave assurances of all help to Tipu Sultan and his heirs against attack from anyone.

'Promise the moon,' Macartney had ordered his Commissioners, 'but get the peace—and then we shall see.' This was the spirit with which the English had entered into the Treaty of Mangalore.

Warren Hastings had prepared a plan of action, following the peace. Scruples had never bothered him. He who had personally contrived the extermination of Rohillas, depradations of Benaras, devastation of Gorakhpur, torture of Oudh princesses and death of Nand Coomar, was not going to be squeamish about the provisions of a treaty with Tipu Sultan. Peace was only a contrivance to get back from a generous Sultan the territories that he had conquered from the English. But Warren Hastings learned his lesson that the English must never in the future underrate the power and might of Tipu Sultan. To meet it, the English must make preparations on a gigantic scale—of men, money and war materials. He reckoned that a minimum period of five years would be required for the English to be ready for a successful challenge to Tipu Sultan, provided that the intervening period was 'not spent away in sloth but in active preparations'. He was also clear in his mind that in the meantime, the English must encourage rebellions, revolts and conspiracies against Tipu Sultan, so that 'we have a weakened foe to face', every assistance and incitement must be given to the Marathas, the Nizam and other powers—big and small—to harass Tipu Sultan.

Warren Hastings conferred with the Nizam who had a simpler and more effective solution to offer.

'Would it not be worthwhile to have Tipu assassinated?' the Nizam had asked.

The Nizam knew of the hero worship that Tipu enjoyed. Somehow he believed that there was something in the blood of the Indian people which made them ascribe such importance to the leader that when the leader dies, everything collapses.

Warren Hastings looked at the Nizam with undisguised affection.

Since then, several hired assassins appeared in Seringapatam. Many were caught and they confessed. Purnaiya spoke once to the Nizam's Chief Minister who hotly denied his master's complicity in the matter. Purnaiya sighed and said: 'Strange that people should go to such lengths to try to kill Tipu Sultan. Yet so easy it is, so simple it is to cause his death.'

The Nizam's Chief Minister pricked his ears. 'How so?' he asked.

'Well, you know,' Purnaiya responded, 'all that your master has to do is to keep a promise—any promise—and surely Tipu Sultan will simply die out of astonishment.'

The assassins did not succeed. But Warren Hasting's policies began to have some effect. The English commenced preparation for a massive war and in the meantime, incited others to rebel against Tipu Sultan. Hastings left the same year (1784). Later, he was to face impeachment proceedings by the British Parliament for his untold cruelties and depradations and for having amassed a vast personal fortune. After a trial of seven years, he was acquitted because the British Parliament held that whatever he had done was very largely in the interests of the English nation and for the consolidation of the English rule in India—and surely in the face of such a glorious objective and achievement, the British Parliament was not going to shed tears over atrocities and misdeeds inflicted on the Indian nation!

Warren Hastings was succeeded by an equally vicious, more avaricious and a craftier person—the acting Governor-General—Sir John Macpherson. About Macpherson, even his successor Lord Cornwallis wrote to the Secretary of State for India in England, referring to his 'ill-earned money', his flimsy cunning and shameless falsehood' and 'his duplicity and low intrigue'. On his return to England, Sir John Macpherson was elected to the British Parliament but was later unseated when it was proved that he had won the elections through bribery, corruption and other malpractices.

Such was the calibre of men who were to safeguard adherence to the provisions of the Treaty of Mangalore. Warren Hastings called it 'a scrap of paper which we must burn one day lest it remind us of our shame' and Sir John Macpherson styled it as 'a grain of sand that will disappear with the first whiff of wind'.

A series of conspiracies erupted. One after another Tipu Sultan witnessed the betrayal by some of his trusted lieutenants, who had been bought over with English gold. Qasim Ali's desertion had hurt Tipu Sultan but what caused him real anguish was the betrayal by Muhammad Ali, a favourite Commander of his father and his own. Muhammad Ali had fought many battles on behalf of the father and the son. He was bluff, hearty, outspoken and courageous. His tragedy was that he loved the traitor Qasim Ali as intensely, and in the same way, as a man can love a woman. When Qasim Ali became a traitor, he dragged Muhammad Ali on the path of treachery. Ghazi Khan's contingent overpowered Muhammad Ali and his troops. He was brought before Tipu Sultan.

'What shall I do with you?' Tipu asked Muhammad Ali.

'You will have me killed, of course,' Muhammad Ali said, with his characteristic courage.

Tipu Sultan did not have him killed. He let him go. He deserved to die but Tipu chose to remember not his present offence but his past services.

Muhammad Ali was overtaken by remorse. Next day, he committed suicide. But what of others, whose treachery Tipu kept pardoning! There were some, whom Tipu not only forgave but also reinstated in their old commands.

Many who loved Tipu Sultan remonstrated with him. Once a traitor, always a traitor, they urged; according to them, the seeming gratitude of the traitor at being pardoned was nothing but a mask to conceal his chagrin at his failure to reap the rewards of his treachery; the insult to his pride at being caught and yet spared was galling; surely, he would desert again when the moment of crisis came. Thus pleaded those who were near and dear to Tipu Sultan. Politely and attentively Tipu heard them. He was convinced that they were right and that he had been wrong to forgive and pardon. He remained in that attitude until the next offender was brought before him—and then suddenly a new crowd of memories came rushing in.

Apart from inciting internal conspiracies, the English also succeeded in encouraging a number of rebellions against Tipu. The Balam ruler, whose family Tipu had spared when he was fifteen, entered into an arrangement with the English. He turned a deaf ear to Tipu's admonitions to cease his refractory conduct. Tipu marched into Balam territory. The ruler fled. Again, the ruler's family surrendered to Tipu.

'He seems to make a habit of leaving his family unguarded,' Tipu said.

'You protected us once. Will you not protect us again?' the wife of the ruler pleaded.

Tipu recalled the ruler and after making him promise to remain loyal, restored the kingdom to him.

After pacifying Balam, Tipu had to march post-haste to Coorg where the English had succeeded in fomenting a serious rebellion against him. The English had standardised their drill for such revolts. They would pour in their money and arms; they would send their agents and emissaries to the rebellious rulers for advice and encouragement; they would promise them physical assistance. When the conflagration took place, they would fail to arrive. The Coorg rebellion was repressed by Tipu Sultan though not without considerable cost and casualties to the Mysore army.

Thus, the English, unseen from a distance, kept up their barrage of harassment against Tipu Sultan. That their guns were fired from the shoulders of others suited them. The pressure on Tipu was kept on, while the English were busy building up their war machine for the eventual showdown with their arch enemy. The greatest stroke of the English genius, however, was the commencement of hostilities between the Nizam and the Marathas on the one hand and Tipu on the other. How the English had laboured and slaved to achieve this! The Nizam was a lackey of the English but the Marathas had an independent policy and a formidable army with a tradition of courage. The English political skill is therefore all the more remarkable that they were able to convince the Marathas that Tipu harboured designs against them, was preparing against them and that Tipu, weakened by internal revolts, could be contained at this stage but any delay would lessen their ability to withstand his onslaughts.

The Marathas and the Nizam began their actual hostilities against Tipu Sultan in May 1786. With skill and enterprise, Tipu commenced his operations. Ignoring their initial gains and the line of their attack, Tipu marched north of Adoni, the Nizam's main stronghold south of Tungabhadra. Adoni fell to his arms. Tipu, contrary to the opinion of his commanders, then succeeded in crossing his army over the swollen and raging Tungabhadra river in 'basket boats'. He dislodged confederates from many places, captured Savnur and several towns. The Marathas were now ready to listen to his overtures for peace, for the Nizam had proved to be a pusillanimous ally and the assistance from the English had failed to materialise. How could it be otherwise? The English were arming themselves in preparation for a major offensive against Tipu Sultan. They did not want to dissipate their energies in this style. Let the Indian powers exhaust themselves against each other was their attitude.

A treaty of peace was signed between the Maratha Peshwa and Tipu Sultan in April 1787. It was a peace which maintained honour of both sides involving restoration of each other's conquests. The Nizam, who had almost faded out of the struggle did not find a mention in the treaty. Tipu Sultan had regarded the pact of the Marathas and the Nizam as an alliance of a lion and a jackal. Why should he dishonour himself by entering into a treaty with a jackal? Unilaterally, however, he restored all the territories of the Nizam which he had conquered.

Tipu had been victorious on many fronts. Could he have insisted on harsher terms for the Marathas? The English had sent him agents suggesting that this was his moment for cutting the Marathas down to size. Frequently, they came to him, carrying gifts, conveying congratulations and incidentally furnishing him with gratuitous advice on how he should go about liquidating the Marathas. He glanced at these agents in cold contempt and dismissed them. To his own officers who thought along the same lines, he said: 'May God give us the wisdom to perceive who our true enemies are. Surely, the Marathas are not. They share this land with us as a part of their birthright.'

Tipu saw the devastation which the war with the Marathas had brought. We must build anew, he thought to himself. Desperately, he needed peace to heal the gaping wounds. There was not much time, he knew, for the real enemy waited the sidelines, watching for an opportunity to strike and kill.

41

THE SURRENDER AT YORKTOWN

LORD CHARLES CORNWALLIS TOOK OVER AS THE ENGLISH Governor-General from Sir John Macpherson in 1786. Personally, he was not dishonest nor corrupt as his predecessors Warren Hastings and Macpherson were. He was not out to amass a fortune for himself. Money meant little to him, women still less. No, his ambitions were of a different kind. His heroes were the early English pioneers who went to America, Canada and Australia, wiping out the entire native races, establishing empires for the British and spreading the civilising message of Christianity. He believed in the survival of the fittest and was convinced that the English nation by reason of its virtue and genius was entitled eternally to its position of greatness. According to him, the inscrutable wisdom of Providence and the inexorable process of historic destiny had so ordained. He loved England as he saw it: proud, free, clothed in imperial honour, industrious, frugal, just, benevolent and temperate. Any challenge to the greatness of his country, he regarded as an offence against the very moral basis of the universe. He was equally convinced that conquest and colonisation by the British belonged to the natural order of events and that the inferior races must be subdued for the greater glory of civilised nations. He knew that the Persians, Greeks, Scythians, Huns, Arabs, Turks and Mongols had broken into India through the north-western mountain walls. All these had become assimilated, in varying degrees, with the Indian culture; their dynasties became Indian dynasties and they looked on India as their home country. But this also he knew that the English, who came across the seas, would be a race apart—cold, distant and indifferent to the memories and traditions of the conquered people; for how else could the ideology of the Empire be maintained?

In his heart, Cornwallis did not harbour hatred or animosity towards Indians. He had no prejudice or bias against them, although he had a lurking suspicion that the colour of man's skin determined the level of his intellect. No, his feelings towards the Indians were not devoid of benevolence. The sense of identifying India with the interests of the Empire gave him sometimes even a feeling akin to affection for the Indians—affection which a master has for his slave. He was an upright soldier, an able administrator and later proved his zeal for reform. He had known of the plunder, graft and misrule by his predecessors and was ashamed of it. He saw the need to evolve some kind of order out of the chaos and anarchy that then prevailed in this unhappy land. But above all, and to the exclusion of everything else, he was conscious of his imperial mission in India. He had developed something in the nature of a religious faith in the paramount importance of his own country and would tolerate no challenge to it. He would therefore view India as an instrument for the greater glory of his own homeland. Yes, reforms would come, but only after the imperial design had been fulfilled and after the British were secure in their complete conquest of India.

Such was the cultural attitude and the imperialistic outlook of Lord Cornwallis who became India's Governor-General in August 1786.

'In short,' said Henry Dundas in a private conversation—Dundas had been advocating the appointment of Lord Cornwallis—'he is a pompus fat sportsman out to gain glory for the empire; he has not the low cunning of Macpherson nor the grasping avarice of Hastings. He is upright, fair, impartial and honourable in all matters—except when he deals with the enemy and then he knows no mercy. Besides, don't forget, he just cannot risk a failure; he has a reputation to repair.'

Yes indeed, Cornwallis had a reputation to repair. On 19 October 1781, had come the most traumatic event of his life. Full of confidence, he had been sent from England to crush the American colonists who were waging against Britain a War of Independence. He had marched with the flower of British troops which were supported moreover by a large number of Canadian fighting men, a strong contingent of pioneers and considerable Red Indian auxiliaries. Yet, he could do nothing against the vision and genius of the American Commander-in-Chief, George Washington. Cornwallis encountered an overwhelming force of Americans, his supplies were low and his communications cut off. None could answer his calls for help and a breakthrough was almost impossible. Choked with tears of shame and rage, he surrendered. His surrender at Yorktown on 19 October 1781, made the outcome of the American War of Independence almost certain and it was now clear that the English were poised on the edge of disaster.

About five years had passed since his humiliating surrender. He had never forgotten that moment of his disgrace—the abject surrender to those whom he had regarded as treasonable criminals defying the authority of their lawful King. The subsequent enquiry exonerated him. His surrender had been unavoidable. But the bitter memory remained. It was a wound that had not healed and pain that had not ceased. Along with his own sorrow and suffering, he had felt an awareness of impending disaster which sharpened his perceptions and heightened his anguish. Then came 1783. The Americans won their War of Independence. He regarded it as a tragedy that was both personal and national. He knew that it was also the year when in a different theatre, another enemy of the British empire—Tipu Sultan—had won resounding victories and that the English had humbly to sue for peace, resulting in the Treaty of Mangalore.

In his heart, he felt anger welling up against Tipu Sultan who had dared to challenge and thwart the British ambition and design. But a wandering question arrested his thoughts. 'If the roles had been reversed, would I have acted differently in his place?' he asked himself. He had heard about Tipu's chivalry, his sense of honour, his courage in battle, his intense patriotism, his gentleness to prisoners and the wounded. He had also heard of his unimpeachable integrity and love for truth and beauty. Cornwallis himself believed in these ideals, practised and cherished them. 'How can I hate him?' he asked himself. 'Is he not an antagonist fashioned in my own mould and worthy of my respect?' Imperiously, almost in anger, he dismissed the question from his mind. The process of historic destiny, he was convinced, has ordained British supremacy and he who opposes it must be crushed without consideration and without mercy. Imperialism must function this way or else it must cease to function. Yes, I must banish from my conscience any trace of feeling for this adversary. But the feeling lingered and he chided himself, adding half- homorously, 'I have come to subdue him, not to praise him.' Suddenly his mood changed and in his heart was a prayer, 'God, give me anger, fury and ruthlessness to smite the enemies of my land. Until then, dry up in my soul the well of compassion and mercy, and grant unto me the strength and the will to fulfil my mission and my purpose.'

Thus came Cornwallis to India. As his boat sailed majestically to Madras, he had thought of his goals and objectives. His was the sure belief that he had the moral right to wreak vengeance upon those that defied his King; that the grand edifice of the Empire must be preserved and strengthened; that the two races—white and brown—must stand on the opposite sides of the fence in terms of superiority and inferiority; that the humiliation in America must be compensated by gains in India and that the blot on his reputation as a soldier and general must be wiped out.

'Five wishes,' he said to himself as he counted these aims on the fingers of his hand. 'Is that asking for too much?' he wondered.

He thought it over. He would compromise and make only one wish so as neither to strain the generosity of the Granter of the wishes nor to appear to be asking for too much. Yes, one single wish—only one. He formulated it in his mind—'The extermination of Tipu Sultan. The rest,' he added, 'will take care of itself.'

His mind was clear. If he achieved that single objective—of exterminating Tipu Sultan—it would involve the fulfilment of all the five wishes. He went over his five wishes again. Yes, each one would be in his grasp, once Tipu was wiped out.

'So, Lord, grant me that one wish,' he had prayed. Surely, God would not hesitate to grant so modest a petition, he thought to himself. Irreverently he smiled, as if gaining a tactical victory by petitioning only for one wish, in the silent knowledge that it would cover the fulfilment of a multitude of aims.

A seagull had settled on the rail of the ship. It called for its mate. Distracted, Cornwallis looked up. He took his rifle. He was an excellent shot. The bird fell, writhed and died. 'That is how, you shall die, Tipu, alone, with none to heed your call,' said Cornwallis to himself.

THE SURRENDER AT YORKTOWN

If another bird, solitary and far away, gave a piercing scream, Cornwallis did not hear it. He was wrapped up in the thoughts of his own glory and honour—and that of the Empire.

The dreams of Cornwallis were not solely his own. He had his urgent and pressing brief from London. The breakaway of the American colonies had shrunk the English Empire, devastated the English morale and depleted its treasury. For Britain, the loss of the American colonies meant the abandonment of a dominion from Hudson Bay to the Gulf of Mexico. This did not end her position as an imperialist, colonising power. She still possessed the Canadian colony, West Indian Islands and many provinces of India. Cornwallis was plainly told by his masters that his mission was to ensure that what was lost in America must be made good in India. The Empire must be extended and the main obstacle to this expansion—Tipu Sultan—must be liquidated. Surely, his masters could not have found a better man than Cornwallis-an able general, a tireless administrator and a man with a surrender to atone for.

'They are testing me,' Cornwallis said to himself, 'and by God, I shall not fail them, Jemima.' Jemima was the name of his wife. She had died a few years earlier but Cornwallis always remembered her in his moments of emotion.

42

RIGHTS OF MAN

(i)

IF THE AMERICAN WAR OF INDEPENDENCE HAD ITS PROFOUND emotional effect on Cornwallis personally and on the future colonial policies of the British government, it was not without its influence on Tipu Sultan. Many were the events and incidents that led to his interest in the war that was fought thousands of miles away.

It was on the eve of Tipu's marriage, when the war in America was still two years away that Hyder Ali had asked: 'All I have is yours, but tell me what is to be your wedding gift from me?'

'All that you have given is enough, more than enough,' was Tipu's reply. But Hyder had insisted. Tipu then had told him that he would like a library to be set up.

Hyder was puzzled. 'Library! You mean books?' he had asked in astonishment.

Hyder himself could not read and write. He knew, of course, of the importance of account books, particularly those that indicated the tax arrears which he still had to collect. He also respected those who spent their time reading the Koran, the Gita, the Talmud, the Bible or the Granth, or the Jap Sahib. Such books, he had thought, at least kept people out of mischief. In any case Goverdhan Pandit and Maulvi Obedullah had already left a large number of them behind and they were now littered in Tipu's large study-room. But if more were needed, certainly, he would not deny his son.

'I will order that all the books in the kingdom be purchased for you,' said the generous Hyder.

Politely, Tipu explained that the project that was in his mind had larger dimensions. 'I would like to begin collecting books of all cultures, of all nations,' Tipu had said. He explained further in response to Hyder's puzzled glance, 'I would like to know how men live elsewhere, how they meet evil, of their battles against it. . . .'

'Battles, certainly,' Hyder had interrupted. 'Who knows, the world may read of your battles too, one day.' The thought pleased Hyder. Then he had a doubt and asked, 'The books from all the world—they are written in different languages, surely?'

Amongst the foreign languages, Tipu knew Persian superbly. He had also studied English and French but could not claim to have mastery over those two languages. He knew that the world expressed itself in many other languages as well.

'Yes,' Tipu replied. 'That is why it will be necessary to have them translated. You see I do not ask for too little.'

'Whatever you ask of me, son, shall always be too little,' was Hyder's fond reply. Enthusiastically, Hyder called Purnaiya.

'My son wants a library,' Hyder told him. 'Let it be the biggest and the best, full of books. Build an entirely new building if need be. Let translators be appointed, many of them, I want. . . .' He wanted to continue with detailed instructions so as to have the satisfaction of personally ordering the fulfilment of his son's wishes but did not know what further details he should give. Then he added, somewhat lamely, 'You do understand, Purnaiya, don't you?'

'Perfectly,' Purnaiya replied with a smile. Hyder looked at Purnaiya with affection. There was some envy in that look also.

'You do understand my son,' said Hyder, 'more than I do, sometimes.'

'To love is to understand,' said Purnaiya, with a broad grin.

'Are you trying to tell me, you wily Brahmin, that you love my son more than I do?'

'Perhaps,' Purnaiya replied unperturbed.

Hyder picked up a thick book from the table and was about to throw it at Purnaiya.

'I thought your son taught you reverence for books,' Purnaiya said laughing.

Hyder laughed and said, 'For books, yes, for you, no.'

Thus began the project of Tipu Sultan's Library which in a decade and a half became one of the finest libraries in the world. Purnaiya appointed Nurul Amin as the Chief Librarian. His Assistant Librarians, Cataloguers, Research and Reference Assistants, were recruited from several countries. French, German, English, Greek and Latin translators were located and appointed.

Apart from the Central Library, Tipu Sultan, with Purnaiya's assistance, set up small libraries throughout the kingdom. 'Reading should be as free as breathing,' he had said. Boys and girls were encouraged to visit libraries and read the books.

Requisitions were sent out all over the world for books. Tipu loved those golden moments when his books would arrive. 'These are my treasures, Purnaiya,' he often said. 'A treasure that shall outlive all gold and silver—a treasure no one would rob or destroy.'

But how wrong he was! When the English finally overtook Seringapatam, his library was one of the first casualties.

(ii)

Men of learning were approached from time to time for suggestions and advice on the books to be acquired for Tipu Sultan's libraries. Amongst them was Pierre Caron de Beaumarchais, the versatile Frenchman, the author of the famous *Barber of Seville* and of *Figaro*, and a fiery advocate of the cause of American liberty. He had even founded a firm—Hortalez and Company—for the supply of arms to the Americans. He was an ardent admirer of liberal thought and a contemporary of Voltaire with a deep attachment for him. It was he who had helped Marquis de Lafayette and other French volunteers to cross over the Atlantic to fight for the American cause.

It was towards the end of 1776 when Count Vergennes, the French Foreign Minister, referred to Beaumarchais the request he had received from Purnaiya, on behalf of Hyder Ali for suggestions for outstanding and learned books on French culture, literature, arts and philosophy.

'You will note, Monsieur de Beaumarchais,' said Count Vergennes, 'that Prime Minister Purnaiya is seeking suggestions for books which are both outstanding and learned. This description would seem to exclude your own books.'

'On the contrary, Count Vergennes,' replied Beaumarchais, 'the description excludes all books other than mine. Still, out of charity, I shall compile a list which includes other authors as well.'

Beaumarchais was amused at the request on behalf of Hyder Ali. 'No doubt, an oriental despot and a tyrant—still if he thirsts for books, he could not be altogether worthless,' thought Beaumarchais. No, he would do better than merely compiling a list. From his own collection, Beaumarchais generously took out a large number of books and some he purchased—all devoted to liberal thought and wedded to the political philosophy which accepted the right of revolution by people against a tyrannical sovereign. 'Let the despot learn what the victims of his despotism think—and let him then quiver with fear if he shall not reform himself,' was the amused thought of Beaumarchais as he began collecting books for Hyder Ali. Then he remembered that Prime Minister Purnaiya's letter, read out to him by Count Vergennes, had also sought information on books which had been translated in the Persian or the Indian languages. Beaumarchais could not think of any but, always a man of inspiration, he turned to his friend Raza Mahdi, a Persian scholar who resided in Paris, read much but wrote little because 'women of Paris, the wines of France and the charms of the world distract me, my dear Pierre'. He, however, undertook to translate the American Declaration of Independence in Persian.

(iii)

Thus it was that in 1778 Tipu Sultan received a large number of books which Monsieur de Beaumarchais had donated to Count Vergennes for the Library of Mysore, and amongst them was the English text, with French and Persian translations, of the Declaration of Independence drawn up by Thomas Jefferson and adopted by the Congress of the United States of America at Philadelphia on 4 July 1776.

Tipu Sultan was deeply stirred by the Declaration. He read enraptured, its sonorous and resounding phrases, its deep conviction of sincerity, its cry for justice, its demand for freedom from tyranny, its righteous indignation and its vengeful wrath at the indignities inflicted on a helpless people, inalienable rights of man, deposition of a tyrant, establishment of freedom from foreign yoke, war in a just cause — were the thoughts that moved him and filled his consciousness.

He read the second paragraph of the Declaration again:

> We hold these truths to be self-evident, that all men are created equal, that they are endowed by their Creator with certain inalienable rights, that among these are life, liberty, and the pursuit of happiness — that to secure these rights, governments are instituted among men, deriving their just powers from the consent of the governed, that whenever any form of government becomes destructive of these ends, it is the right of the people to alter or to abolish it, and to institute new government, laying its foundation on such principles, and organising its powers in such form, as to them shall seem most likely to effect their safety and happiness.

Tipu Sultan read on. He paused at the passage which spoke movingly of the devastation by the unworthy English King.

> He has plundered our seas, ravaged our coasts, burnt our towns, and destroyed the lives of our people.
>
> He is, at this time, transporting large armies of foreign mercenaries to complete the works of death, desolation, and tyranny, already begun with circumstances of cruelty and perfidy, scarcely paralleled in the most barbarous ages. . . .'
>
> In every stage of these oppressions we have petitioned for redress in the most humble terms. Our repeated petitions have been answered only by repeated injury.

A Prince, whose character is thus marked by every act which may define a tyrant, is unfit to be the ruler of a free people.

And then, Tipu Sultan paused again at the final paragraph solemnly declaring the United Colonies as free and independent States and pledging American lives, fortunes and sacred honour in the cause.

He had read it silently at first. Then he read it out to Sayyad Saheb and Purnaiya. 'What do you think of it?' he asked.

'Sounds like treason to me,' Sayyad Saheb ventured. Purnaiya was silent.

'Treason, surely,' rejoined Tipu, 'but treason by who? It seems to me it is the King here who commits treason against his subjects.'

'Rather an extraordinary thought that, isn't it?' Sayyad Saheb questioned.

'No,' Tipu explained that it was not extraordinary at all. There was nothing new nor novel about it. It was exactly in line with political reality as it existed in ancient India . 'What is thrilling here is that the ancient Indian concept of kingship should come to be transformed into deeds far away in the United States of America, spelling disaster for a colonising, imperial power.'

He told Sayyad Saheb then of the Indian theory of kingship, which involved no heavenly prototype but looked back to a social contract between the king and his people. He narrated to him the legend:

> At the dawn of birth of mankind, humanity lived on an immaterial plane, singing and dancing on air in a sort of fairyland, needing neither food nor clothing. There was no private property or family or government or laws or authority. Gradually, thereafter the process of

cosmic decay began and mankind became earthbound, acquiring the urge for food and shelter. As men lost their primeval glory, class distinctions arose, and they entered into covenants with one another, accepting the institutions of private property and family, In order that these covenants were adhered to, that private property was respected and that family was protected, people met together and decided to appoint one man from among them to maintain order in return for a share of the produce of their fields and herds. He was called 'the Great Chosen One' [Mahasammata], and he received the title of Raja because he pleased the people—from the verb Ranjayati ['he pleases'].

That was, Tipu Sultan explained, the theory of kingship in ancient India, the world's earliest version of the contractual theory of the State, implying that the main purpose of government is to establish order, and that the King, as head of the government, is the first social servant, and ultimately dependent on the suffrage of his subjects.

Sayyad Saheb and Purnaiya had retired. Tipu read the Declaration again. He knew that in ancient Indian thought also only one strand was evident on the question of the origin of monarchy—that the King was appointed for, and owed his continuance to, the needs of the people. It was his duty to protect the law and govern righteously. If he failed in that duty, he was no longer the King. Tipu Sultan recalled the passages from *Arthasastra* which spoke of the election of the first King Manu Vaivaswata. Yes, it was the people's pleasure to bring the King and their pleasure to part with him if he failed to fulfil the contract. The mystical theory of kingship or the 'divine rights of kings' was alien to early Indian thought, Tipu Sultan knew. But he also knew that beginning with the

Greeks, many foreign invaders had come with their disruptive influences. He remembered the coronation songs from the *Atharva Veda* and its many references to election of the Kings by the people; and the consecration hymns from the *Rig Veda* which spoke of the need of people's approval if kingship is to be continued.

Tipu's mind now turned to Indian rulers of several States and the English colonisers. He thought of their divine pretensions, of their contempt for the people and of their utter disregard for the hopes and aspirations of the masses. To Tipu Sultan, the American Declaration of Independence, therefore, came like a breath of fresh air, transforming into deeds, a concept of Indian thought in which he fervently deeply believed.

(iv)

Later, Tipu Sultan enquired about the progress of the American War of Independence. He heard of Benjamin Franklin, the envoy of the American insurgents who with his simple manners, plain speaking and home-spun suit was able to charm the French society. He learned of the young French noblemen who, even though France had not yet declared war against England, went to join George Washington to fight for American Independence. Many told him of Franklin's efforts to get assistance from the French government and of his difficult pecuniary position.

Then came to Mysore the Reverend Christian Frederick Schwartz. This gentleman, born in Prussia, had come out to India to work with the Protestant Mission in a Danish possession. Later, he discovered in himself a natural talent for intrigue, diplomacy and spying. He also found that these activities paid far more than religious devotions. He became ready to serve whosoever paid him the most, and often he acted as a double agent. He was an interesting conversationalist and carried out regular correspondence with many acquaintances in foreign countries. Often, his news was well ahead of official despatches. Tipu Sultan who had not till then known of the shady side of his character was impressed with this seemingly pious man who could give so much information on what was happening throughout the world. Of Franklin, Schwartz had spoken as of an old friend. He dwelt on his patriotism and learning, on his trials and tribulations, particularly in getting monetary assistance from the French. Next day, Tipu Sultan entrusted to Schwartz a large sum of money as donation to Franklin. Schwartz who was quite certain that his own need was greater—at least more important—than Franklin's naturally kept the money for himself. Tipu Sultan received a letter from Paris purporting to bear Franklin's signature. The letter had fulsome praise for Tipu Sultan and his father, spoke of Franklin's almost life long ambition of paying respects to them in person and meanwhile asked for more money. The letter, so full of high flattery and low servility, had sorely disappointed Tipu who had formulated entirely a different picture of Franklin in his mind. Subsequently, Tipu came to know that it was a forgery contrived by the confidence trickster Schwartz. He laughed at his own foolishness at being taken in by the rogue. Thereafter, Schwartz kept the longest possible distance between Tipu Sultan and himself and soon blossomed into a full-fledged English intelligence agent. He began calling himself an English missionary and changed his name to Swartz. He later, wrote scurrilously about Hyder Ali and Tipu Sultan. Much of that writing has come down to us, though it strangely omits the incident when Sayyad Saheb captured Swartz, trussed him up on a horse and brought him to Tipu more dead than alive.

'You seem rather tongue-tied this morning, you rogue,' Tipu asked Swartz, who was shivering, though not from cold.

'Well, what about our money to Benjamin Franklin?' Tipu continued. 'I hear he hasn't got it yet.'

Schwartz pleaded that he had forgotten it but that he would send it on to Franklin immediately.

'But you did remember to send me a forged letter?' Tipu reminded him. 'Out with the money, right now.'

'Sayyad Saheb has robbed me of all,' was the pitiful reply.

'Good,' Tipu replied. 'Let that be between you and Sayyad Saheb. What about my money for our American friend?'

'Will you let me go if I pay?' Schwartz asked.

'Who knows!' said Tipu with a smile.

'Let me go then and within seven days the amount will be on its way to you, I promise,' Schwartz said.

'You and your promises!' laughed Tipu. 'Sayyad Saheb, let a gibbet be prepared. This man has entertained us while he lived, let him now entertain us while he dies.' Tipu was bluffing but how was Schwartz to know!

Schwartz begged for mercy but getting no response, finally wrote out notes to two of his bankers. Messengers left for the bankers. Meanwhile, Schwartz remained in Tipu Sultan's camp. Tipu ordered a new suit of clothes for him, saw to it that he got good food and attention to his personal wants. In a day or two Schwartz regained his old assurance and style.

'Come, entertain us, with all the news,' Tipu invited him.

Sayyad Saheb intervened: 'Let Zaman [Tipu's barber] be prepared to sharpen his razor to cut his tongue out, in case he tells any lies.'

Timorously, Schwartz joined in the laughter but then his nervousness disappeared as he began to tell Tipu Sultan of the news from faraway lands, embellishing then often with gossip and personal comments. Some of the factual information that he furnished was known to Tipu Sultan already for, at his suggestion, Purnaiya had been collecting not only books and manuscripts for his library but had also established a chain of correspondents for regular flow of news. Still, Schwartz had for him many interesting bits of gossip and news. He described the surrender of Cornwallis at Yorktown. He talked of the surrender of the British army under General Burgoyne to the Americans at Saratoga in 1777 as if he had been there personally watching the scene. He spoke of the opposition by Louis XVI, the King of France, to joining the alliance with the American rebels and how he was foiled by his own wife, Queen Marie Antoinette and by his Prime Minister Compte de Maurepas, a cynical old man who was interested only in maintaining his position by intriguing among the factions of Versailles. He also said much of Benjamin Franklin and of the affection in which he was held. Of this, however, Schwartz was certain that the American cause was doomed. When Tipu Sultan intervened to express a contrary hope, Schwartz began to appreciate that Americans had a chance and later even professed to be convinced that their cause would triumph. But the French, the allies of the Americans, he was sure, were doomed.

Both the bankers responded to notes sent to them by Schwartz. He had written to two of them in fear, as a sort of insurance, lest one of them defaulted. The result was that the messengers returned bringing to Tipu Sultan twice the amount that Franklin should have received. Tipu Sultan returned half of it to Schwartz. When the time came for Schwartz to part, Tipu presented him with a horse and gave him also the rest of the money that his bankers had sent, saying, 'You have entertained us with your stories. Take all this as a gift. I shall settle accounts with Franklin.'

Schwartz left, promising good behaviour in the future, though he was not called upon to do so. 'I shall sin no more,' he said. But he continued to sin. So deep-rooted was his rascality that a sense of gratitude was alien to him. In any case, if asked, he would have hotly denied that gratitude was a basic ingredient of a human being. Of dogs, certainly; of horses and elephants, possibly; but of men, no—he would have said. It was Schwartz who travelled the length and breadth of the country gathering intelligence for the English, inciting rebellions by local chiefs against the Kingdom of Mysore, encouraging English commanders, notably William Fullarton, to violate the Treaty of Mangalore by attacking Coimbatore. Also, it was Schwartz who spread the falsehood about Hyder Ali's last advice—a dying injunction—to Tipu Sultan. The story was that when Tipu was performing the last rites for his father's body, he found a scrap of paper hidden in Hyder's turban, on which was written, 'I have gained nothing by the war with the English, but now alas I am no longer alive... the English will certainly follow you and carry the war in your country.... Better to make peace with the English on whatever terms you can procure....'

What was the purpose of such falsehood? Mere mischief? Wishful thinking? Perhaps; or was it intended to show to the world that so invincible was the might of the English that it was recognised even by a formidable ruler like Hyder Ali—Hyder Ali of whom Edmund Burke had said in 1783 'indubitably one of the greatest princes as well as the greatest warrior that India ever produced... mild and equitable... one of the first politicians of his day.'

(v)

Sayyad Saheb watched Schwartz leave. 'Interesting rogue,' he said, 'but I agree with him about France. Whether the Americans succeed or not, the French it seems to me are doomed.'

'How so?' Purnaiya asked.

'When a monarchy chooses to support an anarchy,' said Sayyad Saheb, 'the flood tide of history will wash away that monarchy as well.'

'Anarchy! Monarchy! are these not words?' Tipu Sultan asked. 'What you call anarchy appears to me to be a just cry for liberty. And monarchy—why, can you not conceive of a monarchy that is benevolent and enlightened, responsive to the aspirations of the people and their just demands?

'But,' Purnaiya intervened, 'that is not the picture I have of the French monarchy. They are in this war with the Americans not for the cry of liberty but to settle old scores with England. Don't forget they have gone into this war after the English defeat is in sight. Surely, the French are not fighting for a cause or for a principle.'

'Perhaps,' rejoined Tipu, 'but what about America? Will you say that their anguish is coated with greed, too? Will they ever, you think, settle down to their old ways of corruption and injustice after the English have been driven out of their land?'

'I do not know, Tipu Sultan,' Purnaiya replied. 'America is a young nation. Youth forgets. Drunk with power, prosperity and arrogance, who knows to what excesses they would go after they have been liberated. Do not forget her past?'

'Her past!' Tipu said, 'it has been nothing but misery heaped by the unworthy and tyrannical English King.'

'I beg of you, Tipu Sultan,' said Purnaiya, 'look a little deeper in the past.'

Tipu looked at him with a question in his glance. 'Yes,' said Purnaiya. 'The American nation sits on the vast graveyard of the Red Indian race. Was there ever a greater slaughter in the entire history of humanity? I doubt it. They called them savages and murdered them by the millions with callous barbarism and brutality until they wiped out the whole race. The whole race, if you please. What about the right of that race to life, liberty and the pursuit of happiness, and their inalienable right of equality? Why did the Americans not give to their hapless, helpless victims what they now seek from their cruel master? Yes, I repeat, Tipu Sultan, what about the anguish of the Red Indian race that cries out voiceless?'

Sayyad Saheb was delighted. Never once had he seen Purnaiya in anger—always he had kept his composure but now he saw him livid with rage. 'It is good to see Purnaiya worked up,' he said.

Purnaiya laughed but without heartiness. 'We worry,' he said soberly, 'about matters that do not concern us. You asked me about America. Yes, she shall be free. No longer will she suffer from British brigandage. She will have a stirring awakening, a period of vast intellectual activity and surely she will march ahead, with gigantic strides in the economic field. I can see her evolving a just and honourable way of life—but how long will she remain that way, I do not know. Will her love for justice, freedom and equality be permanent and immortal, I do not know; will it apply to entire humanity again or will it be self-centred, I do not know.'

Tipu loved Purnaiya when he spoke like this. 'But what is your feeling?' he asked.

'I really don't know,' said Purnaiya, 'but this much I say to you that a nation that is born out of violence and bloodshed against an unarmed, peace-loving people and lays claim to the land of the race it has exterminated by guile, treachery, brutality and barbarism has much to atone for.'

Tipu Sultan recalled the ringing tone of sincerity and dignity in the American Declaration of Independence. These Americans were men of honour, he was certain, and the path they would take would be not only of glory in the future but of atonement for the past.

(vi)

In 1783, while Mangalore was about to fall to Tipu Sultan's arms, the French contingent which was supporting him withdrew from battle as soon as the news reached of the Treaty of Versailles which brought to a close the Seven Years' War between England and France and which also ended England's colonial rule over the American colonies. United States of America was now a free nation. Tipu Sultan rejoiced. At his orders, a salute of 108 guns was fired to greet the birth of the new nation across the seas. He regretted particularly now that Schwartz should have defrauded Franklin and that he himself should not have had the time to send his modest donation. He wondered if Franklin or the United States knew of his good wishes. He even wondered if good wishes had a part to play in the success or failure of a campaign. On 4 July 1783 the anniversary of the Declaration of American Independence, the salute of 108 guns was repeated in Mysore.

Many wondered that an event so far away should so interest their Sultan. When the one effect of the event was the desertion by the French contingent in the midst of an action against the English at Mangalore, surely the event could not be worthy of jubilation. Even the French themselves were surprised and sullen about it. 'Is the Sultan celebtrating our withdrawal; were we of such little consequence?' they asked. The French knew that the Indian forces were indignant about their withdrawal and had openly hinted that the French had been bribed by the English and their agent Schwartz to do so. Should the Sultan add insult to injury by such celebrations? they asked. Some Indians had been ragging the French that it was Sultan's way of congratulating himself on getting rid of the troublesome French.

'No,' said Tipu Sultan to the assembly which he had called to bid farewell to the French officers—Bussy, Lallee, Boudelot, Gourgaud and others.

'You served my interests as long as you could. Now your interests call you elsewhere. I bid you farewell. We part as friends. I have nothing but kind words, kind thoughts for you. I rejoice over an event whereas you should rejoice more, for it was your arms, your ships, your soldiers who fought for the cause of liberty in America.' To this large assembly of Indian and French officers, Tipu Sultan read out portions from the American Declaration. He spoke to them then of the colonies across the Atlantic that had striven for freedom from English tyranny and inhumanity; of France which fought for the freedom, not for gain or power but to uphold a principle; of America which was now free and independent to pursue the lofty ideals of her Declaration; he told them of the language of Locke, Montesquieu, Rousseau, Voltaire and Benjamin Franklin; of the liberal thought of ancient India which clearly enunciated the principle that the contract with the sovereign was dissolved if the sovereign failed in his duty to uphold justice and the fundamental rights of his people and that in such a case people not only had the right but also an obligation to remove the tyrant by revolution, if need be. He told them of the oath of the Indian kings at the time of their coronation to serve the people—'May I be deprived of heaven, of life, and of offspring if I oppress you. In the happinness of my subjects lies my happiness, in their welfare my welfare; whatever pleases myself I shall consider as not good, but whatever pleases my subjects I shall consider as good.'

Tipu Sultan concluded his address by telling them: 'That is why I rejoice my friends, over the victory of France, over the victory of America—for in that victory is the triumph for the rights of Man.' He continued, 'I know that the time has come for us to part, for such is the decision of your Government and I shall not try to detain you. But, when you go back to your country, go with this knowledge and carry this hope to your countrymen that though you have seen in India the crumbling ruins of a proud civilisation, a day shall surely dawn when this country shall regain its lost heritage. Every blow that was struck in the cause of American liberty, by Americans, by Frenchmen, was a blow in the cause of liberty throughout the world, in France, India and elsewhere — and so long as a single insolent and savage tyrant remains, the struggle shall continue.'

These simple war-hardened soldiers of France had come across the seas to India — most of them to seek their fortunes, some in search of glory, a few in pursuit of adventure. They were neither scholars nor intellectuals, they were unlettered men with little knowledge of history or political theory. Did they have an understanding of what Tipu Sultan was telling them? No one knows. But what is known is that in France, six years thence when the royal prison fortress of Bastille was stormed and when the French Revolution flowered to proclaim the abolition of a tyrannical monarchy, amongst those who took up the banner of Liberty, Equality and Fraternity were many who had listened to Tipu Sultan's address on that day. As Gourgaud lay dying in Paris from the bullets of the Kings's militia, he said, 'Let Tipu Sultan know that I died for a dream that he inspired.'

43

THE MAULVI FROM MUSCAT

'THANK YOU, MY SON, ISLAM DOES NOT HAVE A TRUER SON,' SAID Maulvi Al Amin to Tipu Sultan. He had come from Muscat, with letters of commendation that left no doubt about his worth, consequence and erudition. Tipu Sultan gave him a large donation for the mosque which he was to construct in Muscat. Also, he gave him a purse containing one thousand pagodas as a personal gift.

Later, Maulvi moved around in Mysore and other parts of India. After a year, on his way back to Muscat, he again called on Tipu Sultan. Exchange of courtesies over, he sought permission to raise a matter with Tipu Sultan.

'I have been to many parts of this country — where the Hindu kings reign, where the British rule and where sons of Islam hold their sway. Many were the differences in their customs, laws and practices. One factor alone was constant. The Hindu kings support their temples and their Gods; the Christians their churches and their Jesus; and the Muslims their Prophet and their mosques. Yet, here in your Kingdom of Mysore, you give freely not only to Islam and its mosques — which is your duty and your pleasure — but also to the infidels and their temples.'

THE MAULVI FROM MUSCAT

'Yes,' Tipu Sultan replied softly, as if that was all the answer that was needed.

'But does not the one cancel the other?' enquired the Maulvi.

Tipu Sultan walked to the balcony and looked at the magnificent temple of Sri Ranganatha situated within the fort of Seringapatam.

'I have grown up under the shadow of that temple,' he told the Maulvi. Then he looked at the clock and added, 'In a short while, you will hear the temple bells and the hymns of the Brahmin priests. Hear them and tell me if they cancel your faith in Islam? They have not affected mine.'

'No, son, you take my words literally,' said the Maulvi smiling. 'What I intended to convey was that a single-minded support to one's own religion is necessary as is indeed evidenced by the practice of sovereigns all over the world. If you support your own religion and also that of another with the same patronage and funds, the result is that both grow side by side and your own religion does not advance beyond the other.'

'That is to presuppose that there is rivalry or hostility between religions,' said Tipu Sultan.

'There can be no question of rivalry as such between the religions since ours is the one and true religion while others merely masquerade as religions. All the more reason that a true son of Islam should not recognise the existence of another religion, much less support it.'

The bells of Sri Ranganatha temple could now be heard. The hymns had begun. Silently, Tipu Sultan looked at the Maulvi. He was wondering how a theologian of Maulvi's fame could have expressed such a thought.

'If you forgive the presumption,' said Tipu Sultan after a long pause, 'I would like your permission to remind you of what is said in the Quran—that in the Garden of Wisdom bloom many flowers, but they all bear within their fragrant hearts the Nectar of One Immortal Love and likewise it is with all the different religions in the world.'

After another pause, Tipu asked, 'Is it also not said that when the Light of Love illumines the soul, all His Messengers are honoured, and none are scorned?—and is it not true that Prophet Muhammad himself said: 'We believe in Allah and what has been handed down to us, and what has been given to Abraham and Ishamel, to Moses and Jesus, and what has been given to the prophets from the Lord. We do not discriminate between them.' Therefore, is it not the essence and spirit of the Quran that their God and My God are one?'

'Son,' said Maulvi, 'we go deep in theology and some day it shall delight me to sit by your side to discourse on it. But as you know I am also the temporal adviser of the Imam of Muscat. Princes of many lands have often honoured me for worldly advice. It is because of the love which my illustrious ruler bears towards you and the respect in which I hold you that I presume to submit my advice. Allow me to continue. Today the Hindu temples and the Hindu Brahmins are supported by your magnificent donations even more so than our mosques. Time and again one hears of your protection of the Hindu customs and their religion. Assume that all these energies and funds were diverted to your own people, will you not have their loyal, fervent, fanatic support—to dispose of their lives, fortunes and honour in your cause. True, both the communities are now wedded to your cause but the fury and fervour that you can whip up by single-minded and exclusive devotion to your own people will be thousand-fold and every battle you have to fight will be regarded as a crusade or a holy war. Besides, I do believe that this time-honoured practice which other kings follow must be rooted in wisdom.'

Tipu Sultan replied with a courteous smile: 'I have no doubt that they are wise in their ways. But then there are perhaps some differences between their goals and mine. You said I should support the religion of my own people. Here comes the difference. Who are my people?'

Then Tipu Sultan answered his own question. 'All of them,' he said, and the wave of his hand clearly went towards the temple that could be seen from the balcony. 'Yes,' he continued, 'those that ring the temple bells and those that pray in the mosques—they are my people and this land is theirs and mine.'

The Maulvi bowed but Tipu Sultan had not finished. 'There is another difference,' he said. 'You suggested creation of disunity as a means of achieving power but that is to assume that attainment of power is to be regarded as a goal which is higher than that of achieving unity. Then perhaps your suggestion also involves benevolence to one community and coupled with it, the persecution of another to achieve certain ends. Here, Sir, it seems to me, we have a fundamental difference of opinion, with regard to the connection between the means and the end. To me, means and the end are convertible terms in spiritual and philosophical sense and I cannot conceive that questionable methods can bring about the realisation of a result that is worthwhile. Let me finally say that I am born of this soil which has given birth and nurtured many religions. What do these religions teach me? That all men are brothers. I have a Prime Minister—Purnaiya—who is a Hindu. My father appointed many Hindus to high posts and so have I—not merely because they are Hindus, nor to seek a balance of power but because of their merit. I have conferred grants on temples, given gifts to Brahmins, installed their idols, assisted in construction and maintenance of their magnificent temples throughout the Kingdom, because believe me, I am convinced that both as King and an Indian I am duty-bound and honour-bound to do so. I have read with respect the Hindu system of philosophy, their Vedas and their Shastras. They regard all religions as containing the essential elements of truth in them and enjoin an attitude of respect and reverence towards them all. The Quran, I believe, teaches me likewise. Tell me, have I misunderstood the Quran?'

'No, son, you have not misunderstood the Quran,' said Maulvi Al Amin, and added softly, almost as an afterthought, 'though many others have.'

The Maulvi and Tipu Sultan parted from each other with an embrace. The Maulvi tarried in Seringapatam for seven days more; with what doubts and convictions he left, no one knows. But on the day of his departure, the temple of Sri Ranganatha of Seringapatam received an anonymous donation of a purse containing one thousand pagodas. A short-shrivelled man had stood outside the gate of the temple, accosted a devotee entering in, handed him a purse, begged him to place it before the idol and then walked away as if urgent business called him elsewhere. It is said that the description of the stranger fitted that of the Maulvi and that the purse was the same which Tipu Sultan had gifted to the old man.

44

FOUR YEARS OF ONE MAN

THE SHIP BRINGING LORD CORNWALLIS SAILED INTO MADRAS AS Tipu Sultan was crossing over the flooded Tungabhadra river to deal with the Nizam and the Marathas. For weeks, Cornwallis stayed in Madras to assess Tipu's military situation and then he moved to Calcutta.

In six months I shall begin my operations, Cornwallis had thought to himself; another six months should suffice to crush the Tiger; let him not recover from the wounds that the Nizam and the Marathas shall have inflicted on him; meanwhile let him also suffer from the pressure of internal revolts and conspiracies; yes, six months to wipe the shame and agony of the humiliation at Yorktown; to rehabilitate my military reputation; to achieve glory; to make good the loss of the Empire from treachery across the Atlantic.

But it was not to be. Tipu Sultan was emerging victorious. Even the internal revolts were subsiding. There was a general movement of repudiation and everyone was holding that only under compulsion did he fail to discharge his duties to Sultan.

Warren Hastings had been correct, Cornwallis thought; to annihilate Tipu Sultan, it was necessary to have patience and preparation; yes, utmost preparation.

Vast storehouses of materials and ammunitions had already been piled up since 1784 when Tipu Sultan had dictated the peace treaty to the English; not enough, thought Cornwallis; much more remained to be done if Tipu Sultan had to be wiped out; meanwhile he must silence the proddings of his heart that urged instant action against Sultan. The demands from England were also getting frequent and peremptory. He dreaded the despatches from London. Often, they asked, 'How long will you take to avenge America?' 'Will you wait, until the Oriental despot [Tipu] himself begins the attack?' 'Macpherson's account leaves no doubt that things have been made easy and comfortable for you since he has embroiled Tipu with formidable Indian powers like the Marathas and the Nizam with whom he is now engaged in a bitter war; one thrust from you and he is at your mercy. What are you waiting for?'

'Patience, patience,' he urged. 'Tipu is stronger than you think.' To himself he added, 'One Yorktown is enough for me.'

Later, he thought: 'I must join Tipu Sultan if I cannot beat him.' He was sure that a stab in the back would, then, be easier. He sent his emissary to Tipu loaded with gifts, compliments and a suggestion that the valiant Tipu Sultan and the gallant English forces must join together to teach the Marathas and the Nizam a lesson. Courteously, Tipu Sultan heard the emissary of Cornwallis.

'Thank your noble Lord,' said Tipu Sultan. 'Tell him that I pray for peace. Too long have I been on battlefields in the midst of grief and pain, surrounded by corpses, to wish for anything else. But if it be that I am forced into a war I shall face it. Then let my enemies beware.' Then Sultan added, slowly but in a ringing voice as if afraid that any of his words might not be heard: 'But of this I am certain, that God shall not allow that day to dawn when I have to fight alongside the English to face the Indians.'

This was the reply that the emissary of Lord Cornwallis took to his master.

Impassively, Lord Cornwallis heard the reply. Macartney and James Anderson were present.

'Arrogant bastard,' said Anderson. 'Thinks he can beat them all—the Marathas, the Nizam, the Coorgis, the Poligars—all by himself.'

'Is that your impression also from Tipu's reply?' Cornwallis asked looking at Macartney.

'Something like it,' replied Macartney. 'Don't you think so?'

'Perhaps,' said Cornwallis, thoughtfully, 'But I think he wants to tell us that we are a race apart,' He now raised his voice, 'So we are, by God, we are—and so shall we remain.'

Cornwallis began his feverish preparations for the great campaign against Tipu Sultan. Always a man of indomitable energy and tremendous organisational skill it now seemed as if a missionary zeal was goading him. Troops, reserve corps, horses, fodder, storehouses of ammunition, guns, siege trains, bridge-building materials, pontoons, wagons, bullocks to carry them, began to be assembled. He was determined to have superiority in numbers, superiority in equipment and pile weight upon weight. Tipu's lands were fertile and green, he knew, but still he must not rely on them. He must set up his own granaries. He must have a gigantic array of troops. Strength. Speed. A war machine that cannot fail.

Also, I must secure alliances with the Nizam and the Marathas, said Cornwallis to himself. He almost smiled in contemplation of what would happen to the Nizam and the Marathas after Tipu Sultan is liquidated. He chided himself for looking so far ahead. One step is enough, the rest inevitable.

Cornwallis was not without a sense of personal kindness or humanity. He knew what was involved in collecting vast storehouses for the campaign against Tipu Sultan. He had a clear idea of the pitiless suffering to which he was subjecting the people of the provinces under the control of the English. But he had a mission to fulfil, a goal to achieve. Besides, these men who had to toil and groan, suffer the lash and be bonded in service, were not white, after all. His orders to his Governors and Administrators were crisp and clear. Let the country be laid waste with fire and sword if need be, but the targets must be met. Taxes, more taxes, fines, confiscations—increase them; and use any means but collect them.

'Let them,' said Cornwallis to himself, 'suffer now. I shall make up for all their sorrows; I shall give them a good government and enlightened reforms; I shall wipe out the memory of their sufferings; but let nothing stand between me and my victory against Tipu.' Indeed, in his mind he had thought of various measures to alleviate the pitiable condition of the helpless, hapless people over whom he ruled. Some of these measures he had already initiated; others would have to wait until he had fully armed himself against Tipu. His predecessors had power and wealth. They were interested in dividends, plunder and treasures, and not in the improvement or even protection of those who had come under their sway. But Cornwallis looked ahead and knew that for the future of the English empire, an orderly government and enlightened reforms must replace the present anarchy and chaos in India. But his reformist zeal, he knew, will have to wait until his conquests were secure. Four years passed. The storehouses grew.

45

FOUR YEARS OF ANOTHER MAN

(i)

'IF YOU LOVE ME, SHOULD YOU NOT PUT UP WITH MY WEAKNESS sometimes?' asked Tipu Sultan.

The question was addressed to Mir Sadik who had bitterly complained about Tipu's practice of pardoning those who had been guilty of treason or conspiracy against the Kingdom of Mysore.

'When you give unmerited pardon, you endanger the very essence of your power,' Mir Sadik had complained. 'Howsoever profuse your generosity, your justice must be severe.'

Tipu Sultan himself did not know clearly why, when the guilt of the traitor was proven beyond any doubt, he still hesitated to pass the sentence of death. He was certain in his mind that Mir Sadik was right—a King who knows how to reward must also know how to punish. Why then this weakness?

'Perhaps I think of their past services, their friendship to my father and to me,' he rationalised.

'Friendship is a word that should mean nothing to a king,' Mir Sadik had urged. 'The king must be as hard as irons.

Otherwise they—the very criminals that you spare—will bite your hand, mock at you. The King reigns only through the fear he inspires.'

'Fear?' Tipu asked. 'And you think that people's affections have no role to play in the strength of the Kingdom?'

Mir Sadik looked at Tipu Sultan with incredulity. To his mind, the thought which Tipu had expressed was far too ludicrous to deserve a response. Still, it seemed, Tipu wanted an answer.

'Affection of the people—idle words these,' said Mir Sadik and then added, 'trust no one, Tipu Sultan, no one, not even me.'

'I hope I shall cease to exist if the day comes when I have to distrust you,' replied Tipu.

Prophecy? who knows!

(ii)

The conversation between Tipu Sultan and Mir Sadik had come about as the result of pardon granted to sixteen veteran commanders of Mysore who, lured by gold and promises, were smuggling Mysorean arms to the English. Amongst them were men who had served his father. Now they were assisting the English in piling up their weapons of destruction to be aimed at Mysore. At the head of the conspiracy were Mir Ibrahim and Arshad Beg. Both had openly and unashamedly wept when Hyder Ali had died. Often, Arshad Beg had risked his life for Hyder's cause. Mir Ibrahim had picked up Hyder from the field of battle when his horse had been shot under him and while the enemy bullets rained, he shielded him with his body. Mir Ibrahim still limped from the wound he received on that day.

No, Tipu said to himself, he could not consign such men to death, whatever their present treachery. He remembered what

Mir Sadik had said. 'Only those who are feared are loved. The sword of the king inspires affection, not his tenderness. Above all, a king must make himself feared.'

'True perhaps but how do I stifle another voice that bids me otherwise?' Tipu wondered.

(iii)

Mir Sadik was not the only one bewildered by Tipu Sultan's tenderness towards those caught in an act of treason. 'A king must not permit himself to be guided by sentiment,' they had said. Still, generosity to old servants was perhaps understandable. But what was Tipu Sultan up to, ordering that courts be established to try offenders, that written records of trials should be maintained, that clear testimony of witnesses to the crime must be available, that the accused must not be presumed guilty until so proved and must have the benefit of the doubt, that those who accuse falsely must themselves be tried, that death sentences must not be passed, that for every punishment, an appeal shall lie, that between the conclusion of the trial and the final sentence a period of a fortnight must elapse to permit the judge time for cool reflection. . . .

What utter and absolute nonsense, they muttered to themselves, though in their approach to Tipu Sultan, they were polite and respectful. Justice, they argued, must be swift and simple. What greater proof can there be of a man's guilt than the fact that the man has been arrested, charged, brought before an administrator and sentenced? What will happen to the discretionary powers and patronage of administrators and governors, if they were to be hampered with rules of procedures, testimony and other unnecesary paraphernalia? Surely, those seasoned men, grown old in the service of Hyder Ali and his son, could at a glance discover if the accused carried on his face the evidence of guilt.

Like his father, Tipu Sultan was always ready and accessible to discuss such matters with his commanders, governors and others. The only difference was that Hyder's language was deliberately tough and sometimes flippant, his laugh rich and deep while Tipu Sultan listened attentively, said little, laughed even less. Even in his annoyance there was none of that blazing intensity that seared his father's countenance. Tipu treated himself as an equal amongst equals in such discussions. He did not try to win these arguments by virtue of his rank but by appeal to reason. Still, the sad note that survives is that while every word that his father had uttered was clear to them, much of what Tipu Sultan said mystified them. How could these men, grown old and wise in the ways of the world, understand this man who played not on their emotions of glory, greed and adventure but appealed to something abstract and intangible, such as the rights of citizens to justice and fairplay; if indeed people had rights, well let them go about enforcing them; surely the existence of the right presupposes the ability to enforce it; power, power alone, generates and guarantees the rights; in any case the strong are always benevolent.

But with sorrow, they heard the contrary view. 'Power without law is chaos,' said Tipu Sultan. 'Without law an individual perishes. Governments also so perish.'

As to the instant ability of the governors, administrators and commanders to judge, Tipu Sultan related a story of Manu, the ancient law-giver:

> A farmer had planted cucumber seeds. They sprouted and produced long vines which extended into another farmer's land who claimed them because they were actually within the boundaries of his property. The first farmer claimed the cucumbers as his own since they

received their sustenance from the roots in his own land. A quarrel arose between the two and it came before Manu for decision. Instantly, Manu ruled that the second farmer was right. The cucumbers were his, for they were on his land. The award of the cucumbers was so given but later Manu worried about it and finally he concluded that his award was wrong. Out of his remorse for the error, he resigned as a judge and, in penance, went into seclusion.

'If a law-giver like Manu could make a mistake, are you less likely to?' asked Tipu. 'Would you atone for it, as he did?'

'I promise you, I will never make a mistake in a matter that deals with cucumbers,' Krishna Rao intervened, to take away the heaviness of the conversation.

'If that be so,' replied Tipu, I shall give orders that all my commanders and governors can deal with all matters relating to cucumbers, unfettered. But when it comes to matters of life and liberty of people, surely some caution is necessary.'

It was like talking to a rock—firm and inflexible, the commanders and governors felt

'Meanwhile our privileges disappear,' they grumbled amongst themselves.

(iv)

.... Looting a conquered enemy enriches a few, impoverishes the nation and dishonours the entire army. Wars must be linked to battlefields. Do not carry it to innocent civilians. Honour their women, respect their religion and protect their children and the infirm.

From Tipu Sultan's decree in 1783, repeated in 1785, 1787 and possibly more often.

'What kind of a man is he, this kill-joy?' grumbled the commanders. Much of the loot went into their own coffers. Only a little portion went into the treasury. And then, the joy of it, the thrill of it—all gone. The delighted yells of soldiery, their joyous anticipation over the women to pick, the treasures to plunder, their happy abandon after the conquest—all gone.

Maha Mirza Khan sympathised with the commanders who complained, but he advised against speaking to Tipu Sultan about it. 'Who knows,' he said, 'Sultan might think of adding another paragraph to the Decree saying that our victorious armies, immediately after a successful battle, should go into the mosques and temples and remain there praying until called for the next battle.'

(v)

Flogging and whipping—be they to extract confessions or as punishment—are repugnant to humanity and reason. They do not achieve their purpose. They degrade the victim. They dishonour the person in whose name they are ordered (himsel?).

From Tipu Sultan's Decree issued in 1786.

'Maha Mirza, what do you suggest we do next time we find a criminal?' Mir Jabbar asked.

'Why, simple,' rejoined Maha Mirza, 'have you not read the Decree?'

'To my everlasting sorrow, I have,' said Mir Jabbar, 'but unfortunately it says what we have not to do.'

'To me, the Decree is complete in all respects,' Maha Mirza replied with a laugh. 'You just haven't read it properly.'

'Enlighten me, dear friend,' Mir Jabbar urged.

'With pleasure,' said Maha Mirza. 'See, it talks of humanity and reason. All you have to do is to find a criminal and appeal to his humanity and reason. If he still refuses, just read out to him the Royal Decree. Which criminal will resist it?'

Mir Jabbar joined in the laughter. The joke over, he fumed. Perhaps, some of our commanders who now smuggle arms to the English will also send them their whips and lashes—having no further use for them—and perhaps the English could use them later against the Mysoreans.

(vi)

No man shall be punished save in accordance with law. The law of immemorial custom and as enshrined in our traditions shall be honoured by us. So that people may know the extent and the rigour of the law, as also their rights, duties, obligations and responsibilities, we have decided that codification of law shall be undertaken. . . . Accordingly, we have established a Committee of Ministers under Prime Minister Purnaiya . . .

From Tipu Sultan's Proclamation in 1786.

'Yes, of course,' Bairam Khan replied. 'You shall be given a gift of law books. Pity, you cannot read and write. But let it not worry you. Your tenants will read out to you the law which you are to dispense to them and then they can even write the judgements for you. Simple, isn't it?'

'Very simple. But tell me, doesn't Sultan realise that such laws weaken our authority with people?'

'Perhaps he does and that is possibly why he promulgates such laws.'

(vii)

All praise and glory be to the most high God, who breathing life into a handful of clay gave it the form of man, and who has raised some chosen individuals to rank and power, riches and rule, in order that they might administer to the feeble, the helpless and destitute, and promote the welfare of the people.

From Tipu's proclamation in 1783.

To quarrel with our subjects is to war with ourselves. They are our shield and our Buckler; and it is they who furnish us with all things. Reserve the hostile strength of our Empire, exclusively for its foreign enemies ...

From Tipu's Code of Law and Conduct, 1787.

Naturally, these proclamations were applauded by commanders, governors, administrators and the nobility. There was nothing ominous in their elegant phrases, no call to action, no duty to perform. It was merely the poet in their Sultan's temperament taking charge. They ordered that these proclamations be read out by the town crier and be exhibited at all public places. Then they wanted to forget about them.

They were not allowed to. Wave after wave of new regulations came in—a tenant or a cultivator or his heirs cannot be evicted from land if rent continues to be paid; land must be cultivated otherwise the landlord loses it; the tenant shall not pay rent for the first three years for newly cultivated land; in hard times, if rains fail or if the irrigation system does not function, rents had to be reduced or altogether waived; productivity of land and prosperity of the peasant were of foremost concern and ... so on and so forth.

How was nobility to greet such measures? They to whom the right of indiscriminate intrusion into the lives of tenants and peasants had become a badge of rank, were now called upon to submit themselves to the rule of law! It horrified them that trivialities such as the rights of masses should occupy the royal mind, when the English across the borders were piling up their weapons of destruction. To remit rents and taxes, when Cornwallis was using all means—possible and impossible—to increase the English treasury in preparation for the onslaught against Mysore!

And finally, oh! the disgrace of it. All districts were to have elected councils with the right to petition direct to the king. Every citizen could also petition to the king. Shivji's staff of secretaries would make summaries of those and Tipu Sultan would dictate orders. Since everyone was equal before the law and none was to have special treatment, oral petitions at a private audience or at the Council Table could not be entertained.

With seething anger, the lords of the kingdom pondered over these measures which sought to strike a mortal blow at their highly valued privileges and perquisites in pursuit of some strange ideas of justice and equality. Mir Sadik remonstrated with Tipu Sultan. The king should not, he begged, interfere with the privileges of the ruling classes. The nobility alone is useful to the king to raise taxes, to mobilise the armies and to serve as watchdogs for the kingdom. It is through these men of substance that the efforts of the masses can be directed to the greatest good of the Kingdom but if their authority and leadership disappear, will the people not lose their sense of direction?

Was there anger in Tipu Sultan's reply? He spoke of the antagonism between the interests of the rich and of the poor. 'Should those who own wealth not behave like trustees holding their riches on behalf of the poor?' he asked. 'Should not the purpose of the kingdom be that under it the weakest should have the same opportunity as the strongest?'

His words were not just for Mir Sadik. There was sorrow in his tone as he spoke to the entire Council of Ministers. His words went to the hunger and misery of the poor, to the diamond rings and the gold of the rich, to the laws that made a poor man's crime punishable by torture and death but if committed by the rich, not punishable at all.

'Are we to learn nothing from the past?' asked Tipu Sultan. 'Are we to learn nothing from the history of honour and the tradition of nobility of this country? Can we not grasp the basic truth that power resides in the people and that we are only trustees of that power? By what moral right can we exist independently of the people, clothe ourselves in arrogance and bend their will to our coersion?

'For over a thousand decades in the past, this country resolutely valued individual freedom and social justice unto the least and the lowliest. The kings then fell into loose and easy ways. Drunk with power they forgot the sanctity of their given word. In the name of security, they initially restricted and then destroyed liberty. On the pretext of defending their frontiers, they raised taxes and confiscated wealth, all—so that they and their sycophants could lead a life of ease, pleasure and luxury. And the result? The invaders came; the corrupt rulers fled to be replaced by a tyranny far more cruel and rapacious. I beg of you to read the history of your heritage. You will then believe that there is a law more inexorable than any law made by man. It is the law of death for a nation which ignores the rights of its citizens.

'Is that to be our goal?' Tipu Sultan asked.

There was no answer.

(viii)

...For the social, economic and moral good of our people, there shall be total prohibition on distilling and selling of liquor. Licences shall be issued for limited quantities strictly for sale to foreigners....

From Tipu's Revenue Regulations of 1787.

...Your report, stating you had strictly prohibited the distilling and vending liquors and had moreover made over the whole body of vinters enter into written engagements to desist from selling liquors is understood. You must make the distillers also execute similar agreements and then assist them to take up some other occupation...

Tipu Sultan's letter to Gulam Hyder, Amildar of Bangalore, dated 4 January 1787.

...This is a matter in which we must be undeterred and undaunted by financial considerations. Total prohibition is very near to my heart. It is not a question of religion alone. We must think of the economic wellbeing and the moral height of our people and the need to build the character of our youth. I appreciate your concern for immediate financial loss but should we not look ahead? Is the gain to our treasury to be rated higher than the health and morality of our people...

Memorandum of Tipu Sultan to Mir Sadik, 1787.

Undoubtedly the prohibition policy involved tremendous economic loss to the State Treasury. Those who were actually engaged in distilling or selling liquor and lost their employment as the result of the introduction of prohibition were given financial assistance to begin with and later alternative employment. But who could make up for the loss suffered by a few influential families which largely controlled the liquor industry!

(ix)

From Tipu Sultan's letter in 1785 to the Governor of Malabar—

It pained me to see some women of Malabar going about with their breasts uncovered. Such a spectacle offends the sight and aesthetics; certainly it is repugnant to good taste and morality. You had explained that these women belonged to a tribe whose custom enjoined that they should not cover themselves above the waist. But since then I have been wondering. Is it a question of immemorial custom or is it a question of poverty of the tribe? If it is the latter, I would like you to supply their wants so that their women should be decently draped. If, however, it is a question of time-honoured custom, I would like you to try and use your influence with the religious leaders of the tribe to see if such a custom can be done away with. For this purpose, I wish you to use friendly persuasion without giving any offence to their religious susceptibilities. The arguments that you might employ in this regard will naturally depend upon the foundations on which this custom is rooted. But you may keep the following in view:

— Do customs of this tribe impose any corresponding disability on males also? If not, such a disability on women alone is contrary to principles of justice and is therefore discriminatory.

— Did this custom originate because of poverty of the tribe? Or, did it originate as a punishment by a King? In either case, the kingdom can now intervene to help.
— Even if the custom is based neither on poverty nor on punishment but is rooted in antiquity, how would the sons of the tribe feel about their elders who permitted their mothers to go about half-naked, exposed to ridicule and disgust of bystanders?'

'Tell me, Maha Mirza Khan,' said Ziauddin, 'I hear the ladies of Malai Tribe are to be clothed from head to foot. What will you feast your eyes on when you go next for your vacation to Malabar?'

'The pleasure of not feasting my eyes on your countenance might make up for whatever I miss if I go on a vacation to Malabar.'

'But tell me, should we be worrying about clothing our dainty damsels of the Malai Tribe when the enemy clothes himself in armour of iron and steel?'

'Should you not ask Sultan about it?' asked Maha Mirza Khan with a smile.

'You have his ear, I am told,' replied Ziauddin.

Yes, I have his ear, thought Maha Mirza Khan to himself, but there is another voice he hears, above all others—a voice that comes into his heart, from the Unknown, unbidden, while we—we speak in vain.

(x)

From Tipu Sultan's address to the Council of Ministers in 1789 —

'... The Pharoas built the Pyramids with the labour of their slaves. The entire route of the Great Wall of China is littered with the blood and bones of men and women forced to work under the whip and the lash of the slave drivers. Countless millions were enslaved and chained, and thousands upon thousands bled and died to make it possible that the magnificent structures of Imperial Rome, Babylon, Greece and Carthage should be built To my mind, every great work of art and architecture—be it in countries to the East of India or in the west—is a monument not so much to the memory of the men who ordered them to be built but to the agony and toil, blood and tears of those unfortunates who were driven to death in the effort to build it.

What does such a monument standing impassive, in brick or stone, commemorate? What is its message to all wayfarers who pass it? I believe its message is that here around it is the ruin of an empire, founded on tyranny and anguish of people, driven from their homes, chained and enslaved so that a vain and haughty emperor might harbour illusions of his glory.

And what is the tradition of this proud land which we call India? Its entire architecture, from the Taj Mahal of recent times to the ancient Sanchi Stupa of 2000 years ago, was built by free and devoted men. But why stop there? Go back into thousands of years of the history of our people. Can you tell me of a single structure, of a single monument, of a single edifice built in this land by forced labour? You cannot, for I know it that for 2000 years—nay, even from prehistoric times—this country refrained from imitating the foreign custom of forcing people to donate free labour.

I mention this to you because I received a letter from the Governor of Malabar that in his province are excellent workmen whom he has put to work without payment on government buildings. Knowing of my project to extend the Darya Daulat palace, he has offered them to me. To him I shall say that this palace commissioned by my father with love shall not be sullied by labour forced from unwilling hands. I shall also order that for all their past work on public buildings, those workmen shall be paid and that henceforth none in my kingdom shall permit or order such forced labour.

'Since receiving that letter, I have heard that frequently such labour is being requisitioned by Amildars either on their own or at the request of several departments. Therefore, I say this to you, let strict instructions be issued forthwith, for I see in such a practice the beginnings of a system of slavery.

There can be no glory or achievement if the foundation of our palaces, roads and dams are mingled with the tears and blood of humanity...

'Tell me, Purnaiya,' asked Mir Sadik, 'is everything that is Indian always good?'
'By no means, we have no such exclusive monoply over virtue,' Purnaiya replied.
'Is everything that is rooted in antiquity always good?' was Mir Sadik's second question.
'By no means, the ancients had their barbarism as well. But why these riddles?' Purnaiya asked.
'Oh, for no reason; merely wanted to engage your giant intellect into forced labour without payment.'
'My pleasure.'

(xi)

From Tipu Sultan's circular to all Amildars, 1788—

...Agriculture is the lifeblood of the nation. This land, rich and fertile, will reward those that work on it. Famine and want are either the result of sloth and ignorance or of corruption. The 127 Regulations of this Revenue Code are intended for your immediate implementation. In particular, your urgent attention is drawn to the provisions which relate to cash advances to needy peasants for buying ploughs, steps for taking over derelict land and protection to the cultivator and his descendants. Non-traditional crops must be specially encouraged and the formula for tax concessions to those who grow crops such as sugar cane, betel and cocoanut must be brought into effect without delay. Also essential it is to encourage the planting of valuable trees—mangoes and the like—at the rate of 200 per village and careful protection of teak, sandal, and other timber for internal needs and for export.

The Code is illustrative and not exhaustive. For instance, one amildar has decided that where peasants are convicted of certain minor offences as are only punishable by fines, such fines can be commuted if the person charged with the fine agrees to plant two mangoe and two almond trees in front of his village, and water and tend them till they are the height of three feet. We approve of such measures. Thus amildars must rely on their ingenuity consistent with local conditions (but without ignoring the rights of the people) to stimulate agricultural growth. Any measures so introduced should be reported so that consideration can be given to their incorporation in the Code as also to reward the amildars concerned.

Inscription on the foundation stone laid by Tipu Sultan for the dam on the Cauveri river, 1790 —

...'This dam is being constructed by the Khudadad Government, at the cost of lacs of pagodas, in the name of God. Anyone who brings under cultivation any uncultivated land and grows crops, vegetables or fruits by irrigating it with water from this dam will be given all encouragement and concessions by the Khudadad Government... the newly cultivated land shall belong to the cultivator and his descendants... and no one shall dispossess him....

'Tell me, why does our Sultan write so much?'
'So that we may read so much.'
'The cultivators offer no gifts.'
'No, they prefer to receive them.'
'And how long are we to keep on protecting them?'
'As long as the earth and sky last, for it is the wish of our Sultan that none shall dispossess the cultivator.'
'I shall not last that long, myself.'
'Many others won't.'
'Thank the Lord.'

(xii)

From Tipu Sultan's Declaration, 1787 —

... Religious tolerance is the fundamental tenet of the Holy Quran.

— The Quran holds that there can be no compulsion in religion. The right discretion is henceforth distinct from error.
— The Quran calls upon you not to revile the idols of another religion for it says: revile not those unto whom they pray beside Allah lest they wrongfully revile Allah through ignorance. . . .
— The Quran enjoins on you not to argue with the People of the Scripture, save with such of them as do wrong.
— The Quran expects you to vie with each other in good works and says: for each We have appointed a divine law and a traced out way. Had Allah willed He could have made you one community . . . so vie one with another in good works.
— The Quran requires you to say to people of scripture: We believe in that which has been revealed unto us and revealed unto you; our God and your God is one and unto Him we surrender.

We hold this God-given law dear to our heart, based as it is on human dignity, reason and brotherhood of man. With reverence we have also read the Vedas of the Hindus. They proclaim their faith in universal unity and express the belief that God is one although He bears many names.

It distresses us therefore that some persons wearing the garb of religion have crossed into the frontiers of the kingdom to preach the false and ungodly doctrine of hatred between the various religions. We hereby declare that from this day, it shall not be lawful in the Kingdom of Mysore and for any Mysorean beyond this realm to discriminate against anyone on the basis of religion, caste or creed....

'Well, well,' said Nur Khan to Krishna Rao. 'I loved you because I loved you but henceforth I love you because the law so requires.'
'Honoured.'
'But, Krishna Rao, tell me why does the Decree apply only to Mysore or Mysoreans?'
'Those are the natural limits of the law that can be promulgated by Sultan.'
'So the English beyond the borders are not affected. They continue to revile your idols, and defile our mosques while their missionaries convert your people and mine into Christianity.'

(xiii)

Extract from Tipu Sultan's address at the special audience of the representatives from Trade, Commerce and Industry, 1788—

... I am proud of the spiritual and cultural advancement of our people. That is their glory and their greatness. Let no Kingdom—past or present—claim the credit for that continuity which has flourished in this land for thousands of decades. What then is to be the role of our social structure, of the government and of its various agencies? It is my belief that our basic task is to guarantee material welfare of our people—full employment and the satisfaction of their needs for food, clothing, housing, education of natural justice and human rights can be honoured unless people are assured of economic wealth.

Our economic and commercial policies must be based on growth and dynamism. It is not enough merely to improve our methods of production of the traditional items. We must diversify into new fields of activity suited to the richness of our soil and the genius of our people.

Let me mention two or three avenues in which real progress is possible:

— I have given detailed instructions for the establishment of silk industry in Mysore. Silk worms and men well versed in the art of rearing them have already arrived from foreign lands to train our people. Eighteen centres have been set up for development of the industry. Many more are needed. Every encouragement is being given to plantation of mulberry trees. I would like you to take direct interest in this developmental activity. My goal is clear: I want Mysore to be the foremost amongst silk producing nations.
— A pearl fishery is being established on the Malabar coast. Expert pearl divers are coming to Mysore from foreign lands. They will be with us for a short while until our own people can be trained. Believe me, there is glitter and romance in those pearls—and there is wealth and profit in them. Government is prepared to subsidise your training the youth in this field of work. You will also be assisted in case you suffer any financial losses in the pioneering years. Can I count on your cooperation?
— We must improve our breed of horses and mules. For this purpose, we have imported horses and asses of excellent stock from Arabia. These would

not be for sale but shall be given over free of charge to those of you who can guarantee special attention to such breeding.

These are only a few instances of our desire to diversify the economic activity of the kingdom. Many more such steps can be thought of and I am hopeful that during your deliberations you will devise concrete and constructive measures in this regard. You can be assured of fullest cooperation from the Government in your quest for tapping new sources of wealth, quality-control and improved methods of production. In your prosperity is the prosperity of the nation and a swifter realisation of our goal that every citizen of this Kingdom must be usefully and gainfully employed....

'Well, well,' said Lakshman. 'Our Sultan, I was sure, is a nationalist. But here he goes around getting worms, horses and asses from abroad. What about the feelings of our own worms and beasts? Won't the foreign worms and asses lord over them?'

Purnaiya joined in the laughter while Burhan-ud-din said, 'Don't worry, I am told that these silk worms and even the horses and asses from abroad have a very friendly disposition. You will find in them jolly companions for yourself, who will really appreciate your sense of humour.'

'Thank you,' said the irrepressible Lakshman. 'You really reassure me. I was worried that these foreign silk worms and asses might deprive our own worms and beasts of their rightful place in our country.'

'You need not worry,' laughed Purnaiya. 'I have been assured that they have no imperial designs.'

It was then left to Mulki Muhammad to convert a meaningless joke into a meaningful seriousness, and he asked, 'Did not the Englishmen who came to India first as traders give the impression that they had no imperial designs?'

'Thank you for this lesson in history,' said Lakshman. 'We shall no doubt profit from it.'

(xiv)

'How was the trip?' asked Mulki Muhammad from Lakshman who had returned with the Sultan after a tour of southern districts.

'Excellent.'

'And did you also remember the promise to visit my father's tomb?' Mulki asked.

'Oh yes; I placed flowers on it as you asked me. The Sultan also gave me a wreath of flowers to be placed on it on his behalf.'

'Oh, how kind of him—and how thoughtful!' said Mulki with rapture.

'You know our Sultan. He loves you and he is always so kind but really I felt very sorry when he said some harsh things about your father,' Lakshman said.

'About my father! Impossible. He loved him,' Mulki was aghast.

'Exactly. That is why I was surprised that he should say such things in the town in which your father lived and died. And he said them while speaking to town elders who no doubt revere your father's memory.'

'But how—what did he say?' asked Mulki, ready now to shed tears.

'Well you know, Sultan was making a speech to town elders and I think he got carried away by the impulse of the moment,' Lakshman replied.

'But what did Sultan say?'

'You know he was inaugurating the Education campaign,' replied Lakshman unhurriedly, 'and he said in his speech—now I would like to quote his exact words—he said, that a man who does not educate his children fails in his duty as a father and as a citizen.'

'Then?' asked Mulki, as if waiting for the axe to fall.

'Then nothing,' replied Lakshman. 'Everyone applauded and surely everyone must have clearly understood that the reference was to your father and yourself, his uneducated son.'

If Lakshman did not get a beating, it was because he could run faster and bolt the door behind himself. Through the door, Mulki shouted: 'You fatherless wretch; you who never learned to read and write! You think you have the right to call me uneducated!'

'Well, why not?' Lakshman called back. 'Be reasonable. Neither of us can read and write but you have four uneducated sons while I have only three. Tell me now, who is more uneducated?'

Soon Tipu Sultan's campaign to have 'a school every four miles was catching on. Amongst the many thousands who were enrolled into these schools were seven children—four of Mulki Muhammad and three of Lakshman.

(xv)

'Can you tell me why our Sultan has developed this passion for exports?' asked Mansoor Ali. 'Is it to make our sandalwood, rice, cardamoms, ivory and textiles scarce in our own land?'

'No, my friend,' said Krishna Rao. He explained to him the intricacies and advantages of foreign trade, and concluded by saying, 'so you see, exports mean larger production, greater wealth and higher flexibility for imports.'

'Then will you please tell me, if exports are such a great thing, why did we not export for all these hundreds of years?'

'My dear friend, the tragedy of the past hundreds of years was that enlightened men like you and me were not there.'

(xvi)

'Why should Sultan be spending good money by opening factories and trading posts at Cutch, Ormuz, Jeddah, Aden, Basra and so many other places? Why can't the foreign traders come and buy here? And, why can't our traders go to those countries to do their buying and selling?'

'Of course, they can. Sultan has ordered that a trader intending to export will be entitled to free passage. Our factories and trading posts are there to help in bulk sale and bulk purchases to secure the best rates for ourselves.'

But in point of fact the trading posts did hurt some privileged traders. The bulk trading by these posts and their ready buffer stocks meant that the traders could not manipulate prices or create sudden shortages.

(xvii)

'What did you bring from France, Osman Khan?' asked Jamaludin. Osman Khan was the leader of the delegation which Tipu Sultan had sent to France.

'The honour of an audience with King Louis XVI and Queen Marie Antoinnetee, with the Comtesse d' Artois and Madame Elizabeth in attendance,' said Osman Khan.

'Is that all?'

'Well, not all. We have a promise of seeds of flowers and plants of various kinds. Also, the French King promised to send many technicians and artisans.'

'But no military help?'

'No. That was not the object of the delegation. In any case, the French King was much too preoccupied for that.'

'What should have made him so preoccupied?'

'The French, it seems to me, are always preoccupied when you make a request to them,' was Osman Khan's reply, but he was being somewhat unfair. The fall of the Bastille was only a few months away.

'What about the embassies that we have sent to so many other countries—to Turkey, Persia, Muscat and so on?'

'Their purpose was strictly commercial.'

'But any success?'

'Yes, of course. Only remember that these are the beginnings that Sultan has made for achieving closer international links. Do not judge the whole thing by the result of the first step.'

'Oh, I am prepared to judge them, most generously all the way through, if only I can be sent to such charming places like Paris.'

'Paris, I am sure, will be delighted to welcome a man of your intellectual horizons,' replied Osman with a chuckle.

(xviii)

'Will you tell me, Sankhlaji, why have you imposed restrictions on hunting and shooting? We are not short of ammunition, are we?' 'Oh, no there is plenty of it, Munir Khan.'

'Then, why this foolish order?'

'It is by the command of Tipu Sultan.'

'I apologise. I spoke in haste. But do tell me, why?'

'Sultan feels that animals and birds are a part of God's creation. He fears that their wanton destruction will upset Nature's balance. Hence, sanctuaries are to be established, hunting of some animals has been prohibited and for the rest, their breeding season is to be respected. Still there is plenty of scope for hunting and shooting. Read the entire order carefully. There are many exceptions and relaxations.'

'I wanted to keep my eyes trained on my gun, dear friend, and the birds and beasts that pass by; not on your order. Still if it is the wish of Tipu Sultan, who am I to question it?'

'I am impressed by your most commendable restraint,' concluded Sankhlaji, in a voice heavy with irony. He had an urge to tell Munir Khan that Sultan had even ordered relocation of an ammunition factory from the banks of the Cauveri river, although such location facilitated transportation, on the ground that the fish in the river died as the result of sulpher wastes being thrown into the river. Munir Khan's face, he thought, would look like a dead fish itself if he was confronted with such a story. Soon, it occurred to Sankhlaji that some dead fish looked far more pleasant than Munir Khan's live face. This brought a smile to his lips and in that happy frame of mind he went back to his work, to plan for the establishment of sanctuaries throughout the Kingdom of Mysore.

(xix)

'Why this tremendous activity for road construction?'

'To provide employment and also to keep the wheels moving.'

'Wheels?'

'Yes, don't you know Sultan has ordered all carts to be fitted with wheels. Things move faster; the animals suffer less.'

'Good for animals.'

'Good for every one. You too.'

'How? I don't have goods to move.'

'No, but you have yourself to move. Easy to do that, with good roads and rest-houses to be built every ten miles.'

'Rest houses! What for?'

'So that people may go out, tour and travel, and see for themselves the beauty and grandeur of this glorious country, to identify themselves with the land—its hopes, its people and its customs.'

'Very laudable indeed. But the road that is easy for me to traverse—is it not easy for the enemy also to cross?'

'Not with valliant soldiers like you to guard our frontiers, surely.'

46

THE HOUR STRIKES

'THE HOUR HAS STRUCK, I THINK,' SAID MAJOR GENERAL Medows.

He was sitting next to Cornwallis. Around the table were seven others. For weeks now they had been working late into the night, scrutinising reports and examining despatches. Yes, the granaries were full and so were the arsenals and storehouses. The war machine was ready—ready to strike a mortal blow at Tipu Sultan's empire.

Every one around the table except Cornwallis nodded. He was thinking of the four years that had passed. How he had fretted, chafed, fumed and raged, to drive his officers to extract the impossible! Famine stalked the countryside, ghastly and staggering, and people died in their thousands daily for lack of food; men and women forced by bayonets died from exhaustion; they were replaced by others but the projects went on, uninterrupted. He had wondered if it was practicable to go to such lengths with human beings. Yes, it was, he had concluded; some would adjust themselves to any form of suffering so long as they were permitted to survive; others would work day and night for a handful of rice so that their children might not starve; in any case the lash and the whip worked wonders with them all; the strangest notion that these barbarians had was that famine and other disasters were the work of God, not of man; so they died, a lingering death, dropping often where they worked, waiting for a little food to be handed to them—and sometimes it came too late. Did they die with accusation on their lips, revolt in their hearts and wrath in their souls against an unjust God to whom they attributed their plight? No; they did not lose their anchor of faith, they prayed to God, praised him, gloried in him and even in their last breath of life was resignation and acceptance of things as they are—and perhaps hope beyond.

I am the one, thought Cornwallis to himself, who has crushed and distorted their lives, placed on their forehead the mark of a beast, and on their backs the whip of a slave driver. An exhilarating sense of power surged within him; it was my well of strength—yes, I held the key—mine were the springs—that bent them to my will and made them do my bidding. By all means, let them place the burden of their suffering on God but I shall make sure—yes doubly sure—that for the victory against Tipu Sultan, mine—and mine alone-shall be the credit; I shall not share it even with You, God; too long have I waited.

His mood changed and an entirely different feeling swept over him. It was as if he was searching his soul and seeking forgiveness from someone within. How have I clothed myself with such arrogance? How did such callousness seep into my consciousness? How did I become deaf to the cries of those on whom this havoc has been wrought? How did such brutal indifference creep into me? Have I not sinned; Have I not fallen short of the glory of God; have I not shattered my own beliefs and ideals? No, no, no. He tried to wave his misgivings away and reassure himself. I am but an instrument of the historic process and my mission is to assist in achieving the destiny of the supremacy of my race. I merely give shape to the will and the command of my masters. Of what avail my own individual feelings and beliefs! Have I not yet learned to suppress them? Is it not treason if they come in the way of the greatness and the ideology of the Empire?

Cornwallis, of course, did not know it then that in the centuries of horrors which were still to come, many people, who undertook the task of dehumanising and brutalising their fellowmen, would, when accused, be seeking to appease God and Man with the plea that they merely followed the will and the command of a superior authority—and thus they would rationalise their crime against humanity and seek to shift from their conscience the blame and the stigma for the ghettos, concentration camps, assassinations, gas chambers and genocide.

He interrupted his thoughts to look at the men around him. It was clear from his questioning glance that he had not heard what had been said.

'I said the hour has struck,' repeated General Medows. 'Your targets have all been met—and exceeded.'

'Yes, so I see,' replied Cornwallis.

'And Tipu stands almost deserted with more and more of his commanders ready to abandon him,' said General Abercromby.

'Strange, isn't it?'

'No, not strange, he has lost touch with his people.'

'With his people, did you say?'

'Well, I mean, the few people that matter—people with wealth, commands, influence and land. I wasn't thinking of the uncounted millions of his empire who love and revere him. Their love and reverence would count for much if wars were won on the basis of prayers and blessings.'

'That at least is strange, is it not, that he should have alienated the high and mighty who are backed by sword and wealth, only to find a place in the hearts of the vast multitude which counts for nothing?'

'Well, a King with a notion that under his Kingdom the weakest should have the same opportunity as the strongest—what else does he deserve? He combines economics with ethics and sees no distinction between them; he asks the wealthy to shed privilege, protects the cultivator, remits taxes, and when the landlords complain, he talks to them of social justice; they who have risen to wealth or inherited fortunes—he asks them to act as trustees for people's welfare! No wonder they fear that some day he will be asking beggars to mount horses and take the rod of authority.'

How amazing is the spirit of this King, thought Cornwallis, not without an emotion of envy.

'Yes,' said Cornwallis, waving away this irrelevant discussion and looking at the charts before him. 'We are ready and the moment has almost arrived.'

'Almost?'

'We still have to wait to bind the Marathas and the Nizam into firm alliances. They must sign the pact of our joint war against Tipu Sultan. I am meeting the Nizam next week.'

'Will his signature mean much?'

'What I have offered him will mean much—one-third of Tipu's territory that we shall conquer.'

'So much to a shifty, vascillating villain?'

'Language, language,' cautioned Cornwallis, but with a smile and tone that spelt perfect understanding. 'It is good to enrich friends,' continued Cornwallis. 'They always come in useful if later we need to borrow.'

All shared the smile that lit up Cornwallis' face.

'There is another thing we need before we march against Tipu Sultan—yes, we need an excuse,' said Cornwallis.

'Excuse, for what?'

'For the attack, of course.'

'Surely, that is not necessary.'

'My dear friend, just now you told me that Tipu Sultan combines economics with ethics. I too have a failing. I like to combine politics with good appearances. An honourable excuse is always necessary to lend honour to any action.'

'Well, let us say that Tipu Sultan is arming himself against us, or better still he attacked us.'

'Will that appear plausible?' Cornwallis asked.

'Does that matter?'

'In my book it does. Wars, my friend, are always fought for a noble cause, not for ignoble conquest—to defend an ideal, to uphold a principle, to protect a worthy ally....'

'Let us say, he attacked the Nizam, our worthy ally.'

'Alas, he is neither worthy nor an ally yet. Besides, who would believe it? The Nizam is no chicken that we should have rushed to his help without an axe to grind. No, let us think of someone smaller, someone helpless, someone who cannot defend himself against Tipu Sultan and we go in like valiant knights protecting the weak against the strong.'

Three or four alternatives were considered and rejected.

'What about Travancore? We have some sort of a pact with its ruler though he is already scheming with the Dutch. Why can't we say that he is our helpless ally whom Tipu is harassing.'

'Not a bad idea,' said Cornwallis, concluding the meeting.

The English messengers left for Travancore the next day.

47

OUR FAITHFUL ALLY

THE PACT BETWEEN THE ENGLISH AND THE NIZAM WAS SIGNED and sealed.

'I think I will have another bath this morning,' said Cornwallis as soon as the Nizam had left.

'Anyone who has had long and sustained conversation with the Nizam needs one,' said John Kennaway who was the English Resident at the Court of the Nizam.

'I agree,' said Cornwallis, and then he asked, 'Tell me, does the Nizam ever speak the truth?'

'I am informed on most reliable authority that the Nizam speaks the truth always, invariably and without fail—but only in his sleep.'

'And, never otherwise?'

'Well, if he has to tell the truth, he takes good care to conceal it among so many lies that it is not too easy to find it out.'

'I can believe that.'

'It is not really his fault I think, someone taught him at an early age that language was devised by Man not to express a thought but to conceal it.'

48

THE SHADOW OF AN AXE

THE DEBATE WENT ON IN THE MARATHA CAMP.

'With my own eyes I have seen,' said Pant. 'Their preparations are complete. They have provided for every contingency. They have enough to feed and equip their fighting forces for years. I tell you, today the English army is invincible.'

'Then why do they have this overpowering urge to conclude an alliance with us? Why do they not finish off Tipu Sultan on their own?' asked Nana Phadnavis.

'This Lord Cornwallis is a cautious man. He wants to be doubly sure. He does not have your courage nor your spirit of adventure,' replied Pant.

With good humour Nana ignored the sarcasm and said, 'I grant you what you have said about the English preparations; they are there for everyone to see; many others have also confirmed your reports. But the question that is in my mind is: Can we not remain neutral?'

'How is it possible to remain neutral? Whatever the dangers of war, surely the risks of neutrality are greater.'

'And, how have you arrived at this profound conclusion?'

'Through wisdom, of course.'

'Please share it with me.'

'You are playing games with me, Nana Saheb. But let me explain: if we remain neutral, do you realise what will happen? The English who today count on us for help, will bear us a grudge and hold us in contempt. Tipu Sultan, on the other hand, will despise us for our cowardice. What use will the English have later for a faithless friend and what use will Tipu Sultan have for an enemy who is so timid? After this war when the English and Tipu Sultan have settled their scores with each other, we who shared our fortunes neither with one nor with the other, will be pounced upon by whoever is victorious. Is it not better then to come out boldly, without hesitation on the English side?'

'And, if the English side loses?'

'That is beyond the realms of possibility, but even if we so assume, do you think that Tipu Sultan's victory against the English can be decisive? By no means—and they will wait to strike again. What then will be the result? To the English you will be their greatest ally. They will nurse your friendship and value your alliance as never before. And, Tipu Sultan? Why, he will move heaven and earth to gain your goodwill. He will give much for your neutrality, and much more for your assistance.'

'Assume for a moment that I accept your proposition that the English are bound to emerge victorious—does it not mean that their power will then be so great, so formidable as to cause us to fear it? Are you asking me that we should help them to consolidate that very power which could be used against us, later?'

'But that is where you miscalculate. It is not the English alone who will come out powerful from this conflict. We too. We get an equal share of the spoils and the territory. Our strength advances along with the English strength. They get stronger;

we get stronger. But have you thought of the other scenerio as well, if we are not in the fight at all? The English themselves emerge victorious, grab everything for themselves with none to share. How much stronger do they then become? And how long will they wait to make us their very first victim? Nothing will restrain them. Not even their gratitude for any past alliance.'

'And gratitude for the past—you think will have a restraining influence on the English designs for the future?'

'Perhaps not; but the real restraint will come from our added strength. And, how do we go about adding to our strength, except by joining the English against Tipu Sultan and claiming our equal share?'

Nana Phadnavis remained silent, thinking. Pant pressed on. 'Don't forget, the Nizam has also joined them.'

'The Nizam,' said Nana with contempt. 'The Nizam will stop at neither lies nor deceit. He bathes in them as if they were his natural element.'

'Do not dismiss the Nizam so lightly. He has wealth and power—also an army well trained by foreigners. Incidentally,' continued Pant with a smile, 'his astrologers have told him that he shall live to be the wealthiest ruler.'

'Live! I doubt it. He might die as the wealthiest ruler though.'

'Is there a difference?'

'Oh, yes, a world of difference—of life and death.'

'Let us not digress. I must repeat, it would be a folly, a tragedy, if you permit the opportunity of a pact with the English to escape us. Neither the English nor the Nizam nor anyone else must get too powerful, if we have to survive. We don't want to fall a prey. . . .'

'Let us sleep over it.'

'Malet [the English Agent at Poona] is getting restive. We dare not lose too much time.'

'I don't intend to. Tomorrow shall be the day of decision.'
'So be it.'

A week later the documents for the pact with the English against Tipu Sultan were brought to Nana Phadnavis for signature. To Tukoji Holkar who looked on with sadness, he said, 'I know what you feel. I feel the same way; but what choice do we have? We must join those who are to be victorious and of this there is no doubt. Survival of the Maratha nation depends on it.

'Forgive me, Nana Saheb. To me, it seems we appease the crocodile for a brief moment, feed it with a lamb today so that he may wait till tomorrow to swallow us.'

There was a long pause during which no one spoke. Each was thinking his own thoughts.

'May God prove you wrong,' finally Nana said.

'May God prove me wrong,' said Tukoji Holkar.

Nana picked up the pen and signed the pact. Malet, the English Agent, was in the midst of a speech, congratulating the sagacity, wisdom and statesmanship of Nana Saheb. Abruptly, Nana bowed to the company and left. I must wash my hand, he thought to himself; perhaps the ink had spilt on it or perhaps not.

In the courtyard, the shadow of the palace arch fell against the bright sunlight, the shadow showed only half the arch. It looked like a giant axe etched on the white marble floor. The head of the axe reached the Maratha flag proudly fluttering in the centre of courtyard. Nana saw his own shadow advancing to reach the axe. Momentarily, he shuddered, changed his direction and wanted to smile away some vague thought troubling him. His lips moved, but the smile? . . . It was not there.

49

THE GOVERNOR-GENERAL FROM FRANCE

'BONDS OF FRIENDSHIP AND GRATITUDE ARE VERY GOOD IN THEIR own way,' said Comte de Conway, the French Governor-General in the East, 'but when you have come a certain distance, you must ignore them. An alliance which has ceased to be useful is a nuisance.'

'Will it not tarnish the good name and honour of France, if we fail to support Tipu Sultan. We have pledged our word to him,' de Fresne had the temerity to ask.

'Only a fool fights a losing battle. Nothing tarnishes the good name and honour of a nation as much as a defeat. Surely, in these unsettled times no one expects us to keep faith when it does not suit our purpose and our interests.'

'Tipu Sultan expects us to.'

'The more fool he.'

'So we turn our back to him. Is that your final decision?'

'Yes, though I must say that your expression is not very well chosen. Never turn your back to anyone if you wish to avoid a stab in the back.'

'They say Tipu Sultan never stabs in the back.'

'I know; he has no doubt some special advice from Heavens above, but we—well we have to follow the customs of the earth that gave us birth.'

'Very true; so how do we break with Tipu?'

'Oh, my dear innocent friend, we don't break. We continue our protestations of friendship—louder and louder when he is around and softer and softer when he is not; but. . . .'

'But what?'

'But there should be no connection—none whatever—between our protestations of friendship and the action that we have to take.'

'And what is the action we have to take?'

'Circumstances will dictate that. For the moment, the English are too strong for us to oppose them. There can be no question of siding with Tipu Sultan but maybe, we can render a service or two to the English.'

'What for?'

'Services are rendered only for one reason—for one consideration alone. The first thought has to be: how can they be useful to us? Surely, you are not thinking that services can be rendered out of philanthrophy or altruism?'

Something in the glance of his companion irritated Comte de Conway. 'Why are you looking at me like this?' he asked. 'Are you condemning my motives?'

'Oh, no. On the contrary, I am admiring your subtlety.'

'Thank you, you flatter me.'

Later, Comte de Conway, the French Governor-General in the East, wrote to Cornwallis with positive assurances that the French would not support Tipu Sultan, adding: 'His Majesty, the King of France, had been pleased, with that magnificence and generosity which characterises him, to receive the Ambassadors, which Tipu Sultan thought proper to send to France, but it is a matter of certainty that no sort of engagement has been entered into.... The faith of France, the honour of the nation and her well-known interest, all must positively prescribe to us a strict neutrality.'

Cornwallis smiled at the phrase in the last sentence, 'the faith of France, the honour of the nation and her well-known interest'. Yes, all this had been bought by the bribe he had already sent to Comte. de Conway who was no doubt thinking of his own 'well-known interest'. How much more would he need, wondered Cornwallis, to move from the position of neutrality to come over actively to our side? Not too much, Cornwallis answered himself. Well, it shall be given, Cornwallis decided. It was. A 'loan' of one hundred thousand rupees sufficed. Another ten thousand went to de Fresne. That silenced his misgivings. 'Conscience is a troublesome thing but, fortunately, it can be bought,' concluded Cornwallis.

50

STAND UP AND BE COUNTED

'WAR NOW IS INEVITABLE,' SAID LAKSHMAN TO PURNAIYA.

'And how has your juvenile mind reached so weighty a conclusion?' Purnaiya asked.

'So says everyone.'

'Oh, I thought you were being original, as usual.'

Lakshman smiled. Normally he initiated jests and rarely was he at the receiving end. But he was serious now.

'I see the procession of English agents coming into our court, each vying with the other in protesting peaceful intentions of Cornwallis,' said Lakshman.

'Maybe, they mean what they say,' countered Purnaiya.

'Don't play with me, Purnaiya. You know of their massive preparations across our borders. You are the one who is having sleepless nights over those and. . . .'

'Sleep, my friend, is the luxury of youth. As I grow older, I snatch at every excuse to keep me awake. The time to sleep will come, soon enough.'

Lakshman ignored Purnaiya's remark and continued, 'And what doubt can be there now, after the statement by Cornwallis which came out today?'

'Really?' asked Purnaiya. 'I thought I had read the statement very carefully over and over again. I found it beautifully phrased. Nothing ominous in it. It spoke of everlasting friendship of the English for Tipu Sultan and their conviction that ahead of them was an era of peace, cooperation, goodwill, cordiality and mutual respect between the Kingdom of Mysore and the English Sovereign.

Did you not notice how it heaped scorn on those that had vainly and unsuccessfully tried to drive a wedge between Tipu Sultan and the English. The trouble with you, Lakshman, is that you cannot read and you form your conjectures on what you hear second-hand. Why, the statement clearly denies all rumours about a possible clash. It is an official denial.'

'Yet, you were the one who told us once: Believe only that of the English what they themselves officially deny.'

Purnaiya smiled. 'It was wrong of me to implant such a dangerous thought in your immature mind.'

'Purnaiya, please, I beg of you. I am serious. Please listen to me.'

'What else have I been doing for so long? What is it you wish to know?'

'Only one question—Can Sultan win this war?'

The smile left Purnaiya's face. His voice was angry now. 'You ask—Can Sultan win this war? Whose war is this? I ask you. Is it Sultan's war alone? Or is it yours and mine and of every one of this nation? Please have the goodness to phrase your question correctly.'

'You know what I meant. Why play mental gymnastics with me? Can you conceive of me identifying ourselves apart from Sultan?'

'There are those who have,' said Purnaiya.

Lakshman felt the cold ferocity in Purnaiya's voice. He looked at Purnaiya. The eyes were bloodshot but alert, set in an austere face wasted with worry, strain and overwork. Everyone had known that Prime Minister Purnaiya did not even sleep. Days and nights he spent with secretaries, commanders, couriers, rushing here, inspecting there and making preparations to avert the English threat that loomed over them all. His pleasantries of a few minutes ago, Lakshman knew now, were a cloak to mask the cry that stirred within him as if to say that Mysore, Sultan and the nation he loved with all his heart, were in danger.

Both were silent now but it was as though a dialogue continued between them, unspoken. Lakshman broke the pause.

'For every single traitor, there shall be ten thousand who shall shed their blood in our cause. Remember that.' 'I shall remember. I shall count them all,' softly Purnaiya replied. No, there was no trace of humour in his face, nor in his heart. He meant it.

51

THE GRAND ARMY

(i)

THE KINGDOM OF MYSORE BECAME AN ARMED CAMP, SWEPT WITH violent winds of war.

Cornwallis appointed Major-General William Medows to take over the command of what was called the Grand army, the finest so far put into action by the English in India. Medows was formerly the English Governor in Bombay, subsequently became Governor of Madras and was due to take over as Governor-General from Cornwallis on his retirement.

Fondly, Medows watched the Grand Army as it passed in review. Cornwallis had not exaggerated its size, the magnificence of its provisions, the splendour of its uniforms and above all the vastness of its equipment!

'Come back with victory,' said Cornwallis.

'I shall be back,' said Medows with confidence.

'With victory,' Cornwallis emphasised.

'With your Sultan in chains, have no fear.'

The English Grand Army marched. From a different direction, the Maratha army marched. The Nizam waited and watched. He saw the English advance, unharmed. He saw the Marathas advance, unmolested. He gave the signal to his own army to advance. Three daggers from different directions, all aimed at the heart of Tipu Sultan. The French laughed with their dagger sheathed, waiting for the moment to join the three. Unofficially they gave their soldiers leave of absence to join the armies of any of the three, as mercenaries. Comte de Conway jingled the coins in the gold bag which Cornwallis had just sent him.

(ii)

Medows at the head of the English Grand Army began his march in May 1790. He occupied the frontier post of Karur, abandoned by the Mysoreans. Then he advanced to Aravakurichi, a weak fort guarded by a garrison of thirty men. In the opposite direction, from a distance, Tipu Sultan's messenger watched the English batteries firing on the fort. He was too late with his message for the garrison to abandon the fort and regroup in a stronger position a few miles behind. They were already in the midst of battle. 'For God's sake, put up the white flag,' he shouted, though he knew that his voice would not carry that far. At night, the firing still continued but stealthily he crept to the fort. Of the thirty, twenty-four had died, two were mortally wounded and four remained to return the fire. He was the fifth and the only one who did not bleed from a wound. He chose to forget about the white flag. Too dark for the enemy to see it in any case, he argued with himself. He died with his hand on the gun before the dawn broke. The English troops rushed at the fort which had ceased to return the fire. There were no survivors.

Medows entered into Coimbatore. It had been completely evacuated. No one to fight back, none to rape but plenty to pillage. From there, he sent strong columns in three different directions—Colonel James Stuart to attack Dindigul, Colonel Oldham to Erode and Colonel Floyd towards Mysore.

The Killedar (Commandant) of Dindigul, Hyder Abbas, bold and defiant, refused to surrender. To the person who had brought the message from the English, he said: 'Tell your Commander that it is not possible to account to Tipu Sultan for the surrender of a fort like Dindigul so long as I have a single drop of blood in my veins; therefore, if any other person comes on that errand, I will blow him from a cannon.' Colonel Stuart received the answer, cursed Hyder Abbas and let loose his artillery but even after two days of cannonading, it had little effect on the fort. The cannon fire continued until at last a minor breach was effected and the English then decided upon an assault Their repeated attacks, however, failed against the strength of the fortifications, coupled with the valour of the resolute Commandant who personally headed his best troops at the breach.

'What do we do now?' asked Major Skelly.

'Shed tears over our fallen comrades; and be prepared for a patient, painful siege,' was Stuart's rueful reply.

But that night, a courier from General Medows arrived. He was accompanied by an old man. After a long conversation with Stuart, the old man proceeded to the fort with a message and a white flag. He was of sufficient consequence to be granted immediate entry. Next morning, the fort surrendered.

The old man who had taken the message to Hyder Abbas was his uncle, Shah Abbas—his mother's brother—with whom he and his widowed mother had lived for long. Shah Abbas was now in the pay of the English. Respectfully, Hyder Abbas listened to him. He did not have too much ammunition nor too many troops, he argued with himself, whereas the English had a formidable force. Now he was being offered a future lined with gold. Well, why not? He capitulated. His future? He died with a bullet from his own brother. His brother also killed himself and his dying words to his mother were'... forgive me mother... to restore family honour.... Let the earth cover him and me, his crime and my crime.... May God and Sultan forgive me.' The mother died from the shock at the loss of both the sons. Yes, the family honour was restored, but the family? Extinguished.

Treachery! Treachery! It strikes again. The garrison at Palghat also surrendered to Colonel Stuart, though it could have withstood the siege for several weeks, if not for several months. Colonel Oldham captured Erode and secured the line of English advance. Colonel Floyd reached thirteen miles from Gajalhati on the route to Mysore.

Then came Tipu Sultan, in person. Floyd had to be stopped. The Gajalhati pass had to be closed to the English, the route to Mysore had to be protected. Like a whirlwind, Sultan charged at the head of his army. The massive English columns stood their ground against the impact. Mysore army wavered, charged again. Hundreds died. The banner of Tipu Sultan fell down as Mujahid Hussain who carried it was shot dead. A cry of dismay broke through Sultan's army at the disappearance of the banner. Has Sultan fallen? Burhan-ud-din picked up the banner. The regiments which had broken ranks and were retreating in disorder rallied. Burhan-ud-din shouted a command to close ranks. 'Forward, forward with God, forward with Sultan, faster, faster,' he shouted. Some heard and followed him. Others did not. Burhan-ud-din spurred his horse and charged. The banner fluttered high in the air. Tipu Sultan's army saw the banner now proudly where the enemy lines were earlier. An enthusiastic shout went up. Tipu held aloft his sword. The cavalry surged forward. Through cannonade, bursting shells, smoke, cries of the dying and the wounded, they rushed, with Tipu in the forefront. Tipu shouted at Burhan-ud-din, who was far ahead, to fall back. None could hear him. Those behind thought he was commanding them to follow him—and they followed. They fell on the English, slashed them where they stood. The English retreated beyond the ravine slowly at first and then they ran. Their dead and wounded, their guns and armour, they left behind. Tipu Sultan's victory was complete.

Burhan-ud-din was dead.

(iii)

Ghazi Khan found Burhan-ud-din's body, wrapped it in the fallen banner and carried it on his powerful outstretched arms like a child. The jubilant shouts of 'victory', 'victory' by the Mysoreans faltered to a stop as he reached Tipu Sultan and placed the body before him. A spasm passed Tipu's face but soon he steadied himself. He bent low to kiss the cold forehead. His head was now erect. There was no sign of emotion on his face. 'Let Ruqayya Banu be informed,' he said, in a voice that was gentle and soft.

Yes, Ruqayya Banu, wife of Tipu Sultan and sister of Burhan-ud-din; let her be informed that her brother was dead. These names, even his own, flashed in Sultan's mind, as if they belonged to strangers—strangers whom he had known in some dim distant past. Grief, Ghazi Khan knew, takes many forms; unspoken grief casts a spell that can reach the core of the heart. He groped for something to say.

'He died a martyr's death,' Ghazi Khan ended by saying.

'Yes,' Tipu replied softly, his eyes still on Burhan-ud-din's face. Then he lifted his eyes and they met Ghazi Khan's, wet with tears. 'Many,' said Tipu, his voice breaking suddenly, 'many died as martyrs today; many, is it not?'

Ghazi Khan nodded. The hurt was in the open now. It would heal. He motioned to all to leave Sultan, alone with his sorrow. They left.

'Be with me,' said Tipu Sultan to Ghazi Khan as he was about to leave.

'Always,' said Ghazi Khan, gathering Tipu in his embrace. 'Always,' he repeated, choked with emotion.

'I denied her much. Now I deny her this,' said Tipu.

Ghazi Khan understood that Tipu spoke of Ruqayya.

'I will ask Salim to be near her,' Ghazi Khan said.

Tipu remembered Salim vividly—Salim, the matchmaker, Burhan-ud-din's son who had divulged to Tipu Sultan the secret of Ruqayya's heart—years back.

'Farewell, my friend, farewell, my brother,' said Sultan, when later Ghazi Khan brought the decorated stretcher to take Burhan-ud-din's body. Then he wept, and his tears were not for those who were dead but for those who lived.

(iv)

Later, many said that Sultan committed a grave blunder by not pursuing Floyd's forces who were retreating in disorder. He could have annihilated them and struck a lasting blow to the English campaign. They were right. There were some who knew of the grief of Sultan at the loss of his valiant commander, kinsman and friend, Burhan-ud-din. But, so what? they argued. By what right does a king allow his private sorrow to override his public vengeance! A king's blood must be cold; his action, ruthless; his heart, of stone; his soul, of iron; and his dream, of power. How else can a king be fitted for supreme power? Can a king love, can he have friends, can he shed tears? No, no, no.

(v)

Floyd's detachments retreated to the protecting walls of Coimbatore. Meanwhile, General Medows, in the hope that Floyd would keep Tipu Sultan engaged, moved northwards to get between him and Seringapatam.

Lull in the Mysorean camp. Then Tipu Sultan fell back and having recrossed Bhavani river, he waited for Medows. The English General watched in dismay the Mysorean forces on the opposite bank, protected not only by the river but also by two strong forts. Floyd, who was expected to keep Tipu Sultan engaged, had failed in his task. The road to Seringapatam was closed, with Tipu Sultan himself barring the way. Medows who did not believe in heroics was certainly not prepared to join issue with Sultan without the divisions of Floyd and Stuart joining him. He took the safer course and returned to Coimbatore. Floyd joined him on the way and later Stuart's divisions also reached from Palghat and finally Oldham's. Thus, almost the entire Grand Army was reunited. Now, it was ready for its march to Seringapatam. Its first target: the Bhavani river where Tipu was entrenched.

Tipu Sultan struck before the Grand Army could move out of Coimbatore. He occupied Erode, which surrendered immediately on his approach. Then began a long series of battles with astonishing rapidity. Dharapuram fell to Tipu's arms and several other foils occupied by the English garrison capitulated. Medows knew from his scouts that the bulk of Tipu Sultan's forces were guarding the way to Seringapatam. The Mysorean army was also locked in battle with the armies of the Nizam and the Marathas. Sultan himself was accompanied by a slender force. Well, why not pursue Sultan and wipe him out altogether? thought Medows to himself. Who would then bar the way to Seringapatam? All that was needed was to overtake Sultan and bring him to action in the open country. Surely, he would not be able to withstand the onslaught of the Grand Army—'a force far superior in numbers and equipment to any'.

What Medows forgot to reckon with was that his vast army encumbered by huge equipment and stores could not move as fast as Tipu's cavalry. Clumsily, the Grand Army pursued the small Mysorean force led by Tipu Sultan. In vain, it toiled to catch up with him. 'Making three marches for one of ours,' as the English put it, Sultan took off at top speed for Carnatic, often marching back to be within a few miles of the enemy. Thus, he kept alive the English hope of their being able to capture him but in the end he baffled them by his swift and elusive marches and counter-marches. The English did not suffer too many casualties in men but all along the route they had to abandon guns and equipment against the rapidity of Tipu's marches. The chase went on and meanwhile the plans of Medows for the invasion of Mysore were foiled. Also, Tipu Sultan was able to invade the Carnatic.

Months went by. The year wore on. All that the English succeeded in was to pillage and then burn each village and town through which they passed.

'They will burn many more,' Mir Sadik said.

'They are without pity,' Tipu commented.

'So should you be,' Mir Sadik said.

52

TWO YEARS OF WAR

(i)

LORD CORNWALLIS WAS IRRITATED BEYOND ENDURANCE. HIS devout hope that the campaign would be over in six months was frustrated. Also he was alarmed. The campaign had failed. General Medows was defeated. Carnatic lay at the mercy of Tipu Sultan. The Nizam and the Marathas openly sneered at the defeats of their allies.

'We have lost time and our adversary has gained reputation which are the two most valuable things in war,' wrote Cornwallis. At this rate, he feared, the Nizam and the Marathas would conclude separate peace with Tipu Sultan.

General Medows was relieved of the command. Himself, Cornwallis assumed command of the Grand Army, with Medows as second-in-command.

'I shall leave this place only as a conqueror or as a corpse,' said Cornwallis.'

But he was not only a valiant man. He was also prudent. Word went to all the English provinces. More men, more material poured in. With Comte de Conway, the French

Governor-General in India, he had a heart-to-heart talk. More French mercenaries were promised. The conversation then moved to Frenchmen who had already been in Sultan's service for several years from the time of Hyder Ali.

'You wish me to use our influence so that they leave Sultan's service?' Comte de Conway asked.

'Your influence, yes. To leave Sultan's service, no,' Cornwallis replied.

It took Comte de Conway only a moment to understand. Then he purred with pleasure.

'Milord, your subtlety! It has no equal,' he said to Cornwallis.

Whereas Medows had been a man of violent bombast, arrogance, vanity and pride, Cornwallis was a patient, persuasive organiser who recognised that he could succeed in the war against Tipu Sultan only if he coordinated his activities in every detail with his allies—the Marathas and the Nizam. Between Medows and the allies there had been little coordination on strategy. Each had fought his own battles, often at cross-purposes with the other. When Cornwallis assumed personal command a new era began. The history of doubts and suspicion ended. Medows had been obsessed with the idea of being the first to humble Tipu and reach Seringapatam ahead of his allies, while Cornwallis was a realist who believed that only by joint action could the allies succeed against Tipu Sultan. When it came to argument, Cornwallis was prepared to lay down a bag of gold on the table. Under the cloak of his immense prestige and wealth began a systematic and coordinated planning amongst the three confederates.

The iron ring around Tipu Sultan tightened. War was resumed in the tortured terrain of Mysore, unprecedented in scope, fury, bloodshed and destruction. To the Mysoreans, Cornwallis made it clear—he would be stern and unforgiving, know no mercy, give no quarter and leave a trail of devastation, if he met any opposition. Sack, rapine and death were to be the penalties for resistance. But to those who desert the cause of Tipu Sultan—and some did—he would be generous beyond their dreams.

(ii)

'Sultan has no existence apart from his people,' said Lakshman in an impassioned speech. 'His joys and grief are your joys and grief. His dreams are your dreams. In the glory, honour and pride of his people is his glory, honour and pride. Come then, gather under his banner, sure in the knowledge that whatever shall be denied to him shall be denied to you and whatever he shall secure shall be rendered unto you. Therefore, I say this to you, let this Kingdom be cleansed of treason and treachery; let the entire nation be prepared to face the villainous enemy from within and without; let us rise to dignity and heroism—belief injustice and love of the country; let us show our scars with honour and pride.... Let us then be resolved to perish rather than lose our liberty....' Lakshman concluded his speech amidst ringing applause.

'You made a very fine speech this morning,' Purnaiya told him. 'Did you hear it?' asked Lakshman, gratified but surprised.

'There are some who did. They were moved, I am told,' said Purnaiya.

'Oh, on great occasions, I am all for expression of noble sentiments. It is only my misfortune that the company I often keep,' here he paused pointing to Mulki Muhammad, 'tarnishes my genius and puts flippancies in my mouth instead.'

'Then I am about to do you a favour—to place considerable distance between you and Mulki Muhammad.'

'How is that? We belong to the same regiment. We are being recalled next Friday.'

'No, your orders are being cancelled. You are to tour the length and breadth of Mysore, to make fine speeches, to appeal to the patriotic fervour of the people, to caution them against treachery and to ensure that they are united—heart and soul—to face the onslaught of the invader.'

'Purnaiyaji, I am a soldier—a cavalry commander. I charge at the head of troops with a sword in hand. Remember? And you, you ask me to go about making fine and flowery speeches—just because I got carried away and made one or two in Seringapatam!'

'Personally, if you ask me,' Mulki Muhammad intervened, 'I would say that his speeches never impressed me but then his soldiering impresses me even less. So I would regard the decision as very sound.'

'Shut up. No one asked you,' Lakshman told him.

Purnaiya ignored the intervention and spoke to Lakshman about defections and disunity. He told him of the sorry level to which Mysore had sunk and of the need to revive in the heart and spirit of the people, the voice of national memory. Against the continued onslaughts of three great armies, the nation had to be inspired to accomplish the impossible.

He dismissed Lakshman's further protests and finally ended with the dictum: 'Orders are orders,' against which of course Lakshman could say no more. To relieve him of his disappointment Purnaiya told him that he would be in this new assignment for only three or four months.

'Three or four months?' Lakshman cried. 'By then the war will be over.' He then relapsed into a jest. 'It is Cornwallis who is leading the English now. You must realise that he is the very soul of politeness. He left England specially for America to surrender at Yorktown. Here he comes now, I am sure, to surrender to Sultan at the very first opportunity. What chance will I have to draw my sword?'

'You will have every chance,' Purnaiya replied. 'I promise you—and never underestimate your enemy. We have the Marathas against us, the Nizam against us, everyone against us and Cornwallis who leads a huge army is himself a great General.'

'His exploits then are a well-kept secret, it seems. I have not met anyone who was on the losing side against him. Did he kill them all? And you think my speeches will have better effect than my bullets.'

Mulki Muhammad intervened with a laugh. 'Oh, most certainly,' he said. 'When you make a speech, you merely waste your breath, but when you shoot out bullets, you waste ammunition, so atrocious is your aim. We are short of ammunition, you know.'

'One thing is clear. We are not short of fools,' was Lakshman's retort.

Purnaiya ignored both of them. 'The spirit of freedom stands weeping at the door,' he said. 'Three great powers have hurled themselves against us. Still, they can never succeed if our people stand united, if they are conscious of their role in history, if they have faith in their destiny. How are our people to understand this? By an inspiration? By a dream? By a vision? No, Lakshman, they must be told. Let this be your mission. Men are moved more by ideas than by the sword.'

'A sword which I shall not wield for the great General opposing us will have surrendered by the time I finish my speeches.'

But Cornwallis had no intention to surrender and Lakshman was to get an opportunity to draw the sword. Cornwallis was at that moment advancing on Bangalore. The town fell after heavy fighting. The Mysoreans withdrew into the fort. A free hand was given to the English soldiers to loot and pillage, rape and outrage.

Lakshman saw the huge swarms of frightened refugees who had fled Bangalore. He heard their harrowing tales. 'To arms,' he cried to the peasantry, and collecting a small contingent of untrained men, barely armed, he marched to Bangalore. With the fall of Bangalore, he knew, the heart of Mysore was threatened. This was no time to worry about Purnaiya's instructions to concentrate on making barren political speeches to people. No, the time had come for action—to submit to the obligations of conscience. He must act like a commander in the field and help where his help would count the most. Yes, this was the time to join Sultan who would no doubt himself be rushing to the rescue of Bangalore.

Tipu Sultan waited at a distance. The Mysoreans were in the invulnerable, impregnable fort of Bangalore. He was confident that it would withstand the most fierce assault It was equipped and stocked to resist a grim siege for months on end. The fall of Bangalore had been a grievous blow but it could be turned to advantage. The English would be caught in cross-fire from the fort and from Tipu Sultan's forces.

But it was not to be. The French contingent in the fort, which was in Tipu Sultan's service, guided the English through a circuitous route. Secretly, all night, the English climbed the rampart which was under the French guard. At dawn the French and the English attacked the garrison. The gallant Commandant Bahadur Khan was their first target. They called on him to surrender. He refused and rushed at them with his sword. He was killed instantaneously. The cannons inside the fort were fired to effect the breach in order to permit the English forces to enter in.

Lakshman had reached the outskirts of the Bangalore fort that night. Cautiously, he had crept to the fort by dawn and was now a witness to the tragic drama—the fort walls breached from inside, the English flag fluttering from one of the ramparts and thousands of English troops entering the breach without resistance. He commanded his men to rush to the fort. Blindly they followed him. They grappled with the English at the breach in an almost hand-to-hand fight. They were easily recognisable, in their peasant dress, and mainly the arms they had were those that they could snatch from the English. They were slaughtered. Some, with Lakshman, were able to push their way into the fort. They were slaughtered there. Lakshman took the fallen sword of Bahadur Khan, after his own had been broken. The sword went through one English man, then a second, then a third—and then a pistol shot hit Lakshman in the chest. He fell down. No, there was no pain, no feeling of pain even. Above him was a dark cloud in the sky, impassive and immovable. 'I could do nothing for Sultan. Will Purnaiya count me?' he asked the cloud. The cloud did not answer.

Lakshman died.

(iii)

Possession of Bangalore was the richest prize for the English. Their self-confidence and of their confederates—the Marathas and the Nizam—soared in this hour of triumph. For Tipu Sultan it was an open, seeping wound. He now girded himself for the blows he knew would come. They came. But Tipu Sultan was not defeated and he had no intention of surrendering. On the contrary, he seemed more than ever determined to carry on the struggle to the bitter end and with all the resources he could muster.

All over Mysore, fierce battles raged. Through mud, blood and horror of war, the Mysoreans—gasping and almost spent from months and months of furious and unrelenting combat—proved that they had the capacity to absorb terrible casualties and great defeats. They fought on—and on—in a hopeless situation, in bitterness and desperation, with thousands of men, generals, officers and others dying in the course of each battle. Every English conquest was accompanied by slaughter of civilians; prisoners were tortured until they were maimed; whatever could not be taken away was burnt. Children and old men were killed for sport. Women, for rape. Like demons with unrestricted power, the conquerors went about, razing this, murdering those who came in their way and defiling holy places.

Nana Phadnavis saw the cruelties, which the English and the Nizam perpetrated. It came to him anew that he had nothing in common with these rapacious men—crazed by power and bound by no scruple. Cornwallis listened to him with politeness and the Nizam with a grin. There was nothing that Nana Phadnavis could do except to remind his own forces to continue the Maratha traditions of mercy, honour and chivalry.

✾

These were the chapters of heart-broken lament of Mysore as if written by the flowing waters of the Cauveri river. The historians stood by, their eyes dazzled by the reflection of the sun, their pens dry. Much later, they were followed by other historians. Generously, the English gave them their own books and diaries to read.

'Enough,' said one historian, copying from the books loaned by the English.

'Enough,' agreed the chorus of historians.

The Cauveri flowed on.

(iv)

'They are beaten,' said Abercromby. He was referring to the armies of Mysore.

'Yes, but they don't know it,' Cornwallis said.

'Are they mad? They'll all die.'

'Sometimes,' said Cornwallis softly almost to himself. 'Sometimes, people choose to die.'

Abercromby could not understand. 'What do you mean?' he asked.

'I am not quite sure if I understand what I mean.'

Abercromby shrugged his shoulders. 'They should capitulate, obviously,' he said.

'They should; but will they?'

No, Mysore did not capitulate. Grimly Tipu Sultan fought on. All the time he was within striking distance of the English forces, fighting with courage, harassing them, destroying their baggage and inflicting heavy losses on them. His cavalry was wearing off the English. Many of his generals were also fired with the same courage. Fatah Hyder destroyed enemy forces and captured Gurrakonda. Qamar-ud-din reoccupied Coimbatore after heavy fighting. Cornwallis retreated before Seringapatam against Tipu Sultan's spirited resistance.

In its scale, in its slaughter, in its pillage, in its marches and counter-marches, in the number of battles fought, in the exertion of the combatants, this war far surpassed by magnitude and intensity any that had been fought before throughout the country.

The Mysoreans continued their struggle, radiating the faith of their Sultan.

Cornwallis looked wearily at the devastated countryside. For twelve months he had been by himself in the field. Often, thinking of the Mysoreans, he had caught himself saying:

'What choice do they have except to capitulate'—'or else they would all die bleeding to death with vultures to feed on them and without a choice to determine if they would be buried or cremated.'

To the Bishop of Lichfield and Coventry, wrote Cornwallis: 'My spirits are almost worn out and if I cannot soon overcome Tipu, I think the plagues and mortifications of this most difficult war will overcome me.'

Thus did the second year of the war—1791—pass away. But what does one do to a nation that is all but defeated but will not recognise the fact-and fights on undeterred!

53

THUS DIED A HORSE

'I SHOULD HATE HIM,' SAID RUQAYYA BANU, HER HAND ON DILKUSH the Second, the favourite horse of Tipu Sultan. 'Always he takes you away from me.'

Tipu Sultan smiled at his wife. 'But he brings me back, too,' he replied.

'Yes, that, he does,' affectionately Ruqayya rubbed Dilkush. 'But then you pass more time with him than with me.'

'Your protest, madam, has been noted,' said Tipu.

'Oh, no,' Ruqayya rejoined. 'I alone shall decide the moment of my protest and I shall choose the method of my protest.'

'And when shall that be?' Tipu asked.

'When the strangers are outside our gates,' Ruqayya replied. Tipu Sultan looked around. There was none. It was a courtyard which only ladies of the house and Sultan could use. Then he understood. Ruqayya was thinking of the invading armies. Gently Tipu kissed Ruqayya on her forehead and soon she saw Dilkush the Second disappearing from view, proudly bearing her husband and his master.

The ring of the enemies was now closing round Sultan from all sides. At the head of a small body of Mysore cavalry, he charged, cutting off a great part of Cornwallis' camp equipage. Suddenly, a cannon ball flew aimed directly at the Sultan. Did Dilkush the Second see it before Sultan did? Without warning, the horse pricked up his ears and raised his forelegs high up in the air. Tipu fell on the ground. Dilkush the Second caught the cannon ball. He died but not before he had seen Sultan helped to another horse. Then the writhing agony stopped. He closed his eyes.

Thus died a horse who some say had full comprehension of all that was said, thought and felt by its rider.

54

FAREWELL, RUQAYYA

FEBRUARY, 1792. THE SIEGE OF SERINGAPATAM BEGAN. FROM THE Diary of Puran Chand:

9 February 1792

— *The English forces and their confederates continued today their heavy cannonade against the Seringapatam fort. Shells bursting all over.*
— *Several enemy columns tried to rush to the fort. They were repulsed and compelled to retire with heavy losses.*
— *Today it is said that another contingent of fifty-seven Europeans who were in Sultan's service deserted to the English. Amongst them, I know only two personally— Monsieur Blevette and Monsieur Lefolu—who were in the service of the Kingdom from the time of Sultan's departed father.*
— *Late in the night, one of the enemy shells burst when Ruqayya Banu, the beloved wife of Tipu Sultan, was on her rounds lo console the wives of soldiers who had fallen. It is said that she has been hurt. God, will you not protect her!*

Ruqayya was dead. She died while her husband held her hand and looked into her shining liquid eyes. Her last thought had been to be buried in the clothes she had worn on the day she got married. Her last action—to kiss her husband's hand. The perpetual sparkle of her eyes was now no more. Tipu Sultan remembered the last time they had held hands. They had smiled, talked to each other of nothing and had felt that this was worth all the separation they had endured. How short was that moment of happiness! Now she was gone. He remembered her letters, quite innocent of punctuation, scrawled at a tremendous speed, very long and packed with entertaining laughter. How she babbled, light-heartedly, this vivacious, gleeful girl—half-woman, half-child—to while away her husband's cares! Often, she was noisily energetic with unclouded naturalness, throwing her arms round his neck, chattering away, while he listened to her enraptured. Yet, Tipu Sultan knew that she carried in her heart a deep anxiety—a terror that she shared alone with his mother, Fakhr-un-Nissa. But with him she was gay. Love had so planted itself in her heart that none of the storms that assailed her came to the surface when he was with her. When he was sad, she came with a burst of song, free as waves. She would wait for him to smile—and her joy would then shine with a light—the eye-kissing light, the heart-sweetening light. When his mood was dark and his soul in despair, she brought a lamp near his heart to caress his melancholy away. Yes, hers was a great love which lightened each of his burdens. Tipu remembered the definition she had once attempted of love—a passion which balances the entire world against the person loved and finds the world much lighter.

Tipu laid kisses like a necklace round Ruqayya's throat. Then he closed the window at which Ruqayya used to wait, watching for him to return. She would listen to the hoof beats of Dilkush the Second coming closer and closer. At the end of it she would not greet her husband first. To Dilkush she would address her question: 'Why did you take that long, Dilkush?' Dilkush would bow his head as if he alone deserved the reproof; he would raise his head and consider himself forgiven only when she would place her hand on him. This was the secret between the horse and Ruqayya—he was to take the blame for his master's delay.

Now both were gone. Dilkush and then Ruqayya.

Fakhr-un-Nissa came into the room. She saw her son in the calmness of extreme shock. 'Come to your mother, Son,' she sobbed. 'We shall weep together.' In her arms now was not Tipu Sultan, the King of Mysore, but a little son that was born to her, blessed by Sachal Fakir, Saint Tipu Mastan Oulia.

55

WHERE ARE MY PEOPLE?

IT WAS THE DAY AFTER RUQAYYA BANU'S DEATH.
Purnaiya took over command of the defence of the embattled city of Seringapatam. Tipu Sultan was in high fever. Fakhr-un-Nissa sat by his side. She barred entry to anyone who would discuss State business with him.

The Tower of Somerpeet was the immediate target of the English. It was the keystone of Seringapatam fortifications. Under orders from Cornwallis, his second-in-command General Medows mounted a furious attack on the Tower. Its Commander, Sayyad Ghaffar, fought back. Medows was repulsed with heavy losses. But soon he was back—this time with massive support from the forces of the Nizam and the Marathas. Sayyad Ghaffar was in a good defensive position but he had little chance against the rnassive three-pronged attack. Peril threatened. It was to be a great victory for Medows, and almost the last gasp for a country that had fought this war for two years. Ghaffar's columns wavered against enemy waves. He knew he could not expect help. Purnaiya was engaged against the central army, which Cornwallis himself led. In any case, if help had to come it would have to be through open spaces on which the English cannons were trained. Purnaiya received his message: 'All is lost. I shall die fighting. If my dead body is in a fit condition, let it be placed at Sultan's feet. Otherwise, tell him I died as befits a soldier. Will you embrace my sons for me? Tell Moin that I have gone to defeat Bade Mian in a game of chess.' (Moin was the youngest son of Sayyad Ghaffar and Bade Mian, his father, who had died recently; in spite of all moral support from Moin, Ghaffar invariably lost at chess.)

But suddenly Purnaiya came—not so much because Sayyad Ghaffar's life was at stake but to protect the strategic Tower which was in danger of falling in the English hands. He tore across open spaces, his forces braving deadly cannon fire, and attacked from the rear. It was the shock rather than the weight of the attack that unnerved Medows. He ordered his forces to fall back to face the new attack but the confusion had set in. The forces of the Nizam and the Marathas saw what looked like an English withdrawal. They did not like the sound of guns behind them. They turned back, coming directly into the range of two of Sayyad Ghaffar's cannons which hitherto had been silent. From then on, all order and discipline ceased. The forces of the Nizam and the Marathas were in headlong flight. Panic seized the English. Their confederates ran in different directions while they were locked in combat with Purnaiya's forces. Sayyad Ghaffar had continued his cannonade even though there was danger of his hitting the Mysoreans as well. He was obsessed only with one thought—that night should set in, so that he could repair the damage to the Tower and replace some of his unserviceable guns; nothing else mattered to him.

Medows had ordered his troops to stand firm but some had already run off with retreating confederates. The battle with Purnaiya's forces had taken its toll. Guns from the fort were playing havoc with the English. Their objective of seizing the Tower was no longer capable of achievement. Medows ordered withdrawal.

Sayyad Ghaffar saw it as a miracle. He cried, 'Oh, God, God, may I die, be blinded, be deprived of all that is near and dear to me, if ever I doubt your mercy.'

And, Purnaiya? He said nothing. He was lying unconscious with a bullet wound. The bullet had pierced his shoulder. For a long while through blood, shock and throbbing pain, he had remained conscious. Mulki Muhammad had remained by his side. He saw the English retreat and then he fainted in Mulki Muhammad's arms.

The Tower was saved.

Purnaiya had left Ghazi Khan to face the central column led by Cornwallis while he had gone to Sayyad Ghaffar's assistance.

If Cornwallis had known how the forces against him had been depleted, he would have instantaneously attacked. It was Ghazi Khan's bravado which misled him. From the shelter of the protecting walls of the fort, Ghazi Khan charged at the head of cavalry as if he commanded a massive force and could well afford to stand losses. He came into the open field and went back in good order giving an impression that he did not have a care in the world but had come out simply to reconnoitre the battle positions as a prelude to mounting a heavy assault An assault in the open was just what Cornwallis wished. He ordered his forces to regroup and relocate the position of the guns. All the cannons from the fort opened fire—another sure sign of an imminent attack. There was brisk movement of banners behind the fort walls as if each division was getting ready with its ceremonial before rushing out in battle. Lull from the English side. They waited and watched.

Meanwhile, Ghazi Khan was lying on a bed with a bullet wound in his thigh. He had received it during his brief heroic excursion outside; if the bullet made him wince, neither his comrades near him nor the enemy at a distance saw it. He had raised himself on his horse, lifted his right hand as if to salute the opposing forces before returning to the fort.

Ghazi Khan cursed the doctor while the poor man was trying his best to offer medical aid. Mir Sadik looked on.

'That was a foolish thing you did,' Mir Sadik said.

'What makes you think I did it,' replied Ghazi Khan, deliberately misunderstanding him. 'The English shot at me.'

'You know what I mean; rushing out in the open; showing off as if you were on parade; it was a foolish thing to do,' said Mir Sadik, with some irritation.

'I am a foolish man,' Ghazi Khan agreed good-naturedly. Then he groaned against the doctor's ministrations.

'Yes, you have a bullet to show for it,' was the unfeeling response of Mir Sadik.

'Oh, no, that doesn't prove any foolishness,' Ghazi Khan protested.

'What else?'

'The bullet merely proves that I am a fat man—which I am. A fat man makes, I am told, an easy target.' He laughed, but winced as his laughter strained his wound. 'But, see,' he added hoarsely, 'a fat man also protects those that follow him—like a wall. We had hardly any casualties.'

'Fifteen died,' Mir Sadik reminded him.

'So that thousands may survive,' rejoined Ghazi Khan with a weak smile, but soon he relapsed into oaths against the doctor, 'You..., you..., you....' But the doctor was jubilant. He had found the bullet. He looked as if single-handed he had won the entire war. Mir Sadik moved on.

Cornwallis still waited and watched. Then came to him the news of Medow's debacle. Trust that blithering idiot to convert a victory into a defeat, he thought to himself. Now, God knows what the Marathas and the Nizam's army would be up to, he wondered. Further parleys with them were unavoidable. He ordered his buglers to sound a withdrawal.

Mir Sadik had just tiptoed out of Tipu Sultan's room. The fever would take some days to break, the doctors had said. Mir Sadik saw Purnaiya brought in, unconscious. The overall command now fell on him. He sent word for the Council of Ministers and senior commanders to meet in the Council Chamber that very night.

In the eyes of Cornwallis, General Medows possessed three great virtues; first, he loathed Indians and although Cornwallis did not fully share the emotion, this was all to the good in the interests of empire building; second, Medows detested Tipu Sultan recognising in him the greatest danger to the Empire and he had therefore put himself body and soul into the massive accumulation of men and materials that went to build the Grand Army; and third, he was an incompetent general which meant that the success of Cornwallis would be all the more appreciated. On the strength of these virtues, Cornwallis naturally loved and valued him. He was second-in-command and he was expected to succeed Cornwallis as Governor-General on his retirement. Cornwallis, who knew the ways of the world, was aware of intrigues by those who are designated to succeed. But such was the calibre of Medows that he would never be a threat to the great Cornwallis. No one would call upon Cornwallis to retire prematurely to give Medows an early chance to succeed. What is more, Medows himself had a dog-like affection for Cornwallis. No wonder, therefore, that he had endeared himself to Cornwallis.

It was with utter sadness therefore that Cornwallis learned that Medows had tried to commit suicide. The defeat at the hands of the slender Mysorean force had been too much for him. He had commanded formidable forces supported by the armies of the Nizam and the Marathas. The fall of the Tower of Somerpeet was regarded as a foregone conclusion. Instead, he had returned not as a victorious general but in a headlong flight—defeated and disgraced. He decided to blow his brains out. Then, as was characteristic with him, the pistol went off prematurely, wounding him 'between the breast bone and the navel.' Before he could fire a second time, Colonel Malcolm, who had rushed into the tent on hearing the shot, snatched the pistol from him. The wound was not fatal.

Like wildfire, the news spread to the camps of the Nizam and the Marathas of the depths to which English morale had fallen that their generals were now on the path of suicide.

The English looked about sullenly. They were promised an easy victory as with all other Indian powers. Two years they had slaved in mud and filth, through horror and bloodshed. The end?—even their glorious generals had lost their heart and spirit!

Cornwallis surveyed the situation with anguish. His own lieutenants saw nothing but an endless siege ahead of them before Tipu Sultan could be defeated. The armies of the Marathas and the Nizam were ready to parley with Tipu Sultan and, if the dialogue was not successful, they could withdraw for the moment to return the next year in greater force.

There was wisdom in that thought, Cornwallis conceded. It will not be retreat without reward. The pillage of the entire country awaited him.

'The night will give us counsel. Let us meet tomorrow at noon and make the final decision then,' said Cornwallis to his confederates, the Marathas and the Nizam.

Tipu Sultan woke up at midnight. Twenty-four hours had passed since Ruqayya Banu was dead. He raised his head and looked around in surprise. He had a curious sensation that he was seeing shadows. What was Fakhr-un-Nissa doing here with her rosary—and the doctor? Then he remembered. A spasm passed across his face. Calmly he asked what the time was. They told him. He jumped out of the bed. The doctor tried to restrain him. It was of no avail. Fakhr-un-Nissa looked pleadingly. She said nothing. She was the wife of a king and the mother of a King. There was duty to be done, she knew.

Tipu's steps faltered. They supported him for a moment. Then he shook off help and walked slowly to the Council Chamber. The Conference was already in progress with Mir Sadik presiding. The ministers, who were informed only a moment earlier that Tipu Sultan was about to join them, were now silent. Sultan entered the Council Chamber, pale and haggard. They rose to greet him. He waved away their words of sympathy over Ruqayya Banu's death. It was as if he seemed to say that he came to them like their King and comrade—not as a lover and a husband.

'Please continue,' he said. Mir Sadik continued his statement. Tipu Sultan kept his eyes on maps and charts prepared for the day showing the progress of the siege, placement of guns, casualty figures, positioning and strength of armies and other related details. He now interrupted him.

'The position is not so hopeless, Mir Sadik,' Tipu Sultan said, for Mir Sadik had painted a picture of utter defeat for Mysoreans. 'Have you studied these charts?' asked Tipu after a pause.

'I had them prepared myself, Sultan.' That was true for otherwise it was under Purnaiya's orders that Hari Rao used to prepare them. Today, the orders had come from Mir Sadik and they also bore Mir Sadik's signature and not Purnaiya's.

'And, your conclusion?' asked Tipu Sultan, unnecessarily.

'I shall bow to your judgement; we all shall, Sultan.'

'It is your assessment that I am seeking.'

Mir Sadik spoke at length. To begin with, he was cautious. He spoke of sacrifices which Mysoreans had made in the war. He dwelt on their love for Sultan, their devotion for him, their efforts and sufferings in his cause. Again, Tipu Sultan interrupted him.

'Please, do not speak of devotion to me,' said Tipu. 'I want nothing of it for myself but for the cause. The cause—and please remember it—is bigger than me, bigger than all of us here.'

'I will not dispute that with you, Sultan, but you are dear to our hearts and so is the cause. Both are integrated and identified with each other. Forgive me therefore if I speak of both in the same breath. The point I was making was....'

Mir Sadik continued. The Kingdom could, in his view, impose no further sacrifices on the Mysoreans. Mysore was in a death grip, riddled by defeats, drained by desertions and short of supplies. The remnants of the Mysore army had stood up in an epic struggle against three mighty armies but now they were near annihilation. The civilians had also shouldered a heavy burden of unprecedented bloodshed, fury and destruction. The city of Seringapatam was under a siege that would strangle the entire nation. The country would collapse—never perhaps to recover—if it was not given a moment to breathe. This war must end. Peace must return to heal the wounds so that Mysore can fight again. Else it will fall, with all its lifeblood washed away, without a hope of recovery.

Tipu Sultan listened to Mir Sadik with rapt attention. From time to time he looked at the others. They averted their eyes but it was clear that they agreed with Mir Sadik.

'Tell me, Mir Sadik,' softly Tipu asked, 'when have I not been ready for peace? I offered it on the day when the English marched on us, suddenly, without warning and without provocation. I have always renewed my request, time and again. What have I been offered in return? The sword, the gun, the devastation of my kingdom.'

Mir Sadik did not reply immediately. He was trying to formulate the words for his thoughts. Finally he said, 'Peace could then have come by both sides withdrawing from each other's territory. Now the English would demand a price, so will their confederates, for they are at our very gates. They have inexhaustible supplies of men and equipment while we are drained to the dregs.'

'What about Lakshman's brigades?' Tipu Sultan asked. 'They have been coming in to reinforce our armies.'

'Peasants, mostly. Untrained without arms. Yes, these brigades were coming at first in large numbers. Now it is a trickle. Lakshman himself is nowhere to be found.'

'Where is he?' Tipu asked.

'No one knows. Some say he died,' replied Mir Sadik. And then he added, 'There are others who say that he has deserted.'

'No one says so,' came the angry, ringing voice of Mulki Muhammad sitting in a chair far away. He now rose, and added, 'If anyone does say it, he deserves to have his tongue cut out.'

Tipu said nothing.

'You are voicing my own sentiments, Mulki Muhammad,' said Mir Sadik. The words were warm but the tone, icy. 'Still,' he added, 'Sultan is entitled to all information and even a rumour—howsoever unfortunate and unfounded—affecting those that are near and dear to us.'

'If Lakshman is missing, how is it that his brigades still keep arriving?' asked Tipu Sultan. 'Is it not possible that, unknown to us, he is active in some far corner of the Kingdom?'

'No, Sultan,' replied Mir Sadik. 'We have made the most anxious and searching enquiries. He really is missing. His brigades keep coming because right in the beginning he lectured to many men and sent them out in different parts of the country to spread your message. Out of love for you and for the cause, there are many who readily respond to that message and they are sent to us as Lakshman's brigades. The name has caught on, even though Lakshman himself cannot be found.'

There was a pause during which Tipu Sultan looked at Mulki Muhammad. Already, Mulki Muhammad had realised the enormity of his offence in raising his voice in such distinguished company. Mir Sadik would not forgive him but that did not worry him too much. Tipu Sultan might have felt hurt and that did worry him. He looked crest-fallen.

'Mulki Muhammad,' Tipu began, 'be assured of my conviction—and I beiieve it with all my heart and soul—that if Lakshman lives, he lives in honour and if he is dead, he died with honour. Never, never shall I believe otherwise nor shall I permit anyone else to believe otherwise.'

Tipu Sultan now turned to Mir Sadik and asked: 'And, what then is your final advice?'

'My advice, such as it is worth, is to begin immediate parleys with the English and their confederates, to be ready to offer a little cash indemnity, to make a concession here and there and somehow avert this terrible catastrophe that hangs on us all.'

'You feel that they would be satisfied with a little cash indemnity and not demand our territory?' asked Tipu.

'We can try. There are three powers against us. This is our advantage,' replied Mir Sadik.

'I thought you said earlier that was what was against us?'

'In a war, yes. But when it comes to peace negotiations, we can drive a wedge and create dissensions amongst them. Each will be seeking an advantage for himself and will be ready to forsake others.'

'So three greedy jackals are to be feared less than one jackal when it comes to negotiating peace?' Tipu Sultan asked.

'Yes, though you put it differently and more colourfully than I did,' said Mir Sadik, with a smile.

Tipu Sultan did not smile. He looked at all of them, their faces gloomy, their eyes downcast as if agreeing with Mir Sadik but wishing to spare Sultan the pain of voicing their agreement.

'I must consult Purnaiya also. Where is he?' asked Sultan. He had seen Purnaiya's chair empty. It had not surprised him. Often, Purnaiya was absent from such meetings, so occupied he used to be with other duties.

For a moment, Mir Sadik did not reply. Then he said slowly: 'He is wounded. Unconscious.'

'Oh, God,' Tipu said to himself, but the cry was audible.

'The doctors have not lost hope of saving his life,' Mir Sadik said in a tone least likely to reassure.

Tipu now looked at other empty chairs.

'And, Ghazi Khan?' he asked in fear.

Mir Sadik nodded, sadly. 'Ghazi Khan is down, too. A bullet pierced him. But his condition is not as bad as Purnaiya's.'

'Anyone else?' asked Tipu. It was as if he was forcing himself to speak.

'There are many empty chairs at this meeting, Sultan,' said Mir Sadik, avoiding a direct answer to Tipu Sultan's question. 'These two days have been days of tragedy—nights too.' Thus was Tipu reminded again of Ruqayya. Mir Sadik continued: 'Just now I spoke to you, frankly, but with deep anguish in my heart. It is my love for you that permitted me the liberty of being so candid with you. If God gave me a choice I would have preferred to die rather than speak to you as I did, suggesting negotiations with a cruel aggressor. But I see these empty chairs as you do, I see dark and dismal days ahead of Mysore, I see that the blood of our fallen brothers will have been shed in vain unless... unless we pause for a brief moment and buy peace so that our people can recover breath to be able to fight again. Whatever be your decision, Sultan, whether you value my advice or not, this I beg of you, forgive me if you think that I have transgressed. Blame, then, not me but my love for you.' Mir Sadik's voice was choked with emotion and his eyes filled with tears as he concluded.

Tipu left his chair, put his arm around Mir Sadik.

'I value your advice, Mir Sadik,' said Tipu Sultan. 'Equally, I am proud to have your affection.'

There was silence for a minute. Tipu Sultan looked at Purnaiya's empty chair, then Ghazi Khan's and then several others'.

'Let parleys begin with our enemies,' said Tipu Sultan in a voice that shook with emotion. Then he steadied himself and added, 'You take charge of it, Mir Sadik.'

Mir Sadik bowed. He looked as if a hammer blow had struck him full in the face but in his heart surged a wave of happiness.

56

PREPARATIONS FOR PEACE

(i)

CORNWALLIS ALMOST WEPT WITH RELIEF, SO TERRIBLE HAD BEEN the strain of many years of weariness and desperate danger. Yes, his long night of agony was over, the clouds had disappeared and the sun was shining again.

Mir Sadik had visited him late in the night, shortly after the fateful meeting in the Council Chamber. He crossed into the enemy lines without waiting for a safe conduct, accompanied by two men, one carrying a lantern and the other a white flag. He was challenged and then escorted respectfully to Cornwallis as soon as he revealed his identity. That such a high-ranking emissary should come to them from Tipu Sultan puzzled even the soldiers escorting him to their Commander-in-Chief.

This was the first time that Cornwallis and Mir Sadik had met. Still, it did not take them long to understand each other perfectly. Joint crimes and shared secrets form bonds more powerful than love and friendship.

Now Mir Sadik had left. To himself, Cornwallis reflected that a question which had long puzzled him had finally been resolved in his mind. Luck was the prime mover of the world. Courage, bravery, idealism, intellect, hope or expectation had little to do with it. One more day of resistance from Tipu Sultan, or even silence, the English and their confederates would have been ready to depart. Cornwallis had never been able to explain to himself the undeserved reverse in America leading to his surrender at Yorktown. Now came this unexpected stroke of providence that Sultan himself should sue for peace at the moment when the English and their allies had lost all hopes of victory.

Suddenly, Sultan's sun had set.

(ii)

What was to be a dismal conference between Cornwallis and his confederates at noon became a meeting of joy.

Cornwallis, with supreme self-confidence announced that the Mysoreans were on the edge of disaster, their Sultan had weakened and soon the enemy would send negotiators to settle formally the terms of peace.

Hari Pant, the Maratha Commander-in-Chief, agreed to halt his preparations for withdrawal.

The Nizam swore that he had in any case decided to fight Tipu Sultan to the finish, even alone if the English and the Marathas withdrew. Graciously, the Nizam added that now that his gallantry and determination had compelled Sultan to seek peace, he would readily offer his advice, counsel and guidance with the aim of securing lasting benefits for all the three allies.

Cornwallis smiled. The Marathas laughed. The Nizam in ecstasy watched the arrival of Tipu Sultan's official negotiators.

(iii)

'To negotiate from strength, it is necessary to amass strength, display it, parade it and keep it in view all the time for the enemy to see it. Let it strike terror in his heart. More readily, then, he will come to terms—our terms.'

This was the advice of Cornwallis to his allies. 'Whether we were to win the war or lose it—whether we were to stand firm or withdraw—are not the issues that should cloud our minds any longer. What we have now to do is to win the negotiations for peace.'

Word went out to the English provinces, to the Maratha capital and to the Nizam's dominions: 'The peace negotiations are on but send troops, more arms. Let them share in the joy of victory. They shall march to Seringapatam unmolested without resistance.'

Mir Sadik disbanded Lakshman's Brigades. 'Go back to your lands for the greater prosperity of the Kingdom,' he said to them. 'Peace is coming. Peace with honour. Go, spread the word that it was your will and your sense of sacrifice that helped to bring an end to this terrible war. Go to your loved ones who wait for you, long for you. Sultan thanks you all. Above all, he begs you to remember that the nation is hungry, needs food; to your withered lands therefore must go your undivided attention.'

They left.

Many commanders were also sent back with their contingents to their home stations. 'Peace is coming. Peace with honour,' Mir Sadik repeated to them. 'Your duty lies elsewhere. Go back to your commands. See to the restoration of law and order. See that the peasant is encouraged to till the land. See to it that the withdrawing enemy forces do not pillage. Guard the interests of the Kingdom.'

'Let the wounded and the sick receive all attention,' Mir Sadik commanded. He had them evacuated from the city of Seringapatam and neighbouring areas, brought them into the fort to receive attention from the court physicians.

'What a courageous man!' said some of Mir Sadik who knew that he had gone to Cornwallis, no doubt under instructions from Sultan, almost unattended, without a safe conduct and unconcerned about stray bullets flying out in that embattled zone.

'What a statesman!' said others. The war was not over. Yet, Mir Sadik looked to the future, prepared for peace and, well in advance, took all the steps to make that peace meaningful and prosperous.

'What a humanitarian!' This was to extol Mir Sadik's concern for the sick and wounded whom he had brought into the fort.

But the Mysoreans had rung their peace bells too soon. A solid wall of steel faced them. The enemy forces and their equipment grew day by day. And, the Mysoreans? They were dispersing to pursue their peace-time vocations. The Mysorean peace negotiators heard with dismay the growing demands. They saw the attitude of the enemy stiffen. Cornwallis now met them with cold ferocity. Gone were his smiles and courtesy with which negotiations had begun. He made new demands, impossible demands. Meanwhile his forces swelled.

The shouts of joy that had reverberated through Mysore were stilled. Dread set in. Some who had left Seringapatam, returned without orders. Many wavered and waited for the orders that never came. Many more went to their homes, lands and families in the hope that they would be left alone. They did not understand the significance of what was happening. How does one revive a broken spirit? How does one call for war, resistance and sacrifice after proclaiming peace with honour? How does a war-weary nation mobilise itself for battle immediately after it had disbanded its brigades and dispersed its commanders? No, the stretched string had snapped.

Tipu Sultan looked on in agony. The enemy activity was enormously intensified with plentiful supplies and reinforcements. More and more of their troops were rushing into Seringapatam with surprising energy and unheard of speed. Steadily at first and speedily thereafter the Mysorean forces were melting away.

'Why have so many deserted us, Mir Sadik?' Tipu asked.

Mir Sadik's head was bowed. He did not reply. His face reflected a despair he could not permit his lips to utter.

'So many sick and wounded in the fort and so many dying,' Tipu commented.

'Yes, and countless more outside,' Mir Sadik said, as if with an involuntary shudder.

'Peace must come quickly. We need it. You were right,' Tipu said.

'No, I fear I was wrong.'

'How so?' Tipu asked.

'I have halted the negotiations,' Mir Sadik replied. 'The price the English and their allies are seeking today—I would rather cut off my tongue before I discuss it with them.'

'New demands again! What is it that they want now?'

'What is it that they want?' Mir Sadik repeated the question. 'Everything—or almost everything. They will respect your life and person but that is all. If it was a question of money, gold or silver, yes, I am prepared to be generous. But they want our territory—our towns, our forts to be handed over to them.'

Tipu Sultan did not reply. Mir Sadik continued. 'Sultan, this war is not over. I fear we have to continue the fight. The struggle will be grim, I know. Our chances of survival are slim, that also I know. But then the alternative—what is it? To voluntarily give up our land and call it a peace. These few days of truce have given us some respite. We are in no worse position today than we were on the day we began negotiations.'

'Yet, so many desertions have taken place since then,' Sultan observed with sadness.

'True, but would they have been any the less, if war had been on? More, but not less.'

'Let us discuss it. Purnaiya is still helpless but let us all meet in the Council Chamber this evening.'

(iv)

At the meeting in the Council Chamber, Mir Sadik made his report. First, the routine news—the number of those amongst the sick and wounded in the fort who died during the week, the rising tempo of desertions, steps taken to halt desertions including arrests and measures taken to improve fortifications. Then he reported on the negotiations with the English and their allies. He had met with demands which he considered incompatible with the honour of Mysore and Tipu Sultan. He himself, Mir Sadik explained, had suggested peace negotiations hoping that the enemy would not adopt an unreasonable attitude and in any case a few days of truce were necessary to reappraise the situation as also to repair the damage. Now he felt convinced of the impossibility of continuing the negotiations on the lines demanded by the enemy. Better to lay down life rather than submit to such shameful terms, he concluded.

They all heard in silence. Ghazi Khan who had been well enough to attend broke the silence.'

'These are fine phrases and feelings, no doubt, but the main question is: What is the military siutation?'

Mir Sadik looked gratefully to Ghazi Khan. He had found the silence oppressive. He was beginning to believe that his audience had come to accept his last observation—to fight on and to reject a humiliating peace.

'Your question is pertinent, Ghazi Khan,' Mir Sadik replied. 'I am no military expert and I bow to your superior judgement and certainly to Sultan's. You have not been circulating amongst us due to your injury. Otherwise, you would have assessed it yourself without any help from me. I can only tell you what can be culled from what the various commands have placed before me. Our troops. . . .' Here, he gave facts and figures of the strength and the weakness of the Mysore armies contrasting it in every detail with the superiority of the enemy forces.

Mir Sadik recited figures and statistics without reference to his notes. He was aware of each little detail. Nothing had escaped him. It was a grim account. He was dealing with figures without reaching conclusions. Yet, the one conclusion which was inescapable was that Mysore did not have a chance, if his figures were correct—and they were, as everyone present there knew that. It was only towards the end that some emotion entered into his voice and he said, 'I have told you the military situation as I see it; but let me add, we went into this war with one single aim and that was to drive the invader out. What shall we have achieved if the peace that they seek to dictate to us should defeat that very aim?'

It was Ghazi Khan who again broke the silence. 'How did we come to this sorry pass?' he asked.

Mir Sadik took time to answer. He looked at Ghazi Khan directly in the face. Then his glance lingered on the military commanders sitting by his side. When he spoke, there was no anger in his voice, not even a hint of accusation. It was as if the irrelevancy of the question irritated him. 'This is a question, Ghazi Khan', said Mir Sadik, 'which I must leave to you and to our military commanders to determine. I for one blame nobody, no one. But I do ask you this: Are we to hide behind the curtain of the past groping to find someone on whom to place the guilt of our misfortunes or are we to face the future? And I say this to you that often, Sultan has led us through many battles, victoriously, against overwhelming odds and superior forces. Why then this mood of despair? Why should the future appear to us to be dark, and dismal? Why have we lost hope? Why? I submit I am no military expert but....'

Mir Sadik did not complete the sentence but what he left unsaid was eloquent enough. It was as if he was battling to stifle an accusation and did not want to say anything which should imply an aspersion against military leadership or its morale. Yet, the implication was clear and unmistakable.

Thereafter, Mir Sadik sat impassively as the debate dragged on. He did not need to utter another word. His exposition of their own military weakness and enemy strength had been both accurate and brilliant. They could find no fault with it. His figures of desertions, though somewhat fanciful and exaggerated, could not be challenged. The legion of the sick and wounded in the fort was for everyone to see and on this score, Mir Sadik's figures had been conservative. Also, it was clear that Mir Sadik had done everything possible to resist the demands of the English during the negotiations—negotiations which were begun under the direct orders from his sovereign. Equally clear was the evidence of his courage. Here was a man who, when all seemed lost, chose not the easy path but sought to inspire his colleagues to resume resistance despite the growing might of the enemy.

The debate went on. No, there was no doubt about the conclusion that was emerging. Only it was difficult to put the desolate, inevitable decision in words. The heroic exhortation of Mir Sadik notwithstanding, it was clear that the military situation was such that Mysore could not put up a vigorous defence. It was essential therefore that negotiations must be resumed and peace must be restored. It was one thing to use the last of one's energy in a bid to repel the invader if there was even the slightest chance of being able to do that, but quite another to expend oneself in rowing towards certain destruction. The question was: Can Mysore, whose people by their love, their efforts and their sufferings have preserved the Kingdom, be called upon to take on greater burdens? Can further sacrifices be imposed on them? To what purpose, to what end, to what useless, senseless inconsequence? Should the lifeblood of the nation be allowed to dry up? Is it not better to come to terms rather than face annihilation? Why, had not Sultan dictated peace to the English before and here they were now fighting once more. Surely, the roles can be reversed again. While one lives, there is hope. But only so long as one lives.

(v)

Cornwallis toyed with the idea of delaying peace negotiations, while the English reinforcements streamed in. This might be the best opportunity to crush Tipu Sultan for ever, he thought. Hari Pant, the Maratha Commander-in-Chief advised him against it. 'Do not push the Tiger too far,' said Hari Pant. 'He might turn back and attack.' Nana Phadnavis also wrote to Cornwallis saying that such a course might involve them into a prolonged war in which the Maratha forces were not prepared to join and that he might have to withdraw his armies, if the war continued. Cornwallis knew that without the Maratha support, the English would not be able to move forward, much less defeat Tipu Sultan. He remembered the frustrations of the past two years during which the Mysoreans had carried out a gallant struggle against a powerful combination. He laid aside his dream of total conquest. In any case, Cornwallis knew that it was an idle dream. He could visualise the ferocity with which Sultan would fight if faced with a war to the finish. At the moment, the Tiger was unaware of his strength. If he discovered it. ... No, the English victory would come not so much on the battlefield but on the negotiating table where he would have to deal with Mir Sadik. What was really disquieting was that Purnaiya's condition was reported to be improving. Already, he had gained consciousness. Soon, he might be up and running. Cornwallis did not relish the idea of Purnaiya being in charge of negotiations from Sultan's side. He had developed a fondness for Mir Sadik.

57

LET MY SONS GO

(i)

THE PRELIMINARY TREATY OF SERINGAPATAM WAS SIGNED ON 26 February 1792. In accordance with the articles of the Treaty, Tipu Sultan was to cede half of his dominions to the English and their confederates as also to pay a cash indemnity of thirty-three million rupees of which half was to be paid immediately and the remainder in twelve months. What was more, he was to hand over to the English two of his sons—Abdul Khaliq aged eight and Muiz-ud-din aged five as hostages to guarantee fulfilment of the Treaty. The original draft of the Treaty as submitted by Mir Sadik to Sultan had spoken of 'acceptable guarantees'. Later it was changed to read 'acceptable hostages for fulfilment of the Treaty and due payment of cash indemnity.' Finally, the demand came that the only hostages acceptable to the English would be the two sons of Sultan.

Mir Sadik had rushed to Tipu Sultan and told him of the impossible demand of the English. That Mir Sadik was incoherent at first and had to repeat his statement, was understandable.

'It was not my understanding,' said Tipu Sultan calmly, 'that they wish to have my children as hostages. No, that surely was not my understanding.'

'Nor mine,' Mir Sadik replied. 'We must reject the demand and face the consequences, whatever they be.'

'Who did you think they originally wanted as hostages?' asked Tipu.

'Surely, not your sons,' replied Mir Sadik. 'I thought maybe they had in mind some of your officers or governors, even me or Purnaiya, if he was well enough. But your sons, impossible.'

'Let us consider it,' said Tipu.

'Consider what?' Mir Sadik asked, aghast.

'We shall discuss it this evening,' was Tipu Sultan's reply.

That evening Tipu Sultan discussed the matter with an assembly of his senior commanders and ministers. They were horrified at the mere suggestion and urged its instant rejection. But Tipu Sultan had something to say. He addressed himself to Mir Sadik.

'You told me of your earlier impression that they might have wanted you or Purnaiya as hostages. Tell me if I could part with you and Purnaiya, should I hesitate to part with my children?'

'But this is impossible,' Mir Sadik replied. 'It is your children they are seeking. The five-year-old Muiz-ud-din and the eight-year-old Abdul Khaliq. Your children!'

In the pindrop silence that followed, Tipu said something which was incomprehensible to most of them. 'King Naaga gave a thousand cows in charity,' said Tipu, 'but among them was a cow which did not belong to him and thus he fell from grace.' They all looked at Tipu in astonishment while he continued. 'King Usinara of the Sibis gave the flesh of his own body to protect a pigeon which a hawk claimed as its rightful prey and he now rejoices in heaven.'

'So be it,' Tipu concluded. 'Let my sons be given as hostages.'

The articles of the preliminary Treaty were so finalised. Tipu Sultan's two sons, Muiz-ud-din and Abdul Khaliq, were delivered as hostages to the English to guarantee fulfilment of the Treaty. Half the cash indemnity was also paid. The remainder was payable in three instalments within twelve months after the definitive Treaty was finalised.

(ii)

The preliminary Treaty was followed by the definitive Treaty of Seringapatam on 19 March 1792. During the interval between the preliminary and the definitive Treaty, Cornwallis had shown his mettle. To him a hostage was a hostage and when the negotiation of the definitive Treaty ran into trouble, the princes began to be treated as prisoners-of-war.

All politeness and courtesies were withdrawn from them. Their Mysore guard was disarmed and imprisoned and the children were to be ready to proceed to the Carnatic. They were actually put into palanquins and taken a short distance down the Bangalore road, under the escort of Captain Welch's battalion. They were then allowed to encamp while their father's answer was awaited. News was leaked to Tipu Sultan of their imprisonment and of the possibility of harsher measures against them. This, in spite of the fact that in the preliminaries it had been agreed by Cornwallis that if the negotiations broke down, the hostages would be returned. Cornwallis now made it clear that he had every intention of keeping the two children as prisoners unless and until their father proved to be pliant. Tipu Sultan had already agreed to a cash indemnity of thirty-three million rupees. He had also paid half of it and the remainder was to be paid in the next twelve months. The quarrel had however arisen on the demarcation of the territories to be surrendered to the English and their allies. In the preliminaries, it had even been agreed that the English would claim only the territories adjacent to their own possessions. Now they laid claim on many others including Coorg.

Tipu complained, not without reason—and the English historians have so admitted—that to demand from him a territory 'which approached his very capital, and was not contiguous to the country of any of the allies, was a real infringement of the preliminary articles.' As it is, there was no mention of Coorg in the preliminaries and at the time of signing the armistice Coorg was not included in the list of territories to be ceded to the English.

'To which of the English possessions is Coorg adjacent?' Tipu asked. 'Why do they not ask for the key of Seringapatam? They know that I would have sooner died in the battle than consent to such a cession, and they dared not bring it forward until they had treacherously obtained possession of my children and my treasure.'

But Tipu Sultan knew of the danger in which his two sons stood. The English made it clear that neither the children would be returned nor the cash indemnity, in spite of the provisions of the preliminary Treaty. Also, there were threats of harm to children and the worst among them was that they would be brought up in another religion. Tipu Sultan agreed to the surrender of Coorg and set his seal on the definitive Treaty of Seringapatam.

(iii)

Punctually, Tipu Sultan had met all his obligations under the Treaty. Well before the twelve months were over, he was able to deliver the remainder of the cash indemnity payable to the

English and the allies. His sons were not returned to him for more than two years. The reunion took place at Devanhalli, Tipu Sultan's birth place, on 29 February 1794. Silently, the boys bowed, placing their hands on their father's feet and he gently raised them with his hands on their chins, kissing them on their foreheads. Then he buried his face into theirs, moist with each other's tears.

58

WHO IS YOUR ENEMY?

AT THE TIME OF SIGNING THE TREATY, CORNWALLIS HAD OFFERED one of Tipu Sultan's sons to the Marathas as a hostage. His objective was by no means altruistic. He wanted the Marathas to be tarred with the same brush. If Cornwallis was repelled by barbarism of the Nizam, equally was he irritated by the Maratha reputation for honour and chivalry. Let the Marathas also share the judgement of history for keeping a child as a hostage, thought Cornwallis to himself. But Hari Pant, the Maratha Commander-in-Chief, declined the offer.

'This will give you the best lever against Tipu Sultan for all time to come,' Cornwallis insisted.

'Thank you, but no. We need no children as a lever,' Hari Pant replied firmly.

'Think it over. Consult Nana Phadnavis, if you wish,' Cornwallis suggested.

'On this matter, I know Nana's mind as I know mine.'

Cornwallis hid his chagrin under a silky smile and said no more.

Later, Hari Pant sent a personal message to Tipu Sultan with which he associated Nana Phadnavis expressing regret that he was a party to a treaty by which Sultan's children were taken as hostages but pleading that he had no choice in view of the insistence of the allies. Gratefully, Tipu Sultan acknowledged the message.

Before Hari Pant left, Tipu Sultan paid him a visit. Hari Pant expressed himself even more forcefully on the ignominy attached to a war that victimises children as hostages. 'I feel equally guilty,' said Hari Pant, 'and the fact that we had left Lord Cornwallis in complete charge of the peace negotiations does not justify the offence.' They parted warmly.

'You have been,' said Hari Pant to Tipu Sultan, 'our enemy for long on the battlefield but please be assured of my respect and of the esteem of the Maratha nation for you, personally.'

Tipu Sultan warned him in prophetic words: 'You must realise I am not at all your enemy. Your real enemy is the Englishman of whom you must beware.'

59

A SWEETMEAT AFTER A MEAL

THE WAR HAD BEEN STARTED BY THE ENGLISH UNDER THE PRETENCE of protecting the ruler of Travancore who was supposed to have been attacked by Tipu Sultan. Remarkably, however, no further mention of Travancore is to be found in the official records of the war or in the articles of the Treaty.

Abercromby had reminded Cornwallis of the need to make a mention of Travancore in the Treaty.

'What for?' asked Cornwallis.

'We are supposed to have started the war for the benefit of Travancore.'

'We are certainly not going to end it for their benefit.'

'No, I was only thinking that our paper-work should be in order.'

'Oh, paper-work? Well let us charge Travancore the expenses of the war. Why mess about with the Treaty? Or, is it your intention that to satisfy ourselves on paper, we should pass on to Travancore a portion of what we gain from Tipu Sultan?' asked Cornwallis.

'Far from it,' replied Abercromby with a smile.

The matter did not end there. Even though Travancore did not find a mention in the Treaty, it had to pay two and a half million rupees to the English towards the expenses of the war for the privilege of providing an excuse to begin the hostilities against Tipu Sultan.

Later, Cornwallis was told of the bitter complaint of the ruler of Travancore. 'How can the English, my traditional friends, deprive me of so much after having obtained such tremendous reparations from Tipu Sultan,' wailed the Travancore ruler.

'Tell him,' said Cornwallis, 'that howsoever heavy and wholesome a meal, I love a sweetmeat after it. Will he disappoint me?'

The Travancore ruler did not disappoint him. He dared not.

60

TORCH FOR TOMORROW

IN THE DEPTHS OF HIS SOUL WAS A CRY OF DESPAIR THAT TIPU Sultan could not silence. He peered into the future and could see only dark clouds veiling Mysore's destiny. They were treacherous and thunderous, shot with deadly lightning. A cold feeling had stolen over him that he—he alone—was to blame. Why did I not rise to dignity and heroism? he asked himself. Why did I agree to conclude a peace rather than sacrifice myself for my belief in justice and love of my country? Why did I ignore the voice of national memory? Have I not betrayed the nation and the people who endured patiently the most intolerable hardships and contributed their sons, their wealth, their stores and everything they had? Why did I not, at the cost of my own life, strike the last blow for what I hold to be dear? Why am I alive today on a pedestal of countless corpses, whose life was snuffed out at my bidding? So many died for my cause—but I live, why?

To an extent he knew the answer. He had wanted peace, a breathing spell for his tortured, agonised people who had suffered untold brutalities and defilement at the hands of a merciless enemy for two years. Sick with horror, he had seen the English set up new and ghastly standards of barbarity in which neither women nor children were spared. The days of Timur and Nadir Shah had been eclipsed by the new terror. The English were not alone. The Marathas had remained aloof from savagery but the Nizam was a faithful ally and follower of the English. Together they had participated in wholesale massacres, burning and looting. Yes, Tipu had wanted peace to repair the ravages of the war, to gain time to heal the wounds. But what was this peace? he asked himself. The peace of the desert? The peace of the grave?—peace that dismembered his Kingdom, half of which went into slavery to the English and their allies. Tipu Sultan could foresee what the English would do in the provinces ceded to them by this peace. Already they had given up all pretence of moderation and were ready to tear up humanity in an orgy of devastation. In Tipu Sultan's heart was a silent pitiless cry that he had failed his people and that the burden of his failure fell on the bent shoulders and broken bodies of those who were now in the territories surrendered to the English. They were slaves now—those simple-hearted people of his who had trusted him, ventured to look up to him, to hope, to dream of better times; they, whose hearts beat in unison with him, who had roused themselves to action at his command and had proved their loyalty to the cause of freedom with which he had fired their imagination. What had this peace achieved then? A nation half-free and half-slave. Was this not to be a prelude to total slavery? Thrice before the English had broken their treaties with Mysore. Will they not violate their pledges again? Who will come out victorious then?—war-torn, dismembered Mysore or those who had enriched themselves with its loot and plunder? Why did I then hesitate at the last moment? Tipu asked himself. Why did I not stake my all? Was it to cling to life, to prolong my hours, waiting for another invasion and total conquest? What future can emerge from such a peace?

Tipu Sultan knew that the English would come again, with bigger and better guns, with larger armies more ably led. He could see catastrophe and disaster advancing with rapid strides while Mysore and the whole of India lay helpless and inert. All around him he could see the crumbling ruin of a once-proud civilisation scattered like a vast heap of garbage. A brooding sense of inevitable disaster which he would not be able to avert, an awesome awareness of impending tragedy against which he would be helpless, grew upon him. Why then did I not march with the last of my columns to lay down my life? That was the question he repeatedly asked himself.

He remembered what Mir Sadik had once said: 'Death is the supreme evil and must be postponed for as long as possible.' No, Tipu Sultan knew that life without liberty for one's people, a life of slavery was a far greater evil. A country without freedom is conceivable only as a country bereft of soul. Without it, wealth, power, knowledge, fame, culture, virtue and even life counted for little. If this peace meant the end of all his aspirations, his impulses, his wishes and his ideals, would it not have been better to continue the war to the bitter end?

There were not many to whom Tipu Sultan had spoken of the arrows that pierced his heart. Though always kind, thoughtful and accessible to others' needs, he did not make friends easily. He was what his childhood had made him—grave, meditative and reserved. But in the citadel of his guarded heart he knew that this was the heaviest of all the burdens he had to bear and that he would have to bear it for every moment of the life that was left to him.

Purnaiya and Mir Sadik knew of Sultan's agony. He had unburdened his heart to them. Purnaiya understood. Mir Sadik was puzzled but said nothing.

Later, Mir Sadik asked Purnaiya: 'What would he have achieved other than death if he had chosen to make the last stand? I tell you I saw it all while you were peacefully sleeping with the physicians tickling you all over. The position was utterly hopeless. Fortunately, the English themselves did not know how hopeless it was; otherwise, we would have got still harsher terms. But tell me what would his death have achieved? The whole of Mysore—every inch of our territory—would have come under the oppressor's heel, is it not?'

Purnaiya did not reply. Mir Sadik continued. 'All our main positions were falling in the hands of the enemy. We did not have the troops to drive them back. Everyday our men were deserting and it was impossible to stop them. So tell me how would it have helped our cause if Sultan had shed his own blood?'

Purnaiya still did not reply. Mir Sadik repeated his question. 'Do tell me, Purnaiya,' Mir Sadik said almost teasingly, 'you who see originality and depth in the lightest word of Sultan, do tell me how his death would have helped his cause?'

Purnaiya looked out of the window. He spoke now in a detached voice as if speaking of something that did not concern him deeply. 'There is an intangible force, Mir Sadik. It is called the spirit of the army, the morale of the army. It is this force which moves the army to give its last breath to achieve something without counting the cost to itself, which makes the men feel that they are a part of something bigger and nobler than themselves. If the leader of the people is ready for the supreme sacrifice, the men, howsoever exhausted and unnerved, take courage and comfort. There comes a time when it becomes necessary to take cognisance of that force and to guide it in our favour. Do not overlook the mysterious, indefinable bond that has always existed between Sultan and his armies. It is not really so mysterious after all; the feeling that lies deep in the soul of Tipu Sultan lies in the soul of every Indian. They know what he is fighting for—even if they cannot express themselves in elegant phrases. So, Mir Sadik, it is not always a question of the number of men killed or the positions captured but of the tenacity and of the moral force with which the leader and his men fight.'

'And, you think that this is relevant,' asked Mir Sadik hotly, 'in the light of the judgement of all our military experts who unanimously advised Sultan against any further fight; when everyone knew that we had no chance of survival if we continued the war.'

'Perhaps, you are right,' Purnaiya responded. 'Perhaps, it is not relevant. In fact I do not think that Sultan's painful dejection is caused by this aspect at all.'

'What else, then?'

'He feels that he should have sacrificed himself in the conflict.'

'But why, to what end?'

'I doubt, Mir Sadik, if you will understand it all. I myself do not comprehend it fully.'

'Do test my intelligence for a change,' said Mir Sadik with a smile.

Purnaiya did not return the smile. 'It is my belief,' he said, 'and Sultan has not expressed himself as such, but it is my belief that Sultan feels that he should have died fighting for the freedom of his country. His death would have symbolised the sacrifice of India—not only the sacrifice of the present generation of Indians but also that of the past, the present and the future.'

'Rather a strange thought, is it not?'

'Perhaps, not. This is the hour of humiliation for a country that was at one time at the height of power and glory in both material and spiritual terms. What is happening today? Our compatriots fearfully kiss the hands of the English conquerors who put them in chains of slavery! Every Indian ruler—each one of them—big and small except Tipu Sultan has joined the English, at one time or another, in a war against Indian kings. Even now two Indian powers—the Marathas and the Nizam—hurled themselves against us on the side of the English. Every time the English march, they march with Indians to crush Indians. And what does the Indian ruler do when faced by the English advance? Abjectly, he begs for mercy and accepts their servitude. Tell me, has a single Indian ruler died in the field of battle, fighting the English? No. It does not even occur to our rulers that for their national aspirations, for their honour and the integrity of their land, they must fight and, if need be, die. No, they are satisfied if their life is spared, if the women of their household are not molested and if their personal fortune is protected. It is just not in fashion for a ruler to die for his country. That job must belong to a common, hired soldier. Was India always thus? Then, why has she come to this sorry pass? Is it not necessary to arouse her national conscience? It is this aspect, I think which is in Sultan's thoughts. If he stood up and died fighting for the cause, will not his sacrifice have a cleansing effect? Will it not succeed in building a bigger barrier against a cruel invader? Will not people say that here died a king for a cause that he believed in and hold him out as an example for other rulers to follow? Will it not shame other kings into action? Will not their ancestral pride stir into their minds the memories of a glorious past and contempt for these years of shame and humiliation through which they are now passing? Will the legion of slaves of this country then fail to rise against the brutal conqueror who has come to destroy the heritage of the nation and enslave its people? How, tell me how, will the nation be seized by patriotic fervour without examples of heroism and sacrifice by the rulers themselves? Then, and only then, can the entire nation rise, to brave hunger, sword, fire and death in order to drive this plague of locusts out. Sultan would consider the sacrifice of his life insignificant if it could help in the process of restoration of this nation as it was once—proud, free, virtuous, honest, just and full of faith.'

'I see,' said Mir Sadik, 'so all that Sultan had to do was to sacrifice his life. Other rulers then would have rushed to pick up the fallen torch, instantaneously. Is that what you mean?'

'It is not a question of what I mean. I think this is the thought in Sultan's mind. And when you say "instantaneously", please remember that this is a relative term. What is instantaneous in the life of a nation with a history of thousands of years? As I said, it is my belief that in Sultan's conception such a sacrifice was not necessarily limited to the present generation. His mind, I think, was directed to the future, as well—to generations beyond his own lifetime.'

'Tell me, Purnaiya, did Sultan so express this thought to you?'

'No, to be frank, he did not. His agony, he mentioned to me as to you. The interpretation of what lies behind those piled-up torments is mine,'

'You know, Purnaiya,' said Mir Sadik, clear in his mind now that he could afford to be openly critical since the thought that Purnaiya had expressed was his own and not Sultan's, 'no one is more fond of you than I am but I do believe that with all your experience and age, you do have a juvenile mind in some matters. I do hope that you do not speak to Sultan on these lines. Let me tell you this though, a sacrifice by Sultan would have been of no avail. A nation which has reached the abyss that confronts India is doomed. By their greed, by their dissensions, by their disunity, by their petty ambitions, the rulers of this country have seen to it that never can it retreat from the doom that awaits it, If in their hour of this adversity, they cannot unite and are at each other's throats, do you think that they will unite at any other time? Evil grows. It does not subside. It rises like a flood. Even if the English were to release their stranglehold on India and depart in peace, do you think that will convert this country into a promised land of your dreams? No. The rulers of this country would begin anew their game of baiting each other and soon will look upon another foreigner to help them out. Do remember, a leper cannot remove the marks of his disease and a dead man does not rise again.'

'You do not believe in the ultimate triumph of virtue?'

'I do, I do, but only if it is supported by bigger and better guns. If good happens to triumph over evil, believe me, it is so not because it is good but because it has greater might.'

'And, what about the judgement of history?' Purnaiya asked.

'History is written as a conqueror wishes it to be written. It is nothing but a fiction agreed upon by the victor. Even statues are erected to commemorate the conqueror, not the conquered. Do you know at whose expense? At the expense of the conquered nation. Does history care by what misdeeds a king comes to power and by what crimes he retains it? No, the historian is a mercenary, as good as any other tradesman who sells his wares to the highest bidder.'

'Surely, you do believe that a sacrifice does achieve something.'

'Depends on the kind of sacrifice you are talking about. If a man chooses to burn himself, yes, it will light up a dark corner of this earth for a brief moment but soon he will be consumed and turned into dust and ashes. Such a sacrifice will avail us nothing. But enough of this, Purnaiya. Virtue, truth, righteousness, sacrifice and all these noble words and phrases have their place in a discussion on theology, but do they affect the destiny of nations? It is inconceivable that power can be attained or retained without villainy, treachery or crime. This is the very basis, the very foundation of power. Men will respect you, honour you, admire you, extol you not because of your inherent virtue but because of the might of the armies that back you. Those who are victorious in battle are virtuous, not the other way round.'

'How utterly, how terribly wrong you are, Mir Sadik,' Purnaiya replied gently. 'Do not, please, commit the grievous error of losing faith in Man. True, the insolence of might has humbled us for the moment. Yes, this is the hour of our humiliation and defeat. But a day will dawn, when this nation will reconquer its lost heritage. It may not happen in your lifetime or mine. But surely, it will come to pass. Then the world will remember that there lived a king like Tipu Sultan in that shameful period of India's history who alone and unaided challenged the might of the English. This will be the immortal memory that Tipu Sultan will have imprinted on the ages to come.'

61

AMBITION OF HIS MASTERS

MAJOR-GENERAL WILLIAM MEDOWS WHO HAD EARLIER BEEN designated as successor to Cornwallis could no longer be considered for appointment as Governor-General due to severe blows he had suffered against Tipu Sultan's armies. His attempted suicide after a defeat at Seringapatam had also brought discredit to him. The English paid him a handsome compliment by saying that 'his sense of honour is too refined and too highly strained to submit to the common errors and disappointments incidental to our nature,' and instead they appointed Sir John Shore to succeed Lord Cornwallis as the Governor-General of India.

Sir John had been an apt pupil of Warren Hastings in his intrigues and machinations and in the words of Edmund Burke, 'was materially concerned as a principal actor and party in certain of the offences charged upon Hastings.' Still, he was content to leave Tipu Sultan alone. The English themselves had gone through a period of tremendous anxiety during the war with Tipu Sultan. They also needed peace in order to consolidate their gains before launching on fresh schemes of aggrandisement and conquest. Sir John therefore confined himself to his favourite field of action—intrigue. He contrived the death of Mahadji Sindhia, the downfall of Nana Phadnavis at the hands of Bajirao, annexation of Rohilkhand and even obtained the Nizam's consent for maintaining the English army in his territories, thereby ensuring that the Nizam who was till then an ally became thereafter a faithful servant. But assiduously, Sir John steered clear of Tipu Sultan. An intrigue would not succeed here, he knew; a war would be needed.

Then came Richard Wellesley, Earl of Mornington, a staunch imperialist, pledged to a policy of aggression and aggrandisement, fully armed and fully briefed by Prime Minister Pitt with elaborate plans for the establishment of the British Indian empire. Wellesley wrote to Lady Anne Bernard describing his mission thus:

> I will heap kingdoms upon kingdoms, victory upon victory, revenue upon revenue; I will accumulate glory and wealth and power, until the ambition and avarice even of my master shall cry mercy.

But it is not enough to conquer forts, towns and cities, Wellesley felt. To build a lasting empire, one must build stronger chains around the people. He took immediate steps to propagate Christianity in India. Sunday began to be observed as a holiday throughout the English possessions. The Bible was translated in all Indian languages. All schools which did not make instruction in Christian religion as compulsory part of their curriculum were to be closed down. Christian missionaries began to arrive in India in ever-increasing numbers. A systematic defilement and ridicule of Hinduism and Islam began.

62

MONARCHY AND THE MASSES

WELLESLEY KNEW THAT HE HAD TO CRUSH TIPU SULTAN. Cornwallis had been wrong in assuming that Tipu would never be able to rise from the ravages of the war inflicted on him. Cornwallis even thought that Tipu would not be able to pay the war indemnity in full because the territory left to him was so devastated that it would not bring in that much revenue. That would have been the excuse for annexing all the territory that remained with Tipu Sultan. But it was not to be. While Mir Sadik was drafting stringent taxation proposals in order to collect on behalf of Sultan the tremendous revenue needed to pay the war indemnity, the amount was already in the hands of Sultan. Voluntary contributions had come from all parts of his empire. Farmers, weavers, soldiers, artisans, merchants, even the poorest of the poor came in with a donation. The war had rendered them destitute, their homes had been destroyed, their farms had been burnt, their livestock had been taken away, their wealth had been plundered but still each of them found a few rupees hidden here and there. Women took off their ornaments, men their rings and many an ancient family hierloom was sold. They knew that Sultan's two sons were in English custody and would not be released until the war indemnity was paid in full. Each household felt that its own two sons were so involved. Spontaneously, each village without consulting another and without any concerted plan set up a collection centre, and little by little but in almost unending stream, contributions flowed into Sultan's treasury. Fully and punctually was Tipu thus able to discharge the war indemnity.

When the first of these contributions had been received by Tipu Sultan he had been moved to tears. It touched his heart that these poor men who had suffered so much should now part with the last of their possessions for his sake. Later, as contributions poured in from every part of the country, he began to cherish a feeling that he could not describe. It was not mere gratitude. No. In his heart was joy and elation that his people returned his love. Always he had been reserved and reticent. The love he had felt for his people in his heart was reflected in his actions, not on his lips. Now the people also said nothing but the message in their action was loud and clear. No longer did Tipu Sultan see any difference or distance between the monarchy and the masses. Every action of his, he promised himself, would be directed to the good of his people.

He saw the suffering and adversity of his people, pale and emaciated children, men without shelter, without food and often without hope. He grieved in his very soul to see their sorrows. But mere grief was not enough, he knew. He had to do his part, to put his shoulder to the wheel, to bring hope and cheer to their hearts and to make his country respected.

Yes, Tipu Sultan had roused himself. Instead of sinking under his misfortune, he exerted all his energies to repair the ravages of war. His foremost task, he knew, was to encourage political and administrative efficiency, to restore cultivation of land and revive arts, crafts and industries which had been devastated. With renewed self-confidence, vigour, and extraordinary speed, he removed all traces of the devastation and disorganisation wrought by the war so that his government soon became strong and efficient. The peasantry of his dominions was protected and its labours encouraged and rewarded. He banished all luxury and waste from his court. Himself, he slept on a coarse bed and dressed simply without ostentation. His ministers and amildars had clear instructions to go slow on tax collections from those who had suffered during the war and in particular he insisted that immediate redress must be given to all those who suffered loss or damage on account of serving in his cause. He also called upon them to consider if any of the taxes payable by his people could be abolished and if any reform was possible to reduce the burden on them, both as to the amounts levied and the mode of collection. To his own officers he was strict and clearly laid down that if they did any unjust act or failed to administer justice righteously, or if any grievance was inflicted by them, severe punishment would be meted out to them. No one could plead that he did an act of injustice on account of Sultan for he ordered that if, in order to favour or benefit the Kingdom, any injustice had been done it must be redressed at once, regardless of every other consideration.

It is not surprising therefore that Sultan's dominions were soon restored to their former prosperity.

All this was gall and wormwood to the English, who watched the flourishing conditions of Mysore with rising envy and apprehension.

All this was gall and wormwood to the privileged classes serving Sultan—his administrators, governors, military commanders—who had to tread warily and keep in check the temptation to trample on the masses.

63

IS MY STRENGTH MY WEAKNESS?

WELLESLEY KNEW THAT HE HAD TO LIQUIDATE TIPU SULTAN. YET, he hesitated before taking the first step towards his destiny. In his heart he felt cold anger against a ruler who alone, amongst all Indian princes, resisted his blandishments to join the English against others. Why, I could make him rich and powerful and I do need an ally like Tipu who would not break faith, Wellesley had said to himself.

Fortune, power and riches are inconstant, Tipu had argued with himself, but a stain on one's honour is permanent, eternal, which no feat of arms or penance can wipe away—and would it not be dishonourable to fight against one's own people and to throw them at the mercy of an alien invader?

Wellesley did not show his anger. He bided his time and made his preparations. To his officers he made it clear that nothing should be done which should arouse Sultan's suspicions.

'We must closely follow the classical tactical method of winning the victim's trust,' said Wellesley.

'You do fear him, don't you?' asked Harris shrewdly.

'Of course, I fear him,' Wellesley replied. 'Yes, I fear him greatly. He is not like other rulers of India that we have known.

I fear also the example he sets to other rulers. Fortunately, all of them are far too pusillanimous to follow his example; but in the long run such an example can have a disruptive influence on the empire. Also, we have been wrong once before where he is concerned. It is costly to repeat mistakes.'

'What mistakes?'

'Cornwallis had said that Sultan is so crippled that he would never be able to rise and that his provinces would be bleak and barren. See how they now glow with prosperity and strength.'

'And weakness, too.'

'What weakness?'

'He has the strength of his people behind him; yes, he is a man of the people. Their heart beats in unison with his. But look at his weakness, too. The nobility, the aristocracy, the governors, commanders, men of privilege, wealth and position will never forgive him. They who were lords and masters of the people are now there to administer to the wants, wishes and welfare of the people. In economic terms, it is possible to gain some advantage through such a system but when a crisis comes or war threatens, what happens? Who is to lead the people? Those who are disenchanted with the master and are ready to desert him? A man of privilege will forgive everything except the loss of his privilege. Tipu Sultan may make the finest speeches to fire people's loyalty but who is to lead his people into action? He, alone by himself? So what you see as Tipu Sultan's strength is also his weakness. Yes, they call him Tiger and indeed, he is brave as a tiger but he can lose his Kingdom by this folly.'

Wellesley nodded his head approvingly, as if he was aware of this. But he had learned something new.

Soon, Wellesley appointed a Commission of five officers composed of his brother Colonel Wellesley, Colonel Close,

Colonel Agnew, Captain Malcolm and Captain Macaulay with the object of winning Tipu's commanders over to the English. He considered it 'both just and expedient to do so'. He had not hoped for too much from the efforts of the Commission. Its success, however, astounded him most pleasantly. It was this Commission which contributed so very largely to the ultimate defeat and downfall of Tipu Sultan.

Meanwhile, Wellesley's letters to Tipu Sultan were full of sugar and honey, giving him every assurance of friendship and goodwill. Wellesley had made up his mind to show 'sweepingly dishonest cordiality' until he was ready to declare war for which he had already started swift and serious preparations.

64

THE PRICE OF LAUGHTER

TIPU SULTAN HAD SCRUPULOUSLY ADHERED TO THE PROVISIONS of the 1792 Treaty. He had failed to provide an excuse for attacking him. An excuse had therefore to be invented. It would not be in keeping with the English character and traditions to attack without an excuse.

Tipu Sultan had sent Muhammed Ibrahim and Hussain Ali Khan to the Isle of France to press his request to General Malartic, the French Governor-General for French artisans. The purpose of their visit was intended to be purely commercial. They left Mangalore in October 1797, and reached Port Louis in January 1798. Tipu Sultan knew and certainly General Malartic knew that he had no troops to offer. He had a little more than six hundred men who were less than adequate for the defence of the island itself. Yet, the General after discussing with Tipu's envoys the question of artisans took up with them questions of military importance including a defensive and offensive alliance. These two men pleaded ignorance of those matters since they had no brief on the subject but politely agreed that an alliance with the French would be all to the good and that they would report their conversation with General Malartic to Tipu Sultan.

Now, why did General Malartic who had himself been vainly pleading to France for reinforcements to his own island engage in a discussion with a commercial delegation from Mysore about a defensive and offensive alliance with Tipu Sultan? Was it merely polite conversation or an urge to assure the envoys of Sultan of his sympathy for their cause or was he simply boasting that he was of sufficient consequence to enter into a defensive and offensive alliance with the great Sultan? No. He was trying to lay a foundation for a proclamation which he was paid to issue.

Wellesley had learnt of Tipu Sultan's project of sending a commercial delegation to the Isle of France. The English agents led by Colonel Agnew reached there earlier. Colonel Agnew suggested to General Malartic that he should also discuss military matters with Tipu's envoys and issue a proclamation at the end of their visit. The General was embarrassed. He declined at first.

'I am a Frenchman, a man of honour,' said General Malartic.

The English agents assured him that they recognised him as a man of honour and the amount to be paid for his services would therefore be correspondingly higher.

General Malartic continued to protest. 'I would be ridiculed. If negotiations for a military alliance were to take place, naturally they would be kept secret both by Tipu Sultan and by the French government. And, you are asking me to issue a public proclamation. I have never heard of a nation doing that. I would be laughed at.'

The English appreciated the force of his arguments and promised to increase the price commensurate with his embarrassment at being laughed at. Finally, he was persuaded. Thus, on 30 January 1798, General Malartic issued a proclamation that 'two ambassadors had come from Mysore to enter into an offensive and defensive alliance with the French and to secure military assistance for expelling the English from India. Tipu Sultan would maintain the French troops as long as the war lasted, and furnish them with everything, except wine.'

The excuse—flimsy though it was—for the war, was ready. But Wellesley still had many preparations to make before launching the offensive.

65

UNTIL FURTHER NOTICE

WELLESLEY CONTINUED HIS POSE OF FRIENDSHIP WITH TIPU SULTAN. He, of course, new of the text of the Malartic proclamation of 30 January 1798, even before General Malartic himself became aware of it, since the proclamation was drafted under Wellesley's orders. Immediately after the issue of the proclamation, he received a copy. Also, the proclamation was reported by many newspapers, though it appeared in a Calcutta newspaper somewhat late—on 8 June 1798. However, even thereafter Wellesley continued his policy of cordiality with Tipu Sultan in order to lull him into a false sense of security. On 14 June 1798, Wellesley wrote to Tipu Sultan a charming letter about a minor dispute between the English and Sultan over the district of Wynad, which the English had earlier claimed, was wrongfully in possession of Sultan.

'Being anxious,' wrote Wellesley to Sultan, 'to afford you every proof in my power of my sincere wish to maintain the good understanding which had so long subsisted between your Highness and the Company....' Wellesley further suggested the settlement of dispute by means of 'a reasonable and temperate discussion which is the most friendly as well as the most prudent course, and will always defeat the views of interested and designing persons, who may wish to foment jealousy, and to disturb the blessings of peace.'

Again, Wellesley wrote on 8 August 1798, informing Tipu Sultan that he recognised his claim to Wynad, because it had not been ceded to the English by the Treaty of Seringapatam in 1792. Thereafter also, he wrote several letters to Tipu Sultan, each gushing with protestations of utmost friendship and mutual understanding. In none of these letters did Wellesley mention the Malartic proclamation.

'I shall use it, when I shall use it,' said Wellesley to his lieutenants, 'and Tipu Sultan continues to be our dearest friend—that is, until further notice.'

66

LETTER FROM NAPOLEON

WELLESLEY WAS READY NOW TO UNLEASH HIS WAR MACHINE. HIS planning was faultless, his preparations impeccable. He had taken precautions against every eventuality. Two years he had waited and he had reason now to congratulate himself for his patience and prudence as he watched his three armies massed under General Harris, Colonel Wellesley and General Stuart. He scrutinised also the long lists of Tipu Sultan's officers bought over by the English and knew that a kingdom honeycombed with so many treacherous cells could not endure.

With that realisation, the tone of his letters to Tipu Sultan began to change. In November 1798, he wrote to Sultan complaining about Sultan's friendship for the French who were striving 'to introduce into your kingdom the principles of anarchy and confusion'. But he ended this letter on a note of flattery, friendship and compliment suggesting also that he would send Major Doveton to Sultan who would put forward proposals for establishing greater friendship for the future.

And, what was to be Major Doveton's role? No doubt, to suggest to Sultan to enter into a treaty with the English on the lines of an alliance which they had concluded with the Nizam a few days earlier. The Nizam who had thought he could trick and deceive all the people all the time had himself been duped. This is how the alliance had come about: Wellesley's predecessor, Sir John Shore, had already obtained the Nizam's consent to maintain an English army in his territories. With that army and with his own much larger army, the Nizam felt safe. None could violate his frontiers while he felt free to march against anyone. But Wellesley had different ideas. Why not disband the Nizam's army and replace it altogether by a new subsidiary army directly under the control and command of the English? The Nizam's Prime Minister, Wazir Azimul Omra, was bribed by Captain Kirkpatrick, the English Resident at the Nizam's Court. Quietly, the venerable Wazir began disbanding the Nizam's army. At the right time the remainder of the Nizam's army revolted. Just at that very moment the English army from Madras arrived on the scene and surrounded Hyderabad. The Nizam was trapped. He asked for Kirkpatrick to see him. Kirkpatrick came immediately followed by four thousand soldiers. The frightened Nizam requested him to withdraw. Kirkpatrick replied, 'I came at your pleasure but shall leave at mine.' Quietly, the Nizam signed the Treaty of Subsidiary Alliance whereby he lost not only his right to maintain his own army but had to station in his dominions and at his expense a large English army. He could no longer appoint any Europeans without the consent of the English. The English even forced him to appoint their nominees as his ministers, as they did later when Wazir Azimul Omra died and the Nizam had to appoint Mir Alam at their insistence.

No, Tipu Sultan was not prepared to become a vassal of the English like the Nizam. To Wellesley's suggestion of sending Major Doveton, he raised no objection but replied that the existing treaties and engagements were enough to preserve peace and promote friendly relations between the powers, and that he could not imagine any other means more effective. Tipu Sultan repeated also his wish to 'maintain the articles of the agreement of peace, and to perpetuate and strengthen the basis of friendship and union' with the English.

Without waiting for Tipu Sultan's reply to reach him, Wellesley left Calcutta for Madras to supervise personally the arrangements for the invasion of Mysore. He was delighted with the arrangements. They were foolproof. Also, he knew that the men beyond the frontiers, in Tipu Sultan's court, bought by English gold, were worth several divisions. He received Sultan's reply, ignored its obvious sincerity and wrote to him on 9 January 1799, referring for the very first time to the Malartic proclamation issued twelve months earlier and accusing Sultan of sending ambassadors to the Isle of France, of actually entering into an offensive and defensive alliance with the French, and of permitting the French troops raised at the island to join his army. Wellesley demanded an explanation within twenty-four hours of the receipt of the letter, otherwise 'dangerous consequences' would result

The velvet glove was now off, completely off. The mailed fist was bared. The tone of Wellesley's letter, its language and its demand that a reply be sent in twenty-four hours, left no doubt of it. From the sudden appearance of such an ultimatum, it was clear that the English intended a treacherous attack.

'Can it have any other motive?' Tipu had asked Purniya.

'None except bad faith, perfidy, a sworn enemity to independent Mysore and the desire to break a solemn treaty.'

But immediately, Tipu Sultan received also another letter from Wellesley. With this letter Wellesley forwarded a letter from Caliph Salim III addressed to 'the Indian Sovereign Tipu Sultan.' The substance of the letter was to advise Tipu Sultan to avoid all hostile activities against the English at French instigation, and offered to adjust satisfactorily any cause of complaint that he may have against them.

In the covering letter, Wellesley accused the French nation which considers 'all the thrones of the world, and every system of civil order and religious faith, as the sport and prey of their boundless ambition, insatiable rapine, and indiscriminate sacrilege.'

Wellesley's objective in sending the second letter was to lull Tipu Sultan into the belief that the threat conveyed in the first letter was not seriously intended and that Wellesley had no aggressive designs against Sultan but merely wanted an assurance that Sultan would not enter into an alliance with the French against the English. Tipu Sultan's reply to Wellesley was therefore without anger and without rancour. He wrote a courteous letter and reverting to Wellesley's suggestion to send Major Doveton to him, he added:

> You will be pleased to despatch Major Doveton (about whose coming your friendly pen has repeatedly written) slightly attended (or un-attended)

Was there a touch of flippancy here—a note of irony? Perhaps, when Sultan asked for Wellesley's emissary to come slightly attended or unattended, he clearly meant that he did not want him to come with the army as Kirkpatrick had done when summoned by the Nizam. Yet, Tipu Sultan had every intention of receiving Major Doveton and he despatched horsemen to the frontier to escort the Major.

But Doveton was not fated to negotiate with Sultan for Wellesley had no intention of waiting for Tipu Sultan's reply. He had directed General Harris to invade Mysore without delay.

Thus began an open act of aggression against Tipu Sultan, in contemptuous violation of solemn treaties.

Strangely enough, the overtures for an offensive and defensive alliance with France did not come from Tipu Sultan on this occasion but from the French themselves. In February 1798, when the English army had already began the invasion of Mysore, a letter was addressed to Tipu Sultan by Napoleon Bonaparte. Its text:

FRENCH REPUBLIC

Liberty   Equality

Headquarters at Cairo, 7th Pluviose
7th Year of the Republic, One and Indivisible

BONAPARTE, Member of the National Convention, General in Chief, to the most Magnificent SULTAN, our greatest friend, TIPPOO SAIB.

You have already been informed of my arrival on the borders of the Red Sea, with an innumerable and invincible Army, full of the desire of delivering you from the iron yoke of England.

I eagerly embrace this opportunity of testifying to you the desire I have of being informed by you, by the way of Muscat and Mocha, as to your political situation.

I would further wish you could send some intelligent person to Suez or Cairo, possessing your confidence, with whom I may confer.

May the Almighty increase your Power and destroy your enemies.

NAPOLEON BONAPARTE

Napoleon's letter has survived the ravages of time and has been handed down to history but it never reached. Tipu Sultan. It was to be forwarded by the Sheriff of Mecca, and was intercepted at Jeddah. Significantly it makes no mention of any overtures on the part of Tipu Sultan, much less of any offensive and defensive alliance concluded between the French and Tipu Sultan. However, this was not an aspect which had any relevance in Wellesley's mind. His ambition was power; his dream, a vast empire.

67

NONE SHALL FORGIVE

THREE ENGLISH ARMIES BURST INTO MYSORE. THE CARNATIC ARMY marched under General Harris from Vellore. The Bombay army advanced up to the Western Ghats under General Stuart. The Hyderabad army moved forward under the command of Governor-General's brother, Colonel Arthur Wellesley, the future Duke of Wellingdon, who was destined to defeat Napoleon Bonaparte at the battle of Waterloo. The army of the Nizam, who was independent no more but under the tutelage of the English, marched with Colonel Arthur Wellesley.

The Marathas who had joined the English in the earlier war against Tipu Sultan now remained aloof. Wellesley's predecessor Sir John Shore had contrived the murder of Mahadji Sindhia and had influenced Peshwa Bajirao to imprison Nana Phadnavis. Later, the Peshwa released Nana Phadnavis at the insistence of Doulatrao Sindhia, the courageous grandson of Mahadji Sindhia. A reconciliation took place and Nana Phadnavis was reinstated as the Peshwa's Prime Minister. For a long time Wellesley had his secret envoys intriguing with the Peshwa to join the war against Tipu Sultan. The Peshwa was charmed by Wellesley's suggestions. But Nana Phadnavis and Doulatrao Sindhia firmly opposed a war against Sultan.

'Do you think Sultan has a chance of victory against the English?' he asked Doulatrao Sindhia.

'No, none at all,' Sindhia replied.

'Then why this hesitation to march with the English?' asked the Peshwa. 'Why, when victory and honour await us.'

'Victory, yes; honour, no,' said Sindhia. 'There is no honour in being Wellesley's ally.'

'Victory brings honour, my friend,' said the Peshwa, 'and do not, I beg of you, allow your youth and your romantic temperament to misguide you.'

'But you will allow the treacherous English to guide you?' asked Daulatrao Sindhia. 'Wellesly is a wolf. For two years he was courting Tipu Sultan. Now suddenly comes this war.'

The Peshwa looked at him as if with pity. 'In this world of sin and sorrow, who cares if the English are treacherous and ungrateful or that Wellesley himself is cruel and perfidious? If they succeed, as surely as they will, the world will honour them and Wellesley will go down in history as a great and virtuous man. And Tipu Sultan? The world will either forget him or remember him as a robber and a scoundrel only because he did not succeed. Tell me, Nana Saheb, do you really disagree with me?'

'I do. I beg of you to listen to Daulatrao Sindhia's advice,' Nana replied. 'The Maratha nation has nothing to gain from a victory against Tipu Sultan.'

'Really! Permit me to recall to you,' said the Peshwa with asperity, 'that it was you who decided to side with the English on the last occasion against Tipu Sultan. It was the Maratha arms that won the victory for the English when defeat was staring them in the face. Yes, the decision to go to war then against Tipu Sultan was yours.'

'Yes, mine was the decision,' said Nana Phadnavis softly.

The Peshwa said nothing but looked at him as if expecting Nana to say more. 'Yes, mine was the decision,' Nana repeated, 'and the burden of that guilt shall live with me until my dying day. I do not forgive myself. Nor will the Maratha nation forgive me. No,' Nana paused, lifting his head upwards, 'no one shall.'

They were all silent now. Nana broke the silence as if in answer to a question.

'Yes, he alone could have driven the alien barbarians out of this land. We stayed his hands, blunted his sword, and put the shackles of a dishonourable peace on him.'

'So,' said the Peshwa with heavy irony, 'our great statesman and Prime Minister not only shirks another war but would like to wipe out the last Maratha victory against Tipu Sultan. I suppose you would prefer that the Kingdom of Mysore was as powerful today as it was before the last war.' He laughed but finding none to share his laughter, he glared at Nana.

'If it would avail,' Nana replied, 'I would even at the cost of my life try to restore to the Kingdom of Mysore, the power it once had. You must remember this, that every hour that postpones the defeat of Tipu Sultan, is an hour that prolongs the independence of the Maratha nation. There is another submission I would like to make,' Nana paused and the Peshwa cut in.

'Do, do please make it. I cannot endure the suspense of waiting too long for your gems of wisdom.'

Nana ignored the sarcasm. 'The submission,' continued Nana, 'which I have to make is this: You have seen the vengeance that the English have wreaked on their defeated enemies but it is nothing comparable to what they inflict on their allies and friends; each one has been afflicted with servitude, infamy and poverty.'

'Poverty! Infamy!' said the Peshwa, 'the Nizam, I thought, is rolling in wealth. And, he was always infamous, English or no English.'

'I stand corrected. And, servitude? What do you say to that?' asked Nana.

'I say this that in your old age, your blood has run cold, that you are wanting in faith in the power and resilience of the Maratha nation, that you generalise on the basis of flimsy and transient situations. In short, I can think of no rational motive to which your advice can be ascribed.' There was fury in Peshwa's voice now.

The Peshwa turned to Parashuram Bhau and his son, Appa Saheb, to lead the Maratha army against Tipu Sultan. Both refused.

The Marathas did not march against Tipu Sultan.

68

A SCREAM OF ANGUISH

A SCREAM OF ANGUISH ROSE THROUGHOUT MYSORE AS THE ENGLISH armies advanced. There was a cry of despair, a broken prayer for mercy. The invaders laughed. They had been told that their mission was not only the conquest of territory of the kingdom but to break the spirit of its people, to make their subjection complete. Undefended towns, villages, farms, dwellings, temples and mosques were spoiled and burnt. Women were seized and shared among the men-at-arms. Men and children were slain in a manner to make sport for the soldiery. Every tree served as a gibbet. Victims were strung up, as though for pastime, in the form of figures of eight. Each English battalion boasted of its own 'artists' who came up with new and novel techniques for such amusements. There were some who could not bear the sight of mutilation or the sound of tortured screams and they looked with a touch of horror at their own men who could laugh in the midst of such carnage. Their heads were bent as if from a blow by the realisation that the children who were being massacred were no different from their own; that the women who were being violated were like their own sisters, wives and sweethearts; but they were few and their feeble protests remained unheeded.

A messenger reached Tipu Sultan on all but foundered horse, tumbled from the saddle and gave him the news of the massive and sudden invasion by the English armies, unheralded by a declaration of war, while Sultan was still waiting for the English negotiator Major Doveton to arrive.

The invading English armies marched on. Wellesley crowed about his army which he said 'is unquestionably the best appointed, the most completely equipped, the most amply and liberally supplied, the most perfect in point of discipline, and the most fortunate in the acknowledged experience and abilities of its officers in every department, whichever took the field in India.'

Did Tipu Sultan have a chance? All along the route, Sultan's frontier fortresses surrendered without resistance.

What was happening to Sultan's intelligence system which had been reorganised under Mir Sadik? Sultan had wrong information about the number of troops of the opposing army. They are 'pitifully small', he was told. Even the line of their advance was left to guess work. Worse still, none knew of the surrender of fortresses, and days thereafter supplies were rushed to them. They added up to the English stocks.

News reached him at last of the route of the Bombay army under General Stuart.

Tipu Sultan leaped to one of his sudden swift actions. Mounting his horse Taus, which Ruqayya Banu had presented him after the death of Dilkush the Second, he rushed towards Siddesvara to attack the Bombay army. His men sweated behind him, determined not to be outdone by the tireless man who led them.

But it was not to be a surprise attack. Sixteen hours earlier General Stuart had received a message from a 'friend' from Seringapatam brought by Hashim Khan. He was ready. He had his men under arms. He knew not only the troops that Tipu Sultan commanded but also the plan of attack.

Tipu Sultan advanced to attack, but as he saw the formidable position of the enemy and their preparations, he realised that he was expected. He halted to examine minutely the enemy's position, exposing himself for more than an hour to incessant cannonade. His own light guns made no reply, in order to economise on their limited supply of ammunition. It became clear to Sultan that he would have to change his plan of attack. Quietly and swiftly, he marched through the jungle towards the English flank. General Stuart had not reckoned on Sultan's ability to alter his plans so drastically and his forces remained ready to face a frontal assault By then Sultan's troops had completely surrounded an English brigade in the rear and annihilated it. Ponderously, Stuart's army moved to meet Sultan's threat to his flank but already Tipu Sultan had withdrawn his forces.

It was with a heavy heart that Tipu Sultan left this field of battle. His casualties had been considerable—more than 1,500 men. Among the dead was also his kinsman Muhammad Raza, known as the Benki Nawab (the fiery aristocrat). He it was who had remained with a slender force in the front in order to cover Tipu Sultan's movement to the flank of the enemy, all the while making a demonstration as if he was about to attack. When the English stormed his position, they found him wounded, barely alive. They severed his head from his body and attached it to a long wooden pole as a trophy. Thus died Benki Nawab, a man of fiery temper, hot words and a warm heart. Tipu loved him dearly.

Sultan had also seen for himself how huge the Bombay army was. How had Mir Sadik been given such low estimates of the English forces?

And, where was Sayyad Saheb? Sultan had left him with a large force to watch and harass the movement of the English army of Carnatic under General Harris and to prevent its march to the capital. But the army of the Carnatic marched unmolested. Sayyad Saheb was now in the pay of the English.

And, Qamar-ud-din? He was Sultan's cousin and his trusted General. Twice Qamar-ud-din's forces were on the point of victory and each time he gave an order to his troops to withdraw. His excuse: to save further loss of life but there were many—though Sultan was not amongst them—who began to doubt him.

And, where were so many of Sultan's commanders? Some had taken their forces into the interior as if in pursuit of the enemy through circuitous routes under orders of Sultan. They had not dared to confide their treachery to the units under their command. How could they? Their own men, whose loyalty to Sultan was intense and undivided, would have cut them down. But not all the missing commanders were disloyal. There were some who had received orders in Sultan's name from Sayyad Saheb, Qamar-ud-din, Mir Sadik and others in authority, dispersing them to theatres far away from the front line.

Meanwhile, the huge English army of Carnatic moved on under General Harris, loaded with enormous equipment, supplies, stores and provisions as also with a tremendous train of battering cannon. To carry all this burden, it has ninety-six thousand bullocks. There were even more bullocks, camels and elephants belonging privately to officers and men in the army. As a British officer described it:

> 'The appearance of our army on the march from a neighbouring hill is truly surprising. It may be compared with the emigration of the Isrelites from Egypt; the surrounding plains and towns appear to be in motion. Herds of cattle and flocks of sheep conceal the soil; the route of the troops is marked by the gleaming of their arms, and that of the battering train by a long slow-moving line.

Such a gigantic army may strike terror but it has really very little mobility. Its very bulk and mass make it unwieldy rendering it difficult for it to move rapidly. Its marches have to be tedious and short, its progress slow and halts frequent. How easy it is to harass such an army, halt its progress, destroy the forage it needs, capture its cattle, baggage and military stores! But who was there to do it? The Mysorean commanders had been corrupted. They were in the pay of the English and the army moved on, unmolested. Instead, what the Mysorean commanders did was to send fanciful reports of their heroic attacks on the English and the heavy losses inflicted by them.

Tipu Sultan marched to Malvalli to intercept Harris. He occupied a commanding position which would have prevented Harris from crossing the river. But Sayyad Saheb and Qamar-ud-din persuaded him to fight in an open ground instead of this heavily wooded crossing. The result was that the English were able to cross the river without difficulty. The English then moved to Malvalli. Officers sent forward by Tipu Sultan to reconnoitre brought back reports that the English force was merely an advance guard which could easily be annihilated. Before he learned the truth, the battle had already begun. He had pushed his guns so far forward that he had either to abandon them or fight it out. He led a spirited cavalry charge to cover the withdrawal of the artillery and he succeeded in it but at a heavy cost to his men. His infantry also advanced and stood the charge of enemy bayonets. Qamar-ud-din instead of attacking the English with his cavalry, as directed by Sultan, fell upon a body of Mysoreans and put them all into disorder. Tipu Sultan was able to withdraw with his guns and equipment though he lost one thousand men.

Mir Sadik came to Tipu Sultan with convincing evidence that the English armies were taking the direct route from Bangalore to Seringapatam. Sultan ordered destruction of forage on the direct route and despatched his forces to obstruct the advance but General Harris by marching to the south crossed the Cauveri river to Sosile. Thus, he found ample fodder and came within striking distance of Seringapatam without opposition. With the mass of material, equipment and cattle, the English advance had been miserably slow—hot more than five miles per day and yet they had met no harassment. The Mysore cavalry clearly remained in view under Sayyad Saheb but did not attack the English. Did the Mysorean soldiers and officers sometimes wonder why their commander, Sayyad Saheb, was so inactive when he could easily impede the English advance? Yes, they did, but instantaneously they chased away the doubts from their minds. Clearly, this was a part of a grand design to lure the English on, further and further from their supply base, into a region where their entire army might be surrounded and annihilated without a chance of retreat; and the soldiers could see for themselves that until that moment came, Sayyad Saheb was not prepared to waste the life of a single Mysorean soldier. Some soldiers love a commander who can fire their loyalty with fine speeches, others admire a commander who can win brilliant and spectacular victories in the midst of carnage and bloodshed, but deep down in the heart of every soldier is veneration for a commander who is all the time careful not to sacrifice the lives of his troops. Yes, the soldiers trusted Sayyad Saheb. Who would not? Was he not a kinsman of their Sultan and one of his most trusted commanders? From his calm composure, unnerved by the English advance, it was clear that he had a pre-arranged plan with Tipu Sultan to permit the enemy to move forward to its total destruction. How angry had Sayyad Saheb become, when some of his troops whose enthusiasm he could not restrain had attacked the unweildy English columns! One thousand bullocks in the enemy camp scampered off; broken pots and pans were strewn all over the field; confused and disorderly shooting in the enemy camp; thirty enemy soldiers and three Mysorean soldiers dead; the enemy advance halted for a day and a half. What did Sayyad Saheb do? He ordered that Sunder Lal, the ringleader of the Mysorean attack, be hanged. 'I cannot admire your courage for you have pitted it against the plans and wishes of Sultan,' said Sayyad Saheb to Sunder Lal. Later, he relented and ordered his dismissal from the army. The message was, however, clear and unambiguous: whosoever attempted to bar the English advance would be foiling Sultan's plans and incurring his displeasure.

Again, the intelligence agency of Sultan failed — or did it succeed? Sultan was told authoritatively that Harris would cross over to the island of Seringapatam near the Chendgal fort. All his Sardars vowed to sacrifice their lives if necessary in the expected combat, and Tipu sending Purnaiya and his two eldest sons into the fort to defend it to the last, crossed the river with his army to take up position at Chendgal to meet the expected foe. To his dismay, however, he found that the English, instead of proceeding to the right as he had anticipated, deviated to the left. Meanwhile, Qamar-ud-din's heartening message had also arrived that he would be in a position to intercept General Stuart and prevent him from joining the army of General Harris.

Yes, Qamar-ud-din did reach within striking distance of General Stuart's army. But his intention was not to harass or harm the English. He just wanted to prove to General Stuart that the promise he had received from the English for being made the Nawab of Gurrakonda after the fall of Tipu Sultan was indeed well deserved; and so it was, for Qamar-ud-din not only maintained a discreet distance from the English forces but also sent to General Stuart in response to an urgent request from him, a list of storehouses along the route where rice and other provisions had been hidden by Sultan's forces. The General had been in a quandary. He had found that through loss, theft and fraud, his army had hardly any provisions left. What was worse, he had received messages from General Harris requesting immediate junction between the two English armies but more particularly pleading that his own army would starve unless General Stuart was able to bring a generous supply of provisions. Armed with the list furnished by Qamar-ud-din, General Stuart's forces raided the storehouses and were able to secure large stocks of grain, rice and other necessities. The promise to Qamar-ud-din for grant of Gurrakonda was renewed and he also received cash for all the supplies that the English were able to collect through the list furnished by him. General Stuart suggested to him that General Harris might also appreciate a similar list of such storehouses in his vicinity, 'strictly on cash basis, of course, quite apart from goodwill'. Qamar-ud-din needed no further prompting and proceeded towards Seringapatam.

Tipu Sultan was told that General Stuart's forces had been left crippled and exhausted from Qamar-ud-din's onslaughts and were in no condition to effect a junction with General Harris.

69

DID BANSI LAL DESERT?

THE ENGLISH ARMY UNDER GENERAL HARRIS OCCUPIED A STRONG position. Beyond it lay the grove of palms and coconut trees, called Sultanpet Tope, intersected by deep ditches and watered from a channel running in an easterly direction about a mile from the fort. The grove provided an excellent cover for Sultan's slender force of 'skirmishers and rocket men and enabled them to harass constantly the English pickets. Suddenly, Abdul Shakoor, Sultan's commander in Sultanpet Tope, ordered the evacuation of his forces. Bansi Lal, his second-in-command, wondered why.

'Orders,' Abdul Shakoor barked. Bansi Lal questioned no more and followed Abdul Shakoor with his men. When they were outside the grove, Abdul Shakoor dismissed all of them with instructions to report to the fort and await further orders. Alone, he left in the opposite direction. For a few minutes, Bansi Lal went along with his men but suddenly he stopped and then ran in the opposite direction to overtake Abdul Shakoor. Panting, he reached him and asked: 'Was it orders or was it treachery? Tell me, Abdul, do tell me, please tell me.'

'Are you mad?' Abdul Shakoor asked. 'How dare you impute treachery to me!'

'Then why did we leave such a strategic position unguarded?'

'Orders, you idiot, orders,' shouted Abdul Shakoor, but immediately his anger left him. He smiled, put his hand on Bansi Lal's shoulder and continued, 'How long have you known me, Bansi? Fifteen years. Do you think I would desert Sultan's cause? Do you?'

'Then why do you not come with us to the fort?' Bansi Lal persisted, though much of his suspicion had already disappeared. 'Why are you going in this direction?'

'Again, my foolish friend, I repeat to you that I have to follow orders. Do not question me; question those that give me the orders. I know what I am doing and there is a good reason for all I am doing. Go and ask Sultan, if you wish. I can tell you nothing.'

For a moment Bansi Lal did not speak. He looked at Abdul Shakoor. No, there could be no treachery, not in that open smiling countenance nor in those wistful, honest eyes.

'I misunderstood. Forgive me,' said Bansi Lal, now ashamed of his suspicions and conscious of the enormity of his offence in accusing an old friend who was also his senior officer. 'Do forgive me.'

'A foolish friend has to be forgiven. Go in peace.'

Bansi Lal left. He looked back once to wave his hand at Abdul Shakoor. Next time he looked back was when a bullet from Abdul Shakoor's gun caught him in the neck. Another bullet crashed into his temple. He fell down and Abdul Shakoor approached his fallen body. Shakoor had an impression that Bansi Lal's lips were moving, into a smile and were attempting to formulate a question: 'Was this under orders, too?' He aimed his third bullet directly at Bansi Lal's lips. It was not necessary. Bansi Lal was already dead.

An hour later, the English forces under General Baird crossed into Sultanpet Tope and occupied the deserted grove.

Abdul Shakoor and Bansi Lal were proclaimed by Sultan's Court as traitors and deserters for the evacuation of Sultanpet Tope had been without orders and both were missing.

70

THE DUKE OF WELLINGTON

PURNAIYA SENT A MESSAGE TO SAYYAD SAHEB TO DISLODGE the English from Sultanpet Tope and received a reply that he was much too busy harassing the main forces of General Harris to spare his men for attack on the grove. The Mysorean forces rode out from the fort under Purnaiya himself to attack General Baird. The General who had been assured of peaceful and undisturbed occupation of the grove was forced to flee in his pyjamas. These pyjamas, made of the finest Mysore silk delicately embroidered with a floral design in pink stripes, had come to him as birthday gift from his wife.

Purnaiya was now in command of the grove. At sunset, the English despatched two strong columns under Colonel Wellesley, the future Duke of Wellington, and they attacked in the darkness of the night. They were met with a tremendous fire of musketry and rockets. The English contingent, floundering amidst the trees and water-courses, at last broke and fell back, some being killed and a few taken prisoners. Colonel Wellesley was himself struck on the knee by a spent ball, and narrowly escaped falling into the hands of the Mysoreans. The English withdrew in disorder.

Years later, when Colonel Wellesley had earned many laurels, achieved fame and glory as the Duke of Wellington, he told a friend:

'No, my friend, I do not suffer too much from arrogance. These victories please me, delight me, flatter me, they fill my heart with joy and pride but they do not turn my head. If, perchance, a bout of arrogance attempts to assail me, my mind goes back to the repulse I suffered at Sultanpet Tope. That is enough to teach me humility. For that I am grateful to Purnaiya.'

'Who is Purnaiya?'

'Oh, he was the Prime Minister of Tipu Sultan. He commanded Tipu's forces at Sultanpet Tope. Purnaiya is a forgotten man now.'

'But not Tipu Sultan, though.'

'No, not Tipu Sultan,' responded the Duke of Wellington. 'In fact, I fear, my friend, that Tipu's memory will live long after the world has ceased to remember you and me.'

71

ENEMY WITHIN OUR GATES

(i)

EARLY IN THE MORNING SAYYAD SAHEB ARRIVED AT SULTANPET Tope and congratulated Purnaiya on his victory against Colonel Wellesley's forces.

'But leave the rest to us professionals,' Sayyad Saheb advised. 'You are wanted back in the fort, to be near Sultan.'

'Who is to look after this grove then?' Purnaiya asked. 'You know its importance.'

'I will look after it, of course; what a question!'

'I asked because yesterday you claimed to be busy elsewhere.'

'Yesterday was yesterday. Today is another day.'

'Do I leave any of my troops, here, or can you spare yours?' Purnaiya asked.

'Take them with you. They have fought well and hard. They need a rest. I have enough.'

Purnaiya left for the fort, fully at ease that the veteran commander Sayyad Saheb himself was taking charge of the grove. That night the Sultanpet Tope grove was in the English hands without a shot being fired.

Sayyad Saheb also took command of all the groves in the broken rising ground in front of the English army where protected by deep ditches and tall trees, the Mysoreans could continue to annoy the English and frustrate their efforts to proceed with the siege operations. These groves also fell in the hands of the English within hours of Sayyad Saheb assuming command. Thus, the English were able to establish themselves in strong positions within thousand yards of the Seringapatam fort.

(ii)

Tipu Sultan scrutinised the latest English plans of attack which Mir Sadik made available to him. Mir Sadik was proud of his intelligence agency through which he claimed to obtain such plans. Earlier also, he had obtained a duplicate of the English plan of attack as soon as the war had started. That had been a sketchy plan. Still, clearly it had shown that the attack on the fort would come from the east and south. That plan, marked 'Top Secret', had been signed by the Governor-General Wellesley, General Stuart and General Harris. The latest plan signed by General Stuart and General Harris, though far more elaborate, was also substantially similar in essentials and indicated the attack from the same direction. Meanwhile, Mir Sadik had also told Sultan that he had obtained corroborative information from a Frenchman, a prisoner-of-war, who was an interpreter attached to General Stuart himself. This information, Mir Sadik claimed, left no doubt that the English actually did plan to attack from the east and south. When Sultan desired to see the prisoner, Mir Sadik procrastinated for some time. On being reminded again, Mir Sadik escorted Sultan to a chamber where a European lay in agony and blood, obviously from torture.

'I have witnessed a sight,' Tipu cried in pain, 'which I hope to God I shall never see again.' He left in disgust reminding Mir Sadik of the Decree prohibiting torture or humiliation of prisoners. Later, Mir Sadik pleaded with Sultan for forgiveness urging that he had not been the one to apply torture and that it had been done without his authority by one of his agents who had been severely punished for it.

The incident of the tortured prisoner apart, clearly it was etched in Tipu's mind that the attack would come from the east and south. Most of his defences were also concentrated against an attack in those directions.

After concluding the Treaty of 1792, Tipu Sultan had given little attention to strengthening the defences of Seringapatam, lulled somewhat into the belief the English planned no further mischief against him. It was only when Governor-General Wellesley began this war, suddenly without provocation and without even a formal declaration, that Sultan began to strengthen the fortifications. He hardly had time to do much and obviously could not put a ring of fortifications all around the fort. Therefore, with the exception of a single battery which he had erected on the north-west angle of the fort, all his improvements had been directed to the south and east. What had influenced this decision was the duplicates of the English plan of attack which cleverly his trusted Minister Mir Sadik had obtained to show that those were directions from which the enemy attack would come.

It came as a severe shock to Tipu Sultan that his eastern and southern defences were going to be not of much use. The English attack came from the west and north-west.

The junction of the two English armies under General Stuart and General Harris took place. All the hopes which Qamar-ud-din had given of being able to obstruct the junction were dashed to the ground. Tipu Sultan saw the huge English forces, in an almost unending mass forming a coherent line four miles long less than a thousand yards from the battlements of Seringapatam.

72

HOW DID THEY COME THIS FAR?

MYSORE HAD OFTEN KNOWN DANGER BUT NEVER SO ACUTELY AS now. There had been times of great peril when savage fighting had erupted in the heart of the country but always and with swiftness, it had managed to regain its calm almost nonchalant air. This time it was different; the Seringapatam fort itself was under siege.

Still, there was no panic even though countless refugees were streaming into the already overcrowded fort. They were tense, anxious, shaken, frightened, even desperate before they entered into the fort but once in, they could draw a feeling of security from its high solid walls, and more so from the presence of Tipu Sultan himself. They had come in with a cry of help in their hearts; they had seen the stress and agony of the city quivering under the iron heel of the English aggressor; they had escaped the senseless killing, burning and looting; they had witnessed the bloodbath and merciless tearing apart of families. Many had been orphaned. Some had lost a son, a few all their loved ones. They had come swarming out of shattered cities into the sheltering walls of the fort, with tears in their eyes and a cry of pain wrung from their souls by the measureless torment through which they had passed.

Tipu Sultan looked at them with compassion, his heart filled with sadness and resolution. Their response was spontaneous. The red glare went out of their eyes. Their hearts were touched. Their despair left them and their panic disappeared, replaced by a calm strength, a hope and a prayer.

Purnaiya saw the change. He spoke of it to Mir Sadik, wondering how Tipu Sultan was able to transform their misery and instil confidence. Politely Mir Sadik heard him but did not fully agree.

'Anxiety, fear, terror,' said Mir Sadik, 'are something physcial—a function of the kidneys, rythm of the heart-beat and pressure of the head. With good food and proper sleep they often fade away. I see nothing strange in it all.'

'No, Mir Sadik, you are wrong,' Purnaiya countered. 'I have seen the change in those terror-stricken men who fled from the pathways of blood. For days and nights even while they were behind the protecting walls of this fort, they were beyond consolation, immersed in their grief over the loved ones they had lost and refusing to be comforted. It was only when they came in the presence of Sultan that they found some solace and a calmness of spirit. I tell you this that there is strange force in him which is ever-replenished in this fort. If only one could bring before him every citizen of Mysore for him to speak to each of them, touch them with his gentle hand and pour his strength into them, I believe....'

'What do you believe?' Mir Sadik interrupted. 'Would the English then leave the vicinity of our fort and march back to their homes? No, my friend, the only force that they recognise comes not from a gentle hand but from the barrel of a gun. And, this strange force that you talk of, tell me of what use is it? Why did it not prevent the English from setting foot into our borders? The enemy is outside our walls now. Would this strange force that you talk of hold them back?'

Purnaiya was silent. Mir Sadik continued, his tone gentler now. 'Do not misunderstand me. I love Sultan more than anyone else, you included, but I cannot be blind to realities.'

'We speak of different things, Mir Sadik,' replied Purnaiya. 'I was not speaking of the military situation but of the comfort and solace that Sultan's presence gives to the distressed.'

'Then you speak of irrelevancies,' Mir Sadik retorted. 'With a naked eye, you can see the enemy from the ramparts of the fort and you waste your breath on speaking of the homeless refugees, filthy ruffians and vagabonds who have swarmed into the fort making our difficult task even more difficult. If I had my way, I would have closed the gates to them but you, you came with those strange orders.'

'They were Sultan's orders.'

'With which you were no doubt in full agreement.'

'That I was.'

'To what end? To block our military movement, to deplete our food stocks?'

'No, to protect the people of the realm.'

'But not the realm itself.'

'The people and the realm are convertible terms. You cannot have one without the other.'

'We grow simple minded in our old age, don't we, Purnaiya? Believe me, to protect the realm what is needed is savagery and sacrifice—and to begin with, sacrifice of one's own people. You cannot shed the blood of the enemy until you have learnt to shed the blood of your own people. Savagery is an art to be practised at home before it can be applied to others.'

'Savagery for the sake of savagery!' said Purnaiya with a smile. 'Bloodshed for the sake of bloodshed! To what end?'

'Believe me, Purnaiya, in bloodshed is based the foundation of power. Can a nation be ever great unless its soil has been watered by rivers of blood? Do understand that the principle of power is based on the simple doctrine that the masses must be made to love the rulers and in turn the rulers must reciprocate by imposing sacrifices on them. For the ruler to return love for love would be a pointless, senseless, self-defeating exchange. Every man, be he savage or civilised, needs a master—someone to think for him, thrash him, bind him in chains, someone to fight for, to die for. People exist for their leaders and not the other way round. In fact, as I see it, the main purpose of the existence of the people is to furnish their leaders with a platform for their orations and proclamations, and to provide high officials with magnificent perquisites as also opportunities for their ruler to lead a glorious, resplendent life. Sacrifice is man's destiny and he has no other rights. Should people ever forget that, the ruler must step in to hold their imagination in check initially with slogans and then with promises, guarantees and even gratification of some of their basic necessities; he can cajole, charm, reward, threaten, lie, exhort, and even give them scapegoats to divert their attention or beguile them with parades and celebrations so that their fascinated gaze is eternally fixed upon power enthroned but finally, if all these fail, the ruler must intervene to secure obedience with fire and sword.'

'And, the power of the sword, you think, will conquer the power of the spirit?' Purnaiya asked.

'In this world, yes; what happens in regions of heaven and hell, I do not know, but we shall know soon—very soon.'

'Very soon? How so?'

Mir Sadik waved his hand towards the outer wall of the fort beyond which the English had massed their troops.

'Surely, you don't think,' asked Mir Sadik, 'that we have a chance. If the English could come this far, will this fort hold them back:"

'But, Mir Sadik, we are strongest here. They will rot there wasting their fire power until their ammunition is over, until their food stocks are exhausted and until their spirits wear out. By God, I know we did not lure the English to come this far but do you think they will have a walkover now? Impossible. They will be panting for peace in a month or two. This siege cannot succeed. Sultan himself is in charge. Our walls are well protected and our best troops are here.'

'Our best troops were elsewhere, too,' Mir Sadik retorted. 'What happened? Did you expect the English to come this far so swiftly?'

'That I did not,' said Purnaiya with a troubled expression.

With mocking eyes, Mir Sadik looked at Purnaiya and then said gently, 'Come with me, Purnaiya.'

They went near the ramparts of the fort from which they could see by the light of the moon, the enemy troops spread out into the vast distance.

'It is like an ocean,' said Mir Sadik, 'and there we were in solitary splendour speaking of the mysterious influence which Sultan wields.'

'No, I do not doubt the existence of his influence,' Mir Sadik continued in answer to a questioning glance from Purnaiya. 'I merely question the utility of such influence in the prevailing times. His is an influence which relates to the spirit of man, to the moral well-being of humanity. Men who wield such influence do not found kingdoms on earth nor build empires. They are hounded out, betrayed, nailed to the cross, beheaded or assassinated. God does not protect them—they who call themselves the Sons of God or the Messengers of the Lord. Sometimes, I believe that even if God is all powerful, He begins to suffer from jealousy at the eminence and respect that His Messengers begin to enjoy on earth and therefore fails to protect them in the hour of their need. Tell me, Purnaiya,' there was mockery now in Mir Sadik's tone, 'does this discussion on philosophy bore you?'

'Philosophy! I thought what you said smacked of blasphemy and often of treason. One thing is clear that you have lost all hope and are mortally afraid of the outcome of this war. I can only hope that whilst speaking to others you have shown some restraint. Fear is a disease that can prove to be contagious, you know.'

'Purnaiya,' Mir Sadik's tone was earnest now, almost pained without a trace of mockery, 'you are the only one to whom I can bare my soul and speak out all that is in my heart. My words are only for you; to others I am silent. Can there ever be a question of our misunderstanding each other? You know there is no treason in me. There never can be. I shall die for Tipu Sultan or with him but I can have no existence apart from him. But you see my agony,' Mir Sadik waved his hand again in the direction of the enemy positions. 'Here they have come, unhindered, unmolested. If they have come this far, how far will they go? Where will they stop? I am not afraid for myself but I am afraid for Tipu Sultan. I think you said that in the end the spirit shall conquer the sword. True, but will Sultan, you and I be there to witness that end. Think about it, Purnaiya, think about it. How did the enemy come this far?'

'There will be time enough to think about it. But presently what are our priorities? Surely, to keep the enemy at bay, to hold him where he is and to tire him out. This is our task, first and foremost, and to this our will and effort have to be directed. The question that you ask is not without relevance. We shall, I hope, answer it some day. But in due season; now we have to concentrate our energies against the threat of the enemy outside our gates. You agree?'

'Yes, of course,' was Mir Sadik's unhesitating response.

As he left him, Purnaiya did not see the expression of cold fury in Mir Sadik's face. It had been a useless, fruitless conversation and the purpose with which Mir Sadik had engaged in it had not been served. The marksman aimed well but the arrows, it seemed, fell far short of the target; Purnaiya, he realised now, was not the one to come under the spell of fear.

'Well, well, what happens to those that will not bend?' Mir Sadik asked himself. 'They will break,' he answered his own question, and then smiled triumphantly as if he had hit upon a truth unparalleled in the history of human thought.

73

WE ARE ASSASSINATED

'HOW DID THE ENEMY COME THIS FAR?'—THIS HAD BEEN MIR Sadik's question.

Although he had not admitted it to Mir Sadik, Purnaiya had already asked himself the very same question over and over again.

The question did not divert him from the main tasks at hand but always it was present in some corner of his restless mind. Many answers flashed before him. They were vague, shapeless and formless. He dared not formulate them with clarity or in words. He was afraid to discuss them with anyone. He knew the trend of these answers that thronged in his mind. They gave him a feeling of icy despair which he would share with no one.

How did the enemy come this far? The appalling, agonising question remained. It was a question that was in Tipu's mind as well. Sad at heart, he wondered how so many had deserted his cause. The lists of deserters published by Qamar-ud-din, Sayyad Saheb and Mir Sadik were getting longer day-by-day. Now, he had even lost contact with Qamar-ud-din, Sayyad Saheb and so many others. Where were they? Tipu Sultan faced Purnaiya with this question:

'Where are they—my commanders and my loyal, trusted men?'

Purnaiya's head sank. He remained silent. There was no need to answer. He knew that to Tipu Sultan he could communicate his feelings without having to put them in words. Tipu continued:

'Yes, Purnaiya, I know of your silent agony and the questions in your mind. You are asking yourself: What was the purpose of those insane retreats when easily our commanders could have held the enemy at bay at hundreds of places? Why were so many well-garrisoned forts abandoned en route by our valiant men? And, those reports of heavy losses inflicted on the enemy, of their being without food and provisions, and suffering from acute shortage of troops and reinforcements! Why were these reports, without sense and substance sent to us? Were we not told that the two English armies cannot combine?—that the losses inflicted on each of them have been far too heavy? And did not a courier come everyday with an eye-witness report of the route taken by the enemy? Yet, suddenly we see the endless masses of enemy troops appearing from the opposite direction! Are we to believe that our commanders have suddenly become irresolute, cowardly, dense and dilatory or do we have to believe something even worse—that they led these visitors of ours on to Seringapatam fort in a masterly fashion?'

The voice was calm, the tone gentle, perhaps only the eyes betrayed the anguish that he felt in the depth of his soul.

'This . . . this I did not expect,' said Purnaiya. He did not know what he was going to say. Abruptly he stopped; then he asked hoarsely, almost in a whisper: 'Do you, do you know the answer?'

'I think I do,' Tipu Sultan replied. He remained plunged in thought. He was going over in his mind the whole of this strange war in which the enemy had not won a single decisive battle and yet had captured his forts, put to flight and scattered so many of his trusted commanders with well-disciplined, well-ordered troops and had even reached the very gates of Seringapatam fort. Then he looked at Purnaiya, saw his dejection and smiled. 'If it is any consolation to you,' Tipu said, 'though I fear it is not, let me say that I agree with you.'

Purnaiya who had expressed no opinion, advanced no views, wondered what Tipu Sultan meant. Tipu answered his questioning glance: 'Did you not say once, Purnaiya, that no outside power can crush us?'

'And so?' the question shot out from Purnaiya's lips, involuntarily.

'And so this, that it is not an outside power that is going to crush us. The peril is within us, the sickness is within us, and the enemy ... the enemy is within us.'

'The enemy is within us,' Purnaiya repeated slowly as if trying to understand the import of those words.

'Yes, this country shall not be conquered from without. It shall be defeated from within.'

'But why?' Purnaiya asked. A pointless question for he knew the answer.

'Why! The one lesson which past history of this unhappy land gives us is that it is not courage that we lack. It is not intellect or intelligence that we lack. It is not vigour or dynamism that we lack. We do not even lack cunning. God knows we have some fine practitioners of that. It is Unity. We have never faced the same way to see the truth. Even in this deeply disturbed period of our history, when annihilation faces the independence of this proud land, each goes his own way, possessed by disunity. There was a time when India was united and strong and we went out to the world to spread the message of truth and love. Then came the dawn of a new age, a dark age, when this nation lost the will to preserve itself, torn by greed, jealousy, intrigue and narrow animosities that goaded us into warfare with each other. Thus, have we fallen prey to every petty invader who chose to plunder us. You see in this sorry plight of today a repetition of that historical process and you see in it also a lesson for the future. For I tell you this, that India shall be free again though it will be long after you and I are no more. . . .'

Purnaiya was about to interrupt, but a motion of Tipu's hand stopped him.

'Yes,' continued Tipu, 'India will emerge free and independent long after we have perished. From the soil enriched with our blood shall rise men and women who shall dare all and sacrifice everything. They shall challenge the wrath and might of the English empire and shake it to its very foundations. They shall force the aggressor to depart and, yes, India shall be free. But freedom is not fulfilment. The question that tears at my heart is: What will be the face of India then? Will our countrymen learn something from the past or will they be blind to the warnings and tread the same old paths of disunity and destruction? Will they preserve the soul of the country or will they let it rot with linguistic, communal and petty tribal rivalries? Will they set up provinces or divisions with each casting a stone at the other or will they be guided towards the common goal of greatness through individual, collective and cooperative effort?'

'Is this the moment to think of the future?' Purnaiya asked.

'My mind always thinks of the future, tries to pierce its veil and adorn it with the ornaments of my choice. Yet, a doubt creeps into my mind: Shall we always be thus? Will stupidity, selfishness and the temptation of greed which has now overtaken us, continue to dog us? Will each part of

India try to tear the eyes of the other; will neighbour rise against neighbour and brother against brother; will each of its provinces or divisions try to march forward in isolation from the rest; will they attempt to propagate their own citizenship on narrow regional considerations? Will every part of India come under the sway of corrupt, ambitious and petty leaders mouthing slogans and platitudes and exhorting the people to make sacrifices while they line their own pockets and purses? If that happens, many will fall away, betray one another, hate one another and I can see the tragedies that lie before this land. It shall then be no different from being the plaything of a foreign conqueror.'

'This is no moment to think of the distant future, nor of the remote past,' Purnaiya intervened. 'I beg of you to direct your mind to our present situation.'

'Present situation!' Tipu repeated. A rueful smile replaced his faraway look. 'Presently, I told you, the hour of our humiliation has arrived. This land, which I love more than my soul, is dying an un-natural death. We have been assassinated—yes, by the enemy within us.'

74

THE DESTINY OF OUR LAND

PURNAIYA HAD HEARD TIPU SULTAN, HUSHED AND SOLEMN, HIS mind in a turmoil. The hour of our humiliation has arrived, Tipu had said. We have been assassinated, he had added. In despair, Purnaiya asked himself: Has Sultan lost all hope? The enemy guns were silent. Soon, the night would end and the shelling would start, but in his own heart Purnaiya heard the thunder of a thousand guns. Suddenly, in a shrill voice he said, 'The enemy is outside the fort, not inside. We can hold them there, They shall not conquer us while we live.'

'Yes, that they shall not,' Tipu replied. 'They shall not conquer us as long as I live; this I can promise you, but this also I know that here I shall die resisting their attack.'

'Do not say that, Tipu, my son.'

How had Purnaiya relapsed into this form of familiar address which he had never used after Tipu ascended the throne!

'Time and events shall not wait, Purnaiya. I cannot alter their inevitable course.'

'If ever it should come to pass that your life is in danger, you will have to leave the fort. Those arrangements have already been made.'

'I know. I have had them cancelled.'

'But, why?'

'Purnaiya, just now you said that they shall not conquer us while we live. You contradict yourself.'

'I do not contradict myself. I spoke of my life and the lives of my colleagues—our officers and our soldiers; not yours.'

'On the assumption that my life is more precious than others?'

'Yes, of course. You are our King, you wear the Crown, you carry the rod of authority, you bear the torch; in you lie all our hopes and dreams. With you gone, what remains? You have to go elsewhere.'

'Elsewhere! where? To do what? To prolong the hour of humiliation and defeat?—to kiss the hand of the conqueror and ask him to bind me lovingly in his chains? If a soldier can die why is it so inconceivable that the King also should die?'

'Death is always the companion of soldiers.'

'Today it is the companion of every Indian.'

Tipu continued. 'No, Purnaiya, what had before seemed to me only a possibility has now become necessary and inevitable; I too would like to die as courageously as any of my soldiers. Is sacrifice only to be theirs? By what right do I command my men to die for my cause if I should be afraid to lay down my own life? In the face of a common calamity, is the King to escape sacrifice and suffering? And why should I prolong the hours when there is no more profit in them? I should only make myself ridiculous—in the eyes of others and of my own—if I cling to life needlessly. Would you advise a Tiger to follow the lifestyle of a jackal; would you?'

'I am advising nothing of the sort,' Purnaiya said in some heat. In measured tones he added, 'I am advising you to live for the glory and greatness of India.'

'The glory and greatness of India is a cause worth living for; but do not forget, it is also a cause worth dying for.'

Tipu was touched by the misery in Purnaiya's expression. He reached out his hand and placed it affectionately on Purnaiya's shoulder. 'Then why is it, Purnaiya, that those that love me give me advice against my nature? Should life be held so precious? Should death be regarded so dreadful? I always regarded death as an awakening. But assume that life is precious—why, all the more reason to sacrifice it for a cause greater than life. Why should you and Mir Sadik militate against my decision?'

Purnaiya pricked his ears. 'Has Mir Sadik been saying what I said to you?'

'Not exactly, but I think his advice also relates to a grand design to save my life. He feels that I must take the world as it is, come to terms with it, live within the conditions that life offers. He rejects the theory—in fact he laughs at it—that man is true to himself only when he surpasses the limitations that nature has imposed on him.'

'But what was his advice?' Purnaiya asked with impatience.

'He suggests that I should come to terms with the English.'

'But you have tried that—all along you have tried that. The conditions they offer are impossible.'

'Yes, on those impossible conditions Mir Sadik wants me to come to terms with the English.'

'To be a vassal of the English! To be dependent on them, to live in their chains!'

'See, your gorge rises too; and yet your advice is not vastly different when you ask me to save my life.'

A transformation was taking place in Purnaiya—on his face and in his mind. The brooding dejection left him. It was as if an answer to a vital question which had eluded him for years had suddenly dawned on him.

'Tipu, I know what you would choose if it is ever a question of choice between your death and dishonour; I shall be untrue to you, to myself and to all that I have believed in, if ever I should advise you against that choice. Lay down your life, if you have to. More than any Indian ruler you have dared a dream and if death is to come, you can have no regret, for you shall live, Tipu, you shall always live. You who alone challenged the might of a terrible enemy who comes to enslave this proud, sensitive land.'

Tipu smiled. 'Thank you for this charming speech. Sometimes, you act as if the sun rises and sets on my head. Do not, I beg of you, elevate me beyond my deserts. We spoke of the duty of kings and common soldiers. Death, you must remember, does not respect rank or status; it makes humans out of princes and demigods. Can you really see any difference between the death of a king and that of a soldier?'

'It is in the memory of man—in the imprint on future ages—that the sacrifice of a valiant king remains.'

'Even of a defeated king?' Tipu asked.

'Defeat, victory—are these not of transient, trivial, secondary importance? What is important is the sacrifice for a nation. The world cherishes many memories, with enduring affection and respect. These are not of conquerors and victors in the battlefield, no, but rather of those who went down fighting for the ideal they believed in and the cause that was just. Will a nation for whom you sacrifice your life ever commit the mistake—nay, tragedy—of ignoring it? Will it ever forget you?'

'Why don't you understand that it is not I who must be remembered but the cause?'

'That is exactly what I mean. The cause of freedom of the country, its moral uplift, its greatness, its glory are linked with your name.'

'No, Purnaiya, no, I am not the first, nor shall I be the last. Many strong shoulders have in the past borne the load of greatness of this country. Many hereafter will have to bear that load. The nation is greater than the greatest of us all because countless generations have nurtured it with their love, tenderness, blood, sweat and sacrifice. If I did not have faith in the coming generations, if I did not feel that they would pick up the fallen torch, if I feared that they would be without commitment to the cause of their nation, I would have an empty, sinking feeling in my heart and an apprehension that I would die in vain. But that is not so. A day will dawn when our people will shed fear. With that gone, the very foundation of English terrorism and deception will disappear. My faith in the destiny of this nation is unshaken and in that lies my dream, my happiness and my bliss.'

75

PROFILE OF A TRAITOR?

PURNAIYA LEFT SERINGAPATAM FORT THREE DAYS BEFORE THE final assault began.

'I have a favour to beg of you,' Tipu Sultan had told Purnaiya.

'Do not beg what you can command,' Purnaiya said. 'Ask for anything in my power, it is yours.'

'Then I ask that we part company and....'

Purnaiya misunderstood. 'You have decided to leave the fort, then?' he asked.

Tipu shook his head. 'No, I shall never leave the fort; but you have to.'

Purnaiya looked at Tipu Sultan in disbelief, his mind in a turmoil. Was Sultan blaming him for the disaster that awaited Mysore? He lowered his face so that Sultan might not see his agony but the voice was calm and controlled.

'If it is from want of faith in me, my lord,' began Purnaiya formally, 'you can relieve me of my command, strip me of all my honour and position, but my years of service entitle me to the privilege of dying here with you when the blow falls. How have I deserved banishment?'

'Purnaiya, please, try to hear me fully. Do not interrupt, I beg of you. Maybe, then you will not misunderstand. How can there be any want of faith in you? You had much to give. You gave it all. But I have still to seek a service, a favour from you. Please listen.'

Purnaiya thereafter heard Tipu Sultan in stunned silence. Tipu reminded him of the conversation of the other day—of the assassination of India by the enemy from within, of how the country was weakened by intrigue and treachery before it was struck down by the alien invader, of how it was poisoned from within before it was smitten from without.

'Now we stand alone in the breach, facing the monstrous force of an enemy who comes to enslave this nation. Will anyone stand up to them after we are defeated? No, all the remaining unravished kingdoms shall also be torn to pieces in a few months, if not in weeks—and the tyranny of the conquerer will be all the more complete for he shall be acting through Indian rulers who, like the Nizam, will be their puppets carrying out with obedience and without question their orders.'

Purnaiya did not interrupt. Tipu continued: 'Therefore, I want you out of this fort. I want you to be safe—so that you may live to serve the next ruler of Mysore, to instill in him the spirit of resistance, to inspire in him the dream of unity of India so that once again the Kingdom of Mysore may stand forward as the champion of the freedom of India and the rights of man.'

'What makes you doubt that your Crown Prince has not already been fired by the same dream?' Purnaiya asked. 'Why do you fear that he will fail? I know him as well as you, Sultan, and I assure you, you need have no apprehensions. I shall watch him from the heavens above and, this I know, I shall be proud of him.'

'Do you really believe that the Crown Prince has any chance of succeeding to my throne? If the English are victorious, you think they will permit my dynasty to continue? No, Purnaiya, they will want to wipe out, for ever, my name and my family. Be sure of that.'

'Alright, if not the Crown Prince, if not a member of your family, who then will the English choose to succeed you?'

'That will not pose a tremendous problem for the English. They can pick up any upstart—anyone from the nobility or from my court who is ready to sell his soul to them; or they can pick up some one from the old royalty.'

'Exactly, and what use will that new ruler have for my services? How will I go about inspiring the lofty dream into a soul that has already been mortgaged to the English? Do you think that such a ruler will permit me to come within his earshot?'

'Purnaiya, do not underrate yourself. You are known far beyond this realm as one of the ablest administrators. Repeatedly several princes have asked for your services. If you leave this fort, alive and well, ahead of the final assault, no one will think that your loyalty towards me is so deep-rooted that you will not faithfully serve another master. Why, the English themselves would be clamouring to get your services. The English have a talent for choosing their servants well.'

'Tipu, do not mask your words. Be open with me, as you have always been. You want me to wear the mantle of betrayal to you, so that I am in the market to serve another master after you. Is that what you mean?—that the world shall know me as a traitor and as a deserter to your cause so that the English may embrace me to their bosom and allow me to serve the next ruler of Mysore? Is it really your wish that I should appear to all the world as a dishonourable traitor and a common scoundrel, and should lose my self-respect along with the respect of all my fellow-men? Is this then the reward of my life-long devotion to you and to your illustrious father that I now, in the closing years of my life, have to wear the garb of treachery!'

'Wear whatever garb you have to,' Tipu replied in a tone that was pitiless and crisp, 'and does it matter so long as you are conscious that you serve a noble and an unfolding purpose to help a nation—your own—which is threatened, which has fallen on its knees and is bleeding from its wounds?'

'You ask for the impossible. I shall not be known as a deserter.'

'You echoed my feelings once that you loved your country more than your soul, didn't you? So, what are you prepared to sacrifice for it? Your life, yes. But your sacrifice stops there. You set definite limits to it. Your fair name must be preserved. That is beyond the pale of sacrifice, is it?'

'Tipu, please understand me,' replied Purnaiya almost piteously. 'My life is of no value to me unless it is spent in your service and by your side. If you have to die in battle, I want to be near you, to hold you in my arms, to smooth your brow, to wipe your blood, to wash your body and . . . and then, then I do not wish to live for another day.'

If Tipu was moved by the appeal in Purnaiya's voice, he did not show it. 'Agree then,' said Tipu coldly, 'that my analysis is correct that you bind yourself to me but not to the cause that we should both cherish.'

'Where is the room for analysis or hair-splitting?' Purnaiya asked wearily. 'Enough if we die resisting the same enemy and for the same purpose.'

'Each man has his own destiny, Purnaiya. From each, a different sacrifice is called for. For me the moment is fast approaching when I might have to part with the world. Soon, the English will begin their final assault. I know that I am not invulnerable or under special protection of heaven. I know therefore that I am in danger—and this is the danger from which I shall not run away. We have talked of this before. The unalterable, inevitable course of my destiny leads me to the necessity to sacrifice my life—to die for a cause bigger than an individual's life; but for you....'

'For me, yes, for me, for the same cause why is the privilege to die to be denied to me?'

'Dying is not a privilege, Purnaiya. It is a necessity; understand that. As I was saying, before you interrupted, for me the time is coming to part with the world, to die; but for you, that time is not yet. You must live to guide and warn the succeeding rulers of this land. For this you must live.'

'I must live, damned, condemned and scorned with the finger of accusation raised against me for abandoning you at the hour of your greatest need! Is it not better to die?'

'Your death will avail nothing. It will be an empty gesture of agony which will add to the pain of this country. There is still much before us, a great deal lies ahead. How can you think of dying when the cause remains, when there are promises to keep and when duty inescapable beckons! We are not fighting for ourselves alone. How can we then think of ourselves alone? And remember, when the day dawns—as surely it will dawn—the spirit of India will turn with understanding and tenderness to men like you who in this tragic hour did not desert the cause of their nation.'

Purnaiya was silent. Tipu continued: 'Do not, for a moment, believe that a lie has greater currency and will for ever cloud and overwhelm the truth. God grant that you may live to tell the truth but even if you do not, will the historians not have a true perception? Surely, history will then turn to you with comprehension and the nation with gratitude.'

Purnaiya's eyes were covered by a film of moisture and he seemed to be looking far away. He made one more effort to plead.

'You make a terrible demand. I beg you to revoke it.'

'I made it clear to you at the very beginning, Purnaiya, that I was not giving a command. I was begging for a favour. By what right can I control your freedom of action when I shall be no more! Yet, this I know that if you live to work for the recovery of this fallen land, then I shall await the impending assault undismayed; and if I die, I shall have died only in my body, while my spirit shall remain alive, vibrating with hope.'

Two days after this conversation, at five o'clock in the morning when it was still quite dark, Purnaiya left Seringapatam fort. He had wept when parting from Tipu Sultan. It was their last meeting, he knew. He had dried his tears now. He walked erect and composed, past the gate which the sentries had opened for him. His servant followed him with two horses. The Guard Commander warned him to hurry since the shelling would soon start. Purnaiya responded with a melancholy smile and asked him not to worry. How was the Guard Commander to know that Purnaiya would have welcomed with all his heart and soul the release which the English shells and bullets would have given him!'

On the night that followed Purnaiya's departure, Mir Sadik called for a meeting of commanders. To them he made the following announcement:

'Tipu Sultan has ordered me to carry out all functions and responsibilities of Purnaiya Saheb in addition to my own. In full consciousness of my responsibilities I assume the leadership of the armies of Mysore. All those responsible to Purnaiya Saheb shall henceforth be solely responsible to me. I shall make many changes. It is the desire of Tipu Sultan that I do so. I shall ask for unquestioning obedience. My first task is to make arrangements for the defence of the realm against the impending English onslaught and to protect our men and women from unnecessary destruction. I repeat that I shall make changes—sweeping changes. I shall appreciate your understanding but I do not ask for it. All I ask is that everyone carries out my orders fully and faithfully. Whosoever fails to do so will be deemed guilty of impeding the accomplishment of the task before us. He shall pay for it with his head. From each and all of you, I must expect unquestioning obedience. This I ask of you, demand of you, in the name of, and by the authority invested in me, by Tipu Sultan.'

The meeting was dismissed. Never before had the commanders been addressed in such peremptory manner. Not by Mir Sadik, not by Purnaiya and certainly not by Tipu Sultan. Why were they being treated like raw soldiers on parade ground, they wondered. The situation must be far more grim than they thought it was if Mir Sadik should forsake his customary sense of delicate irony and start behaving like a Sergeant Major who has to deal with woodenheaded recruits. In silence they began to leave the meeting. Only Rudad Khan hazarded a question:

'Mir Sadik, may I ask where is Purnaiya Saheb?' It was a question in everyone's mind. They all halted to listen to the reply.

'It was not the purpose of this meeting to discuss the whereabouts of Purnaiya Saheb,' replied Mir Sadik frostily.

They left, their hearts rent with perplexity. Why did Mir Sadik refuse to answer? Where had Purnaiya gone? Where is he now? Had he really taken the awesome step to desert his master? Purnaiya himself! They looked at each other with covert dejection, dreading to ask the question. A ghastly, nightmarish feeling stole over them all. Each felt cut off from the other, alone, helpless . . . and afraid!

Back in their quarters, some wept, not because of any personal grief but in sympathy with the emotion which they thought must have filled Sultan's soul on hearing of Purnaiya's defection. Those were tears of love, compassion and tenderness. There were others, however, many others, who began to brood on different matters—their own safety, their own future and their own wellbeing. Their minds and conscience darkened.

76

THE LAST DAY

MYSORE'S LAST DAY DAWNED. NO ONE IT SEEMED REALISED THAT it would come so soon. No one knew what awaited the city.

How did that fateful day arrive so soon—with such sharp suddenness and breathtaking rapidity?

Immediately in the wake of Purnaiya's departure came sudden changes of command. That evening itself, under Mir Sadik's orders several units were shifted from one position to another; many commanders were separated from their men and given charge of new units; often, while an order was being implemented, it was countermanded by another or drastically modified; units which had remained intact for years were being scattered; troops asked to report to a commander sometimes found to their dismay that the officer could not be located within the fort; and if he was eventually located, he himself had instructions to report elsewhere to take up new duties. In swift succession one order followed another, each by itself seemingly sensible but in their totality they led to confusion and bewilderment.

All night Mir Sadik worked, fully awake, leaning on his elbow contemplating the next order to be issued. Sometimes, he left his room to inspect this position or that. The commanders would then murmur to him their difficulties over conflicting orders. Some even cautioned him against dispersal of units. Mir Sadik would look at them in distress, saying little but his expression and tone clearly implied that he had little choice in the matter, that he himself was under orders, and that much of what was happening was incomprehensible to him also. Everyone could see that this valiant, tireless man was living through terrible moments of anxiety and stress. He had to supervise the entire army and the defence effort. Was it fair to trouble him with trivial complaints? The commanders remained silent. But not Ghazi Khan.

In the middle of the night, Ghazi Khan charged into Mir Sadik's chamber and demanded to know why Syed Ghaffar had been relieved of his command at Mahtab Bagh, which was the key bastion of the fort.

Even for Mir Sadik it was not easy to trifle with Ghazi Khan who had been a colleague and confidant of Hyder Ali, perceptor and military tutor of Tipu Sultan, and was now the military guardian of Tipu's eldest son, the Crown Prince Fath Hyder. With a smile and a wave of his hand, Mir Sadik politely motioned the indignant Ghazi Khan to a chair. Ghazi Khan remained standing and repeated his question.

'Enormous and extremely difficult things are demanded of us, these days,' parried Mir Sadik.

'That is not an answer to my question,' retorted Ghazi Khan.

'Oh, your question! Well, I thought the reason for relieving Syed Ghaffar at Mahtab Bagh is evident.'

'Do please enlighten me.'

'Surely, Ghazi Khan, you know the danger we are in. We need Syed Ghaffar in the fort itself. He is loyal, valiant and stouthearted.'

'I see. So you surrender the key bastion of Mahtab Bagh, your sure defence against the enemy, to that clown Shustari.'

'Zainul Abidin Shustari is not a clown and you know it,' Mir Sadik replied solemnly. Then as if wishing to lighten the conversation, he added, 'Surely, Ghazi Khan, you know Shustari has even written a famous military manual *Falh-ul-Mujahidin* [The Triumph of the Holy Warriors].'

'I have read it. I repeat he is a clown and I beg of you to remove him from Mahtab Bagh forthwith. Let Syed Ghaffar be reinstated in his command there.'

'Please, Ghazi Khan, try and believe me, that it is a considered view that we need Syed Ghaffar here. Obviously, he cannot be in two places at the same time, can he?'

'Do you realise that if you leave Mahtab Bagh to the mercy of the enemy, you only hasten their entry into the fort. It is a dangerous move, and if you think about it, it is a stupid one.'

'I do not resent your strong language, Ghazi Khan. I know you are inspired by the same spirit of commitment which we all share. But allow me to say this with utmost respect to you that I am in overall command. The responsibility for such orders lies with me.'

'Is that so? Somehow I had the impression that Tipu Sultan is in overall command.'

Mir Sadik smiled as if relishing the heavy sarcasm employed by Ghazi Khan. 'Of course, Sultan is in overall command. The order to relieve Syed Ghaffar was issued in his name.'

'With his knowledge?'

'Do you really think that such an order can be issued without his knowledge and concurrence?'

Ghazi Khan looked crestfallen, and Mir Sadik was convinced that he was at the end of an irritating conversation. But it was not to be.

'Well, then, let us speak to him,' said Ghazi Khan.
'Speak to who?'
'To Tipu Sultan.'
'To what end?'
'To tell him to rescind the order.'
'Do you think this is the time to trouble Tipu Sultan? Hasn't he enough worries?'
'Worries! I tell you, his worries will multiply if Shustari continues in Mahtab Bagh.'
'But, Ghazi Khan, are you implying that the decision was made without careful consideration?'
'Of course, I told you it was a stupid decision!'
'And, you propose to tell Sultan that.'
'Listen, Mir Sadik, have you ever known Sultan to be afraid of hearing or knowing the hard truth? The final decision is his, that is true, but has he not always invited criticism and even contradiction? Has he not asked us to put fearlessly before him our candid views? How can we remain silent now? The strategic importance of Mahtab Bagh is clearly discernible even to a blind eye. To keep a buffoon like Shustari in charge there is to court certain disaster. Yes, there can be no doubt that the order Sultan has asked you to issue is a blunder, and we must tell him that. You really want to know what I think of this order?'
'Please, do tell me,' said the polite Mir Sadik, continuing to smile. 'But I would enjoy listening to you if you sit down.'
Ghazi Khan sat down in the chair.
'You do not drink, Mir Sadik, and Sultan does not drink. Otherwise, I would have said that two drunken men have met together to formulate this fantastic order.'
Mir Sadik laughed as if hugely enjoying the joke. Ghazi Khan looked pleased with himself.
'Well, well, what do we do now?' Mir Sadik asked.

'We go to Sultan and ask him to revoke the order.'
'Now?'
'Of course.'
'Let's do it tomorrow. It is late now.'
'Tomorrow it might be too late.'
'You are incorrigible, Ghazi Khan,' said Mir Sadik with a winning smile. 'Really, you convince me against my better judgement. But let us not trouble Sultan now. I will tell you what I will do. I will call Syed Ghaffar and tell him to take over Mahtab Bagh again immediately. But tomorrow morning you and I shall talk to Sultan. If he disagrees, we will call Syed Ghaffar back, but I am sure he will agree. Come to think of it, I was too weak with Sultan. I should have protested more strongly. Still, let us not trouble him now. What do you say?'
'Suits me fine, so long as you send Syed Ghaffar back.'
'This very instant.'
'Thanks.'
They shook hands. Before Ghazi Khan disengaged his hand, he heard Mir Sadik ordering the sentry to call Syed Ghaffar.
Ghazi Khan was about to leave. Mir Sadik detained him.
'When will you be in your quarters?' Mir Sadik asked.
'In an hour or so, why?'
'There is something about Commandant Mir Nadim, I have to discuss with you.'
'What has he been up to?'
'That is what I wish to discuss with you. Informally. Some papers have come into my hands.'
'Treachery?'
'I fear so, but I cannot be certain. Besides, there are three or four persons who have some damaging information about him. I am meeting them in the next half an hour. After I have talked to them, I want to see you. Maybe, I will bring them along also to you.'

'I can come over to your chamber in an hour's time, if you wish,' Ghazi Khan offered.

'No, I will come to you. Comings and goings to my chamber are often watched. There will be no one else about in your quarters, I take it.'

'No one except my old servant and the ceremonial guard.'

'Better dismiss them for the night.'

'Oh, they are reliable enough.'

'Still . . . if even the Commandant Mir Nadim can be suspected, tell me can we honestly say that anyone is free from suspicion? Dismiss them or better still send them away on an errand.'

'If you insist. But they would think that in my old age I am expecting a clandestine visit from a lady in my quarters. You are running my reputation, you know.'

'On the contrary, this will enhance your well-known reputation for virility.

'When should I expect you?'

'After one hour, but bear with me if I am a little late.'

Two hours later there was a gentle knock at Ghazi Khan's door. Ghazi Khan opened the door. Four men entered, bowed and one of them handed over a thick sealed envelope to Ghazi Khan. 'Mir Sadik asked us to report to you and to hand this over to you.'

'Where is Mir Sadik?' Ghazi Khan asked, puzzled.

'He will be here in a few minutes. Meanwhile, he requested that you glance over these papers.'

Looking at the envelope, Ghazi Khan walked to the table where the lantern was placed. Discreetly his visitors followed and stood behind him. Ghazi Khan broke the seal on the envelope but before he could draw out the papers, a savage blow from an iron hammer smashed into his skull. He reacted instantly. Although his body was slipping to the floor, his hand clutched the lantern and he turned towards his assailants. He dashed the lantern in the face of the man who had given him the envelope. With an inward smile he heard the moan of the stricken man but by then the three others had surrounded him and were bludgeoning him on his head with what looked like short iron pipes. His legs folded and he sank to the floor. It was not pain that he felt but anger at his helplessness. Then there was stillness and peace. He was dead.

At Mir Sadik's orders, well before the dawn broke, and much ahead of the usual hour, the Mysorean batteries started cannonading the enemy positions. The English dutifully returned the fire. It was late in the morning that Ghazi Khan's battered body was found in a spot which had suffered from heavy shelling by the English.

The body was washed and dressed. For some time it had been laid on the embalming table. Lovingly, men skilled in the art had prepared the body for the last journey and restored for its countenance the vigour, nobility and dignity which marked it during the lifetime of this great soldier. The body was now placed into an open coffin for everyone to see and to pay their last respects to it.

Mournfully, Mir Sadik carried the news of the tragedy to Tipu Sultan. Silently, Tipu Sultan prayed before the coffin. Then he bent to kiss the cold brow. There were no tears in his eyes. But his voice trembled when he spoke. What he said was little and the words were incomprehensible even to those who heard them. 'You were to guide me through the valley, were you not?' was what he had said, looking at the austere countenance of the soldier in the coffin.

'Do not panic,' was Mir Sadik's advice to every command post he inspected. 'I know you are troubled by the fact that so many have deserted the cause. But keep up your spirits and your moral force. There are still countless men who will do their duty and be guided by Sultan's ideal of glory and sacrifice.'

Glory and sacrifice! Fine words indeed! But he recited them as a ritual, as if he had no hope of being able to convince anyone, least of all himself. He was telling them not to panic, but the effect on his listeners was quite the opposite. Was the panic, they wondered, already so widespread that Mir Sadik had to exhort against it? Were there so many deserters, indeed? If they did not know it before, they knew it now—and minds which were not troubled before, began to be troubled. When he so addressed them, Mir Sadik spoke in low, mournful tones as if afraid of being overheard; he would first glance in the direction in which the English had set up their fortifications, then to the men around him and finally in the opposite direction giving an uncomfortable impression that he knew of many amongst his own compatriots who would like to be as far away as a man can run and as deep as a man can hide. If anyone raised a specific question, he chose to be vague and evasive as if he had no plan of any sort and was apprehensive of everything. It was only when he was in his own chamber that his sharp decisiveness and self-confidence returned to him. Then he clothed himself in a blanket of paper-work—long reports for Tipu Sultan and a barrage of orders for commanders and troops.

To every command post, Mir Sadik sent an order that an attack might be expected any moment, day or night. The troops were placed on a twenty-four-hour alert, to be ready all the time, dressed, belted and shod, with their guns and muskets about them. The spectacle was impressive to begin with, but after two days (and nights), the soldiers, pale and weary with dark rings around their eyes, had enough of it. They cursed the alert bell that sounded after sunset every quarter of an hour; they cursed the night guards who with drummers went about supervising the alert; their nerves were frayed and their bodies tired; hesitancy could be seen on their faces; their desire for duty, victory and glory weakened and they longed for rest, tranquillity and home. Some abandoned their posts instantaneously. Others followed. The trickle became a flood and mass desertions began.

Shustari surrendered the Mahtab Bagh bastion to the English without a fight. The way was now clear for the enemy to storm the main fort. Still Sultan's flag continued to fly from Mahtab Bagh and hardly anyone in the fort knew that it was in enemy's hands. But Mir Sadik did. He called Syed Ghaffar.

'I am worried about Mahtab Bagh,' Mir Sadik told him.

'Really!' was the sarcastic response of Syed Ghaffar who had not forgotten what he regarded as an affront of being relieved from his command post at Mahtab Bagh.

'Yes,' said Mir Sadik, ignoring the sarcasm. 'I fear, Shustari may let us down.'

'Oh, no, never. I believe he is even now fully engrossed in writing a new book. It promises to be a masterpiece, I am informed. No, Shustari will never let us down, believe me, and Mysore will be the envy of the world in the field of literature.'

'Do not joke, please, Syed Ghaffar. You know we had to have you here. When Purnaiya left, think of the void in Tipu Sultan's heart. Think of his sorrow; think of his fear. If he wanted his trusted officers near him, do you blame him? I knew he was lonely and wanted strong men and stout hearts near at hand. When he asked for you, I did not protest, though I knew that Mahtab Bagh needed you and not Shustari.'

Syed Ghaffar was touched. Still he asked: 'But why did you have to send Shustari, of all persons? For the might of his pen?'

'Because, Syed Ghaffar, I did not want to send anyone very senior or highly competent who would resent being recalled after a day or two. I regarded this as purely a temporary arrangement which could not last beyond forty-eight hours.'

'And now?' Syed Ghaffar enquired, keeping his hopes in check.

'Now you must take over Mahtab Bagh again. Shustari has instructions to hand over to you his command.'

'Well, let me hope he has not made an utter mess of it,' said Syed Ghaffar, happily. Then a thought crossed his mind. 'You called me here when Purnaiya left. Now, Ghazi Khan—may God rest his soul—is no more. What about Sultan's wishes in the matter?'

'I have spoken to him. He has steeled his heart. He knows that our safety lies in the protection of Mahtab Bagh. It is at his orders that I am asking you to leave for Mahtab Bagh.'

'I shall leave immediately.'

'Leave after an hour. I have promised Shustari that you will relieve him sharp at two o'clock. Posterity will damn me if he were to write in one of his books that I broke my promise,' said Mir Sadik with a smile.

'Oh, we can't let that be said, never. Nor do I wish to be damned in his book for being unpunctual,' replied Syed Ghaffar, returning the smile.

An hour later Syed Ghaffar left for Mahtab Bagh. As he approached his goal, the cannon in the bastion, now in English hands, was trained on him. The first cannon ball tore off his legs. He fell on his back and sank onto the ground, wet with his blood. His eyes were open. The cannon boomed again and again. He did not hear it. Nor did he see the cannon balls falling around him. He could only see the lofty, infinite sky above himself. But soon his eyes shifted. He saw Sultan's flag come down from the bastion and the English flag go up. He tried to stir and utter a protest. He could neither move nor moan. An intolerable pain overcame him. He made a supreme effort to keep his eyes open, with a prayer in his heart that somehow Sultan's flag should reappear and the English flag should vanish. Until then I shall not die, he promised himself. Mercifully, the benevolent, measureless sky smiled on him and he imagined that he could see above him countless flags flying high up in the air. He could not see their colours, nor their design, but he was convinced that they were his flags—the flags of his country. In that moment of bliss and with the sure knowledge that these flags would fly for ever and ever, he died, at peace with himself and with the universe.

'We are beset by indiscipline and desertions,' complained the commanders to Mir Sadik.

'You blame me for that! I, who do not personally command a single soldier! What are you commanders for?' was the haughty retort of Mir Sadik. But soon enough his tone softened and he added, 'I know I am in charge. The blame is mine—and mine alone. I, I alone must bear the burden.'

'The burden belongs to all of us,' said Bhaskar.

'Thank you,' Mir Sadik replied, and then he reverted to his favourite theme. 'Let the rats who are deserting, desert. We shall be all the more strong if we are purged of their presence. Can we really hope that they, who wish to sneak away, will ever stand up and fight? No, their very presence amongst us weakens us. However, do not let it worry you. In a day or two such cowards and poltroons will have lost the opportunity to escape.'

'How so? Have you thought of a means of stopping them?'

'The ring of steel is closing round the fort. Everywhere the English are erecting their cannons and batteries. Anyone trying to sneak out of the fort from whatever direction will be mowed down by them.'

'But why? Surely, the English will welcome deserters.'

'How would they know that they are genuine deserters? In a day or two, as soon as I have completed certain arrangements, I propose to send out a number of sorties, each containing a few men. Some will go with the appearance of deserters and others even with a flag of truce but they will all be armed to fire on the English positions and create confusion and chaos. The least that will be achieved is that no longer will the English be able to distinguish between a genuine deserter and a camouflaged combatant.'

'Mir Saheb, will Sultan ever permit the violation of the flag of truce?' Bhaskar asked. 'And how can you achieve anything by sending these small groups against the English? You will be sending our brave men to certain death.'

'Death is around us, everywhere. One can die out there in the open or one can die here within the fort itself. What is the difference?'

My God, wondered Bhaskar to himself, is it really at the back of Mir Sadik's mind that we are all waiting to be slaughtered here. No, the words that he had used were different, quite different. Bhaskar looked at others and feared that their minds also had been arrested by the same thought.

'I beg of you to reconsider your scheme of sending out unsupported sorties to face the English guns,' pleaded Bhaskar.

'Oh, I haven't finalised my views on it yet. I was only thinking aloud with you all.'

'Also, if you permit the boldness,' Bhaskar said, 'may I submit that secrecy can never be maintained if such thoughts are exchanged in so large a gathering. The English often have a way of knowing much of what is being said here.'

Mir Sadik gazed at Bhaskar as if he had not understood. Then quietly he said: 'You are right, my son. Thank you for reminding me. Yes, there are traitors amongst us.'

Bhaskar had something more to say: 'It is also my fear that many desertions are caused because of the dispersal of units. Commanders do not know who their new men are and the troops do not know who their new commanders are. Many units are floating about like lost sheep and no one seems to be responsible for anyone.'

'There is much in what you say. Dispersals are going to stop. Units must remain intact. I have spoken to Sultan about it,' Mir Sadik replied. Abruptly then he left.

No one spoke to another after Mir Sadik left. Each was wrapped in his own thoughts. Each tried to recall Mir Sadik's exact words. No, there was nothing ominous in those words but somehow they had stirred the unspoken fears of these men. Slowly, the fears were taking shape and the message was beginning to be loud and clear: Death is around us all; those that remain must wait to be slaughtered; those who do not desert immediately may not be able to desert at all; the ring of steel is closing round the fort. The ring of steel. The ring of steel. The ring of....

'Mir Sadik, gold, silver and other treasures are still stocked in the fort,' said Tipu Sultan. 'Why not evacuate these? I had suggested it last week.'

'We have plenty of time.'

'Still, why not be prudent; later it might be too late. We must not take the risk—howsoever remote—of their falling into the English hands.'

'That shall never happen. I shall begin its evacuation in a day or two but not in a rushed manner, lest it gives an appearance of panic.'

'Good, but do begin it, as you say, in a day or two.'

'I repeat I must see Sultan,' Balram insisted.

'I beg of you, do not embarrass me. Go, get the authorisation from Mir Sadik,' replied Zafar Ali, Captain of the Guard. He was an old friend of Balram but he had clear instructions not to permit any one in Sultan's presence without Mir Sadik's authorisation.

'But Mir Sadik has refused,' Balram pleaded.

'So must I, regretfully.'

'It is a matter of life and death, Zafar.'

'Yes, my life and my death, if I permit you in without authorisation.'

'When has this madness begun of barring entry to Sultan's presence?'

'Since last two days.'

'Whose orders, Sultan's or Mir Sadik's?'

'Surely, they speak with the same voice.'

'But why?'

'Why, what? You mean why do they speak with the same voice?'

'No, you ass, I am asking what is the sense in barring access to Sultan?'

'Balram, why are you so dense? Sultan has one thousand things to do. The fort is under siege; we are in danger; can't you realise that? Sultan does not get time even to eat or to rest. He has hundreds of visitors, dozens of reports to read, numerous charts to study; also he has to inspect troops and has endless meetings with Mir Sadik and others. But still, people like you come along and keep wondering why Sultan is not as easily accessible as before! I think it was a sensible order that Mir Sadik issued to bar entry to Sultan's presence.'

'But can't you realise that I have something serious to say to him.'

'When has it been that you are not serious? The trouble with you is that you look into the mirror far too often and cannot therefore laugh at the world. Alright, if you have got something serious why don't you speak to Mir Sadik? He still keeps sending streams of people to Sultan. Why would he discriminate against you?'

'I have tried. He apparently does not take serious notice of what I have to say and will not permit me to see Sultan. He just won't listen to me.'

'Let me try to be as wise as he is, and not listen to you.'

'But it is a serious matter. The fort wall has been breached and no one is telling Sultan about it.'

'Has the fort wall really been breached?'

'Yes, with my own eyes I have seen it.'

'That is serious, but don't go about believing that Sultan has not been told. Mir Sadik sends a report almost every hour. How will he fail to inform him of that?'

'Then, why has Sultan not come near the wall to inspect it? Is that believable? I think he has just not been informed. I must see him.'

'And I, my friend, keep telling you that you cannot. Show me the authorisation from Mir Sadik and I shall personally escort you to the door, open it for you, and even bow low to you as you walk in.'

'Let me see Shivji, then, at least.' Shivji was Tipu Sultan's Secretary.

'Shivji! poor man! He is more hardpressed than Sultan. He is awake when Sultan is awake. Thereafter he guards Sultan's sleep as well; but I will pass on your message to him sometime today.'

'No, no, now itself.'

'No, not now. He is busy with Sultan at this moment.'

Balram left in a temper. He was headed now for Mir Sadik's chamber, to try again. When he had gone a few steps, he saw Sultan at a distance coming out of his study accompanied by

Mir Nadim and some others. At the top of his voice, Balram shouted: 'Sultan, Sultan, stop, hear me.' The group halted. Mir Nadim and others glared at Balram in disgust. Sultan also looked at him, mildly puzzled.

'Who is he?' Sultan asked, not recognising him at a distance.

'Some idiot wanting your attention,' replied Mir Nadim. 'Let us go along. The guards will look after him.'

'No, let us see what it is about,' said Tipu Sultan, and then he added, 'Oh, it is Balram, son of Mahipal. Let him approach.'

When Balram reached them, Tipu asked, 'What is troubling you, Balram?'

'A breach, the wall is breached,' said Balram. He was out of breath; shouting, running and excitement had taken their toll.

'Calm yourself, give yourself a moment, and then say quietly what you have to say.'

Meanwhile, Mir Nadim whispered something to a guard who detached himself from the group to report to Mir Sadik.

'Forgive me, Sultan,' Balram began after a pause, 'for having presumed to appear before you so indecorously, but I had something urgent to say.'

'I am waiting to hear it,' said Sultan with a smile. 'We can all dispense with decorum if you have something worthwhile to say—as I am sure you have.'

'I fear, Sultan, that there has been a breach in the fort wall and that no one has kept you informed,' Balram blurted out.

'What treachery is this that I should not have been informed? Does Mir Sadik know about it?' Tipu asked with sternness.

'Not treachery, Sultan, I am sure; but out of consideration for you they have kept it from you.'

'Strange consideration indeed! But are you sure there is a breach?'

'I have seen it myself.'
'Where exactly?'
Balram explained.
'Is the breach serious?' Tipu asked.
'You should see it. I fear it is.'
'Let us go and see it,' Tipu said. 'You come with us, Balram. You too, Mir Nadim. Let Mir Sadik be sent for. He should also join us.'

Mir Sadik was already approaching. 'I have to speak to you,' he told Sultan. His tone made it clear that he wanted privacy. Others fell back. Sultan and he were alone now, out of earshot of others.

'Syed Ghaffar is dead,' Mir Sadik told him.

Tipu was silent. He felt an agonising pain as if something was being rent within his heart. Death had taken so many away and now his most loyal, trusted friend and commander. A silent cry of loneliness was running through his whole being. But when he looked at the sorrow-stricken face of Mir Sadik, he instantly overcame his own grief. After a long pause, softly he asked, 'How did he die?'

'Gloriously defending Mahtab Bagh.'

Tipu was silent again. Then with an effort he asked: 'Mahtab Bagh has fallen?'

'I am afraid so.'

Another long pause followed. 'Syed Ghaffar's body,' said Mir Sadik, 'has been brought to the fort. It has been placed in the outer courtyard. It was his wish,' continued Mir Sadik, his voice breaking, 'his last wish, that his body should be immediately taken in Sultan's presence, so that he pays his respects to you.'

'We shall go to pay our respects to him,' Sultan said, his eyes brimming with tears. 'Come with me.'

Sultan walked with Mir Sadik in the direction of the outer courtyard but after a short while he stopped, remembering something and mentioned to the group behind him. Mir Nadim, Shivji, Balram and others who waited at a distance hurried to join him.

'I go,' said Tipu Sultan to them, 'to pay my respects to Syed Ghaffar who became martyr today. Balram, you meet me outside my study in three-quarters of an hour. We shall go together to see the breach.'

Tipu Sultan and Mir Sadik hurried along, followed by many. Balram was about to follow when Mir Nadim asked him to stay back. 'I want to talk to you,' said Mir Nadim. Balram waited. For a moment, however, Mir Nadim said nothing, wrapped up in his own thoughts.

'Terrible news, Syed Ghaffar's death,' said Mir Nadim at last. Balram nodded, sharing his sorrow.

'And what is this about the breach in the fort wall?' asked Mir Nadim as if hurt. 'Should you not have reported to me? After all, I am the Commandant of the fort. I should have been informed.'

'Mir Nadim, I tried, believe me, I tried. I just could not find you. Ask Jabbar and Khaliq. I begged them to let me know as soon as you could be found.'

'I see; well, in that case, I cannot blame you. I can only have praise for your alertness,' said Mir Nadim graciously. 'But, tell me, did you inform Jabbar and Khaliq about what you had to convey to me?'

'How could I! I didn't want the news of the breach to be known to others. It would have caused some panic, if the news went round.'

'Young man, you will go far,' Mir Nadim said with evident admiration. 'Come now with me to my study and let us draw the exact location of the breach on a chart. Meanwhile, I must also find out if Mir Sadik has taken any action; otherwise we must rush our engineers, builders and workmen for an instantaneous repair job.'

Quickly they went to Mir Nadimi's study. Mir Nadim motioned Balram to a chair. On the desk were writing materials and several charts of the fort walls with indications of their technical specifications, strength and materials used for each section.

'I will be with you in a moment,' said Mir Nadim and he left while Balram became busy with the charts.

Noiselessly, from the door behind the desk three men entered into the study. Balram did not look up until someone pulled his hair. A silken rope went round his neck. Balram's body went leaping into the air, hitting against the desk which fell off. The chair clattered to the floor. But the silken rope remained, pulled harder and tighter, cutting into his skin and choking his breath. The strangler motioned to his companions. One gripped Balram's hands and the other held his body against the desk. Balram's eyes bulged as the rope was pulled tighter; then his body went limp, his struggles ceased.

The strangler removed the rope. One of his companions asked: 'Is it over, Khaliq?'

'Of course,' Khaliq replied. He kissed the silken rope and put it in his pocket.

'It would have been much simpler to have run the sword through him.'

'My dear Jabbar, you know that our Commandant, Mir Nadim Saheb, does not like blood in his study.'

'And I have no taste for being a party to a strangling.'

'It is an acquired taste that only developed minds can appreciate. The real trouble with you is that you have no artistic instincts.'

Mir Nadim waited outside Tipu Sultan's study. The horses were kept ready to take them to the fort walls. Tipu arrived with Mir Sadik, after having paid his last homage to Syed Ghaffar.

His mind was still on the tragic loss of his trusted friend and the danger that faced the fort with the loss of Mahtab Bagh. Seeing Mir Nadim and others, he instantly forgot his own grief 'Where is Balram?' he asked.

Mir Nadim looked around. 'I don't know. He left with me a chart showing the exact location of the breach that is worrying him. Maybe, he has gone ahead to the fort walls. Shall I send someone to find him?'

'No, not necessary,' replied Tipu Sultan. 'Let us go. You lead us to the breach or whatever it is. We will find Balram there.'

They mounted their horses. 'So much has been happening,' said Tipu to Mir Sadik, 'that I forgot to ask you. Is this breach serious?'

'Not at all. It is skin deep, not even that. Balram wasted my time. Now he is wasting yours. We can really call off this visit to the walls.'

'No, let it be. If I don't see it for myself, the doubt might persist.'

They continued to ride, without speaking.

Suddenly, Tipu Sultan asked: 'Why is Mir Nadim taking us through such devious route?'

'We are getting near the walls. I think he is trying to avoid the danger of enemy shells,' replied Mir Sadik.

'Oh, our good Commandant knows where they would fall and where they would not. Excellent.'

Finally, Mir Nadim led them to a section of the wall indicated on the chart which was supposed to have been given to him by Balram. They dismounted. The place was well-guarded and everywhere Sultan's soldiers could be seen.

'Please, do not expose yourself,' Mir Nadim prayed to Tipu Sultan—a prayer that went unheeded.

There was a slight, superficial damage to the wall but by no stretch off imagination could it be called a breach. The wall was somewhat disfigured having borne the concentrated brunt of hundreds of shells but its strength had not been affected. A few masons in an hour or two could have restored its looks and provided for it the coat of outer plaster which had been shaken off from the wall.

'This is no breach. Are you sure this is the section to which Balram was referring?' Tipu asked.

'Yes. He brought me here, at this very spot, this morning itself,' replied Mir Sadik.

'But what a silly thing to do!' said Tipu.

'Exactly, but in a way I think the fault is mine, too.'

'How so?'

'Balram heard from someone about this alleged breach. He came to me. We came here together and inspected it. He then asked me if it was serious. Now this is where I made my mistake. Instead of putting his mind at ease, I said yes, it was serious and I added that every shell that falls against our walls, every bullet that hits our men, every hurt, harm or misfortune that assails us is serious, and to guard against that men like Balram must fight with renewed vigour and zeal.'

'I hope it teaches you to guard against such lectures in the future,' said Tipu in good humour, now that the dread of a serious breach in the fort walls was not real.

'Oh, most assuredly, because the moment I completed my lecture, he became almost obsessed with the idea that I must report this so-called breach to you. When finally I agreed, he waited so that you might come to inspect the wall yourself.'

'But now I have come and he is not here!'

'Yes, that is surprising,' replied Mir Sadik. 'How do you account for that, Mir Nadim?'

Mir Nadim shrugged his shoulders. 'Maybe, he got some sense at last or someone finally was able to convince him that this breach was no breach. May I request that we leave.'

'Yes,' replied Tipu Sultan. 'Though I am wondering how a sensible lad like Balram came to make such a strange assessment. Why?'

'Well, he may just be wanting to draw your attention to himself or perhaps...' Mir Nadim tapped his forehead and added, 'so much is happening nowadays. Things are not easy. Anybody's nerves can be frayed.'

Sombrely, Tipu nodded and mounted his horse. Mir Sadik followed with Mir Nadim.

'See that no one gets near the real breach until the moment arrives,' quietly said Mir Sadik to Mir Nadim.

'I have already seen to it.'

'Make doubly sure,' said Mir Sadik, and then went faster to reach Tipu Sultan's side.

On the pretext of distributing pay to soldiers, a pay parade was held to which Mir Sadik's protege, Commandant Mir Nadim, called all the troops stationed at or near the fort walls. It was not the pay-day but everyone was told that due to troubled times ahead, it might not be possible to hold pay parades regularly for some months and therefore the generous Sultan had decided that on this pay parade, the salary for next three months would be disbursed. Pay for the next three months! They all rushed to join the pay parade.

Thus, they paved the way for the last, fateful day of Mysore.

77

THE LAST HOUR

AT THE GAPING BREACH IN THE FORT WALL STOOD SAYYAD SAHEB. He it was who had earlier along with Qamar-ud-din shared the treacherous burden of guiding the English to the very gates of Seringapatam. On him, Sultan had imposed the command of a huge army with the task of impeding the English advance. But the English had made tempting offers to him, enough to silence his conscience and he, as the result, had not only avoided harassing the English forces but had facilitated their advance in every possible way by surrendering strong, invulnerable posts to them as also by making available food, provisions and stores for their men and cattle. It was fitting that he should be in the vanguard of those who were to signal to the English to enter the fort and take it over. The rest was expected to follow a predetermined pattern. Sayyad Saheb would welcome the English troops. He would lead them inside the fort. His own position, status and dignity were sufficient to secure obedience from any stray units of the Mysorean troops if he called upon them to lay down their arms. If not, well, the English could intervene. Thus, he would lead the English troops in an orderly fashion to Mir Sadik who would welcome them, proclaiming himself at the same time the Sultan of Mysore and a friend of the English. Meanwhile, Mir Sadik and Mir Nadim would have already rendered Tipu Sultan helpless either through imprisonment or.... For himself, Sayyad Saheb saw vision of honours, titles, estates and riches.

These were the thoughts that ran in Sayyad Saheb's mind as he along with sixty others waved his white handkerchief as a prearranged signal to the English to come over. The English troops were assembled in trenches and were waiting in readiness for such a signal. Immediately, the English troops moved. From the trench to the bank of the river was one hundred yards. The river itself, rocky and varying in depth from ankle-deep to waist-deep, measured 280 yards more; beyond that again was a stone wall, then a ditch some sixty yards wide, and finally the breach. Yet, in less than seven minutes, a handful of men succeeded in planting the British flag on the summit above the breach. The rest of the English troops then poured in.

Thus, unknown to Tipu Sultan, unknown to the main body of the Mysorean forces, the English had reached and captured the breach. The entire passage from the trenches to the breach was exposed to heavy Mysorean guns. But the guns were silent and unmanned. Not a single Mysorean soldier died at the breach. None was even present except the traitors who had signalled to the English. Balram alone had died for it—in vain, to draw Sultan's attention to it.

The English assault began. Sayyad Saheb did not get an opportunity of graciously welcoming the English. The on-rushing English soldiers saw him as one of the enemy and treated him to a rifle butt. An English officer, Major Dallas, picked him up and murmured, 'Sayyad Saheb!' He was given a little water and recovered somewhat but he was in no condition to assist or escort the English troops. Dallas left him, therefore, and went to join his men. Sayyad Saheb watched him go. With the exception of an English sepoy, who had painfully sprained his leg, he was alone in the breach. Then he laughed either because his mind was unhinged or because of a curious sense of humour. 'You English,' he told the sepoy, 'are barbarians. Go, call the troops, I shall lead them.'

The English sepoy ignored him, though his musket was ready in case he was threatened. Sayyad Saheb was disgusted at the lack of response from the sepoy. He staggered to his feet to walk away. He fell over the battlements into the ditch and was drowned in knee-deep water.

The English divided themselves into two columns. The right column was to attack the southern rampart while the left column was to direct itself to the northern rampart. Both were to meet at the eastern gate. Rapidly, the columns moved. No resistance. The mockery of the pay parade was still going on. The outer hall in which all troops were to keep arms before joining the pay parade was securely barred and locked. The English advance continued.

Suddenly, like an explosion, the news reverberated that the English attack on the fort had begun, that they had captured a breach, hoisted their flag on the outer ramparts and seized the inner rampart, well within the fort. Tipu Sultan was then in the city behind the fort. He had just finished his midday meal when the news reached him. He washed his hands, mounted his horse and rushed to the fort with the few officers and men who were then with him and entered the fort through the back door.

A short crisp announcement was made at the pay parade under orders from Mir Nadim. It said, 'Sultan has decided to parley with the English who are now already in the fort. Soldiers, do not offer any resistance. Do not try to secure your arms. Remain where you are.'

Mir Nadim's messengers and scouts were all over, reciting similar messages to all command posts. Additionally, the message to them said, 'All the gates are open; leave the fort if you want, as soon as you can.'

Confusion. Pandemonium. It was less—much less—than an hour ago that the English had risen out of trenches and within this brief period, the breach, the outer and the inner ramparts and every part of the fortifications was occupied by them. Seven minutes, it has taken for the English to rise from the trenches and to capture the breach. When the breach was surmounted, the English came across a second formidable ditch, dividing the outer from the inner rampart. Mir Sadik's men brought the planks to serve as bridges. No opposition; no resistance. So entirely abandoned was the inner or second rampart and the surrounding area that a small party of only twenty-eight men of His Majesty's regiment, crossing the inner ditch, a little to the right of the breach, got possession of all the guns and batteries in the western bunker. This took no more than a few minutes. Again, the three bunkers within the south face, from which it was apprehended that the attack by the right column would receive tremendous annoyance, made no resistance. Those stupendous works were abandoned; the attack by the right column succeeded in getting possession of them, and of the whole of the southern ramparts; and within less than an hour, the English troops arrived upon the eastern face of the fort, capturing the entire ring of fortifications.

Only the palace itself was yet to be molested.

The English were now firing on the demoralised, fleeing and even unarmed men who had offered no resistance but were seeking to escape in accordance with orders issued in the name of Mir Nadim and Mir Sadik.

Tipu Sultan saw the carnage. He knew he was too late. A thought flashed in his mind, 'Should I turn back, the gates are still open.' He had not foreseen the closing act of this war in this fashion. He had imagined himself at the head of a proud, disciplined army which would stand up and fight. True, he had feared that the English army was mightier and that he would ultimately be defeated. But there would have to be a fight, he had imagined and not this inglorious, cowardly, treacherous rout. He dismissed the thought of turning back, altogether from his mind. 'I shall fight, alone, if I have to; yes, alone if I have to. There will always be men to shape the future of the nation and to lead it forward into freedom and fulfilment. For them I must leave an example of devotion to the cause. Let my life end, if it has to, and let the sacrifice serve a generation unborn.'

He tried to rally the troops. Many joined him but when they became exposed to heavy fire of the English detachments from both the inner and the outer ramparts, it spread consternation among them and they fled. Only a handful remained with him.

Some who wanted to join him, could not. The gates had been shut. Mir Nadim had the water-gate closed deliberately so that Sultan might not be able to escape. But it also had the effect of stopping the Mysorean troops from reaching him, and when Tipu ordered the gate to be opened, he was ignored. Mir Nadim, the Commandant of the fort, stood on the roof of the gate, but did not obey his commands.

'I have to answer to my own master, Mir Sadik,' Mir Nadim had shouted back, and then disappeared from view.

Above the din and tumult, Tipu Sultan heard and understood Mir Nadim's answer. His hand went to his heart. On his face was suffering which no one had seen before. Seeing the agony on his face and his hand on his chest, Raja Khan, Tipu's personal physician who was with him, became concerned. Bullets were flying all over. Had one of them caught Tipu Sultan's chest?

'Are you wounded?' Raja Khan asked, drawing Tipu's hand from his chest.

'The wound is not outside, Raja, it is inside, deep inside my heart.'

But the wounds of the flesh were also to come.

Tipu Sultan knew now that he was surrounded by a nightmare of treachery. Still he had a chance to escape. There were some loyal soldiers around him. With them, he could fight his way out but he chose to remain. What is more, he knew of two secret passages which could have led him to safety if he wanted to escape. Hyder Ali had those passages built underground after a palace conspiracy had erupted early during his reign. Only three persons knew of those secret passages—Purnaiya, Ghazi Khan and Tipu Sultan. 'No, I have a promise to keep,' he told himself. He made one last desperate effort to rally his troops. He unleashed his sword and yelled out his battle cry of 'Sarkar-e-Khudadad'. This cry had shaken the English before. In a decade and a half, it had gained legendary force in Mysore. But in less than an hour, it was to perish for ever, and well before the setting of today's sun, it would be heard no more.

One by one his companions fell. Only Raja Khan, his personal physician, and a young soldier were now by his side. Suddenly, from behind, some English soldiers rushed at Tipu and before he could turn round, the young Mysorean lunged at the English with his sword. The English soldiers looking for loot and easy prey ran off leaving the bodies of two of their companions behind. 'Well done, my son, you are my entire army today, are you not? What is your name?' Words choked in the youth's throat. He had often wondered how he would behave and what he would say if Sultan ever noticed him but now that the moment had come, he could not even utter his own name. A shot rang out. It hit the youth in the chest. He was dying. Tipu held him. 'I am Shamaiya's son, My father betrayed you. Forgive him, if you can.'

'Son, you have more than atoned for your father. I call on God to forgive him and to bless you both.' The youth died.

Remnants of a company of Mysorean soldiers came into view. They were trying to escape from the fort: They halted at the sight of Sultan accompanied only by Raja Khan. In astonishment, Chintamani, the leader of the group, asked Sultan: 'What are you doing here, sire?'

'What am I doing here?' Sultan asked in anger. 'I am here to fight the enemy and to die if need be.'

'But Mir Sadik has ordered hoisting of surrender flags all over and we have been asked to lay down arms. He spoke in your name.'

'Mir Sadik is a traitor. Go, my son, escape if you wish to. I shall not hold it against you. I shall fight alone.'

'We shall all fight,' said Chintamani, his eyes wet with tears, and he let out the cry 'Sarkar-e-Khudadad'. His soldiers took up the cry. They formed a ring round Sultan to protect him, their muskets and swords ready. Forward they marched and with their pitiful number, they engaged the English troops.

Meanwhile, Mir Sadik's strongmen, Khaliq and Jabbar, had been going round looking for Sultan. 'See that he is no more,' Mir Sadik had ordered them. While he had seen to it that with the closure of the gates, Sultan's escape was impossible, he was still worried that the English might capture Sultan alive. Who knows then what bargain the perfidious English would drive with the imprisoned Sultan and in the end his own dreams might come to nought. From a distance, Khaliq and Jabbar saw Chintamani's company, fully armed. They had not seen that Sultan was in their midst. Through his blow-horn, Khaliq called out as he had been doing all along: 'Surrender, surrender or escape. The war is over. Lay down your arms. These are Mir Sadik's orders in the name of Sultan.'

Chintamani shouted back: 'Sultan is with us, you coward. Tell that to your treacherous master.'

Brazenly, Khaliq came forward to see if Sultan was really there, his hand ready on the knife which dangled from his belt. He was without fear. He was the right-hand man of Mir Sadik and knew of the dread he inspired. Contemptuously, he looked at Chintamani and his non-descript band of soldiers. Chintamani aimed his musket at his head and fired. Instinctively, Khaliq turned his head. The bullet caught him on his thick clean-shaven skull. Chintamani had an impression that he saw fragments of Khaliq's skull fall before his body hit the ground. Khaliq was dead. Chintamani did not know that the dead man before him was the one who had strangled his younger brother—Balram.

The fleet-footed Jabbar had run off. He was not fond of muskets when they were directed at him. Also, he had to carry the news of Sultan's presence to Mir Sadik.

Tipu Sultan could now guess the errand with which Khaliq and Jabbar had come. A prayer formed itself in his heart. 'Merciful God, spare me the ignominy of dying by the hand of my own countrymen.'

Jabbar found Mir Sadik closeted with the English Officer Commanding, General Baird, and Commandant Mir Nadim. Mir Sadik interrupted the conversation and came towards Jabbar. Then he went back to Baird and without telling him of Sultan's presence, informed him of the spot in which some misguided Mysoreans were trying to congregate in order to offer resistance. 'That will be attended to,' Baird had replied shortly, and his orderlies carried the deadly messages to the English columns.

Meanwhile, Chintamani's company had been joined by several stragglers who at the sight of Sultan vowed to fight by his side.

Baird's instructions were being carried out. From all sides, the English began pouring forth destructive fire in the general direction where the Mysoreans were supposed to be regrouping. The English detachments had now precise instructions from Baird to shoot on all Mysoreans, armed or unarmed, and drive them to the centre from which resistance was suspected so that all could be mowed down in one single sweep. Baird was now getting angry. In a matter of minutes his forces had captured every rampart and every fortification. Mir Sadik had promised him peaceful surrender without any resistance. Everything had been going on according to plan. Meanwhile, Baird had been keeping a careful watch of the time. Victory was unquestionably certain and the conquest of Seringapatam was to be total and complete. But he wanted to go down in history as a Commander who just within one hour's time conquered the famed fort of Seringapatam and dealt a crushing defeat to Mysore and its valiant Sultan. One hour. It would be a record—he knew—that future conquerors would not be able to surpass or even match. Only a few minutes remained for the hour to pass and now came the news of some resistance from Mysoreans! Wipe them out, wipe all of them out. There was another chain of thought in Baird's mind: 'Who would regard it as a glorious victory, if there are not too many casualties? Every one would say that I have got it too easy and that Mir Sadik gave it to me on a platter. Who would then care if I took an hour or half or even less? I was prepared to abide by my agreement not to wreak death and havoc against them; but now they have begun resistance. It might grow. I do not know who is guilty and who is not; let them all taste fire and be afraid, and if the list of their casualties is long, so be it; mine shall be the greater glory.'

Deadly fire even on forces which had surrendered! All the buildings and halls in which the Mysoreans were trapped were set fire to.

Through smoke and fire, in a dense mass the Mysoreans were running and no one could extricate himself from that torrent. Waves of fleeing mob caught up with Chintamani and his men and bore them back. The English guns kept their steady, unwavering fire. From every rampart, the Mysorean cannons, now manned by the English, brust out, heaping flaming death on men whom they were originally designed to protect.

Shekhar was outside the fort. He knew that Sultan was trapped inside and all gates were shut. Mir Nadim's men guarded them. He rounded up twenty men and attacked the gate. The guards took to their heels but the gate was securely locked. They brought a huge wooden log and tried to batter the gate with it. Mir Nadim's men returned now accompanied by many, and fired on them. Shekhar saw most of his companions fall. He escaped with a bullet wound in his left shoulder. He kept running until overcome by weakness and dizziness from loss of blood and lay down by the side of ditch. Painfully, he dabbed the water from the ditch on his face. It revived him a little. Miraculously the blood had stopped flowing.

Suddenly, Shekhar saw Mir Sadik emerging from an inconspicuous side gate. Accompanying him were four English soldiers, one of whom appeared to be of a high rank. Following them were some Mysoreans including Mir Nadim and Jabbar. Without premeditation, without any conscious thought but perhaps fearing that they would kill him if they saw him, he shouted: 'Mir Sadik, Mir Sadik, Sultan wants your help.' Mir Sadik walked towards him briskly, the English and the Mysoreans following him.

'Where is Sultan?' asked Mir Sadik, looking at the wounded man.

'There, there,' he pointed in the direction of some buildings, 'save him, he wants your help. He has given me a message for you.'

'What is the message? Quickly man, quickly,' Mir Sadik bent low to hear the message. He did not want others to hear the message if it dealt with Sultan's whereabouts; it was necessary in his interest that Sultan must be caught dead, not alive....

'It is in my pocket,' Shekhar's eyes moved to his wound as if in pity over his own helplessness.

Immediately, Mir Sadik knelt lower to put his hand in Shekhar's pocket in order to take out the message. Shekhar groaned in pain and blood began to flow from his shoulder. He turned slightly and then leapt. The blade of his dagger found the unprotected throat of Mir Sadik and remained there. Blood gushed over Mir Sadik's tunic and he fell with no more than a gurgle. Shekhar died from a sword thrust from Jabbar. Instead of crying out in pain, he laughed for he knew Mir Sadik was dead. 'Heavens shall hear my laughter,' was his last thought and then he died, his eyes smiling till the end.

The Englishman shrugged his shoulders. Either thinking aloud or sharing his thoughts with his companions, he said: 'Pity, Mir Sadik, you would have made a good ally and a good ruler. Now we will have to look for someone else in your place.'

Even now whenever Mir Sadik's name is mentioned anywhere, where there are men to hear it, they curse it. Many who revere Tipu's memory throw stones towards the spot where Mir Sadik died. But since Shekhar also died at the same spot, those amongst them who know their History well, always say, 'Not for you, Shekhar,' when they cast their stones. It is said that Shekhar's spirit laughs when it hears this. There are, of course, many without knowledge of history who just cast their stones without putting in their reservation about Shekhar. It is said again that Shekhar's spirit laughs at that, too.

Meanwhile, Chintamani's company closed round Tipu Sultan and with difficulty they extricated themselves from the torrent of milling crowds, crazed, wounded and dying men and riderless horses. They made their way to the left. A deadly shower of bullets whistled over them. Many fell and finally Sultan accompanied by Raja Khan, Chintamani and eleven others found himself between the watergate and another archway leading through the inner ramparts into the city. Tipu had already received a bayonet wound. He received his second bayonet wound before he reached the archway. Now, he received his third wound when he was shot in the left breast and his horse was killed under him. Raja Khan begged him to make himself known to the English and surrender to them, but proudly he refused.

'Are you mad? Be silent,' he shouted at Raja Khan and then gently, he told him to look after Chintamani who had fallen. Chintamani was beyond all medical care, Raja Khan told him. Again, Raja Khan begged: 'This is no way to die, alone, unattended and uncared for.'

'No, Raja, no, when I made the promise, I raised no conditions. So be it,' replied Tipu. Raja Khan did not comprehend the words that Tipu uttered. Still, he knew that destiny had set its course and he would not be able to alter it.

The firing became intense now. Around him his companions were falling. Raja Khan alone remained with him. Suddenly, the firing stopped. Tipu wanted to press on. Raja Khan tried to follow him but could not. He himself had been wounded five times. Firing had stopped all over the fort. It was four minutes before the deadline of one hour which Baird had set for himself for the complete conquest of the fort. English detachments and even stray soldiers were now moving about in order to mop up whatever resistance remained. Silence all over, except for the wail of the wounded and the groan of the dying. All resistance had ceased. Only one Mysorean with three wounds in his body was standing up with a sword in his hand to defend Mysore. Only one Mysorean—Tipu Sultan.

A party of English soldiers came. Their eyes caught the richly jewelled sword-belt which the wounded Sultan wore. 'Let us get hold of it,' one of them said, and with swords and musket butts they charged at him. Although he was half-fainting with loss of blood, he smiled knowing that his moment had come. His sword clanged against theirs. Two of them received sword-cuts. An English soldier who had not entered the fight, shouted from the distance. 'Back men, back, let's shoot him and be done with it.' The soldiers backed out from the fray. Then a shot rang out and struck Tipu through the temple.

The last defender of Mysore was dead.

'He fought like a tiger,' said one of the soldiers removing his sword-belt.

He was the Tiger.

When later, he was recognised and his body was recovered, the sword was still firmly clasped in his hand. Many were moved in that moment who were never moved before.

The English Governor-General of India, Richard Wellesley, second Earl of Mornington, was entertaining a select gathering to a dinner when he received the news of the death of Tipu Sultan.

He rose—unsteady from several helpings of whisky and wine—raised his glass and said:

'Ladies and Gentlemen, I drink to the corpse of India.'

RV1799